KRAKEN HUNTERS

TALES OF THE CRYPTO-HUNTER
BOOK 3

R. GUALTIERI

COPYRIGHT © 2020 RICK GUALTIERI

Cover by Damonza: **www.damonza.com**

Published by Freewill Press
Freewill-press.com

DEDICATION

For Katy, an unsinkable spirit in this world and the next.

ACKNOWLEDGEMENTS

A shout out to my Patreon gang: Michael L, Simon, Shari, Tina, Lee, Nicole, Caprice, Nick, and Michael S. Thank you all for sticking by me.

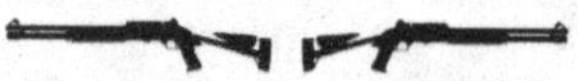

Special thanks to my alpha readers: Eric, Chris, and Mark for helping to make me a wee bit less ignorant regarding some of the technical aspects of this book, including what a toolpusher does.

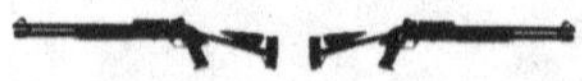

And finally, a big thanks to my beta crew: Aaron, Dave B, Andy, Eric, Jackie, Michael, KJ, and especially Helene, Anthony, and David H. You guys took a hammer to all my plot gremlins, showing no mercy no matter how big or small they were.

PROLOGUE

The leviathan lay upon the ocean floor, almost perfectly camouflaged despite its great bulk.

Fish of all sizes swam by unaware while innumerable crustaceans crawled close enough for it to easily ensnare, but it paid them no mind as it slumbered – lazily enjoying the cool current washing over its massive form.

Soon enough it would rouse and, when it did, the ocean would become a roiling frenzy of quick strikes and torn flesh. But for now it was content.

Once, long ago, its species was more numerous, but declining food sources and aggressive competition had gradually whittled their numbers down. Now, only a handful remained in the depths, and encounters with others of its kind were rare as they were solitary creatures by nature.

Those that survived into adulthood were loath to venture into the shallows, often preferring far deeper waters than the hunting ground which the leviathan had claimed as its own. As a result, they were relatively unknown to the world above, not that the great beast cared about such things.

There, safe in its territory, it was king of all it surveyed – doing as it pleased and fearing nothing.

It was a blissful tranquility that wasn't meant to last.

The ocean floor shuddered, causing the great beast to stir as the sand beneath it shifted and vibrated. Such disturbances were rare but not unknown, an annoyance at best – one that would quickly pass and be forgotten.

Mere moments later, however, a much larger tremor hit, shaking the silty ocean floor and stirring up debris amidst the normally clear waters.

A shockwave from some kind of explosion or eruption soon followed, disturbing the leviathan's sensitive statocysts and bringing with it a torrent of rushing water that roused it, enough to take a cautious look around. Whatever had just occurred had been powerful enough to stun all of the smaller fish swimming nearby. Curious, but ultimately little more than a minor discomfort to a beast of its...

Thrum.

Something unseen jostled it, like a wave of energy passing through its body, electrifying its brain and jolting it fully awake. The creature scanned the surrounding depths with its keen eyesight, yet saw nothing to account for...

Thrum.

Another invisible pulse passed through it, causing it to recoil. Pain and discomfort flared within its mind and it lashed out with its arms, causing the surrounding water to swirl in a chaotic maelstrom.

Several long moments passed and again the invisible enemy struck, driving the creature into a near frenzy. However, it could neither see nor sense where its foe was. All it knew was that it was being attacked and whatever was responsible seemed to be both relentless and beyond its reach.

The minutes drew out, feeling like hours, as more of the strange energy struck the mighty beast, driving its synapses into an uproar. Soon enough, its misery and confusion gave way to rage. It lashed out again with its many arms, striking at anything that moved. In short order, the water grew thick with the blood of any fish unlucky enough to be within the beast's vast reach.

And yet still the thrumming continued, relentlessly tormenting the leviathan with its inexorable power.

It scanned the ocean floor again, looking for something, *anything*, to attack that would stop this assault on its senses. However, all the surviving creatures within the immediate vicinity had fled following its initial fury.

Finding nothing upon which to vent its anger. It began to swim, casting its mammoth form off the ocean floor and toward the surface.

Soon enough, it detected something new, something worthy of its wrath, floating above at the far edge of its domain, daring to intrude where it did not belong. It didn't know if this newcomer was the source of its torment, but it intended to find out with swift and savage finality.

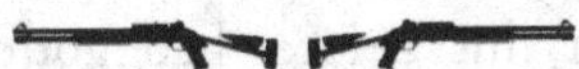

"Say that again, please. I was ... distracted."

Sydney Treco was actually bored out of his mind. This assignment was bullshit and everyone aboard the floating shit-trap known as the San Cristóbal Tortuga knew it. They were out here for one reason and one reason only: to give the illusion that they were doing something worthwhile.

In fact, the only one who seemed excited was the geologist standing in front of him, a Dr. Rigel, or Regal ... some R-word Sydney couldn't be bothered to remember.

"Those sediment samples we collected yesterday," the scientist said, calling up a chart on his laptop, "they're very unusual."

"How so?" There was only one type of unusual that would have roused Sydney's interest and that was confirmation that they'd found a pocket of natural gas, the bigger the better.

"We're not certain yet."

"Come again?"

"We found traces of iridium along with the expected minerals, which in itself is remarkable. But there was something mixed in with it, trace fragments of a metal of unknown origin."

"Unknown origin?" Sydney asked, perking up.

"Well, maybe unknown is too strong a word," the scientist replied, pushing his glasses up on his nose, no doubt to emphasize his nerd credentials. "What I mean is we haven't identified it yet. We're still analyzing the samples, but we think..."

"Oh." Sydney's interest dropped again. Why was this asshole bothering him with this crap? The guy was getting all worked up despite admitting they were still working on it. Was he really that bored, too? The sad thing was, Sydney had seen this before, had gotten his hopes up despite sketchy seismic data. Then, invariably, when the results were double-checked, there was almost always some excuse: contamination, machine error, or human screw-up. Every *fucking* time. It seemed to be the story of his life.

His official title was Offshore Installation Manager. On paper, he was in charge of this expedition by the ZarroGreen Oil and Gas Company Limited, named after its founder Miguel Zarro – one of the richest sons of bitches in South America.

The reality was somewhat less grand, though, and probably the reason he'd been passed over for the far juicier Gulf expedition he'd been hoping for. That Guerrero bitch had never liked him, not since that fuck-up in Bolivia when they'd been forced to abandon a drill site due to one of his team being photographed handling a highly endangered frog. And now, with her recent promotion, she was in prime position to turn the screws.

The result had been his assignment to this floating asylum. That the weather had been perfect only accentuated the fact that he was in the heart of the Caribbean, yet unable to enjoy any of its splendors. Hell, they were barely a hundred miles northwest of Turks and Caicos. One short helicopter ride and he could be relaxing on a beach with drink in hand, but instead he was busy being slowly driven mad.

"So, why exactly are you bothering me with this?" Sydney asked, interrupting some other nonsense the geologist was pontificating about. "Go finish your analysis."

"I just thought you might want to know."

Sydney opened his mouth to correct the over-eager scientist when the cabin shuddered, grinding those thoughts to a halt. A moment later, he felt the ship lurch beneath them, and then the lights began to flicker.

"We're done here," he said with finality, reaching for the phone on his desk even as the geologist beat a hasty retreat. He put the receiver to his ear, impatiently waiting until it was picked up on the other end. "Mind telling me what the hell that was?"

"I don't know," Jenson Greaves, the ship's first mate, replied. "But whatever it is, it's causing everything on the bridge to go haywire."

"Define everything."

"Sonar, geo-positioning, hell, probably the coffee maker, too."

"What the fuck?" Sydney replied, more to himself

than the officer. "Get someone from the floor on the box. I want to know what those clowns are doing."

A minute or so later, Eddie Gunch, the drill crew's toolpusher, got on, although Sydney could barely understand him – the previously crystal clear connection now garbled with static. "We're ... working ... it, Treco."

"Working on what?"

"I'm not... We were jetting ... when ... hit something hard and ... drill kicked in."

"Yeah, and...," Sydney prompted, doing his best to try and fill in the gaps.

"And that's ... shit went nuts. I think ... hit a methane pocket. We're checking things now."

Must've been a hell of a pocket to take out the entire fucking bridge, Sydney thought, not that he gave a rat's ass about the bridge, the crew, or the whole damned ship for that matter. Well, that wasn't entirely true. He cared about it from a budgetary sense. It wouldn't have surprised anyone at headquarters if this operation turned out to be a bust. Hell, it was practically designed to be. But equipment damage was a whole other ball of wax. Shit like that would be dumped on his shoulders in a hot second. "How's the drill?"

"Pretty sure ... stuck... Trying ... retract it now ... some damage."

"Just fucking great."

"Might take ... some time ... know for sure. The controls are..."

"Are what?"

"They're acting ... weird. Not ... respon..."

That was all he got before the line fell dead, the coms apparently following the lead of whatever the hell else was going on.

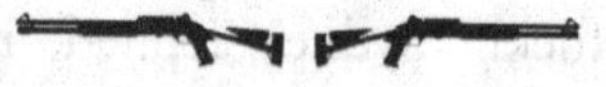

Fucking wonderful! Sydney stepped on deck, heading for the ship's derrick. This was just his luck. The entire operation had been pretty much designed to be a cluster-fuck from the start, but a necessary one. ZarroGreen wasn't about to let their hard-fought drilling rights expire via entropy. They'd lost most of their bids in the Gulf, minus the expedition Sydney had been jockeying for, but had made up for it by greasing pockets all across the Caribbean. Too bad they'd been mostly forced to sideline any real development in the years since, thanks in part to several high profile lawsuits wreaking havoc on their stock price.

But now, those rights were up for renewal and, if ZarroGreen didn't show at least some effort on their part, they could very well lose them.

Sadly, this was, at best, a fishing expedition as far as Sydney was concerned. The seismic survey of the site below them – a narrow shelf between the shallows and where the bottom dropped by several thousand feet – had been noted as having *potential merit* by the higher ups. To Sydney that was shorthand for not having a fucking clue. Problem was, the company was in too big of a rush to risk botching a dig more likely to yield fruit.

The company's top exploratory teams were currently busy elsewhere, their fleet spread too thin. So when the suits finally noticed that the clock was ticking, they did what they could in the fastest and cheapest way possible.

The Tortuga was one of ZarroGreen's oldest drillships, due for decommission by year's end. It seemed the perfect solution: send an old ship that wouldn't be missed to make sure their rights didn't expire. If something was found, great. Better equipment would be called in. Even if not, though, so long as the company could show they'd done their minimum due diligence, ZarroGreen could continue to sit on their rights until they were ready to mount a more serious operation.

Unfortunately, the Tortuga wasn't exactly in topnotch condition. Everything about it was old, rusty, and generally unpleasant.

It wasn't a surprise to anyone aboard when stuff broke down. However, for seemingly everything to go haywire at once was both new and not something Sydney wanted to hear. That meant he needed to kick the drill team's ass until they got their shit back in gear.

As he climbed the stairs to the drill floor, he amused himself with a petty fantasy in which this stupid-ass ship finally gave up the ghost and sank beneath the waves, through no fault of his own of course. He envisioned himself sitting on a beach, a babe on his arm and a drink in his hand, watching it go down like the fucking Titanic.

A few roughnecks passed him on the way, barking out greetings which he didn't return, being too preoccupied with not getting his button down shirt any dirtier than it already was. That was perhaps what he hated most about this rig. Everything, even the control room, felt like it was encrusted in a thin layer of grime.

That included the personnel.

Eddie met him about halfway up. Sydney stopped without offering the toolpusher a hand in greeting. "Please tell me you have good news."

Before Eddie could answer him, though, the ship lurched again, this time far more violently than before.

"I thought you said the drill was stuck."

"It is," Eddie replied, looking around. "That wasn't the..."

The deck shuddered beneath them as emergency klaxons began to blare. From his position, it appeared the ship was now visibly listing to one side.

"What the fuck?" Sydney barked as both men grabbed hold of the railing. "Did something hit us?"

"Way out here?" Eddie replied, holding on with a death grip as they were a good fifty feet above the main deck.

A rogue wave maybe? Sydney knew all about those. But they had a clear view of the horizon. The sea was calm and clear with nothing in sight that could...

Eddie's eyes suddenly opened wide. "What the hell is that?"

Sydney turned to follow his gaze and what he saw made him wonder if maybe the fumes from the derrick were causing him to hallucinate. Surely there was no other rational explanation for what he was seeing.

Something was rising up past them, coming from the sea itself. It appeared to be an impossibly long fleshy mass, covered with massive suckers that scraped along the side of the ship as it continued to climb.

And it wasn't alone.

Sydney immediately recalled a movie he'd seen a few years back, something about pirates and CGI fish men. Whatever was rising from the deep now reminded him of the monstrous beast from that movie, one with tentacles which had...

Whatever these things were, one of them wrapped around the superstructure upon which they stood, bringing with it the groan of tortured metal.

It was crazy, absolutely impossible, yet somehow it was happening, mocking reality all the same – like something out of a drunken sea yarn.

As the ship listed further to the side, Sydney held onto the railing for dear life, but Eddie wasn't nearly so lucky. His grip slipped and he went tumbling past the offshore manager into the open air. For one surreal moment, the toolpusher reached out, as if hoping to catch hold of something by sheer will alone, and then Eddie was gone – slamming into the deck below and staining the rusty metal with his blood.

The ship began to lurch more violently. Sydney was no structural engineer, but it was painfully obvious the rig was beginning to give way under the assault of the nightmare tentacle wrapped around it.

His feet slipped out beneath him as the Tortuga came dangerously close to capsizing, and he found himself hanging by his fingertips over fifty feet above the surface of the water.

The screams and cries of the crew could be heard amidst the fatigue of metal being strained beyond its capacity, but nothing mattered to him beyond his own predicament.

I knew this fucking mission was cursed.

Almost as if in answer to his thoughts, a great mass of orange-brown flesh emerged from the sea below. He had time to glimpse one massive eyeball glaring up at him and then his fingers slipped and he fell – desperately hoping to hit the water instead of the deck, but knowing it would likely be the equivalent of slamming into solid concrete from that height.

Somehow, though, the thought of a quick death wasn't nearly as frightening as the alternative.

PART I

1

Dr. Derek Jenner crept through the thick underbrush, moving quickly but deliberately. A small headlamp provided barely adequate light against the thick Pennsylvania woods.

He bent low, examining the cold ground of the well-traveled game trail. There was no shortage of tracks, but he saw nothing out of the ordinary. He voiced as much. "Doesn't mean anything. This creature is said to be smart. At least as smart as a wolf. Maybe even as smart as a man."

"Over here," a soft voice called from off to his left, nearly inaudible even in the stillness of the woods.

Derek pushed past some brambles to find his tracker Daniela "Danni" Kent down on one knee looking at something on the forest floor. In the glare of his headlamp, her thick blonde hair stood out against the seemingly endless green of the forest, even tied back in a ponytail as it was. "What have you got?"

"Scat," she replied. "Fresh and from something big."

"Get one of the evidence bags so we can have it tested for DNA."

"You got it."

13

She removed her backpack and unzipped it just as there came the crack of a branch breaking from somewhere in front of them. It was impossible to tell exactly where but it had been close and – more importantly – whatever caused it had sounded big.

Derek started to push through the bushes, intent on finding out what it was.

"Wait. This'll just take a minute."

He turned back toward Danni. "Finish up and then follow. Keep your radio on."

"Okay. Just be careful."

He threw her a quick smile. "Always am." Then he stepped through the bushes, knowing he was instantly lost to her sight. Even with their headlamps, they were lucky to see much more than ten feet in front of them.

It was a dangerous proposition when faced with a potentially lethal quarry. The Mongrel Man of Morganberg, as the media had dubbed it, wasn't nearly as well-known as the Beast of Bray Road over in Elkton Wisconsin. However, the local papers had latched onto this creature in recent years as sort of a local celebrity, especially after a few sightings and alleged disappearances.

It was hard to believe, a living breathing werewolf, but that's exactly what eyewitnesses described.

Derek stopped and looked around, surveying the thick vegetation that seemed to be on all sides. It appeared to be a whole lot of nothing, yet he knew that could be deceptive, the bush able to conceal just about anything from sight. Such a beast could be standing mere feet away from him and he would never know until it was too late.

"This far out in the woods," he said aloud, "it's easy to believe. All of those stories that frightened us as children – they all become real out here under the stars. Suddenly, they don't seem so absurd, when you can't reach over and turn on the lights. That's the point where you realize you have a choice: run back home and pray it doesn't catch you or head toward it and hope for the best."

There came the crack of another branch, this one closer than the last. Derek prepared to push through the foliage once more, but then a voice cried out from somewhere in the darkness.

"Ow! Goddamn it!"

Derek stopped moving and sighed. "Cut!"

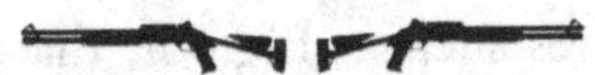

"Relax," Julie Wilhelm, the show's camera operator, said. "We can edit around that."

"I know." Derek let out a sigh. "But I was really hoping to do it all in one take."

"Sorry to disappoint, Mr. Tarantino," Mitchell Harkness, the team's medic replied – his wiry frame stepping out from behind a tree. "I guess we'll have to skip the Emmys again this year."

Derek laughed. "Nobody appreciates our art. You okay by the way?"

Mitchell shrugged, looking embarrassed. "Yeah ... I tripped on a rock."

"Oh no, not a rock," Danni called out, likewise joining them. She'd switched her headlamp to a higher setting, greatly increasing the illumination it provided. "And here Derek said we'd be safe leaving the guns behind."

Derek turned to her and shook his head. "I'm so glad we don't broadcast live." Julie opened her mouth to reply, but he held up a hand. "Yes, I know. I still haven't decided if I want us doing that live Halloween show. Sounds like a waste of time."

"Sounds like?" Danni offered.

"Okay, it'll *definitely* be a waste of time, but the kids will like it."

Whatever locale or legend they picked for the live show, there was one thing they could all count on: it would be far from any actual activity. They'd spend three or four hours traipsing through a dark forest or spooky cave, knowing there wasn't anything out of the ordinary – especially since they'd be the ones to make sure of it first.

In a way it was ironic, he considered. They were one of the few active field teams qualified to track down actual cryptids – creatures such as Bigfoot, that were considered little more than myth and legend by the general public. Yet for the sake of the *reality* show they starred in – *The Crypto-Hunter* – the same show that acted as their cover whenever they were on a real mission, they'd end up wasting an evening doing nothing but chasing their own shadows. This would be spliced in with them turning back to the camera to offer fake *what if* scenarios about what might be out there, always just outside the range of the camera's lens.

As for the Mongrel Man of Morganberg, it was a snipe hunt. Nothing more than a local legend, probably started by drunk teens trying to cover their asses after staying out too late. It was why he and his team were out there unarmed with nothing but their cameras.

Well, maybe not entirely unarmed. Derek checked the concealed shoulder holster he wore beneath his jacket. One could never be too careful. There were, after all, real predators in these woods.

However, he was fairly certain none of them were werewolves. Even his superiors within the Department of Agriculture, keepers of a vast archive filled with data on species unacknowledged by science, agreed on that one. Sure, there was a known squatch clan a few miles to the west, but they were mostly benign. And, so far as he could tell, none were currently in the area where they were filming.

"So what's the word?" Julie asked, setting her camera aside so she could pull some brambles from her auburn hair. "Should we call it a night or keep hunting until the full moon goes down?"

Derek considered their options for a moment. "It's getting late. Let's head back in. We can film the rest of that scene along the way."

"Don't forget, we need to reshoot your intro," she said.

"Why? It sounded fine to me."

"This is why." She turned up the volume on the camera and swung out the viewfinder for them all to see.

"Since man first walked the Earth, people have seen the unexplainable: Lights in the sky, ghosts from the past, monsters in the mist. Do they exist, or are they just our imagination? Science has scoffed at these stories ... until now. My name is Dr. Derek Jenner, and I dare to believe. Together with my team, I will find what is out there. The truth cannot hide from me. I am ... the Crypto Hun ... oh shit. What did I just step in?"

Mitchell snickered. "Good job there, Crapto Hunter."

Derek shook his head. "Yeah, I guess maybe we can record that part again, too."

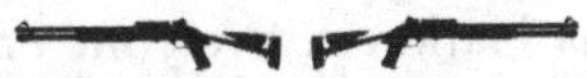

A pair of curious yellow eyes watched the foursome as they turned around and began filming again. Their owner followed them for a short while, moving with barely any sound while listening to their banter ... until finally it veered off and disappeared back into the darkness of the surrounding woods.

2

"Want some?"

Danni turned from where she'd been stoking the campfire to find Mitchell unloading a heavily laden sub sandwich from the cooler.

She smiled. "Not exactly roughing it are you?"

The medic let out a laugh. "The appeal of trail rations is lost upon me."

"Fair enough, but I'll pass, thanks."

"More for me."

"I don't even know where you put it all," she replied, noting his lanky frame.

"Thank Mama Harkness. Everyone on her side is thin as a rail, age be damned. And no, before you say it, life is not fair."

"Good, then I'm volunteering you next time our producers set up a photoshoot."

"Leopard print really doesn't go with my eyes."

She picked up a handful of dead leaves and threw it at him. "Don't start with that shit."

Mitchell opened his mouth, although Danni wasn't sure whether it was to say more or fill it with sandwich.

Either way, he was interrupted by a shrill beeping sound coming from Derek's backpack.

"Is that…?"

"The satnav?" the medic replied. "Sounds like it. What do you think? Wrong number or did they finally remember we exist?"

Danni shrugged. It had been six months of mostly fluff assignments, with a few quick hunts during squatch mating season to break things up.

Still, it was hard to complain after what had happened in New Jersey: the death of their friend Francis and that nightmare ordeal with the Lesterfield family. They'd all needed a break to catch their breaths and heal. Danni was still speaking to a therapist twice a week and would likely continue for a long time to come. The nightmares had finally started to subside, but that didn't mean the memories didn't still pop unbidden into her head when she least wanted them.

She didn't fool herself that their *exile* had anything to do with the trauma they'd suffered, though. Their minders were probably far more concerned with how they'd embarrassed the governor of the Garden State, bringing enough scrutiny down on him to end his career. Sadly, he'd had friends in high places. Though his threat to have the team disbanded hadn't come to pass, she had a feeling their superiors had been forced to pay a heavy political tithe in the grand game of D.C. bureaucracy.

Regardless, they were also the only ones with the satnav's number so, unless some telemarketer had gotten supremely lucky, that meant something was up.

"You going to answer that?" she asked as it continued to beep.

Mitchell responded by popping open a soda to go with his sandwich. "It's all yours, kid." When she did nothing but stare at him, he added, "You're part of the team, too.

Besides, the bean counters don't like me all that much. Long story."

Despite his urging, Danni hesitated. At a few months shy of twenty-one, she was the youngest member of the hilariously named Department of Cryptid Containment by at least a decade. True, Julie was technically her junior from a tenure standpoint, but their superiors hadn't given her nearly the grief Danni had gotten when she'd been recruited. She got the sense the suits in Washington looked at her as little more than a college intern, her status as a badged agent notwithstanding.

The phone continued to ring, but Danni knew better than to hope it went to voicemail. Outside of life or death situations, they were expected to answer.

She glanced at Mitch, narrowing her eyes at the barely concealed smirk on his face, then took a quick look at the surrounding trees, hoping Derek picked that moment to reappear.

No such luck.

It's just a phone. She popped open the flap on Derek's backpack and retrieved the device. Then, with one last withering glare toward Mitch, she answered it. "Hello?" *Gah! Don't be so stupid.* "Um, I mean, Danni Kent speaking..."

"Danni?" the voice from the other end asked. It was, as expected, Norah Caseman, their liaison within the Byzantine bureaucracy of Washington D.C.

"Yes, Agent Caseman," Danni replied, trying to force down her nervousness. It wasn't like she'd never spoken to Norah before. It was more the fact that taking these calls was Derek's job. It didn't feel right to be ... usurping his authority like this.

Okay, that was probably laying it on a bit thick. All she was doing was answering the phone while he was...

"Is Derek there?"

Of course she'd want to talk to him. "Sorry. He's out shooting some footage with Julie, I mean Agent Wilhelm…"

"Just so long as he's not shooting an actual werewolf," Norah replied with a slight chuckle. "I really don't need that kind of paperwork right now."

"Just Crypto-Hunter stuff," Danni said, forcing herself to relax. "I can take a message if you want."

There came a pause from the other end. In her mind, Danni could picture the senior agent shaking her head as she replied, "No. It's nothing you're not going to learn anyway. I'm going to assume it's not exactly a secret that we've been keeping the team on the backburner lately."

"Not really."

"That mess with Yarlberg still has everyone walking on eggshells. That bast... I mean, the *governor* made a lot of noise on his way out the door. Though his allies have been distancing themselves from him publicly, that doesn't mean they're a forgiving bunch. I won't lie. They've been looking for an excuse to sink this program, so I've made it unofficial policy to not give them one."

Danni knew she should keep her mouth shut and listen, yet she couldn't help but ask, "So what changed?"

Norah let out a sigh. "We can't hide forever. Eventually the budgetary committee is going to start asking why we're paying field agents to film a TV show. Mind you, that's not exactly the biggest waste of money I've seen from this administration." She paused, as if realizing she was speaking more freely than was probably warranted. "Nevertheless, you're correct. As soon as you can wrap up there, I need you all on a plane headed south."

Danni raised an eyebrow that only Mitch could see, not that he was paying attention. "Chupacabras? Or are we talking further south than that?"

"Yeah, and a bit wetter as well. I can't believe I'm

saying this, but they need you down in the Bermuda Triangle."

"The ... Bermuda Triangle?" Danni asked after a few moments.

They'd originally been scheduled to fly to the Bahamas following the debacle in New Jersey, she mused, but the mission had gotten deprioritized shortly thereafter, albeit that was probably more due to their *time out* status.

"I know what you're thinking, but this has nothing to do with time vortexes, UFOs, or any of that crap."

"So what's this about, then?" Danni asked, realizing she was starting to get into the groove of talking to their handler, taking on a more businesslike approach and asking the questions she assumed – *hoped* – Derek would ask.

"I don't know if Derek told you or not, but last year, right before the shit hit the fan..."

"You're talking about that giant squid case, right?" Then she quickly added, "Sorry to interrupt."

"Relax," Norah said. "This isn't the military." Then her tone changed, becoming more businesslike. "But yes. Some months back there was an abandoned fishing vessel found with marks in its hull which seemed to suggest an encounter with ... a creature of considerable size. It caused a minor furor with the local press, but then it died down just as quickly."

"So what changed?"

Norah paused, but when she spoke again there was a bit of an edge to her voice. "Have you heard of Zarro-Green Limited?"

"Aren't they an oil company?"

"Among other things. They're a major conglomerate based out of Venezuela. I'll spare you the boring details and get to the point. Yesterday afternoon they abruptly lost contact with one of their drillships in the region. No S.O.S. or anything, and it apparently just dropped off GPS. Their head office didn't waste any time reaching out to both the US and Bahamian governments for assistance in the matter. Fortunately, we had a ship in the area that was able to respond."

"Did they find it?"

"What was left. Mostly bits and pieces."

Danni closed her eyes, trying not to envision it. "Survivors?"

"Just one, and he had quite the story to tell."

Only one?

"Or at least so far as we can tell," Norah continued. "Communication with the rescue ship has been … choppy at best." Again her voice took on an edge. "But it was enough that the agent in charge made the decision to contact my superiors. Agent Caseman was apparently insistent that this was a job for the DoCC."

Wait. Agent Caseman? Before she could ask aloud, though, Danni remembered that Norah's ex-husband Jacob was likewise in the government's employ. She'd thought the tightness in the senior agent's voice had been due to the tragedy, but apparently it hit a bit closer to home, especially since she'd heard the divorce had been fairly recent.

Though Danni had never met the man, she knew he and Derek were friends from way back, which had to make this that much more awkward for their handler.

Norah, however, didn't volunteer any further information on the subject, maintaining a neutral tone as she continued filling Danni in on the details until she was done.

"Pass the word on and tell Derek to call me back if he has any questions."

"Will do."

"Oh, there is one more thing, Danni," the senior agent said.

"Yes?" she replied, curious to hear what Norah had to say.

"How have you been? I mean, I've read the reports, but I wanted to ask you personally."

Danni considered giving her some platitude, but this wasn't a summer internship. She was an agent of the U.S. Government, even if her team was off the books as far as the general populace was aware. "One day at a time," she said at last. "But it helps knowing they won't hurt anyone else ever again."

"I'm sorry I got you all involved in that mess. It should have been a matter for the police or the Bureau. But what's done is done. Off the record, though, I'm glad you bagged those hillbilly bastards."

"Me, too," Danni said, so softly she wasn't sure Norah even heard her.

"All right then. If that's all, then I'll meet you down there."

Danni frowned at the receiver. "Wait, you're going to meet us?"

"Yes. I know it's not standard protocol, but with multiple governments involved, this one has potential to become sticky. So, I've been given my marching orders. I'm to meet your team down there and assess the situation firsthand."

3

"That sounded a lot less fun than my dinner," Mitchell said once Danni ended the call and put the satnav away. "Care to fill me in?"

Danni glared at him sidelong. "I wouldn't want to ruin your digestion with actual work."

"Relax, kid. You did great. Besides, Norah's not exactly a hard-ass, at least not compared to our last liaison..."

He was interrupted by the sound of movement from the surrounding brush. A few moments later, their missing teammates stepped into the clearing, looking no worse for the wear.

"Who's hard ass are we discussing?" Derek asked idly.

"Definitely not his," Julie said, gesturing at Mitch as she started to pack her camera up. "Pretty sure he's allergic to the gym."

"What can I say? My mind is my most potent weapon, aside from my wit of course."

Derek sat down next to him and grinned. "Do I need to make any comments about firing blanks on both accounts, or is that a given?"

"I'd be insulted if you didn't."

He shook his head then turned to Danni. "Everything okay? You look a little pale. Please tell me Mitch didn't offer you any of his vegemite again."

"I did, but she's a food snob."

"One with working taste buds," Danni replied, taking a deep breath. "I'm fine. Norah called. Caught me off guard since you weren't around to answer it."

Derek nodded, raising an eyebrow. "I see. And I assume the senior team member around the fire left you to sink or swim."

"It was just a phone call," Mitch said.

Danni shrugged, but decided not to press the issue. Nerve wracking or not, she'd gotten through the conversation unscathed. "First time in the hotseat jitters I guess."

"I'm sure you did fine," Derek replied. "Besides, Norah likes you." He then inclined his head toward the medic. "Better than him anyway."

Mitchell threw back his head and laughed. "See, I told you."

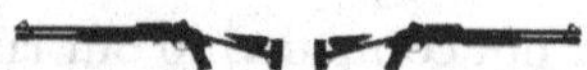

Derek listened intently as Danni brought the team up to speed, warring emotions stirring within him. The fact that they were once again being called in on something political had him worried. His team was used to operating on their own, running solo missions in remote locations where they could do their job unhindered.

It went hand in hand with what they did. After all, one didn't usually hear of Thunderbirds flying around Times Square. The simple fact of the matter was that the prehistoric throwbacks they normally dealt with tended to be found where people mostly weren't.

It was only when their paths crossed and turned bloody that Derek's team was brought in. Their job was simple: save lives, preferably on both sides. Culling a rogue Sasquatch, for example, was regrettable, but doing so not only saved human lives but potentially spared others of its species from the wrath of vengeful locals.

That debacle in New Jersey, though, had been an utter clusterfuck, born from human ego, and resulting in nothing but loss and suffering for so many. Now, to be called in again for a mission in which there were agendas attached...

The very idea threatened to make his blood boil, but that wasn't all.

There was also the locale to consider. Being out at sea would afford them the same anonymity as the deep woods. However, if they were forced to bring their work closer to shore, for whatever reason, that would almost certainly cause an issue. The Bahamas weren't exactly remote. The last thing they needed was to land a big fish, so to speak, in plain sight of thousands of beachgoers.

However, there was also the flipside – the excitement of a new mission. In his time running the team he'd known loss and sorrow. But there was also the joy of having seen things few others had. And it was all because the U.S. government had an interest in keeping extant megafauna off the public's radar, even if his team had never been given a concrete answer as to why.

But that was the government for you. He'd been dealing with them long enough to know that for every report that was eventually declassified, there were ten more that had been redacted enough to look like a game of Madlibs.

After hearing Danni out and considering things, he decided to focus on the positive. Rather than worry about government agendas, they'd do what they did best: assess the situation and do what was needed to rectify it. And if they got to see something new and interesting in the process, well, that was icing on the cake.

The rest, well, Norah could deal with it. They had their job and she had hers.

"Thoughts?" Derek asked once Danni had finished relaying the details. Later on, he planned to call Norah back and ask more questions, but for now it was best to get the others' opinions, including theories on what they were facing.

"I've always favored Speedos over swim trunks myself," Mitchell replied.

"Thoughts on this sea monster, I meant." He held up a hand. "And not that kind of sea monster either."

"Giant squid, maybe?" Julie asked. "Or those bigger ones. What are they called?"

"Colossal squid," Derek offered. "Maybe, but in either case it would need to be considerably larger than any specimen observed to date, not that we haven't seen that before. They also tend to be found in deep water, not at the surface sinking boats."

"So we drop some lines at the continental shelf and do a little sport fishing on Uncle Sam's dime."

Derek turned toward the medic. "Not going to complain if that happens, but there's also the fact that we had a similar case dropped in our lap a few months back."

Danni nodded, "I mentioned that to Norah. She said it got deprioritized."

"Meaning *we* were deprioritized," Derek surmised. "But it still makes me wonder if we're even dealing with the same creature."

"Which is a big if," Julie said. "I mean, this is still just a one-off so far, isn't it? There's no pattern established here. Why even bother calling us in at this point?"

"Apparently we were requested by name. Isn't that right?" Derek inclined his head toward Danni who nodded. "There's also the fact that the missing ship belonged to a member of big oil. Don't doubt that they have a bit more pull than the local fishermen."

Mitch leaned forward. "So, are we just going to ignore the rest?"

"What do you mean?"

"How this is all conveniently happening in the Bermuda Triangle."

"Ah, I see. Is this the part where we put on our tinfoil hats?"

The medic laughed. "Just putting it out there. Ignoring sea monsters for a moment, this isn't the first time people have reported strange things out there ... like, for instance, the radio interference from that rescue ship. All I'm saying is the place has a rep."

"That could simply be a case of broken equipment."

"And this monster might be nothing more than misidentified seaweed, but we're still taking it seriously."

Derek held up a hand. "Point taken. But orders are orders. That said, our first and foremost duty is to assess whether this creature exists and is a threat. That's top priority, above busted radios, smoothing ruffled feathers, or even finding the lost city of Atlantis. Agreed?"

There were nods from all around the campfire.

"All right, good. Then let's wrap up here, head in, and get some research done. I'll touch base with Norah to figure out when our flight's leaving, but knowing our gracious government let's assume it's a red eye."

"You'd think we'd rate better than coach," Julie said from her spot next to Danni on the half-empty McDonnell Douglas MD-88 bound for Atlanta.

"Be thankful," Danni replied, peering at the laptop in front of her. "If it was up to the Adventure Channel we'd be taking a bus."

"Is that schoolwork or..."

"Research. Derek gave me permission to access the archives last night. Figured it would give me a chance to get caught up while we're in the air."

Julie understood that was about as much as Danni could say, at least on a public flight. Though the other travelers appeared to be preoccupied with their own affairs, there was still their cover to maintain. As far as their audience was concerned, they were nothing more than the cast of a run-of-the-mill reality show, chasing shadows in the woods and calling it evidence.

Of course, there were those who thought otherwise, some who'd come perilously close to figuring out the truth. Julie knew full well because she'd been one of them. After her sister had gone missing, she'd been stonewalled by both the police and her own colleagues at WGXP News. In desperation, Julie had turned to the internet, searching for anything that might help her, and learning of some of the crazier theories that abounded in cyberspace.

Then she'd heard that the cast of The Crypto-Hunter was visiting the state, purportedly to conduct an investigation close to where her sister had last been seen.

It had seemed a long shot, but it had paid off – albeit not quite in any way she could've foreseen. Hell, the ordeal had nearly killed them all. In the end, though, they'd pulled through as a team – which in turn had led to her being offered a fulltime position within the DoCC.

Best of all, they'd managed to save her sister.

Sadly, Sophie had since withdrawn from the family,

refusing all attempts at contact. It was heartbreaking, but Julie clung to the hope that her sister just needed time to heal ... much as Danni had.

Speaking of which, it was time to get her mind in gear. Her sister was always in her thoughts these days, but for now she had a job to do.

Besides, as a former reporter, research was right up her alley. It also didn't hurt that her current duties tended to be far more engrossing than the banal human interest stories that had once been her bread and butter.

"Need a study buddy?" she asked the younger woman.

Danni turned toward her and smiled. "You bet. This stuff is usually pretty interesting, but it's still easier staying awake if someone's there to nudge me."

"Then consider me your nudge," Julie said.

She liked Danni. The girl was brave and resourceful, but lacked the cliquish ego one might expect from a college-aged coed. Some of that might've been the sobering reality of what they did, coupled with the fact that the poor girl had lost friends and family along the way.

Julie didn't enjoy prying into other people's business as a habit. However, it was second nature from her reporting days. Not to mention, she'd thought it best to familiarize herself with her new teammates. After all, their lives could very well depend on one another.

She knew that Danni, her brother Harrison, and several of their friends had been in the wrong place at the wrong time. Though the papers had reported it as a bear attack, the truth was far more sinister. An entire town had been left in ruins after a rare strain of rabies had infected a nearby Sasquatch clan. Julie could barely imagine how horrifying that must have been, certainly every bit as terrifying as that affair with the Lesterfields. Yet this girl sitting next to her had survived both.

She hadn't walked away unscathed, though. In the months since, Julie had spied Danni occasionally talking to a picture of her late brother. She remembered doing something similar on sleepless nights, when Sophie had first gone missing. It had been a way of keeping her alive in her heart, no matter what happened. Julie had gotten far luckier with her sibling than Danni had, but she still hoped it helped the poor girl find the peace she deserved. "Find anything good so far?"

Danni showed her what was on her screen. "The St. Augustine Blob of 1896."

Julie stared at the pictures. "Looks like a giant pile of snot."

"Close. It wasn't much more by the time it washed up on the beach. Then it was sucked back out to sea, only to end up beached again a couple days later in even worse shape. But at least the folks who spotted it the second time were smart enough to drag it away from the surf."

Julie nodded. "I think I read about that back in college. Had a boyfriend who was into this stuff."

"Bet he'd love to hear what you're doing now."

"Probably. But some romances are best left unkindled. So what's the scoop?"

"Inconclusive as usual. They've been debating this one for more than a century – going back and forth between a giant squid, rotting whale blubber, and a monster octopus."

"Two of those are scary, one is just gross."

"Pretty much, although it's kinda funny to think that people have been arguing over a pile of whale fat all this time."

"So where did this Coke versus Pepsi debate net out?" Julie asked.

"That's the weird part. Up until the mid-nineteen eighties, most analysis seemed to conclude that it was actually a massive cephalopod. They even gave it a scientific designation, *Otoctopus giganteus*."

"Shouldn't that be spelled...?"

"It isn't a typo," Danni said. "Means giant-eared octopus or something like that, although I'm not really sure why. Either way, someone was trying to jump the gun on naming the species, even though it probably doesn't exist."

"Oh?"

"Yeah. The two most recent studies, one in the nineties and another in the early two-thousands, concluded it was nothing more than blubber after all."

"Except," Derek said in a low voice, glancing back from the row ahead of them, "not all studies are created equal."

Julie raised an eyebrow. "Are you saying there's something funny about them?"

"I'm saying no such thing," he replied with a grin, no doubt due to them being surrounded by other passengers. "I'm simply suggesting that some methodologies leave a bit to be desired whereas others ... are purposely done that way."

"A coverup," Julie whispered. "But why, especially after so long?"

Derek grinned again, then turned to face forward.

"Hold on. I think I know," Danni said, scrolling through the files on her desktop. "I saw this earlier but didn't think anything of it. Ah, here we are." She pointed again to her screen. "There was supposedly an expedition in the mid-nineties, right before that new analysis was done. But it was unrelated, on paper anyway, to the St. Augustine monster."

"So then why do we care?"

"Because it was the same cryptid. The Augustine blob was linked to the legend of the Lusca. According to local myths, it's a massive tentacled creature that supposedly inhabits the blue holes just off the coast of Andros Island."

"And that's what this expedition was looking for," Julie surmised.

"Exactly. A Caribbean-based cryptozoological group got funding from a local tourist magnet to search these so called blue holes and the surrounding waters."

"Did they find anything?"

"That's the kicker," Danni said, shaking her head. She scrolled through her files again, then called up the inflight WiFi and made a few cursory Google searches. "Nope. Just like I thought. There isn't anything after that. Just a few hits about the expedition being planned and then nothing. I can't even find a mention of this group afterward." She glanced at Julie. "That's usually not how these things work. Even when an expedition fails, which they do all the time, there's writeups, speculation, excuses, et cetera. But it's like all record of these guys was expunged after the fact."

"Did something happen to them?"

"Maybe," Danni offered. "These blue holes are known to be dangerous. Even experienced divers have lost their lives in them. But there shouldn't be any reason to hide an accident."

"So you think they found something?"

Danni shrugged. "Or something found them."

"But then why cover it up? I did some digging into the crypto community back before, well, you know," Julie said, mindful of prying ears. "They're not the type to let a blurry photo go unnoticed, much less something more substantial."

"Trust me, I know. If someone had seen so much as a shadow, they'd have been crowing about it left and right. But maybe that means something not only happened to them but that someone else wanted it kept quiet. The question is why?"

Julie considered this for a moment before a possible reason hit her. "I think I might have an idea. I did a piece on popular vacation spots a few years back, pure fluff, but I gave it my due diligence. Anyway, the Bahamas has one of the most thriving economies in the Americas, based entirely off tourism."

"Makes sense. Can't say I'm not looking forward to a beach day or two."

"Same here. But imagine what might happen if a news story broke about something in the water."

Danni inclined her head. "Like in that old movie *Jaws*?"

"Not *that* old," Julie said with a huff. "But yes. A big hungry shark is definitely going to affect the summer crowd."

Danni nodded. "And that was just one. But think of what could happen if word got out that there was perhaps an entire population right off the coast?"

"It might cause a panic. Worse, lots of people would choose to spend their vacation dollars elsewhere."

"Makes sense. And we're talking about something potentially a lot bigger here."

"How much bigger?" Julie asked.

"That's a good question." Danni clicked open another tab on her web browser. "The colossal squid is officially recognized as the world's largest cephalopod species."

Julie nodded. "I saw the photos from when they caught one. Cool looking, but I'm not sure I'd give it odds against anything larger than a speedboat."

"Exactly. Officially, the largest specimen was about thirty feet long and weighed maybe half a ton."

"Big but not sea monster big. What about our pile of snot?"

"A *bit* larger. Assuming it wasn't whale fat, the St Augustine creature was estimated to have an arm span of between seventy five and two hundred feet, with the upper estimates of its live weight in the several dozen ton range."

"Not exactly an accurate measurement."

Danni shrugged. "Best they could do. It was badly decomposed." She then lowered her voice to a whisper. "But think about that estimate. On the low end, it's still pretty damned big. But if they were right about the high end..."

She paused and clicked to open another file.

A reproduction of an old painting appeared on her screen – one depicting a monstrous octopus tearing apart a three-masted sailing ship, beneath which was a single word: *Kraken*.

4

5 *miles off the coast of Nassau*
"So ... what do you think they're doing down there?" Ericka Saliz asked, despite knowing full well what was likely going on below deck in the thirty-five foot cabin cruiser.

"All I know is those had better be damned good sandwiches," her boyfriend Gabriel Jackson replied with a chuckle, looking up from where he sat in the fighting chair, beer in hand and his fishing pole leaning against him – the line cast but so far not a nibble.

They were aboard the Too Loose To Trek, owned by Gabriel's older brother Roy. As an art major, the name of the boat made Ericka cringe, but it was hard to complain about a free vacation to the Bahamas.

The weather was beautiful, barely a cloud in the sky, and the water – at least near the coast – was so clear it was like peering through glass. This far out, trying their hand at deep sea fishing, that wasn't quite the case, but she still couldn't deny it was beautiful.

Roy had invited them down to celebrate both his recent promotion to vice-president at the firm he worked for, as well as his six month anniversary with his wife Maryanne.

Ericka hadn't been too impressed with Maryanne. She was a bit too blonde and bubbly to be anything other than a trophy bride. The fact that Roy could barely keep his hands off her made Ericka slightly uncomfortable. Public displays of affection weren't really her thing. Doubly so since Gabriel was currently eying her in her white string bikini, no doubt hoping to entice her into one of his weird kinks.

"Why don't you come over here and keep me company while we wait for them? We could pretend you're the naughty little mermaid and I'm your prince."

Ugh!

Maryanne had gone below to fetch some snacks while the men were busy casting for sailfish, or trying to. Roy had followed her shortly thereafter. That had been twenty minutes ago. Not helping was the occasional grunt heard from inside the cabin, making her desperately wish she'd stayed back at shore.

Who does that? she thought. *Who invites their brother out fishing and then disappears for a not so quickie?* "Sorry, this little mermaid has no interest in your trident," she replied, stepping onto the narrow walkway leading around the boat. "I'm going to the front to catch some rays."

"It's called the bow," he called back, "or, if we add an extra L, it could be the bl..."

"Keep dreaming, King Neptune," she replied, gripping the railway to keep herself from slipping. Though a swim sounded good, she preferred somewhere where she could still touch the bottom.

As she made her way forward, she was certain she heard a soft moan coming from inside. Ericka stopped to listen, but then realized what she was doing and began heading forward again.

"So gross," she said to herself just as a splash of cold water hit her backside. For a second or two, she lost her grip on the railing – leaving her teetering on the edge before she managed to grab hold again. "Goddamn it, Gabe! That wasn't funny!"

"Huh, what wasn't?" her boyfriend asked, popping his head around the corner.

"You splashed me!"

"Um, no. I was resetting my line ... and grabbing another beer."

"Yes you did. Look at me. I'm all wet."

"How wet are you?" he asked with a leer.

"I swear, Gabe..."

"Relax. You probably just caught some spray. This is the ocean, after all."

"Whatever," she replied with a huff, still certain he was somehow to blame.

Thankfully, there were already some towels spread out on the bow. Maryanne might've been a trophy wife, but at least she realized not all of them were interested in sport fishing.

Ericka lay down, the sun warm against her brown skin, and then called up a playlist on her phone. Nothing but silence greeted her, however, as the app crashed back to the home screen. A few more attempts produced the same result, until she finally gave up in disgust.

"Piece of shit."

She closed her eyes and had just barely settled down when there came a whizzing sound from the back of the boat. For a moment, Ericka wasn't sure what it might be, but then she heard the whoop of joy from her boyfriend and realized it was the reel of his fishing rod.

"I think I got something!"

"That's nice," she whispered, leaning back again. "Keep it to yourself."

"Holy shit! This thing is huge."

She chuckled softly as the boat rocked in the current. "Good luck trying to convince yourself of that."

"What the... Fuuuuuck!" A heavy splash came from the rear of the boat, cutting Gabriel's cry short just as the boat rocked again.

Ericka sat up and looked around, wondering if maybe a wave had hit them, but there wasn't anything to be seen from her vantage point except calm water.

There came more frantic splashing from the back. Giving up on her plans, she let out a sigh and got up again. Knowing Gabriel, he'd gotten too excited and fallen overboard. Either way, she supposed she should go give him a hand. He was a better swimmer than her, but he'd also been drinking.

The boat lurched in the water as she shimmied her way along the side, almost causing her to lose her footing on the slick walkway. It definitely felt like something had hit the boat, but what could they have possibly run into way out here, especially with the engine off?

Ericka stepped onto the firmer footing of the back deck, or whatever it was called. There was probably a proper nautical term for it that Gabriel would be happy to mansplain to her. However, her boyfriend was nowhere to be seen. Neither was his fishing pole. She stepped to the railing, certain she'd see him, pissed off and wet, trying to climb back aboard. But something else caught her eye instead.

A large gelatinous mass was pressed up against the boat. She'd been right, something had hit them after all, no doubt propelled by the tide. Whatever it was, it was fleshy, brownish-red, and huge — easily as wide as the ship itself.

"What the hell?"

Had Gabriel fallen overboard and maybe gotten trapped beneath this thing?

Oh no!

She quickly looked around for something to use to push it away from the boat, spotting a long-handled fishing net nearby. Ericka grabbed it and leaned over the railing, prodding at the mass in the hope of freeing her boyfriend, hoping it wasn't too late to...

In the next second, though, it was as if the sea itself had erupted around her. Water foamed up as the object began to thrash, instantly soaking her in the ensuing spray. In the space of one horrified instant she realized two things: the mass was alive, and it was even larger than she'd first assumed. It rolled over and she caught sight of two massive eyes that seemed to instantly fixate on her.

At first she could do nothing but stare back, then something impossibly strong wrapped around her torso, ripping into her skin and squeezing hard enough to cut off the scream that wanted to escape her lips.

Ericka was lifted from the deck, little more than a child's plaything in this monstrosity's grasp. Acting on nothing but pure instinct, she managed to grab hold of one of the boat's dual fighting chairs, barely halting her progress as massive fleshy appendages rose out of the water from seemingly all around, each at least as long as the boat itself.

They're ... tentacles!

She had one brief moment in which she remembered something Gabriel had tried to get her to watch the other night, some disgusting Japanese cartoon, and then she was overpowered. She was dragged from the chair, losing two fingernails in the process, and lifted off her feet as if she weighed nothing.

Her world briefly became a nightmare roller coaster as

she was swung about, the deck little more than a blur of sickening motion beneath her.

Then, before she could even begin to process what was happening to her, or what had likely happened to Gabriel, she was yanked over the side at breakneck speed, the side of her head colliding with the boat's railing. There came the sickening crunch of bone, followed by the shock of cold water hitting her body, and then she mercifully knew no more.

"Did you feel that?" Roy Jackson asked his wife, rolling his sweat-slicked body off of hers. "I'm pretty sure we rocked the whole fucking boat."

"Jerk," Maryanne replied, punching him lightly on the arm. "I can't believe we did that. Your brother is right outside."

"That's what makes it so awesome," he said with a laugh. He wasn't kidding either. Though he'd locked the door at his wife's insistence, he knew that wasn't foolproof. Someone could have peered through the windows or popped the hatch on the bow. The thought of being caught by his brother or, better yet, Gabe's hot ass girl-friend, had not only caused him to follow his wife down below, but had allowed him to finish so explosively that he was certain he was at least three pounds lighter.

There was no denying it had been the best sex they'd had in months. And though his wife had protested at first, he knew for a fact that she had cum at least twice. The scratches up and down his back were a testament to his performance.

Maryanne grabbed her bikini bottom and began to tie it back on. "You realize they probably know what we were doing, right? It doesn't take that long to carry up a tray of sandwiches."

"You'd be surprised how clueless Gabe can be when he wants to be."

"And Ericka?"

"With any luck my little brother got the hint and decided to make good use of their time alone. For all we know, they could be going at it right now up on deck."

The thought of catching them in the act caused Roy's dick to twitch again. He reached over and grabbed the string of his wife's swim top. "Wanna go watch? Maybe we can get it going from both sides of the door this time."

She slapped his hand away. "Down boy. There's no way you're getting round two while they're still aboard."

Roy was pretty sure he could've convinced her otherwise if he pressed the case, but just then the boat lurched to the side, followed by a muted noise that almost sounded like a tree branch cracking.

"Maybe they're the ones rocking the boat instead," Maryanne said, getting dressed.

"Not unless they're into some really rough stuff." He let out a sigh. "Guess I'd better go take a look. Make sure the moron didn't hook something bigger than he can handle."

He started toward the door when Maryanne cleared her throat from behind him.

"Forgetting something, Romeo?"

He turned to find her holding his swim trunks. "Oh yeah. Might need those."

"Sorry, hun, but I don't think either of them need to see the Loch Ness monster."

The thought of Gabe's girlfriend checking out his junk caused Roy's prick to twitch again. At the speed of thought, he indulged in a quick fantasy of Ericka joining them in the cabin, all while his brother cluelessly chugged beer and waited for a bite on his line.

Realizing he was in danger of getting another raging erection, he quickly slipped his trunks on and tried to think unsexy thoughts – like visiting Maryanne's family during the holidays. *A boner killer if ever there was one.*

He reached for the doorknob when his wife once again caught his attention.

"You'll need this, too." She handed him the platter full of sandwiches.

He took it then, balancing it in one hand, opened the cabin door. "Sorry, bro. Needed to check the bilge pumps," he called out, knowing it was a pathetic lie, but also realizing his brother probably wouldn't question it. Gabe was the type to just go with the flow, a useful trait for times like these.

However, his words were met with nothing but the breeze and the gentle lap of water against the hull.

"Gabe?" He stepped out, seeing nothing but an empty deck, one far emptier than it should've been. "What the fuck?!" One of the fighting chairs was missing, seemingly torn right out of the hull. What the hell had that idiot done to his boat? *I'm gonna kill that little shithead.* Roy put the sandwiches down and turned back. "Hey, Mare. Can you check the hatch, see if they're up front?"

She turned away, grumbling to herself. "I swear, they'd better not be doing anything." A few seconds later, though, she called back, "No one's up here."

Roy looked around. Where the hell had they gone? It was a nice day for a swim, but it would have been stupid for them to take a dip without saying anything first, especially if they'd just caused thousands of dollars in damage to his fucking boat.

Nevertheless, he stepped to the aft rail, leaning on it as he looked out at the vast sea around them. The glare off the water was too bright to see much, though. "Hey, Gabe!" he called out, "are you out...?"

The words died on his lips as his left hand slipped, almost causing him to stumble. He caught himself and stepped back, noting the railing was slick.

Roy's first assumption was that it was simply spray from the ocean, but that quickly gave way to much darker thoughts as he looked down and saw the bright red stain of fresh blood coating his hand.

5

Danni had expected the weather to be nice, but what she found, upon leaving Andros Town International Airport, was beyond even her expectations. If only all their future assignments could be in such a wonderful place.

It was night and day compared to trudging through a cold damp forest. The feel of the morning sun on her face was almost enough to make her forget that the last leg of their journey had been anything but smooth. Danni had been on plenty of rough flights since joining the team, but whatever they'd flown through on their approach to Andros Island had given new meaning to the word turbulence.

The seatbelt sign had come on relatively early during the flight and the attendants had been tight-lipped about it. Even the look on Derek's normally unflappable face had suggested he'd had doubts as to whether the plane would shake itself apart before landing.

But they'd made it safe and sound. And, despite the seat-gripping fear of earlier, she couldn't help but feel a thousand times better stepping foot into the light tropical breeze that spoke of fun, sand, and surf.

Danni knew they were there to do a job, but found herself hoping for at least one free day nevertheless. Maybe she'd get lucky and Mitch would ask her to assist him in setting up his lab, something that almost always resulted in plenty of free time as he was both a workaholic and terrible at delegating assignments.

As usual, they had only their luggage and some Adventure Channel gear with them. However, they'd managed to not be recognized – no doubt their status as d-list celebrities was far less interesting than the tropical paradise they were now entering.

Under normal circumstances, they'd pick up their real gear later. It wasn't uncommon for them to step foot from an airport and find their custom SUVs already waiting for them – black, unmarked, and loaded to the rims with firepower.

However, Derek had dissuaded them from that notion early on in their flight.

"Much as I might miss having easy access to my rifles," he'd told them, "it probably wouldn't do much good against a sea monster. Besides, we'll be meeting up with Jake at some point. Don't doubt for a second that he'll have everything we need."

That ought to be interesting, Danni considered. Supposedly, he was the reason Derek had gotten into this line of work to begin with. However, unlike most of their missions, Jake's ex-wife Norah was also on her way to brief them in person.

Not on her way, already here, Danni noted, recognizing her as she approached from the direction of the short term lot. *Speak of the devil and she shall appear.*

Norah was a fit woman in her early forties, with light

brown skin, a tight smile, and shoulder length dark hair which she normally kept in a tight bun. Today was no exception. In fact, Danni realized, nothing about her appearance, down to her crisp suit, seemed any different than when she was in the office. Truth be told, she stuck out like a sore thumb against all the visitors in shorts and sundresses. If this was her idea of undercover, they were going to have a hard time blending in.

"Enjoying the weather?" Derek greeted as they walked up to her.

"Not really," Norah replied. "Too damned warm for my blood."

"In all fairness, you might be a wee bit overdressed."

"And if this were a pleasure cruise I might agree, Dr. Jenner."

Derek laughed and stepped forward. "It's good to see you, Norah."

For a moment, Danni wasn't sure if the senior agent would keep it formal or not, but after a beat she gave Derek a hug. "Likewise. It's been too long."

"Not by design." Derek stepped back, allowing the other team members to greet her, albeit a bit more formally than he had.

Once they were finished, he asked, "So can I assume our penance has finally been paid?"

She looked away for a moment. "That probably depends on how this mission goes."

"Fair enough," Derek said with a slight shake of his head. "Is Jake here yet?"

Norah frowned. "No. There's been some ... complications."

"Complications?" Danni found herself curious, considering they were talking about Norah's ex, but to the senior agent's credit she barely batted an eye.

"Of the mechanical variety." After a moment, she

added, "I wouldn't worry. They should be underway again soon. In the meantime, how was your flight?"

"About the same, complication-wise," Julie said.

"It wasn't that bad," Derek replied.

Mitchell chuckled. "Says you. I was starting to think that tomorrow's headline would read *Cast of Crypto-Hunter lost in Bermuda Triangle*."

"You assume we'd make the front page. Although, as far as obituaries go I could think of worse."

Danni nudged him with her arm. "Personally, I'd prefer to hold off on mine for another sixty years or so."

"If it means anything," Norah said, "so would I." After another beat she turned and beckoned the group to follow. "That's enough chitchat. The Coastal Defense Force just got word of another incident that we think might be related to the ZarroGreen sinking. I'll brief you on the..."

"Dr. Jenner! Excuse me, Dr. Derek Jenner!"

The group turned to find a tall lanky man heading toward them. He was tanned, had his blonde hair up in a man bun, and was wearing cargo shorts and an unbuttoned shirt. Despite his overall laid back appearance, an expensive looking camera hung from around his neck.

Before he could reach them, however, Norah let out a sigh then moved to intercept him. "There will be time for autographs later, sir. For now, I'll need you to please..."

Rather than stop, however, he neatly sidestepped her. "Sorry, lady, but this is official business."

She looked like she wanted to say something to that, but Derek was ready, a smirk on his face. "You heard the man, it's official business. What can I do for you?"

This was nothing new for the team, playing their parts so as to maintain their cover, but Danni was curious to see how Norah would handle it. In her day to day duties there was no secondary identity to protect. She was a government agent twenty-four / seven. For now, though, all she did was roll her eyes.

The man stopped in front of Derek. "Kerry Klipsch."

Derek took a moment to shake his hand before asking, "And how can I be of assistance, Mr. Klipsch."

"It's just Kerry. Save the mister part for the award show banquets," he said with an exaggerated chuckle. "Anyway, Stant told me what flight you'd be taking and asked me to meet you down here."

Oh no. Danni just barely suppressed a grimace. Stant Bennet was the director of merchandising at the Adventure Channel, as well as one of their producers. He, or his assistant anyway, was always signing them up for conventions and what not. Sadly, he was also the man behind Danni's oft-lamented photoshoot at Chesapeake Bay, leading to record poster sales at the Adventure Channel's online store.

That wouldn't have been so bad, had it not meant her having to sign hundreds of pictures of her half-naked body for the show's adoring and often desperate fans.

However, that shoot was over a year old and sales were beginning to drop again. Stant had been hounding them for new merchandise and it was only through Derek's fine hand at finagling that they'd been able to remain conveniently busy whenever the subject was brought up.

But now Stant had apparently opted to stop playing games and simply ambush them instead. *Stupid.* She should've seen it coming, especially knowing where they were flying to. It was pretty easy to ditch the corporate types when they were deep in the woods, but here in the vacation capital of the world? Danni didn't like her odds, especially since she'd already been planning to hit the beach. All this clown had to do was tail them.

Despite their undercover status, Danni found herself

wishing Norah would flash her badge and tell this guy to take a hike. They could always make up a lie about it later.

She glanced at her teammates. Derek and Mitch both wore knowing looks on their faces, but Julie merely seemed confused. She hadn't been fully indoctrinated into this crap yet, her actual debut on the show only a few weeks old thanks to the Adventure Channel's programming schedule.

She's not going to like this, not one bit.

As she was ruing what was no doubt to come, Kerry took off his sunglasses and introduced himself to the rest of the team. Though his voice was pleasant enough, Danni could see his eyes already working, appraising them all ... but mostly her and Julie. She could almost sense what he was thinking. There'd be plenty of shots of the team as a whole, setting up equipment, getting ready to work, some staged, others candid. Then there would be individual shoots, for the channel's website and official magazine.

That's where things would diverge. There might be a request for one or two pictures of Derek in his swim trunks. After all, there was no point in alienating an entire market segment. However, that segment also wasn't their primary audience. Conversely, she and Julie would probably be offered increasingly smaller swimsuits and asked to pose in ways that had nothing to do with hunting cryptids.

Worst of all, there was likely no way around it. It was the price of fame, minor as theirs might be, as well as part of maintaining their cover. Not to mention, it was in the fine print of their contracts.

The introductions out of the way, Kerry immediately launched into his spiel. "All right, so I know you guys have a tight schedule and I don't want to get in the way..."

"That's great," Derek interrupted. "Because we..."

"So I figured we could shoot first over at Gialia. My

assistant is out there setting things up now. Then, maybe, if there's time before you fly out, we can get some action shots at Zorkos. I bet Stant would go wild for that."

"I'm sure we can work something out," Derek said, gesturing toward Norah. "But for now, we have an interview with Ms..."

"Jackson," Norah replied. "And I'm on a *really* tight schedule."

Not to be dissuaded in the least, Kerry said, "Cool. Well, I don't want to hold you up, but I'm willing to bet you don't need the entire team. If I can just borrow a few folks for now, I'm sure we can get caught up later." Not surprisingly, he turned toward Danni. "Miss. Kent, Ms. Wilhelm, if you'd both be kind enough to follow me, I have a vehicle waiting right over there."

"I ... need my camera operator to record the session," Derek replied, throwing Danni an apologetic glance. "But perhaps Mr. Harkness would be happy to oblige. He can give you a rundown on some of the equipment we typically use on our night hunts and how this episode might differ."

Danni saw the look of disproval Kerry made and instantly knew that wasn't going to fly. "That's great and all, Dr. Jenner, but perhaps Mr. Harkness can help with your task instead. I'm sure someone as technically adept as him can operate a camera."

"I knew I shouldn't have skipped leg day," Mitchell said with a grin, no doubt enjoying this. "But yeah, I'd be happy to run the minicam, chief."

Derek threw him some side eye. "Don't call me chief."

"Awesome!" Kerry exclaimed. "Then I won't hold you up any longer. Ladies, if you'll follow me."

"Hold on," Julie said. "I'm not going anywhere. I mean, I'm not even dressed for this. And I sure as hell didn't pack any..."

"It's all taken care of," Kerry interrupted. "Hair and makeup are waiting for us, as well as wardrobe. Don't worry, the Adventure Channel has all your sizes so we should be good to go."

"Derek...," Julie growled, her tone cold as ice.

"Sorry," he said sheepishly, "but it *is* technically in our contract."

6

Derek would have sooner given his own life than offer up any of his team as sacrificial lambs. That said, Kerry Klipsch's arrival wasn't exactly life or death. Still, he didn't enjoy his friends being exploited.

And he definitely knew he wouldn't enjoy the fallout later, especially with Julie's temper. Still, they all had obligations as part of their TV commitment, even if they didn't particularly care for them.

A smile crossed his face as he remembered his friend and former tracker Chuck. Put that man in the harshest swampland and he'd be right at home, but stuck behind a table signing autographs was his own personal hell, something he hadn't been shy about voicing.

Derek's smile quickly fell, though.

First Chuck and then Francis, both of them lost in the line of duty. If Derek had one personal specter with regards to the dual lives he and his team led, it was that those who died for the cause were often given some public fluff regarding retirement – their real fates covered up as part of the service they all agreed to.

And now here he was, almost full circle ... in a manner

of speaking anyway. It had been some time since he'd seen Jake, far too long as a matter of fact. It had been even longer since they'd worked a case together, not since the early days when the DoCC was first formed.

He remembered it like it was yesterday – that ill-fated research expedition deep in the Amazon rain forest. One moment Derek had been cataloging the effects of deforestation on the indigenous howler monkey population, the next he was locked in a life or death struggle with a creature that time had seemingly forgotten. It was only through dumb luck that he'd stumbled across an undercover CIA operation in the middle of...

"Relax. They'll be fine."

He turned away from the window. "Huh?"

"You looked like you were wool gathering," Norah said from the opposite seat in the back of the oversized black sedan. "I'm pretty sure your team can handle a few photographs."

Undercover they might be, Derek considered, but their transportation was anything but subtle. Once they got through with their initial briefing, he'd have to do something about making sure they were a little more low key as they prepared for this operation. "I know," he said, pulling himself back into the present. "I was just thinking about when Jake and I first met."

"Simpler times," Norah replied, her words implying more than one meaning.

The privacy screen was up between them and the driver, so Derek felt comfortable talking openly. "If you consider being hunted by an angry Megatherium to be simple."

Mitchell grinned at him. "Must've been terrifying facing off against a giant sloth. I bet you almost had to casually saunter to get to safety."

Derek laughed. "You'd be surprised how fast they can move when they're pissed off."

"I'll take your word for it. I saw the photos. That was one hell of a big bastard."

"Not as big as what we're here for," Norah said.

"Yeah, about that. Are you sure we're not just dealing with an accident?"

Norah inclined her head toward the medic. "Pretty sure. The situation has ... progressed while you were in transit."

"How so?" Derek replied, all business now.

"The Royal Defense Force responded to a garbled distress call yesterday from a pleasure craft. Two people were missing, the owner's brother and his girlfriend. There was blood on the deck and the owner reported seeing something large swimming away from the boat."

"And you're sure alcohol wasn't involved?" Mitchell asked.

She shook her head. "First thing they asked. Accidents aren't uncommon, especially when you take basic human stupidity into account. Problem is, stupidity doesn't rip a high-end fighting chair straight out of the deck or leave gouges in the hull just above the water line."

"A whole lot of alcohol, maybe?"

Derek glanced at him then back at Norah. "I think what Mitch is trying to say is it could be circumstantial."

"Yes it could be, but there's been other odd occurrences as well. I'm not sure if they're related or not, but when you've done this job long enough you start to get very leery about labeling anything a coincidence."

"How so?"

"I have a man standing by to brief your team. At the behest of the local government we've brought in a specialist. He's waiting for us at the institute." Upon seeing the raised eyebrow on Derek's face, she clarified, "The Rogers Maritime Institute. That's where we're headed."

Before he could ask anything further, there came a chime from Norah's side. She plucked a cell phone out of her jacket pocket and answered with a curt, "Caseman here."

Derek knew better than to interrupt, especially once he saw Norah's eyes open wide in apparent surprise.

"It did?" she asked. "When? How did it happen?" She continued to listen, nodding to herself as the party on the other end relayed the information to her. "Okay, do what you can. In the meantime, clamp a lid on this. And do not, under any circumstances, let that Guerrero woman know before we arrive. I don't want her boss stirring up more shit until we can assess damage control."

She hung up, looking considerably more annoyed than she had minutes earlier. Though Derek decided to let her take the lead, Mitchell was a bit more forthcoming.

"I take it our formal reception has been cancelled."

"Something like that," Norah replied. "We just got word that one of our helicopters went down about a mile off shore."

"Anything we can do to help?"

"A rescue mission has already been dispatched, but they're not hopeful for survivors. This complicates matters."

Derek and Mitchell shared a glance and then the medic said, "I hope you're not going to tell us a giant squid caused it, because I'm pretty sure I saw that movie last month on Syfy."

Norah shook her head. "Not quite. However, the helicopter just so happened to be carrying the lone survivor of the ZarroGreen accident."

"What can you tell us about this guy?" Derek asked as the car pulled into the lot of the Rogers Maritime Institute – a pair of squat, drably colored buildings far more modest than the name would suggest.

"I don't suppose it hurts, especially since you can't ask him yourself," Norah said. "His name was Sydney Treco. Expedition manager for ZarroGreen. Company man, been with them for over a decade, but apparently not considered one of their rising stars. He wasn't exactly commanding the darling of the fleet."

"Oh?"

"The San Cristóbal Tortuga, one of their older drill-ships. Apparently it was scheduled for decommission later this year, or so I've been told."

"Guess this saves them the effort."

Derek nodded. "Not to mention probably gives them an insurance payout that dwarfs the actual value of the ship itself."

"Still, talk about bad luck, for him anyway," Mitchell said. "Any idea what caused the crash?"

Norah took a deep breath. "Remember what I was saying about strange occurrences? Before they lost contact, the pilot reported instrument malfunctions."

That caught Derek's attention. "Is it me, or does there seem to be a lot of that going on lately?"

"Maybe the State Department's going with lowest bidder again," Mitchell suggested.

Norah shook her head. "Had the Tortuga not experienced the same thing, at least according to Treco's statement, I might almost be willing to accept that and move on."

"Yeah, but what fun would that be?"

Silence descended in the car as they navigated toward the rear of the second building, until Derek said, "Just promise me nobody's going to start throwing out the words Bermuda Triangle at this briefing."

"Can't say that hasn't crossed my mind a dozen or so times during this conversation alone," Mitchell opined.

"Relax," Norah said. "You're here to assess the possibility of bagging a big fish, nothing more."

"Good."

"However," she continued, "I won't lie and say there might not be some overlap. As I said, do this job long enough and you'll soon realize there's no such thing as coincidence."

Whatever research this facility normally conducted appeared to have been co-opted for the time being. Plain-clothed guards stood at all the entrances, their suits making them stand out as much as if they'd been wearing riot gear – at least in Derek's eyes. He and Mitch had to show their IDs at no less than two checkpoints before finally being led toward a conference room.

"Just a bit on the overkill side," the medic commented.

"Perhaps," Norah admitted, "but the local government has agreed to let us take point on this, provided we ensure it doesn't cause any strife to the tourism trade."

"It's always about the Benjamins."

Derek could understand his friend's reticence, but at the same time he knew how the game was played. There was *always* money at stake, the only upside being that the more of it that was at risk the likelier they'd be allowed to finish their job quickly.

Though this assignment wasn't dripping with the same level of political slime as their mission in the Garden State had been, so far anyway, there was still an unpleasant undercurrent. He was rapidly getting the impression of backdoor deals more concerned with cash flow than lives.

Truth be told, as beautiful as this island was, he was already looking forward to moving on, hopefully to something with less strings or oversight attached.

However, as the doors to the conference room opened and the loud voices within began to stream out, he got a sinking feeling that this assignment would neither be quick nor clean.

"Do I need to point out, Ms. Guerrero, your company's negligence in the trans-Andes pipeline disaster three years ago?"

"An interesting choice of words, Mr. Reid. I'm sure you're well aware a multinational grand jury agreed with our assessment that it was an accident, plain and simple. Not to mention, they cited the time, effort, and *expense* ZarroGreen invested in the cleanup."

"What expense? You barely spent a tenth what your CEO took home last year. And it's Doctor Reid, if you'd please."

In Derek's opinion, there was nothing quite like stepping into the middle of a sparring match. And the two combatants appeared ready to go the distance, as distinct in their appearance as they were in their opposing viewpoints if what he'd heard was to be believed.

As his group stepped in, those present paused long enough to turn toward them. There were three already in the conference room, including a suited man who looked to be in over his head. From the way he glanced at Norah,

Derek guessed he worked for her – probably some poor sap assigned babysitting duty until she returned.

Of far greater interest were the two seated at opposite ends of the table, while a wall-mounted screen displayed photos of what appeared to be pieces of wreckage, likely from the ship that had gone down.

"Don't mind us," Mitchell said. "We're just looking for the Keurig machine."

Norah flashed him a quick glare then indicated the two they'd interrupted. "Gentlemen, may I present to you Alvita Guerrero, Senior Vice President of Acquisitions and Exploration for ZarroGreen Limited."

The woman, middle-aged, stout, and with eyes as hard as steel, stood up and offered her hand. She was wearing a crisp suit which made Norah's seem straight off the rack by comparison.

"I'm sorry you had to walk in on that. Dr. Reid and I were in the middle of a spirited discussion, nothing more."

Despite her hard-as-nails look, her voice was surprisingly soft spoken, at least when she wasn't arguing. Derek had been expecting her to sound like a practiced politician, but instead it was more like a beloved neighbor asking how your day was.

He made a mental note not to underestimate her. Those who came across as oily, like the former governor of New Jersey, were easy to keep your guard up around. It was the ones who could disarm you with a few words who needed to be watched. Derek wasn't stupid. He sincerely doubted she'd risen to her current rank by virtue of being everyone's best friend. Still, there was no point in being rude.

"A pleasure, Ms. Guerrero. My name's Derek Jenner, and this is my associate Mitchell Harkness."

"Dr. Derek Jenner," Norah added. "And this is Dr. Llanzo Reid of the Rogers Institute."

He couldn't have been a greater contrast to his sparring partner had he tried. Whereas she was older, crisp, and professional, Reid was dressed as if he'd come to work straight from an all-night bender. Shorts, sandals, and a polo shirt that had seen better days were rounded out by his dark skin, glasses, and the short dreadlocks adorning his head. Judging by the man's youthful appearance, Derek would have been surprised to hear he'd held his Ph.D. for more than a year or two.

"Dr. Reid," Derek said, holding out his hand.

Rather than take it, though, he turned to Norah. "You're kidding, right?"

"Here it comes," Mitchell said, flashing a knowing grin.

Derek barely suppressed a sigh. It was one of the downsides of the cover they maintained. Someone could be the most respected field researcher in the world, but the second their name was linked with Bigfoot, they were immediately dismissed as a crank. It was why so few dared to risk their careers, even if the evidence suggested a mystery worth pursuing.

There was also the fact that he knew damned well that such ridicule was actively encouraged by his employers. After all, the Russians and Chinese weren't the only governments who tried to steer social media to their own benefit.

True, trolling Sasquatch enthusiasts was minor in the grand game of cyber counter terrorism, but it was part of the game nevertheless. And, despite his misgivings toward those who fell for it hook, line, and sinker, he knew what he was getting into when he'd signed on. A minor bit of annoyance was a small price to pay for the things he'd seen.

Nevertheless, he decided to let Norah take the lead.

"You were already briefed, Dr. Reid. I told you we had specialists flying in. Believe me, this is no joke."

"Really? My sixteen year old brother watches their show for God's sake."

"Maybe we can hook him up with an autograph when we're done."

Derek turned to the medic. "Not really helping."

"It's part of my charm."

He decided not to take the bait and instead motioned toward Norah. "I assume the necessary assurances have been obtained."

She nodded, so he stepped forward. Swearing foreign nationals to secrecy could be a dicey proposition, but Derek wasn't worried. Much as a belief in cryptids could expose one to ridicule, so too could *wild* claims of coverups and conspiracies. It wasn't something an established professional like Alvita would likely risk, double that for a man like Llanzo who was likely still building a reputation.

"I can assure you, Doctor, that we're the real deal," he said. "Anything you or your brother may have seen on TV is a carefully formulated lie. So called reality television is anything but most of the time, but in our case what you see is even further from the truth."

Alvita leaned forward. "I have to admit, Doctors Jenner and Harkness, that this is..."

"It's just Mr. Harkness," Mitchell replied as he, Derek, and Norah took their seats.

Alvita smiled at him. "Very well, *Mr.* Harkness. I have to admit it's a bit much to take in. If it weren't for the assurances made by your government, I'd be hard pressed to believe we were actually having this conversation."

Derek couldn't help noting she said nothing about the testimony of her own employee.

"As would I," Llanzo replied. "However, I'm far more

dismayed that we're here to discuss how to kill this creature, assuming it even exists."

"Relax, Doctor," Derek said. "We're not hired guns and this isn't a bug hunt. I'm a conservationist at heart. We're here to assess whatever, if any, threat this alleged creature poses and then respond accordingly."

"Threat?" Alvita asked. "I think the loss of my company's ship as well as nearly all hands aboard already establishes that fact quite clearly."

Derek held up a hand. "The loss of life is regrettable, Ms. Guerrero. You have our deepest sympathies for that. However, we simply don't have enough evidence to assume these incidents were unprovoked."

"*Incidents?*"

Shit! Derek realized a moment too late his faux pas. He'd been right about this one. She'd pounced upon his slip of the tongue without missing a beat.

He turned to Norah, noting the raised eyebrow she gave him. No doubt he'd hear about this later. Still, the point of this briefing was to share information. If she didn't like it, she should've laid down the ground rules ahead of time.

"Nothing conclusive has been determined yet," Norah said after a moment, "but the Coastal Defense Force responded to an S.O.S. off the coast of Nassau earlier, in which..."

"Off the coast?" Llanzo replied.

"How far from where the Tortuga went down?" Alvita asked dispassionately.

"Who cares about that?" the scientist snapped at her. "If this creature is headed toward populated coastal areas..."

"So much for live and let live," Mitchell muttered, albeit not enough under his breath to go unheard.

"I'm not a fool, Mr. Harkness," he shot back.

"Hunting down a once in a lifetime discovery in open waters is one thing, but I'm not sanctimonious enough to suggest we sacrifice human lives."

"Enough!" Norah stood up, drawing all eyes her way. "Nothing we've seen indicates this creature is venturing into populated waters. For all we know these are two unrelated incidents."

"I concur," Derek said. "Until we know more, it'd be best to not jump to any conclusions."

"Very well," Alvita replied, "but there's still Mr. Treco's testimony to take into account. He claimed the Tortuga was attacked by this thing, unprovoked."

"As I've likewise heard. However, I think it safe to say that was a somewhat ... stressful situation. It's entirely possible he was mistaken in his..."

"Agreed," she interrupted. "Which is why we should ask him ourselves once he arrives." She turned to Norah. "A helicopter was dispatched to bring him back to shore for medical treatment, correct? However, I see no reason why we can't speak to him once the doctors are finished."

Derek leaned back in his chair. There was no way he was fielding that one. Despite his public persona as the team's spokesman, he was more than happy to let Norah take the lead here.

Mitchell, no doubt sensing the same thing, likewise settled in, albeit not without tenting his fingers, probably in anticipation of the blowback to come.

"That might be ... a problem, Ms. Guerrero," Norah said at last, obviously realizing this particular buck stopped with her.

"How so?"

"The helicopter ferrying Mr. Treco went down somewhere off shore. A rescue effort is underway but so far there are no signs of survivors."

Alvita frowned at the news, but otherwise remained

calm. "I see. Our underwriters will be disappointed to learn that. I don't suppose you're going to tell me this creature, whatever it may be, was responsible."

"Of course not. All signs point to some sort of malfunction, an accident."

"More equipment malfunctions? You'll forgive me for saying so but, between the ship that rescued Mr. Treco and now this, I'm beginning to wonder if my company should question their faith in the U.S. Navy."

"This isn't a Navy operation." Norah leaned forward in her chair. "And I will remind you, Ms. Guerrero, your own man reported similar issues."

"Similar issues?" Llanzo asked, a troubled look on his face.

Norah turned to face him. "It wasn't the focus of his debriefing, not after the story he told my people, but he claimed the Tortuga was experiencing widespread equipment failure shortly before the ... encounter."

Derek and Mitchell shared a look. He could see in his friend's face what he was thinking, so he was quick to mouth the words, "Don't say it," at him.

Nevertheless, it was hard to deny that something weird was going on.

"I don't think this is a coincidence," Llanzo said a moment later.

"How so?" Alvita asked. "Is this somehow my company's fault again or are you proposing that we're dealing with a beast that's capable of shorting out electronics wherever it goes?"

"Quite the opposite." He turned away from her to face Norah. "Agent Caseman, why did you call me into this meeting?"

"You were already told why."

"Humor me, please."

"Fine. There's been two dolphin beachings in the last

twenty four hours. We recruited you on your institute's behalf to consider the theory that they were fleeing from something, a large predator perhaps."

"Thank you. And if you recall when asked, I informed you such a thing was preposterous. That there was no evidence to suggest anything of the sort."

"I do."

He nodded. "But what if the two are actually related?"

"I don't understand..."

"Go on, Doctor," Derek said, interrupting his boss. He was curious to see where the young scientist was going with this.

"Thank you, Dr. Jenner. Yesterday, right before the first beaching, I was out performing a diagnostic update for one of our sonar arrays. It had started acting strange out of nowhere, randomly throwing back bad data. I thought maybe there was a software issue, but there was nothing wrong that I could find."

"And then these beachings happened."

"Not to mention what happened to that ZarroGreen boat," Mitchell stated, "and then the rescue ship, and the helicopter, too, and let's not forget our airplane."

"What airplane?" Alvita asked.

"We had kind of a stressful flight in."

"Okay," Llanzo said. "So let's think of this from another angle perhaps. Instead of all of this being unrelated, let's try assuming for a moment that they're connected."

"And we're back to a dolphin eating sea monster that somehow zaps helicopters out of the sky," Alvita said dismissively.

"Not necessarily," Derek replied. "It makes more sense if we maybe flip that around. Instead of assuming some creature is responsible, what if something else is causing all of this? Something that's not only making manmade equipment go haywire but is also messing with the local sea life, causing it to go crazy."

"So these dolphins and the creature...?" Norah asked.

"Could be related, but not necessarily as cause and effect. What if both are the effect? What if there's something out there driving them both nuts, causing the dolphins to run ashore and some heretofore unknown creature to lash out?"

"You realize we're back to Bermuda Triangle theories again, right?" Despite his words, however, Mitchell's tone suggested he thought Derek might be on to something.

"Much as I hate to admit it, Occam's razor. Right now it's probably the least crazy theory we have."

"It's still pretty crazy."

"Not arguing."

When no one else at the table offered either suggestions or disagreement, Norah finally asked, "So then what could be causing it?"

"No idea," Derek replied, "but at least it gives us something to test."

"Agreed," Llanzo said. "If there's some phenomenon out there causing this, it should be easy to detect. We could use the institute's research vessel. It's packed with nearly every sensor we have access to."

"Okay," Norah replied. "How do we do this then?"

"Simple," Derek said, only half-jokingly. "We take this boat out, and if everything breaks down then we know we're onto something."

8

"I'm going to kill Derek and then I'm going to kill Norah. And if Mitch even looks at me wrong, I'm going to castrate him for good measure."

"It wasn't *that* bad," Danni said, enjoying the air conditioning as they stepped into the hotel lobby.

"I felt like a piece of meat."

"Hey, at least we got to wear the one pieces for most of it. I've worn dental floss with more fabric than some of the bikinis he had hanging in there." She considered what she'd just said then added, "Okay, fine, not exactly dental floss but you know what I mean."

Julie shook her head. "I know I'm probably overreacting, but all I can think about are my old colleagues coming across me in some calendar. It feels like ... I dropped out of journalism to do porn."

"*Now* you're overreacting," Danni replied. "How different is this than going to the beach? Are you seriously telling me that if we get a day off, you're going to spend it in an overcoat?"

"No."

"Okay then. So you gain a few fans and have to sign

some autographs. Believe me, you have nothing to be ashamed of, lady. You are tight."

Julie stopped walking, a smirk on her face which soon broke into a grin. "That's probably more than I can say for some of the clowns back at WXGP. A few of them would be lucky not to be towed back out to sea."

Danni joined her in a laugh, even if she, too, was annoyed at having been dragged off for a T&A shoot when there was work to do. At least in her case she'd already been there and done that. All of this was new for Julie. "Speaking of which," she said after a few moments, "that whale was something else. What was up with that?"

"I don't know, but it was pretty gruesome from what I could see."

Danni was certain that hadn't been an everyday occurrence. Kerry had been in the middle of posing them at the very edge of the surf, when his assistant suddenly started pointing past them toward the ocean.

As they'd spun around to check out what was going on, she'd caught several questions from nearby beachgoers.

"What's it doing?"

"Is it trying to beach itself?"

"This is so cool. Grab my camera."

They'd spied a large mass jutting from the sea maybe a hundred yards from shore. For one brief moment, Danni was convinced they'd found their quarry ... or it had found them. But then a spray of foam had confirmed that what they were looking at was actually a whale.

The poor thing appeared to be struggling, stuck in the shallows as it was. Several in the crowd stopped their picture taking long enough to wonder aloud whether something could be done to help it.

However, before anyone could do much more than gawk, the sea around the whale began to churn in a froth of frenzied splashing. Again, Danni's first thought was the creature they'd been sent there to find, but then she spotted a fin in the surf followed by another and soon more.

Within seconds, the foamy froth turned red – the beginning of a feeding frenzy. The whale had probably been injured, maybe cutting itself open on the seabed where it became stuck. That in turn had attracted the sharks, lots of them from the look of it.

What started as a curiosity became a panic as those who'd been approaching for a better look quickly turned tail.

Both women had immediately abandoned the shoot to help people back to the safety of the beach. In a nod to humanity, so too had many others, resulting in no more tragedy than some bumps and bruises. Thankfully, the sharks had been far more interested in their easy meal than in any nearby paddle-boarders.

The sharks hadn't been the only ones preoccupied, though. When Danni next caught sight of Kerry, he'd been perched on his assistant's shoulders, a telephoto lens attached to his camera as he tried to document the event. All but forgotten, she and Julie had made good use of the distraction to get dressed and call a cab.

Word of the beaching had spread since then. People in the lobby were talking about the incident, and a TV in the nearby lounge was showing an aerial view of the scene.

Most of what caught Danni's ears as they checked in were vacationers annoyed that the beach might be closed until the carcass could be safely towed out to sea, as if there weren't plenty more places to visit on the island.

A few tidbits of gossip were more interesting, though. Apparently this wasn't the only beaching this week. She learned that a pod of dolphins had recently swum ashore at another location, refusing all efforts to drag them back out to deeper water.

Danni vaguely wondered if it might be related to their monster as they stepped into the elevator and rode up to their floor. She was certain she'd read somewhere about animals beaching themselves to avoid alpha predators, although she couldn't quite remember if it was an actual study or from a novel she'd picked up at some point.

They stepped out in the hall where she turned to face Julie. "We probably shouldn't go very far, at least until we hear from Derek."

Her teammate nodded. "Wasn't planning to. Think maybe I'll grab some lunch then check out the pool."

Danni couldn't help but smirk. "You just spent the last few hours complaining about being in a swimsuit and now you want to put one back on?"

"That's different. I'm *choosing* to put it on. Also, mine is way cuter then anything that clown had. What can I say? Nobody puts baby in a corner."

"What?"

"Probably a bit before your time, *kid*," Julie said with a smile before turning and heading toward her room.

Danni couldn't help but shake her head. One of the downsides of being the youngest on the team were jokes that predated her.

Still, it's not like they questioned her abilities, especially after New Jersey – even if the Garden State had left its mark on her in more ways than one. Danni sighed, noting it was probably a good thing Kerry had agreed to the one piece. She still bore the scars from her encounter with the Lesterfields. True, those could be airbrushed out, but that would only make things feel even more surreal than they already did. Speaking of which...

Danni unlocked her room and stepped inside, finding her luggage already there waiting for her – one of the perks of their job.

Before the door could close, though, she propped it

open, swiveling the security lock so that it caught in the frame. That done, she retrieved her carryon and pulled out the ceramic knife hidden deep inside. Then, holding it in a reverse grip, she made a quick circuit of the room – checking the closet, behind the shower curtain, and beneath the bed.

Only once she was certain she was alone did she allow the door to click closed. It was one of the many open wounds from her time in the Pine Barrens. Still, she considered, it was a lot better now than it had been. For the first three months afterward, she'd slept with a light on, when she could, and a gun always within reach. Being alone was hard, but knowing she was vulnerable while she was asleep had been far more difficult to overcome.

She was young and strong, though. Most importantly, she was unwilling to let them win. It would be a cold day in Hell before her memories of those bastards broke her. That was what she held onto late at night, when the shadows seemed to almost take on a life of their own.

Her sweep finished, she picked up her carryon again and pulled another item from it, a framed picture of her brother – her own personal totem against the bad times. He was smiling in the photo, looking so confident, so strong and alive, just how she wished to remember him.

"I'm getting better, Harrison," she said. "Just a quick check this time, nothing more. No nightmares on the plane either. Oh, and we're finally back in the saddle again. A sea monster this time. How wild is that? Remember when we saw *Clash of the Titans* together as kids? I was scared of the kraken but you thought it was the absolute best. Well, now I might actually get a chance to meet a real one."

She placed the photo on the nightstand by her bed then stepped to the window and drew back the curtains, revealing the bright sunny day. "You'd like it here. If only

I'd suggested someplace like this for spring break instead of Bonanza..." She trailed off, refusing to go there. "No, you're right," she continued, envisioning him rolling his eyes at her silliness. "There's no point in what ifs. All we can do is move forward."

She turned away from the window and wiped her eyes. "God, I hope you're out there somewhere. If I could just know that, even for a second, well, then I don't think being alone would bother me so much." She looked down at the picture and smiled. "Yeah, I know. Time to wrap up this pity party. There's work to be done."

Danni took a few more minutes to unpack. She changed into shorts, sandals, and a tank top before pulling out her laptop. Right before she sat down, though, she hesitated, once again turning toward her brother's smiling face. "You're right. Why the hell am I locking myself up in here? I should go see if Julie wants some company by the pool." She grinned at his photo. "Nobody puts this baby in a corner either."

Danni turned away before stopping and glancing back one last time. "And yes, I promise to look up where that's from."

9

The leviathan floated in a sea of blood and viscera, the act of killing having saturated its complex nervous system with enough neurochemicals to temporarily calm it.

The squeaking things weren't normally its prey. Though it was happy to eat whatever it could catch, it often preferred the slower prey that crawled along the ocean floor. The squeaking things were fast and tended to stay near the surface. They could also be dangerous in large numbers. Though they were no threat to it now, it remembered hiding from them in its youth.

Driven nearly mad by the ceaseless thrumming, it had sensed the pod above and launched itself into their midst. The squeaking things were disoriented, swimming erratically – possibly due to the same thrumming that kept attacking it again and again. It neither knew nor cared. All that mattered was they were slow to respond when it lashed out at them. Calves, females, and even the fully grown bulls were torn to shreds before they could mount a defense, their black and white skin soon red with their own blood.

The attack had been over quickly, perhaps too quickly. As it stuffed another chunk of their blubbery flesh into its beak, so as to replenish the energy it had spent, the thrumming once again became impossible to ignore, sending it into an agony of confusion, pain, and misery.

Intelligent as it was, it didn't know how to make this anguish go away, despite having tried its best to destroy the thing responsible.

After that first burst of confusion and rage, it had killed something large upon the surface, sending dozens of tiny screaming creatures into the water to splash about in a panic. The leviathan had plucked a few of them up, devouring them whole, but it hadn't been satisfying. Though its beak shredded their bodies with ease, they'd tasted quite terrible. That was of little concern, though, as its savage action had somehow served to momentarily dull the pain.

Alas, the reprieve had been far too temporary before the thrumming began to torture it again. The large surface thing, now destroyed, hadn't been the source of its misery after all.

Soon enough, its acute senses began to home in on the true source of the merciless pulses ravaging its mind. The thrumming was coming from the ocean floor, not the surface, something it had missed in its initial confusion.

Though the closer it got, the more miserable it became, it pushed forward to the bottom, letting the misery turn into rage – rage that it planned to use to destroy the source of its anguish.

Even had its eyesight and senses not been keen, it would have been hard pressed to miss the strange sight awaiting it. A veritable sea of the dead floated just above the ocean's bottom, the water there strangely thick and difficult to swim through, leaving scores of fish to hang motionless in the bizarre effluviant. Everything smaller and weaker than it had apparently been driven away or overwhelmed.

Not even the larger predators, eternally hungry as they were, had dared to approach the bottom and the easy meal waiting there. The leviathan was alone in the depths, a king with no kingdom.

There came another pulse, invisible to the eye but more than felt. The creature was stunned by the sheer closeness of it, for a moment able to do little more than twitch as it floated with the dead. As it righted its bulk, though, it saw the sandy bottom shift in time with the thrumming, as if the seabed itself were trying to birth something monstrous.

Some kind of object was sticking out of the sand there, a long proboscis of some sort. Whatever it was, it appeared to be injured – the end of it, about twenty feet above the ocean floor, was seemingly sheared off, leaving it jagged and sharp.

That greatly interested the leviathan. If whatever was down there was already injured then it meant it could be killed that much more easily.

Enduring the pain, it lowered itself to the silty ocean floor and began to thrash its arms and body, squirting a high powered jet of water out beneath it. If whatever was buried in the sand did not wish to come out, then it would simply uncover it.

Soon, the surrounding area became a muddied mess of churned silt, seawater, and dead fish. Despite the thrumming which continued to wrack its body, the creature's size and strength allowed it to clear massive amounts of seabed in a short time as it dug ever deeper, searching for the source of its misery. Until, at last, it uncovered something strange.

Whatever this thing was, if it was even alive, it was covered in a hard smooth shell – not unlike what the thing at the surface had been comprised of before being dragged down to the depths.

The leviathan redoubled its efforts. Its enormous arms uncovered more and more of the thing, eventually unearthing enough to grasp hold of. As it attempted to drag its enemy from the silt, it bit down upon the hard shell with its beak, hoping to pry it open and expose the soft parts within.

However, its efforts were for naught. No matter how hard it bit into the shell, all it could do was scrape the surface, leaving welts and scratches but unable to penetrate it.

Despite the leviathan's vast size and strength, easily the match of even the large squeaking things that roamed the sea, the thing embedded in the ocean floor refused to budge.

The leviathan began to suspect that what it had uncovered was a mere fraction of the thing's true bulk. Perhaps worst of all, the massive thing gave no indication it had even noticed the intrusion, continuing to thrum as it had before – the pulses now stronger than ever thanks to the tons of displaced sand which no longer served to mute its cries.

Soon, exhausted by the effort, frustrated by its failure, and in increasing pain due to its proximity to the thing on the bottom, the leviathan decided to vent its rage elsewhere.

The leviathan was a thinking creature, capable of complex problem solving. On some level it vaguely realized that its attack had only made things worse – each pulse now like a tiny flame setting its nervous system afire.

Many of the larger creatures with whom it shared its habitat had fled – some to the shallower waters, others going deep.

However, despite its pain, it refused to follow them. Unlike its smaller cousins, it was territorial by nature, having claimed a vast range befitting its size. To flee would be to invite others to lay claim upon its hunting grounds.

Such a thing could not be allowed to stand, nor would other intruders be tolerated ... such as the one it sensed now.

There came a hum from a distance, one of the surface things – similar to the one it had killed when the thrumming first started. Normally, it wouldn't have paid it any heed, not even from curiosity. However, in that moment another of those damnable pulses arced through its body causing it to spasm.

Seconds later, its statocysts detected the distant hum sputtering and then ceasing altogether, telling it that the surface thing had likely been crippled by the thrumming.

As it reasserted control over its body, confusion gradually gave way to purpose and then rage.

This other surface thing was crippled, vulnerable. It would pay for daring to intrude where it did not belong, and in doing so its death would serve to ease the leviathan's suffering.

10

Danni finally muted the ringer on her cellphone, hoping that Klipsch took the hint.

"Sorry," she said to Norah, as they manned the communications array of the Rogers Maritime Institute, the building itself nearly empty so they could work unobstructed. "Annoying photographer won't take the hint."

Almost as if on cue, her phone vibrated, telling her a text message had come in. Of course it was Klipsch again, letting her know that he'd rented a sailing yacht on behalf of the Adventure Channel for some action shots out at sea.

She had a feeling what that would likely entail – Derek and Mitchell in either wetsuits or casual boat wear, with her and Julie as the eye candy draped across the deck.

Another text came in a few moments later, informing her that his plan was actually far worse. He'd managed to rent some props from a low budget monster movie shot on location there last year.

Great. Now I can be someone's tentacle porn fantasy, too.

Norah glanced at the younger agent. "I have to admit, some days I'm split between being glad I work behind the scenes and envying your team the spotlight." At Danni's raised eyebrow, she chuckled. "But now isn't one of those times."

Danni couldn't help but laugh. She was still intimidated by the senior agent, but little by little she was forcing herself to loosen up.

Besides, it was either small talk or sit there in silence waiting to hear from Derek and the others. The rest of the team had gone out on the Rogers Will-Do, the institute's research vessel – bad pun of a name notwithstanding.

While she and Julie had been making their escape from Klipsch earlier, the others had made some progress with regards to a plan of action, although Danni wasn't sure what it had to do with actually tracking down their quarry.

By the time she and Julie arrived around mid-afternoon, Norah having finally sent a car to collect them, the group had been deep into discussions regarding the reported equipment malfunctions and whale beachings.

The institute's scientist, a young if somewhat intense doctor, had been arguing for heading out first thing in the morning. However, he'd been overruled. With strange occurrences, monster-related or not, piling up, Norah and Derek both felt that the sooner they could rule out at least some theories the better.

Sadly, Danni had drawn the proverbial short straw. Derek had wanted at least one person to stay behind – to keep their finger on the proverbial pulse in case something new came up.

"Anything happening online?" Norah asked, dragging her back to the present, although her tone suggested she wasn't expecting much.

Danni looked back at her screen, currently full of local newsfeeds. "Not much. There was a brief brownout reported in Congo Town, but nothing major. Otherwise, all seems to be quiet."

The radio too was silent at the moment. Derek had been checking in with them every half hour, but aside from mentioning some footage Julie was busy shooting, there wasn't much of note to report aside from a few erratic sonar pings.

The last bit of interesting news they'd heard had been from Jacob Caseman. His crew had finally managed to sort out their engine problems and were now underway again.

Danni had been in the room while Norah spoke with him over the radio, the connection choppy at best, but she'd at least pretended to not eavesdrop. The conversation had been professional, if somewhat cool. Norah brought him up to speed on what had been happening, mentioning that Derek had commandeered the institute's vessel to test if they could reproduce any of the reported malfunctions.

Jacob had expressed interest in rendezvousing with the smaller vessel, so Norah gave him the Will-Do's last coordinates, even though none of them were sure how long the research vessel would be out.

Danni continued scanning the news, trying to do her part. A low pressure system had formed to the south, but it wasn't expected to amount to much more than some light rain and minor swells. That was good. The last thing they needed was a cliché freak storm muddying up things.

They were still five minutes shy of the next check-in when the radio crackled to life.

"Rogers Will-Do to ... Institute, please copy."

The signal was poor, a lot more staticky than earlier, but Norah was quick to answer. "Maritime Institute, Caseman here. Is that you, Derek? Over."

"Yeah, it's me. I know it's early, but we're having ... trouble. Figured ... let ... know."

"I missed some of that, Derek. Come again."

Danni raised an eyebrow at the word trouble, to which Norah shrugged, her meaning clear. It was too quick to jump to conclusions.

"I ... said ... engine. Reid ... Mitch ... working ... it. Just wanted ... know ... delay ... in returning..."

"You're coming in awfully choppy. Please repeat. It sounds like you said you're having engine troubles. Is that correct? Over."

"Yes ... don't worry ... being worked ... will ... keep ... posted ... over."

The connection cut off abruptly. Norah tried to hail the vessel again but got nothing but static in return.

"That can't be a coincidence," Danni said.

"I can't say I'm not leaning toward that conclusion. For them to go out looking for equipment failure and then to find it ... that's a bit too uncanny for me."

"So what do we do?"

"I'll try to hail Jacob again to let him know. Otherwise we keep doing what we're doing. It sounds like they're working on it."

"But..."

"Relax. If things get bad, they always have the satnav on them."

Danni nodded, unsure of how to feel. However, Derek's voice had sounded unworried, at least the parts she could understand. It was going to be a relatively calm evening and they were aboard a well-stocked vessel. For now, there was little for them to do except wait, and maybe hope that the next time they heard from him it wasn't via S.O.S.

"Did you understand a word of that?"

Derek looked down at the lower deck of the fifty foot research vessel where Mitch had taken on the role of engineer, trying to get the engines restarted. "Not really. Seems like the radio is on the fritz, too."

"Try the phone."

"Already did," Derek remarked, looking down at the Satnav and seeing no connection. This was starting to feel less and less like a coincidence by the minute.

"That's not all," Llanzo said, stepping from the cabin. "GPS is down and I'm pretty sure the side scan sonar array is reporting false positives."

"Pretty sure?"

The scientist shrugged. "Mostly sure. Sorry, that wasn't meant to alarm anyone. What I meant is it's acting strange. Everything appears to be functioning fine one minute, then suddenly it'll be full of contacts that weren't there a moment earlier."

"So we're hunting sea ghosts now?" Mitchell asked, popping up from the access hatch to the trawler's twin diesels. "Pretty sure that's a whole other TV show."

Derek chuckled. "Never hurts to expand our audience a bit."

He wasn't laughing on the inside, however. They'd run into the very same equipment issues they'd gone out there to test, seeming to confirm something strange was indeed going on. Now it was time to regroup back at shore so they could discuss their findings and mount a proper expedition, assuming they could get things back up and running again.

Though he was confident in Mitch's ability, Derek didn't like being a sitting duck.

Fortunately, they hadn't come entirely unprepared, even if the vastness of the ocean suggested a slim chance of randomly bumping into the creature which had attacked the Tortuga. Still, Derek was forced to wonder whether they'd brought enough firepower to dissuade a sea monster on the off chance one found them.

"Maybe we should've brought a couple of proton packs with us," Mitch remarked, dragging Derek's attention back to their conversation.

"Speaking of which," Llanzo said, "it might be out of line for me to ask, especially considering the not so thinly veiled threats your Agent Caseman seems to like throwing around, but how exactly does that work? I mean, how can you do what you do while keeping such a high profile? It seems counterintuitive."

"That's exactly why it works," Mitchell replied from below, continuing to tinker with the engines. "Haven't you ever heard of hiding in plain sight?"

"Of course I have. Most of the creatures in these waters excel at it."

"Let's just hope the thing we're looking for isn't one of them," Julie replied, joining them at the stern. She'd taken advantage of the earlier lull in activity to head to the bow for some footage, at least before their current equipment woes started.

Derek nodded. "Can't say I disagree. The thing is, Dr. Reid, sea life may have millions of years of evolution to fall back on, but what we have is just as powerful: human nature. You see, people are social animals. We have an inherent need to belong. What my team does, our cover anyway, exists on the very fringe of science."

"Yep," Mitchell called back, his voice echoing in the hold. "Whereas early maps had captions like *here be dragons*, you could look at what we do as *here be crackpots*. There's so many shysters and conmen out there trying to shuck fake footprints, it's hard for any real scientist to cast their lot in this field and survive with their reputation intact. But that's what makes it perfect for us. I mean, what's easier to believe: that there's actually a government conspiracy to cover up the existence of cryptids, or that anyone who believes it is simply a nutjob?"

"I suppose," Llanzo replied, adjusting his glasses. "I mean, I'm out here with you and I still barely believe it."

"And why should you?" Derek asked. "Your work involves studying this ecosystem, and now you're being asked to accept a creature that science says can't exist and the fossil record doesn't readily support."

"I get all of that, in a sense of course. But why cover it up to begin with? When mountain gorillas were first discovered the world learned of them. When a new species of insect is found, nobody races to arrest everyone involved."

Mitchell popped up from where he was working and shared a glance with Derek.

"The truth, Doctor," Derek said, "is we don't know either. Our job requires us to be armed with a certain amount of knowledge. But that doesn't mean we're not left with just as many questions as anyone else."

"But there's at least one we don't have to worry about," Mitchell added.

"What's that?"

"Whether or not we have to paddle home. Check it out." He reached down, fiddled with something, and a moment later the twin diesel powerplants roared back to life. "How about that? Good to know if this TV thing ever goes bust that I have a future in the merchant marines."

"How'd you get it running?" Julie asked.

"I didn't," the medic replied. "Technically there was nothing wrong with them. The circuits connecting them to the main controls, however, appear to be a different story."

"Fried?" Derek asked.

"Hard to say. All I know is they're not working right."

Llanzo pursed his lips. "Like the sonar?"

"Pretty much."

"An EMP maybe?" Derek offered.

"If so, it would have to be low level enough to frig with our systems without actually blowing them out." Mitchell shook his head. "The reality is, I have no idea beyond the fact that, mechanically, the engines are fine."

"Wait," Julie said. "So if everything else is going haywire, how come my camera is still working?"

Derek turned toward her. "It is?"

"Yeah, I was just using it. What? You didn't think I was up front taking a nap all this time, did you?"

Mitchell held up his hands. "Hey, this is a judgement free zone."

"Don't make me throw something at you."

"Hold on, I might have an idea," Derek said, cutting off their sniping. "Just give me a second to think." He climbed down from the captain's chair, mulling it over in his mind.

"What have you got?"

Derek grinned at the medic. "Sometimes it helps to be the guy who signs the requisition forms." When Mitchell raised an eyebrow, he explained, "Frank had an accident a couple of years back. He unexpectedly ran into a female squatch while filming some background footage. She was just trying to scare him away from her cubs, but the camera got knocked out of his hands and he lost a couple days' worth of footage."

"Oh yeah. I remember that. He was grumpy for like a week."

"So were our producers. Anyway, afterward he insisted we upgrade to militarized camera gear."

"Guess that explains why it's so heavy," Julie opined. "I thought it was just old."

Derek shrugged. "Frank wasn't playing around. They're not only ruggedized but the internals are shielded, too."

Mitchell let out a chuckle. "Don't tell me he was expecting to run into an electric Sasquatch at some point."

"Not quite. The shielding was just part of the upgrade package. It made him happy and I figured there was no point in grousing about the details."

"Well, then that makes me happy, too," Julie said, hefting the camera back onto her shoulder and stepping to the railing.

"Be careful," Derek called to her. "The deck's kind of slippery."

"I take it you didn't spring for waterproofing," she said over her shoulder.

"Those were the next model up. The budgetary committee's not *that* generous." He turned back to the others. "It's not much, but maybe it gives us something to go on."

"But that still doesn't tell us what's causing it," Llanzo said.

Mitchell shrugged. "Sunspots maybe?"

"One thing at a time," Derek replied. "Figuring out that something odd is happening is step one. Finding what's causing it comes next ... after we get back to port of course."

"Speaking of which," Mitchell said, turning to Llanzo. "I don't suppose the institute has anything like her camera handy, something we could use to test things out, see if it compensates for..."

Llanzo shook his head. "I'm not sure I know of anything that would... Wait a second."

"What is it?" Derek asked when he fell silent.

"Maybe there is." Llanzo's face brightened into a smile. "A couple of years back, while I was still an intern, the institute did some consulting with the Royal Navy. I wasn't privy to the specifics, but part of the agreement involved us evaluating hardened versions of common shipboard systems."

"Why?"

Llanzo shrugged. "One of the rumors was that they were testing a directed energy weapon, but I have no idea if that's true or not. I was merely a grad student at the time. They didn't tell me anything. But that's not the point. The point is..."

"Please tell me the institute didn't throw everything away once they were done."

"That's exactly what I'm getting at. I remember the prototypes being too unwieldy for us to make use of, so they were put into storage. I'm not sure what's there, but if I could maybe dig out a sonar array or..."

"That would at least be something. What do you think, Mitch?"

The medic nodded. "Better than hunting ghosts. Let me just make sure we can still steer this thing, then I say we head in for a refit."

"See to it. I'll try to raise Norah again. Maybe she can put some folks to work back at home base, have that stuff ready for us when we put in."

"Sounds like a plan, chief. Then we can..."

"Um guys," Julie called out. "I hate to interrupt the nerd fest, but I think we have some company."

Derek stepped to her side as she lowered the camera and pointed. Sure enough, there was a dark shadow visible just below the water's surface, a couple dozen yards from the stern.

Something large was moving toward them, and it looked like it was about to surface.

11

The leviathan moved quickly through the sea, propelled by a powerful jet of water as it closed on its prey.

Confused and enraged by the constant barrage against its senses, it realized it had two choices: fight or flee. The latter was out of the question, though. The thing on the surface was the intruder here. To run now would be to cede its territory to a lesser foe, one smaller and weaker than it.

Normally, it was both curious and cautious. Under different circumstances, it might have swum close enough to investigate, then use its speed to jet away once its curiosity was sated. However, its mind was currently in agony and the only way it knew to ease that pain was in the form of swift savage action.

"Any luck with the sonar, Doctor?" Derek asked.

Reid shook his head from his spot at the instrument

cluster. "The reading keeps changing. I can't tell what's a ghost and what's not."

"I'm pretty sure whatever's circling us isn't a ghost. Mitch!"

"Coming!" The medic stepped on deck dragging a waterproof weapons case with him, then used his thumbprint to unlock it. "Step right up, ladies and gentlemen. Grab yourself a prize."

"What kind of *snacks* did Norah pack for us?"

"Not as much as I'd like," Mitchell replied. "This was supposed to be a three hour tour, not a hunting trip."

"Don't remind me."

"Hopefully it's enough to give whatever's out there a bad taste in its mouth."

"Don't tell me it's full of your nude selfies," Derek replied.

Mitchell put a hand over his heart. "You wound me, sir."

"I'm not going to ask." Julie stepped in, putting her camera down. "Ladies first."

Mitchell handed her a Remington Special Purpose Marine shotgun. "Goes with your eyes."

"Thanks, but I'm more concerned with my ass right now."

"Join the club." He grabbed a duplicate weapon for himself then pulled out a Navy issue M4, which he handed to Derek. "And a kewpie doll for our beloved host."

"Appreciated," Derek said, slapping in a magazine. "Doctor?"

"I'd probably just end up shooting myself. I'll man the equipment."

"Okay. Just keep your hand near the throttle. If you hear me give the signal, open it all the way up." He glanced at Mitchell and lowered his voice. "Will it work?"

"It *should*, but it's a spit and bale wire bypass. Just don't hold it against me if we end up getting eaten by a megalodon or something like that."

"Noted."

"Get ready," Julie shouted. "I think it's coming."

The leviathan attacked without mercy, wrapping its tentacles around the exterior of the surface thing. Though the outer shell was tough, the parts of it above water were far more fragile. The brute felt it crumble beneath its grasp as it began to increase the pressure.

As its body broke the surface, sounds flitted across its statocysts, warbling cries similar to those made when it had claimed two of the tiny creatures earlier, from another of the inedible surface things.

Caution had won out in that encounter and it had fled before drowning the rest. However, such concerns were now a thing of the past as the ceaseless thrumming continued to drive it mad.

It remembered those screaming things had tasted foul, but had died easily enough. These ones, however, seemed determined to not go down without a fight.

Tiny flares of misery rippled through a few of its tentacles. Its keen eyes caught sight of some of the tiny creatures attempting to fend it off, attacking it with strange objects that inflicted stinging pinpricks of pain.

Under other circumstances, the assault might have been enough to drive it away. Now it merely served to focus its rage. It would drown them and the inedible thing upon which they stood. They would die knowing they'd been bested by a superior foe, one they should have never dared challenge.

It lashed out with five of its arms, compressing its

powerful muscles until it felt the surface thing's shell finally begin to crack. It used its remaining appendages against the tiny creatures futilely attacking it – crushing two of them, then dragging two more beneath the waves.

In its domain they stood even less chance than they had before, but still they fought ... for a minute or so anyway, their struggles growing ever weaker until they stopped moving altogether.

The leviathan, however, refused to give up its grip on them, lest it be a trick.

At last, the inedible surface thing finally broke apart, crushed beneath its awesome power. Barely recognizable from what it had once been, it sank toward the black depths below.

The leviathan followed moments later, dragging the dead things still in its grasp as if they were gruesome trophies of its recent triumph.

"Out of the way, I want to get this," Julie cried, pushing past Derek and Mitchell.

She'd quickly discarded her gun and grabbed her camera again once they'd spied the sprays of water breeching the surface of the ocean.

Killer whales, a whole pod of them from the look of it.

It was a magnificent sight, one she knew their producers would appreciate.

Albeit probably not as much as their photoshoot, she said to herself, glad to have left Klipsch far behind.

"Guess they weren't ghosts after all," Llanzo said, sounding far more relieved than he had at any point during this journey so far.

The orcas circled the boat a few times, the big bulls coming closest. Julie managed to get the majority of it on camera. It was great footage, the kind you simply couldn't stage. Thank goodness her predecessor had insisted on top notch equipment.

However, majestic as they were, there was something harried about the way the whales moved. Julie was no biologist, but this didn't seem to be a leisurely swim. They were moving too erratically. Then, as abruptly as they'd appeared, the pod began to move off.

"What was that about?" Mitchell asked, once they were gone.

"I think they were checking us out," Llanzo said after a moment.

"Curiosity?" Julie replied, shutting down the camera. Any dialogue they needed to add could be redubbed later. Though they reviewed all footage before sending it to their editors, she'd learned it was a good habit to stop recording before anything potentially incriminating was caught on film.

"I don't think so," Derek said. "Did you see the way they were moving? I don't think they were circling us just to say hi."

Llanzo nodded. "Agreed. And did you notice how the calves were herded into the middle? That's the type of behavior they show when they feel threatened."

"By us or something else?" Julie asked, suddenly glad her gun was still within reach.

"Hard to say, but it certainly seemed like they were giving us the once over. The question is why. I mean, it's not like boats are uncommon in these waters."

"Sonar," Derek offered, turning to Llanzo. "Whales rely on it. Is it possible that whatever's messing up ours is doing the same to theirs? Maybe that's why they were giving us the stink eye, to make sure we weren't something else."

"I'm not sure there's any way to know," he replied.

"Although, I suppose it's possible." He appeared to mull it over. "Probable even. We use our instruments to augment our limited capabilities, but these creatures have adapted to this environment over millions of years. They're attuned to it in ways we've only begun to understand."

"So are you saying we're dealing with messed up whales instead of a...?"

Derek held up his hand, interrupting her. "Nobody's saying anything of the sort, especially since I'm pretty sure killer whales didn't sink that drillship."

"At the same time," Llanzo continued, "the way they were acting toward us. It was as if they were trying to decide whether we were a threat."

"Since they moved off, I'm guessing they decided we're not."

Julie agreed with the medic, but then found herself compelled to ask, "But what if they hadn't?"

There was silence on deck for several long seconds as they all no doubt pondered what might have happened otherwise.

Finally, Derek broke the silence. "I'm going to try the radio again. Mitch, get those engines cranked up. I think it's time for us to head in."

12

"What the hell is going on out there?"

"I wish I knew."

Danni glanced at the senior agent then turned back toward the radio array. Not only hadn't they heard from Derek, but in the last hour it was as if someone had flipped the switch from normal to crazy. As they waited for word from the Rogers Will-do, the ship to shore channels had seemingly gone nuts – even if most of it had been incomprehensible static. There'd been multiple reports of pleasure craft suddenly going dead in the water or experiencing other forms of equipment failure. Far worse had been a frantic mayday call which had cut off abruptly, but not before the panicked operator was able to get out a garbled plea about something beneath his boat.

Norah had placed some calls, trying to get more information from the local authorities. In response, a small craft advisory had been posted. Boaters across the region were being asked to stay close to shore, the *official* rationale being unusual sunspot activity coupled with the storm still developing to the south.

It was a flimsy excuse in Danni's opinion, but better than nothing.

Sadly, according to what Norah had been able to find out, rescue efforts were being hampered by the same issues which were affecting those stricken. Needless to say, it was making an already strange situation worse.

However, just as Danni was opening her browser to see if she could get a read on how far spread this phenomenon might be, a thought hit her. "Wait. What about sailboats?"

The senior agent turned to her. "Excuse me?"

"All those reports of engine failure. A sailboat wouldn't have that issue."

Norah appeared to consider this. "If it were that simple, yes, but we're not just talking a few outboards going dead here. There's radios, navigation, sonar..."

Danni nodded. "All things they didn't have a hundred years ago. Yet somehow sailors managed to get by."

Realization dawned in Norah's eyes. "You mean doing it the old fashioned way? Hmm. Not a bad idea. Quick thinking, Danni. I'll see that the word is passed around. I'm sure there's plenty of local captains who'd be happy to help."

"What about...?"

Norah cut her off at the pass, no doubt anticipating the question. "That's a whole different ball of wax. For starters, we don't know that Derek actually needs any help. And even if he did, our situation's a bit too complicated to warrant sending out some random schooner captain to fetch him."

"Klipsch," Danni said.

"Pardon me?"

"That photographer. He chartered a sailboat. I've got at least half a dozen messages from him about it. He wanted to do a shoot with us out at sea."

Norah raised an eyebrow. "Are you suggesting, Agent Kent, that we perhaps ... commandeer his charter?"

"The boat anyway. We can give him the boot," Danni replied with a grin. "Unless, that is, the Navy or Coast Guard have any sailboats in the area."

Norah shook her head. "Not likely. Besides, I think our superiors would prefer we keep this low profile, at least for the time being. Naval exercises tend to attract attention, even in friendly waters."

"We'd still need a crew, too. Sailing's not exactly my specialty."

"Mine either." Norah's expression, however, suggested she was already thinking past that. "Let me make some calls, see if I can convince the brass over at AUTEC to give some of their personnel the day off. There's gotta be plenty of folks on staff who sail in their spare time." She paused then added, "Off the record of course."

Danni grinned. It was a good idea. The U.S. maintained the nearby lab facility as a testing ground for its submarines and crews. They probably couldn't officially provide help, at least without raising eyebrows, but unofficially...

"Let me put some feelers out," Norah continued, "but we'll keep this idea on the back burner for now. Derek's last check-in didn't seem to indicate an emergency and Jake's ship should be approaching their coordinates soon enough." She no doubt noticed the younger woman bristle at the suggestion because she added, "Take a deep breath. I've known Derek a lot longer than you. If he didn't sound worried, then neither should we."

Danni wanted to believe her. But, even though she'd been a part of the team for less than two years, she'd seen firsthand how quickly a situation could go from being under control to completely FUBAR.

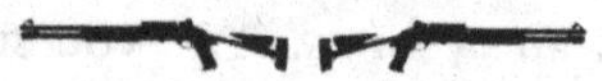

"Would it help if I got out and pushed?" Derek asked.

"Don't start with me," Mitchell growled from the engine compartment. "I thought I had this damned thing fixed."

Llanzo glanced at the instrument cluster from his spot in the captain's chair, all of it now running off battery power. They should have been well on their way back to shore by now. Whatever was going on, though, seemed to be getting worse – bad enough that the engines had once again sputtered and died, not long after their encounter with the orcas.

"Is there anything from your end, Doctor?" Derek asked, looking up.

Llanzo shrugged, more to himself than anyone. "Radar and sonar are both down, and according to the compass north is that way." He pointed toward the southeast. "It doesn't make any sense."

"Welcome to our world. Our job is to make sense of the senseless."

"Yeah," Mitchell added, popping his head up. "Although usually there's dry ground beneath our feet."

"And half the time the weather is freezing," Derek remarked.

"Point taken. At least I can work on my tan while we wait."

The two men shared a laugh, while above Llanzo shook his head. He couldn't understand how they could joke at a time like this. Even ignoring the alleged creature they'd come here to track, what was happening seemed to defy explanation. It was like an EMP combined with a computer virus, yet it seemingly affected sea life, too. It didn't add up in any way he could understand.

It was a conundrum, one that was beyond him.

Conserving the sea life of the Caribbean was his job, his passion. This ... was more like something out of that old TV show he'd watched as a child, *The X-Files*.

"Any luck yet, Mitch?"

"That depends on whether you're still offering to push."

"Um, guys," their camera operator Julie called out. "That might not be necessary. Look!"

What now? Llanzo turned in the captain's seat to find her standing at the stern pointing out to sea. For a moment, he didn't see anything save the endless horizon of ocean meeting the rapidly clouding sky. Then he spied it – little more than a greyish dot just barely visible against an expanse of nothing.

Derek ducked back into the main cabin, returning moments later with a pair of high powered binoculars.

"Definitely not a cruise ship," he announced after taking a look.

"Think it's Jake?" Mitchell asked, popping his head up from the engine compartment again.

"I'd bet your life on it."

The medic laughed at the unfunny joke. "It's about time."

"Do you think they see us?" Julie asked.

"No way to know from this distance," Derek replied, peering through the binoculars again. "But maybe we can up those odds."

"You could try the radio again," she offered. "Even if they can't hear us, maybe you can do that thing they always do in the movies with Morse code."

"Not a bad idea. Anyone here know Morse code?"

Llanzo sighed. "There's a flare gun in the top cabinet right before you reach the galley."

"On it." Derek turned and headed back in.

The ship was almost certainly heading their way,

Llanzo noted. Already it appeared larger in the distance. They must have figured out a way around the electrical issues. Either that or the vessel, obviously much larger than their own, was simply better shielded.

None of that mattered, though, compared to getting back to the institute and reassessing what was happening. As for the so-called beast haunting these waters, it was probably little more than panicked misidentification, brought on by a mix of these occurrences combined with over-active imaginations. Llanzo turned back to the instrument cluster satisfied that was the likely answer.

There was still the issue of figuring out this phenomenon before it wreaked further havoc with the local marine life, but that would hopefully be made easier once they were done searching for mythical sea beasts.

Still, Llanzo found himself unable to relax. He remembered listening as a child as his uncle, a former merchant marine, regaled him with stories of strange happenings at sea – rogue waves, dead calms, a massive shark he claimed to have once seen, and tales of ships getting lost because their compasses refused to work.

That last one was a classic yarn of the Bermuda Triangle, one it was easy to laugh at once he grew older. Yet wasn't that exactly what they were experiencing now, only worse?

That's what bothered him most as his eyes roamed over the malfunctioning displays. He spied a large hit on the sonar screen, almost if the device were mocking his thoughts, then let out a sigh. He was a man of science, not some hustler trying to sell haunted boat rides to tourists. He was used to the unexpected, had trained to deal with it. However, the unexpected was different than the unexplained. Words like strange and weird were for the lay people. A man of his education should be forming hypotheses, not thinking back to the ghost stories his family told as they passed around a bottle of rum.

"Oh knock it off." He slapped the side of the sonar array out of frustration as the ghost reading appeared to close in on their location.

Derek reappeared on deck a minute or so later, flare gun in hand. "Found it."

"Hold that thought," Mitchell called from the engine compartment. "Maybe we can meet them halfway."

"Oh?" the team lead replied, loading the gun.

"Yeah," the medic said, his voice echoing from below deck. "There's a burnt out actuator here. I think if I can bypass it... There!"

A moment later, the engines once again roared to life just as Mitchell popped his head up from the hold. "There we go."

"Finally got it?" Julie asked, sounding doubtful.

"Sue me for being better with DNA sequencers, but I think so. We should have steering and throttle control again. Fingers crossed it'll hold this time."

Derek nodded. "Okay. Just to be safe, let's make sure we have their attention and then see what we can do about it. Either way, it beats swimming back to shore."

He raised the flare gun over his head. Before he could pull the trigger, though, the boat lurched violently to the side, throwing Llanzo from his chair.

"What the hell?"

"Shit!"

Llanzo fell to the upper deck just as the pop of the gun sounded from below, followed by the hiss of the flare discharging.

However, something was wrong. There came a flash of light but it wasn't from above as it should have been. It instead came from the direction of the aft deck. That and the panicked cries of his shipmates told him all he needed to know.

What just happened?

Sadly, there was no answer save that it had been the space of a heartbeat for their situation to turn dire.

"I think you should see this, sir."

Jacob Caseman's second in command turned to him and handed over her binoculars.

"What the hell now?" the senior agent replied under his breath. He lifted the binoculars to his eyes wondering what else could go wrong on this godforsaken mission.

They'd been sailing back to Florida, having neutralized their target – a group of drug runners based out of Cuba – when the call had come in regarding that ZarroGreen ship. Normally, it wouldn't have been their problem. The decommissioned Reliance class cutter was no longer a rescue vessel, having been refitted for more covert operations. However, ZarroGreen had political ties to Washington, so his superiors had okayed the action, no doubt sensing an opportunity to gain clout with the oil conglomerate. It was supposed to be a quick thing – ascertain what happened, then fish out any survivors and shuffle their asses onto a chopper as soon as possible.

Jacob wasn't averse to missions of mercy. If anything, a bit of good karma didn't hurt to balance out the less savory assignments he'd been party to over the course of his long career. Too bad it hadn't gone according to plan.

The Nest, the unofficial nickname of their vessel – outside of an IMO number that was changed every time they put in to port – began experiencing issues shortly thereafter, something his engineer Vakovsky had at first attributed to the ship being almost fifty years old

Then, when they'd finally reached the Tortuga's last known coordinates, they'd found only a single survivor hanging onto some debris, one with a crazy tale to share. Under different circumstances, Jacob might've concluded the man, one Sydney Treco, had come unhinged due to the trauma he'd suffered. However, then Vakovsky had examined the pieces of wreckage and reported odd cylindrical marks in the metal that he couldn't easily explain.

A less experienced agent would have quickly dismissed the evidence as crackpot, but not Jacob. He was well aware that the world contained more than the general public was aware of. Hell, years back he'd been partly responsible for the creation of the somewhat unfortunately named Department of Cryptid-Containment — including recruiting its current leader, a man who also happened to be one of his best friends.

It had been a crazy time in his life, but a satisfying one — something he missed. Too bad his and Derek's work had long since diverged, thanks to the changing priorities of his service.

It also hadn't helped that the dry irony of the U.S. Government had stepped in during the years since, placing Norah as the DoCC's handler within the ATF. It had been a kick to the balls, with Uncle Sam knowing just where to aim.

The reality was his life hadn't been the same since they'd separated. They might've been oil and water during the final years of their marriage, but that didn't mean he hadn't spent many a night awake wishing it had worked out differently. And now, with it over, all he had left was his career and a few close friends.

Bringing Derek into the fold on this, however, had meant contacting Norah first, not that he gave a damn about following the proper channels in a case like this, but because he had no idea how to reach his friend otherwise —

he and his team constantly hopping from one godforsaken location to another.

Norah, for her part, had been a bastion of professionalism when he'd eventually reached her, the delay not helped by the fact that his ship seemed to be slowly dying of old age. But then she'd mentioned that she'd be touching base in person on this one. It was odd for her to volunteer for field work these days, especially on an assignment like this.

He'd gotten off the phone desperately trying not to get his hopes up that she might be using this mission as an excuse to see him, despite his pragmatic side insisting Norah didn't work like that.

Either way, there hadn't been much time for speculation as things had gotten progressively worse from that point on. First the Nest's engines had cut out entirely, leaving them dead in the water, then their chopper had gone down en route to shore – taking the lives of both Treco and Becky Asher, his team's pilot, a seasoned pro he'd have trusted to fly through a hurricane unscathed.

The unlikelihood of these events being little more than bad luck had in turn set his team to chattering like monkeys, speculating about computer viruses and foreign operatives. After all, they were operating outside of U.S. waters. If their cover was blown, that would mean a lot of embarrassment for...

There came a flash of bright red from the water right next to the distant vessel, dragging Jacob out of his ill-timed reverie. "What the hell?"

A misfired flare perhaps? That wasn't like Derek. Jacob had trained his friend himself and knew him to be both a crack shot as well as a stickler for making sure his team was up to speed on their training.

He quickly saw, however, that an errant flare was

perhaps the least of their worries as something large surfaced just off the stern of the other vessel.

Jacob Caseman was a practical man. He didn't waste time trying to fool himself into thinking he was looking at a hunk of blubber or maybe whale spooge.

Instead, he quickly made a mental calculation of the scope of the potential threat, only to realize the other ship was likely outmatched, and with them still too far away to do anything about it.

He lowered the binoculars and turned to his lieutenant.

"See if we can coax some more speed out of this rust bucket, Mac. And then get the fifties ready. I think we're gonna need them."

13

Derek was used to being outmatched.

He'd gone up against thunderbirds, giant ground sloths, squatches and more – most of which dwarfed his six foot frame. But this was the first time he actually felt tiny.

There came a cry from down in the hold, where Mitch had disappeared when the ship first started to list. "Ow! Son of a..."

"You might want to get out of there," he numbly replied to the medic, unable to take his eyes off the creature which had surfaced behind their vessel, so close he could have reached out and touched it had he been insane enough to try.

"What do you think I'm doing?"

"Jules..."

"On it," the camera operator replied, already moving to help Mitch.

Derek barely heard her, though, focused on the beast before him. *Guess it wasn't a squid after all.*

One of the octopus's massive eyes seemed to focus on him, given a demonic glow by the nearby flare still sizzling in the water. Thank goodness he'd missed the deck when the boat had shifted beneath him – a small victory before what appeared to be the main event.

There wasn't time for much more speculation on the matter as a massive tentacle lifted out of the water, followed by another.

"My god!" Llanzo cried from somewhere behind him,

Derek, however, was in no position to answer, being forced to dive for cover as one of the beast's tentacles lashed out and wrapped around the crane housing at the stern.

The ship lurched under the assault, sending him tumbling into the port gunwale before he could regain his footing.

The good news, he noted as he regained his feet, was they hadn't stowed the weapons locker after their encounter with the orcas. Too bad it was over on the starboard side of the deck, past two ... no, make that three grasping tentacles, each of which easily looked strong enough to break him like a twig.

Damn. We should have brought a harpoon to this tentacle fight.

He had a choice, move and fight, or stay there until the monstrous octopus decided he would make far more sporting fare than the hull of the ship.

And he had no doubt that would happen. Regular octopi were known to be highly intelligent, and, well, usually the bigger the creature, the bigger its brain in relation to its smaller cousins.

As he considered his options, he dared a glance behind him, seeing Mitch scramble out of the engine hold with Julie's help, all while Llanzo continued to stare wide-eyed at the creature trying to capsize them.

And doing a pretty damned good job of it, he noted as

the boat lurched violently again, the sound of cracking wood beginning to fill the air.

"Get the doctor below!" Derek commanded.

"But..."

"Now!"

"You heard the boss-man, move it!" Mitchell cried.

There was no time to make sure they followed through on his orders, not with the way the engines were beginning to whine as the back of the ship continued to be beaten to hell. If he didn't do something soon they were going to be swamped, and if that happened...

Gotta time this right.

Derek pushed off from the gunwale, hoping he didn't slip – the deck growing slicker by the second from the spray this thing was kicking up. He launched himself over one tentacle, making a mad dive for the weapons case ... but then all of his forward momentum came to a halt as something impossibly strong grabbed hold of his ankle with near crushing strength.

Derek managed to latch on to the winch's controls as he was dragged back, slowing his progress for a moment but knowing he had no chance of winning against such brute...

A deafening *boom* sounded from close by, drowning out all other noise. A split second later the tentacle let go, sending him tumbling face-first onto the deck.

Derek shook his head, wiping a thin smear of blood from his brow, then looked up to find Julie standing there, shotgun in hand.

She mouthed something at him.

"What?" he cried, barely hearing her over the ringing in his ears.

"I said court-martial me later."

"T-this isn't the army," he replied, scrambling behind her as she fired again.

"Then feel free to write me a sternly worded letter when this is over."

"Heh. Stern ... ship humor," he mumbled, reaching into the locker and grabbing hold of his own weapon."

"What?"

"Never mind."

He stepped up next to her and took stock of the situation, noting she'd clipped one of its tentacles – thankfully enough for it to drop him. Not bad considering it was a moving target. Even better that she'd managed not to hit him.

"What's the plan?" Julie asked, chambering another round as the ship's stern began to drop dangerously low in the water. It was as if the beast were attempting to use its own mass to drag them down.

"I'd tell you to run, but we wouldn't get far." Leveling his rifle, he tried to formulate a strategy that would hopefully keep their oversized foe at bay, for now anyway. Cephalopods weren't exactly his specialty, though, so he decided to keep it simple. "Focus on the arms. I'll keep the head busy."

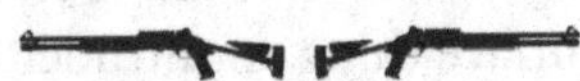

"What do you mean something's attacking them?"

The message which came back was even more garbled than the one before it, but Danni caught enough to understand that Jacob's ship was closing in full-steam ahead on Derek's location, minutes away at most.

It did little to put her mind at ease.

"Come again," Norah replied into the radio. "We didn't catch all of that."

Danni was no stranger to how quickly a situation could turn into a complete clusterfuck. One moment you could be on a relatively uneventful hunt. The next, one of your teammates could be lying dead, shot by a clan of murdering bastards.

And now it was happening again.

No, it isn't, she told herself, trying to force the memories away. *They're dead.*

Whatever was out there with Derek and the others, though, was most certainly not, meaning they couldn't just sit there and hope for the best.

Apparently, she wasn't alone in her thoughts, as Norah put down the radio with a muffled curse and turned toward her.

"I think it's time we paid a visit to your photographer friend and his sailboat."

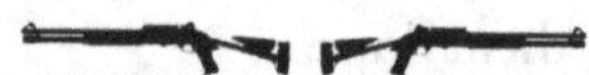

The leviathan was growing frustrated. Already in pain from the near constant thrumming, it had swum in an agonized daze, until at last it had sensed another of the surface things nearby. Though it was no longer certain it was even in its claimed waters, that didn't matter. It was an apex predator. Anywhere it swam became its territory, which made the surface thing an intruder to its domain.

So it had attacked, the violent action temporarily soothing its torment as it sought to destroy this new enemy.

Yet this one was proving difficult. Though only slightly larger than the last foe it had bested, dragging the screaming things aboard to the depths, this surface thing's denizens were seemingly far more effective at defending their nest.

Pinpricks of pain lit up its ganglia as the tiny creatures pecked away at its powerful arms, doing relatively little damage but causing it to become unfocused in its attacks.

As it flailed its arms, trying to figure out how best to

destroy this challenger to its supremacy, sound blared out and then something struck its sensitive siphon, causing it to recoil.

For a moment, no more, it knew fear, but then the rage took hold again, stronger than ever. The leviathan tensed up, preparing to grab hold with more of its arms. The surface thing was already foundering. A bit more effort would be all that was needed to send the annoying screaming things into the water, where they would be easy prey.

Before it could bring its monstrous strength to bear, though, it hesitated, sensing something else approaching – another enemy – something much larger than the surface thing it was battling.

In a daze of red hot rage, it concluded its current foe was nothing, weak prey that had merely gotten lucky. This new challenger, however, would need to be dealt with swiftly and with finality.

Derek and his teammates retreated as far as they could without entering the ship's cabin, affording them a modicum of cover as they continued firing upon the massive octopus.

Julie and Mitch focused on the creature's whipping tentacles, their weapons barely enough to dissuade the beast whenever it tried to grab a solid hold on anything. Derek in the meantime peppered its head with controlled bursts, hoping to blind it or perhaps injure it enough to cause it to break off.

What then? he asked himself, although he had no immediate answer. Despite the ship's engines working again, he didn't like their odds of outrunning this thing should it give chase.

But maybe they didn't need to.

A boat horn sounded from nearby, drawing Derek's attention to the other ship, an old Coast Guard cutter from the looks of it. More important was the fact that it had managed to close a good deal of the distance between them.

No, not Coast Guard, he thought, noting the ship's dull grey colors. However, he was damned glad to see it regardless of its paint job.

"Looks like the calvary has arrived," Mitch cried.

Derek could see crewmen scrambling on the deck of the much larger vessel. "Yep. Now let's just hope they don't decide we're acceptable losses if it means taking this thing out."

Julie glanced sidelong at him. "They wouldn't actually do that, would they?"

Derek tried to shrug, but it turned into a stagger as the stern suddenly bobbed up, nearly knocking them all off their feet.

A moment earlier they'd been dangerously close to the waterline, maybe seconds away from being flooded. All at once, though, the octopus slipped below the surface, letting go of their vessel and dropping back into the sea – leaving them battered but still in better shape than Derek could have ever hoped for.

"Did we just win?" Julie asked.

"Yeah, is this the point where we start talking about swimmin with bow-legged ... ow!" Mitchell flinched as she slapped his arm.

Derek wasn't so quick to drop his guard, though. "I don't know."

The behavior of octopi, unknown species or otherwise, wasn't exactly his wheelhouse, but he'd seen animals crazed out of their mind before – whether by disease or other causes. They typically didn't retreat willingly. If anything, they tended to act like they were cornered, fighting until you killed them or vice versa. If so…

Julie pointed, directing their attention past the stern. "Look!"

Even with the glare of the sun shining off the water the wake was obvious, as was the dark shadow rapidly moving beneath the surface, away from them and toward the cutter.

"Look at the size of it," Mitch remarked.

He wasn't wrong, but that wasn't as important to Derek in that moment so much as the fact that the creature had seemingly decided they were the lesser of two evils.

A small voice in the back of his head reminded him that this thing had supposedly managed to sink a drillship, a vessel considerably larger than both the boat he was currently on as well as the one coming to their aid.

Apparently the crew aboard the other vessel realized this, too, as, a moment later, they opened fire.

14

"Give me some good news, Mac."

McAvee's pause, however, told Jacob everything he needed to know before she even spoke.

"No sign of the creature, sir."

"Is that no sign as in it escaped, or no sign as in we haven't found the body?"

"I ... think it went deep."

"Think?"

"Sonar is still fragged. Readings are all over the place."

Jacob blew out a frustrated breath. Under different circumstances he'd have chewed any of his subordinates a new asshole for bringing him a basket of maybes. He'd trained them better than that. But even he had to admit these were far from ideal conditions, against an enemy they couldn't have anticipated when they'd set sail.

Hell, how would they even know if they'd killed it? Did dead sea monsters float to the top like oversized carnival goldfish? Jacob had seen his fair share of the weird, especially after establishing the DoCC. But these days he was far more at home against human adversaries.

People were predictable, easy to figure out. Monsters that time forgot ... well, Derek was welcome to keep that shit to himself.

"Counter measures?" he asked, not expecting much in return. They were equipped to take down drug smugglers and their cargo, not engage with the *Beast from 20,000 Fathoms*.

It was a rhetorical question anyway. Most of their cache were small arms, with a couple grenade launchers and 50's for when they needed to bring the pain, more than enough for what they typically dealt with. Although, maybe their supply of...

"We could try the ASGs," Andrea McAvee, his second in command, replied, pretty much reading his mind.

Jacob nodded. McAvee was one smart cookie. There was a good reason he'd recruited her out of Caltech some years back.

Their armory included a small cache of anti-swimmer grenades, usable up to a depth of a hundred feet. The problem was they were designed to stun or kill hostile divers of the human variety.

The thing out there wasn't exactly Godzilla, but he'd seen more than enough to know it was considerably larger and faster than any frogman he was likely to ever encounter. It was all a problem of scale. Would an ASG do anything more than tick off that creature, assuming it was even still in the area? After all, it was more than possible his people had managed to drive it...

The ship suddenly lurched to port, almost causing him to lose his footing.

The hell? Either Vakovsky was screwing with the engines again or...

"Sir!" Simmons, another of his operatives, cried, bolting into his office. "Sorry to interrupt, but I think you need to see this."

Jacob didn't hesitate. He simply turned and followed her, having a sinking sensation of what might be awaiting them once they arrived on deck.

Julie was half-tempted to retrieve her camera. Despite knowing there was no way this would ever be allowed to make it to the public eye, the journalist in her felt it should be documented regardless. After all, what were the chances she, or anyone else for that matter, would ever see such a sight again?

However, she remained rooted to the spot next to her teammates, watching the spectacle that was unfolding several hundred yards away.

"Think I saw this on the late show once," Mitchell said, wide-eyed.

"How did it end?" Derek asked.

"Don't know. The special effects sucked, so I turned it off."

"Pity. I think we could all use some inspiration right about now."

Julie shifted over as Dr. Reid joined them, there being little reason to keep him confined to the cabin at this point.

"My god. Is this really happening?" he asked, giving voice to the question they were all likely thinking.

Growing up at the Jersey shore, Julie had seen cutters before, much like the one that had come to their rescue. What was new, though, was the thrashing shape hanging off its side, as if the ship had grown a massive fleshy tumor.

Even at this distance, and against the background of the much larger vessel, the beast seemed huge, like something that had been dredged up from a forgotten world.

Yet, at the same time, it didn't appear all that different from the octopuses she'd seen at the Camden Aquarium, except maybe a magnitude larger.

Had she not been witnessing this with her own eyes, she could've almost fooled herself into thinking she was watching a normal sized octopus attack a toy boat.

The rat-tat-tat of machine gun fire, however, served to drive home just how deadly a game this actually was.

"Why don't they kill it already?" Llanzo asked. "What are they waiting for?"

"I sincerely doubt they aren't trying, Doctor," Derek replied.

Julie's experience wasn't nearly his equal, but even she could understand the chaos that must've been unfolding on the other ship.

No less than five of the beast's monstrous tentacles had latched onto the other vessel, allowing it to pull itself up the side while, at the same time, causing the cutter to list dangerously.

Crew members were scrambling back and forth along the deck, some firing at the beast, others aiding their effort.

Even as she watched, one of the creature's arms whipped about, sending two people flying into the water.

"This isn't good," Derek said at last, stating the obvious – at least in Julie's opinion. "They can barely get a clear shot with that thing whipping around, and it's too close to use heavy ordinance without damaging the ship."

"They're going to capsize, aren't they?" Julie asked.

Mitchell shook his head. "I don't think so. At least not yet. They seem to be handling the extra weight okay for now. But if that thing manages to climb much higher they're going to be in trouble."

"I'd say they're already in trouble." Derek replied. "We need to help them."

"How? What can we possibly do?" Llanzo cried, sounding like he was close to panic.

"Go fishing of course." Derek turned to him and smiled grimly. "Tell me, Doctor, does this ship happen to have a dinghy or maybe a life raft aboard?"

"Are you sure this is gonna work?" Mitchell asked.

"Of course not," Derek said as they examined the stern mounted crane. "How's it look?"

"It's banged up, but the main housing seems intact and it doesn't look like any of the cable is frayed."

"Good."

A few minutes later, Julie and Llanzo returned from the task they'd been given, dropping a heavy steel grappling hook to the deck.

"One dinghy anchor from the hold, as requested," she said.

Derek picked it up and gave it the once over. "Perfect."

"I'm still not sure what you need it for," Llanzo remarked. "It's far too small to injure that creature."

"True," Derek replied, "but we're not trying to hurt it ... directly anyway."

Jacob did his best to steady his aim, while trying not to get swept overboard like several of his men already had. Others were already working on the rescue effort, albeit he was starting to wonder if they might not all need rescuing before this business was done.

That goddamned monster was stuck to the side of his ship like a tick, a heavy one at that. And though Vakovsky had assured him they could handle the load without capsizing, he was having doubts, especially while trying to get a clear shot at what felt like a forty five degree angle.

There came a scream and Jacob whirled in time to see one of his men swept off his feet by a tentacle at least a foot around. Before he could do anything about it, though, the poor bastard was dashed against the forward cabin, his body falling limp in the creature's grasp.

It was insane. This was the twenty-first century for fuck's sake. They weren't on some old whaling ship, months from port and at the mercy of Mother Nature. Yet somehow, despite all their weapons, he felt almost as helpless. So far as he could tell, they'd managed to do little more than piss it off.

If they weren't able to kill it before it could tip them over, they were as good as fucked.

Derek's vessel was no match for this thing, and Jacob more than understood the fine print of his own mission. If they went down, no distress call would be sent – assuming they even could with the Nest's equipment all frigged up.

Bottom line, he and his team were expendable. They all knew that going into this. However, none of them had expected it might be at the hands, so to speak, of a giant fucking octopus.

I can only imagine what they'll put on my tombstone, he grimly considered, a scant moment before those thoughts scattered to the wind at the sound of an incessantly blaring boat horn.

"What the hell?" he muttered to himself, making sure his position was secure before daring a glance.

Derek's boat, a modest-sized trawler with the ridiculous name Rogers Will-Do stenciled on the back, was apparently not as dead in the water as he'd been led to believe. Its engines were revving up. He watched as it began to angle away from them, no doubt preparing to make a run for it.

Good luck, buddy, Jacob thought with a grim smile.

However, the Will-Do's horn continued to sound, and it was soon joined by more – portable air horns. Jacob could see people at the stern, Derek's team no doubt, holding them high and setting them off.

What the hell were the fools doing?

If they were trying to escape while this thing was distracted, they were doing a piss poor job of it, practically announcing their departure with a twenty-one gun salute.

Why would they do something so cataclysmically stupid?

A second later, though, a grin broke out on Jacob's face. Whatever this was, it was too sloppy for a wily son of a bitch like his old friend. That meant Derek was up to something. He wasn't sure what it might be, but he understood one thing.

Whatever plan was going through that crazy bastard's mind, he and his crew needed to be ready to take advantage of it.

Now to only hope it worked.

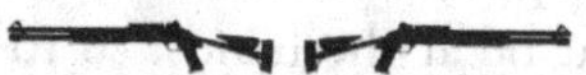

The pain was growing difficult to ignore. Though they were little more than minor stings against the leviathan's flesh, there were a great deal of them, each one igniting a tiny pinprick of fire within its nerve endings.

More annoyingly, this surface thing was proving to be a challenge. And, while it had dispatched several of the screaming things who rode atop it, many more remained to vex its efforts.

Had they been in shallower water, it could have latched onto the rocks below and used them as leverage. But it had been some time since the leviathan had prowled the shallows, its instincts demanding it seek greater depths as it grew ever larger.

Nevertheless, it refused to be bested.

It was straining to pull itself wholly atop the surface thing, so as to attack it full on, when it detected sound vibrations both from the air and the water below. They were different than the thrumming which had sent it into a tortured rage, but annoying nevertheless. Its submerged arms pinpointed the source before it saw what was happening, movement in the water informing it of everything it needed to know.

The other surface thing, the smaller one, was trying to flee.

The leviathan was a thinking creature. Under different circumstances it wouldn't have paid attention to the smaller prey while busy with its larger foe, but the thrumming had driven it to near madness — caused its reason to retreat in favor of savage instinct.

With no further thought beyond its unceasing rage, it released its grasp on the larger thing and turned toward the fleeing one — unleashing a jet of water powerful enough to easily overtake its prey.

This time there would be no escape.

15

Madmen! He was on a ship with madmen.

This wasn't what Llanzo had signed up for. His primary concerns were conservation and research, focusing on the sea life around the island. When the institute's director had first approached him about this assignment he'd almost laughed, only taking it because the experience would look good on his CV.

He'd never imagined that the legend of the Lusca could actually be real, or that he'd be running for his life from it.

Running was only good, though, if there was a chance of escape. Llanzo was no fool. Growing up he'd been a slow runner, slower than the other kids anyway, which had led to a few beatings at the hands of bullies. This was no different. The Rogers Will-Do was a solid vessel for research, but it wasn't built for speed. Acceleration, however, was probably their more pressing concern.

Octopi could reach twenty-two knots in short spurts, regular sized species anyway. But they were dealing with something here that was unknown to science. It might be slower due to its size or evolutionary adaptations may have compensated for that, owing to the fact that such a massive beast would still need to catch prey.

Llanzo had no idea what Jenner was planning as he stood on the other side of the crane, but he found himself praying the beast was a slow swimmer – because there was little doubt it was coming after them.

Mere moments after these crazed fools had put their insane plan into play, the octopus had released its hold on the other ship and turned its attention back their way.

"Give it everything you've got, Mitch!" Derek called to his teammate, who was currently manning the ship's controls.

It was all Llanzo could do to hope the man had been thorough in his repairs. If not...

"What do you think I'm doing?" the medic called back.

"Well, do it faster. It's taking the bait."

You mean us, Llanzo screamed inside his head, wishing he'd never suggested taking the Rogers Will-do out.

As the creature quickly closed the distance between them, he realized this was one mystery he would've been glad to have never learned the truth about.

Derek hadn't been sure his gambit would pay off, but now he was thinking it might've worked a bit too well. The monstrous octopus was definitely coming for them, much faster than anticipated.

Time to reel in this fish ... hopefully. "Turn on the crane, Doctor, if you'd be so kind."

"It's too soon," Llanzo replied. "It's not over the..."

"It's moving a lot faster than that winch will. Trust me, it'll work out."

And if it didn't, Derek silently noted, at least there

wouldn't be much chance for the others to call him out on it.

Llanzo flashed him a doubtful look then pulled the lever, retracting the line they were towing behind them.

In a way, what they were doing was trying to shoot a fish in a barrel. Yes, it was a big fish, but the Atlantic Ocean was the second largest barrel in the world. If their foe deviated in the slightest, going deep or attacking from another angle, they were likely done for.

He took some small solace in knowing that, at worst, they'd at least given the crew of the other ship a chance to regroup.

For now, there was no mistaking the heavy wake rapidly bearing down on them. Either it was the creature or they'd somehow managed to piss off Moby Dick along the way.

A bulbous fleshy mass broke the surface a moment later, answering that question.

Damn, that thing is big. Derek remembered seeing the preserved body of a giant squid at the Smithsonian. This thing made that exhibit look like a bath toy in comparison. Still, large as this creature was, there was something nagging in the back of his mind as he watched it close in.

Now was not the time for introspection, though. Derek steadied himself then took aim with the M4. *Might as well season the pot a bit.* He squeezed the trigger, firing a burst at the octopus.

It was probably little more than a gnat bite to the brute, but he wasn't trying to kill it so much as...

Derek lost his footing and fell as the research vessel shuddered beneath him, decelerating rapidly as the line behind them suddenly pulled taut.

He sat up slightly dazed to see both Llanzo and Julie had fared slightly better, both having managed to grab handholds near where they stood. One upside: at least she hadn't caught his rather ungraceful tumble on film.

More important was what the tortured whine of the winch meant. "Did we hook it?"

"I think it's trying to run," Reid cried, frantically working to reverse the controls.

"Don't!"

"It'll rip the crane right out of the deck," he warned. "If it doesn't drag us under first."

Julie, however, stepped between the doctor and the controls before he could ruin things. "It doesn't matter. We just need to hold it for a few minutes."

Derek threw her a nod of thanks, then he pushed himself to his feet to find the sea behind them whipped into a froth as the massive octopus went absolutely nuts. No doubt about it, they'd managed to hook it good. The question now was whether they could hold it long enough.

The rest, well, it was up to the crew of the other ship.

"Everyone, get to the bow!" Derek ordered, choosing to hope for the best. "We want to be as far away from that thing as possible when the fireworks start."

"Fireworks?" Llanzo asked. "What...?"

"Now, Doctor." Derek grabbed his arm and began guiding him forward.

Mitchell was waiting for them, holding onto the railing as the ship shuddered under the assault. "The taxidermy man, he's going to have a..."

"Oh shut up," Derek replied, pushing past him.

The crazy son of a bitch did it, Jacob mused. In the space of an instant, Derek's plan became crystal clear. They hadn't been trying to run, they'd been trying to hook the damned thing – using their own vessel as a float to keep this big fish from escaping.

Problem was, they likely didn't have long. Jacob wasn't sure whether that big motherfucker could drag the research vessel down or not, but he wasn't about to chance waiting around to find out.

"McAvee, you're in charge of the rescue effort," he said to his lieutenant before turning and raising his voice. "The rest of you, I want every last piece of ordinance we have unloaded into that thing, *now*. 50's, the launchers, even seashells if you have them."

Jacob gave a subconscious nod as his people readied to unleash hell, then he leveled his own M4 at the creature thrashing about in the waters directly to their east. With all the spray it was throwing up, he wasn't sure how much damage he could do, but at this point every little bit counted.

"Open fire!"

The leviathan was enraged beyond anything it had ever known before. With the scent of its own blood in the water and the damnable thrumming continuing to assault its senses, it was driven into a frenzy.

The things which even now challenged it, daring to think they were its equal, would be proven wrong.

It would squeeze the life out of them, squeeze them until they struggled no more. Then it would drag them down to the depths where it would eat its fill before leaving the rest for the scavengers to pick clean.

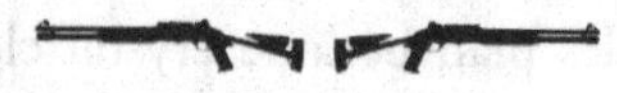

Llanzo had been raised a Christian, though his faith had lapsed in recent years. But if there was indeed a Hell, then surely it couldn't be much worse than this.

He and the others strapped on life preservers at the bow of the Rogers Will-Do, preparing to abandon ship if necessary – a suicidal move at best. However, it was equally dangerous to stay, as explosions and gunfire filled the air. A constant drizzle of sea water rained down on them, although whether from the weapons or the creature's manic struggles, he didn't know.

All he cared about at that moment was surviving, something he was certain was impossible with the madness all around him. As far as he could tell, his choices were staying and being hit by stray gunfire, or getting ripped to pieces by a cephalopod straight from his childhood nightmares.

In that moment he remembered well the tales told to him by his uncle, as he talked about the monstrous beasts that haunted the waters off these islands – wishing to God he hadn't dismissed them as nothing more than tall tales.

Now, as the waterline drew ever closer thanks to the beast's struggles, he realized he was paying the price for his arrogant disbelief.

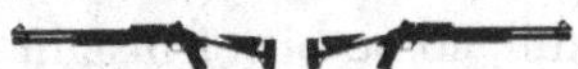

Derek knew it was stupid to pop his head up during a firefight. He'd been in enough to know better. But he also had no delusions of living forever. More than once he'd bested the reaper when it looked like all hope was lost. Hell, last year alone he'd come frightfully close to meeting his end at the hands of that family of crazed zealots. Yet, despite his injuries and the scars he still carried, he'd walked away in the end.

He knew his luck couldn't last forever, but, at the same

time, he needed to know what their situation looked like. As team leader, it was his duty to assess the risks they faced. If he was destined to take the proverbial bullet so that one of his people didn't have to, so be it.

That said, he had no intention of being stupid about it.

An explosion sounded, causing him to duck beneath whatever cover the ship's cabin afforded. He popped his head up again just as a spray of seawater rained down on him.

The octopus continued to struggle, trying to dart every which way, its movements growing panicked as it was peppered with gunfire.

Muzzle flashes lit up across the deck of the cutter as they continued to pour it on.

It was difficult to tell how much damage they were doing with the amount of foam the beast was kicking up, but Derek hoped it was enough.

The crane housing at the stern looked like it was about to give, and black smoke was rising from the hold as the engines were pushed to their limit. Despite all that, the outmatched vessel continued to hold.

It was an incredible sight to see, one straight out of a summer blockbuster. Yet, once again something nagged at the base of his skull, some bit of insight his subconscious wanted him to realize.

Whatever it was, though, it would have to wait. The next few minutes would likely determine their fate. Either the other crew would prevail, or Derek and his shipmates would soon be shaking hands with Davy Jones.

He raised himself up a bit higher, trying to determine which outcome was more likely, only to be overcome by a fury of light and sound as a grenade from the larger ship hit home and exploded, drowning out all sense of anything else.

16

"Listen, lady, I don't know who you think you are, but I chartered this boat and you're not invited. So kindly..."

"Yes, and I'm commandeering that charter, Mr. Klipsch," Norah replied, handing the photographer a stack of paperwork that had been signed off by the local authorities.

The crew they'd requested from AUTEC was already onboard, loading their gear and relieving the current crew of their duties. Danni wasn't sure what they were being told, but the former captain and his crew departed a few minutes later.

"Hey!" Klipsch called after them. "Where are you going?"

"The same place you are," Norah told him. "Somewhere else."

Danni couldn't help but grin, watching from the back of the sedan – the window cracked just enough for her to eavesdrop, but not enough for the photographer to notice her presence.

Though she would have liked to have seen his face as

his plans were ruined, she understood it was best to remain out of sight. It was one thing for him to complain about Norah. He had no idea who she really was. It was quite another, however, if he realized Danni was a part of this.

Still, that didn't make this any less sweet.

"You're enjoying this, aren't you?" Alvita Guerrero asked from the seat across from her, still dressed in a crisp business suit despite the voyage ahead of them.

"I had the displeasure of spending some time with our unwilling *benefactor* yesterday."

"For that show of yours, correct?"

"One of the downsides of being undercover."

"Maybe," Alvita replied, looking wistful, "but I remember the days when I could still fit into a bikini. I'm not sure I would have minded the attention all that much."

Danni raised an eyebrow at the older woman. She'd questioned Norah upon hearing that the ZarroGreen rep had been cleared to accompany them. However, the senior agent had merely shrugged. The oil conglomerate was already a part of this, not to mention their CEO was politically connected. It was unclear what this woman could actually bring to the table with regards to this mission, but this was clearly a decision that was out of their hands.

It was easy to see why Derek hated whenever politics interfered with their job, as if New Jersey hadn't been enough of a wake-up call. At least things appeared a bit different this time. Alvita wasn't some lecherous governor with a Napoleon complex. She also wasn't in charge, which meant the chances of her messing things up were hopefully limited.

Either way, Danni wasn't ready to drop her guard. "I'm not a fan of being a piece of meat."

"Neither am I," Alvita replied with a sweet smile.

"However, I am a fan of using any advantage I have to better my position."

Danni was almost tempted to ask if that meant she'd slept her way to the top, but before she could say anything that would surely come back to bite her, Norah tapped on the window.

Danni glanced past her, expecting to see Klipsch skulking away with his tail between his legs, but instead one of their crew was escorting him aboard.

What the? "Am I missing something," she asked, opening the car door, "or is he headed in the wrong direction?"

"No. He's heading right where he insists on going, although he may come to regret that decision." Norah shook her head. "Seems Mr. Klipsch is not one to go quietly into the night. He threatened to complain to his bosses, the police, the U.S. embassy, and probably the *Weekly World News*, too. This seemed the easiest way to handle things without wasting more time."

"How so, if I may ask?"

"You may. Seems Mr. Klipsch left his equipment aboard, so I'm having him escorted to his cabin while we make final preparations to shove off. Too bad for him we'll be setting sail before he has a chance to depart."

"So ... we're kidnapping him?"

"More like house arrest." Norah shrugged. "I prefer to think of it as buying us the time to properly *explain* how things are going to work, while avoiding any public tantrums."

"Ah." Danni knew the drill, had seen Derek do it at least a dozen times. That said, he was a natural at disarming people with his words. She imagined Norah impatiently badgering Klipsch that he could either sign the affidavits ensuring his silence, or *else* – intimidating the man with not-so-idle threats.

On the flip side, the guy was kind of a self-absorbed asshole. Either way, Danni was far more interested in setting sail than worrying about that jerk.

"Ms. Guerrero," Norah said, moving to block the older woman. "I'd be remiss in not asking you to rethink joining us. My people will do what they can to protect you, but we'll also be out at sea, facing an unknown situation with little backup."

Alvita nodded. "I understand the risks, Agent Caseman, and have duly passed them on to my superiors. However, this crisis started with one of our ships, and I would be derelict in my duties if I failed to provide proper closure to our underwriters."

That sounded like a load of corporate bullshit to Danni but, sadly, it was money that made the world go round. Either way, so long as this woman didn't hamper their rescue efforts it was of little concern to her.

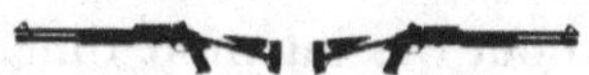

"Now that wasn't such a chore, was it?"

Jacob raised an eyebrow. "You're going to make me regret not hitting you in the crossfire, aren't you?"

"Probably." Derek grinned as he stepped in to give the other man a hug.

Jacob returned it before pulling back with a smile. "Easy now. No making it look like I actually care in front of my team."

"God forbid." Derek took a good look at his friend. Tall, brown-skinned, and covered in lean muscle as usual. The only difference that he could see was that Jake had grown a short beard and his black hair was now turning salt and pepper. "Going grey before your time?"

"This job ages you. If it isn't drug runners, it's a giant fucking squid."

"Octopus."

"Like I care so long as it's dead. The paperwork's your problem. But speaking of problems..." Jacob turned to face Mitchell as the medic finished climbing aboard.

"Long time no see," Mitch replied, shaking his hand.

"You still pissing off everyone under the sun?"

"Whenever humanly possible."

Once that was done, Derek stepped back in to introduce Julie. "And this is the newest member of our team."

"Ms. Wilhelm," Jacob replied. "I read about how you handled yourself in Jersey. Impressive."

"Thank you," she said. "I've likewise heard a lot about you, Agent Caseman."

"All of it lies, I assure you." He then turned back toward Derek. "I was sorry to hear about Frank, man."

"We all were."

"How's his wife holding up?"

"Shakti's a trooper. She's been doing her best to pick up the pieces."

"That's all any of us can hope for with this gig."

Derek wondered if perhaps there was a deeper meaning to his friend's words, but now was probably not the time for that. He glanced over the railing toward the Rogers Will-Do, now alongside the larger ship. With the octopus dead and its body neutrally buoyant, the job of keeping it near the surface had been much easier on the taxed vessel.

Jacob's people were already busy securing the corpse with hooks and tow ropes to allow for a cursory examination, one meant for the Department of Agriculture's archives. After that, it would be disposed of in a more permanent manner.

None of that should have been an issue under normal circumstances, but something about this still felt off to Derek, not the least of which was the aftermath.

He looked over the side, where the body could clearly be seen just below the surface. "Not to put a damper on the pleasantries, but has anyone else noticed what's missing from this picture?"

"Yeah. I keep waiting for the director of this B-movie to show up and yell, 'cut'," Jacob remarked.

Mitchell, however, seemed to pick up on what Derek had been implying. "Where are the sharks?"

Julie glanced at him sidelong. "You want sharks now, too?"

"Not really, but I doubt they care what I want. I meant, where are they? These waters are full of reef sharks, tigers, and hammerheads. Something this large dies and it should be like ringing a dinner bell."

"Maybe they're afraid of it?" Jacob offered. "It's one big fucker."

"Big but dead," Derek replied. "And it's not like they'll turn down a whale."

"Who knows? Not everyone likes calamari."

Below, on the smaller ship, Llanzo could be heard complaining to Jacob's people as he tried to collect samples.

"What do we do about him?" Julie asked. "He's like a kid in a candy store down there, at least now anyway."

Jacob shrugged. "Let him have his fun. Will probably make your work a lot easier. Just so long as he knows to hand over any data he collects."

"Pretty sure Norah already read him the riot act," Derek said, curious to see how his friend would react to his ex-wife's name.

"Well, she can read it to him again, just to be safe." He let out a sigh. "It'll distract her from reading it to me once she gets here."

"Wait. Once she gets here? What do you mean?"

"Yeah. Last communique we got. Was garbled to all

hell, barely understandable, but sounds like she's headed this way, on a sailboat of all things."

Mitchell smirked. "Smart. Wish we'd thought of that."

"Tell me about it. My team's barely holding this old tub together. Shit's been breaking left and right. I'm beginning to think the agency should have scuttled this bucket rather than handing me the keys."

"There's a lot of that going on," Derek replied. "The part about stuff breaking that is."

"So I've heard, in bits and pieces anyway. Walk with me and bring me up to speed."

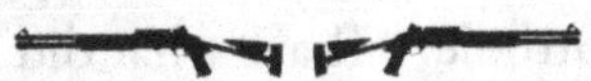

As Derek accompanied his friend below deck, he explained the troubles they'd had on the Rogers Will-Do.

"You're not trying to tell me that thing out there caused all this are you?" Jacob asked once they were in his briefing room.

"Why? Did everything suddenly start working again?"

"Not to my knowledge."

"Then, no, I'm not telling you that." Derek blew out a breath. "I thought it might be EMP-related, but it seems to go beyond that ... at least that we've been able to observe."

"Any theories?"

Derek shook his head. "Sunspots, the aurora borealis, hell, maybe even ghosts for all I know."

"Please tell me that's going in the official report."

"And have Norah skin me alive? No thanks."

This time Jacob grew quiet at the mention of his ex, but only for a few moments. "Didn't want to say anything in front of my people, but how is she?"

Derek took a seat. "Keeping busy so far as I'm aware.

There's been a lot of fires to put out after that clusterfuck in Jersey."

"So I've heard. Please tell me they sent in some black ops to make sure none of those sons of bitches got away."

"If they did, I'd be the last to hear about it. But getting back to your question, she seems well. Definitely not cutting me any slack."

"That sounds like Norah."

"How about you? How are you holding up?"

"As well as can be expected. Not a lot of time to mope. The lifestyle keeps me on my toes." He turned away and looked out the porthole. "That's what did us in, you know. This life, it brings people together, but then assignments change and it tears them apart again."

"Hence why my own dance card remains empty."

"Oh? Nothing going on between you and that fine camera lady? The rumor mill said..."

"Julie?" Derek interrupted, taking a quick look to make sure she wasn't near the door. "I won't bullshit you. Maybe ... if things were different. But right now, after what happened to Frank and Chuck..."

"They knew the risks."

"Doesn't make it easier."

"No, it doesn't. But that doesn't mean you should stop living."

"Better to have loved and lost than to never have loved at all?"

Jacob let out a chuckle. "Your words not mine."

"Seriously, man. You okay?"

"I'll live. Love is ... well, it's no worse than being gut shot. You should try it sometime."

"Getting shot in the gut?"

"The other one."

"We'll see," Derek replied. "It's like you said. This lifestyle doesn't make it easy. Going home covered in squatch stink isn't exactly a good lead-in to date night."

"Ain't no squatches in sight, far as I can see."

"No, but there's plenty of dead octopus."

Jacob laughed before stepping in and clapping his friend on the shoulder. "Then there should be no problem. Just make sure she likes seafood first."

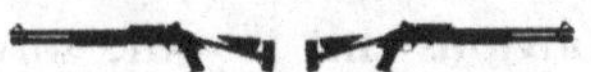

The whine of the chainsaw finally stopped, a necessary evil considering the size of the creature.

Now that the excitement was over, Llanzo was finally able to calm down a bit, although he had a feeling it would be a while before his heart stopped racing every time he heard a swell break against the side of the boat.

The others had all boarded the larger vessel, leaving him to perform his analysis. That was fine by him. Between the cold efficiency of the other crew, coupled with the fact that their ship was unmarked, he had a feeling it was better to focus on his work than ask too many questions.

On the one hand, he was sad they'd been forced to kill such a magnificent creature. Octopi weren't aggressive by nature and he sincerely doubted this subspecies was an exception. Otherwise, with its size and power, he imagined there would be almost no way something like this could have remained hidden until now.

That meant something had been wrong with it, enough to necessitate putting it down. Unfortunate, but it had to be done. Llanzo was no martyr. He loved the sea and its myriad life, but that didn't mean he was eager to throw his away, no matter how incredible a specimen might be.

The cabin door opened and one of the agents from the

other boat, McAvee or something like that, entered carrying a hunk of tentacle nearly a foot across. "I have the sample you requested, Doctor."

"Excellent. Please put it down over there."

She did as asked then stepped back to allow him to take a closer look. "So what do you think about all of this?"

"I think it's incredible," he replied. "I've barely begun, but it's already obvious this is some sort of superspecies. Just this sample alone tells me it dwarfs the mass of the largest Pacific Octopus on record."

"I have to admit, it's pretty amazing."

Amazing was one word for it. He thought back to how close the creature had come to sinking them. The octopi family were fascinating in their abilities, but he doubted any of the other species had ever capsized a rowboat, much less anything larger.

Llanzo began to study the tentacle fragment when he realized McAvee was still behind him. "That will be all, thanks."

"I'm sorry, sir. My orders are to ensure that all notes and data are duly catalogued."

You mean confiscated. He kept that thought to himself, though.

Knowing all his work here would be shunted into some vault, never again to be seen by the scientific community, greatly concerned him. However, he also knew what he'd been getting into. Complaining about it now would do neither him nor his career any good.

At least he was able to take some solace from the fact that *he* would know the truth. And perhaps that knowledge would enable him to one day study a creature like this again, hopefully in a way that wasn't hampered by shadowy government figures.

Llanzo decided to focus on the positive as he worked,

taking care to memorize every important detail as he continued his analysis. In some ways, this was a dream come true, discovering a brand new species, an apex predator at that. For surely there was nothing in these waters, outside of perhaps the sperm whale, that could hope to compete with a beast of this size.

He finished measuring the circumference of the tentacle then placed it onto the nearby scale so as to record its weight.

As he set it down and made a note of the reading, the overhead bulbs in the cabin dimmed slightly. Red lights began to flash on some of the instrumentation. Llanzo sighed and stepped back for the moment. Whatever phenomenon had been affecting their electrical systems was no doubt continuing to plague them.

He shook his head and glanced at McAvee. "Please inform your superiors that we should be putting into port as soon as possible so we can retrofit your systems."

"What do you mean?"

"Ah. I thought Jenner would have mentioned it. We may have some equipment back at the institute that might have a better chance of withstanding..." He trailed off as his eyes caught sight of the scale again. "What in the name of...?"

"Withstanding what, Doctor?"

Her question, however, was suddenly the furthest thing from Llanzo's mind as he focused on the reading in front of him.

"It's simply not possible."

17

"Okay, it's a couple of killer whales. Cute. Your point?"

"The point isn't the whales," Derek explained, "but the fact that the footage, all digital I might add, is perfect. That was our first clue, especially with almost everything else aboard the ship going haywire."

Jacob nodded. "Same as it's doing here."

"Exactly."

"But you said it's not an EMP?"

Mitchell shook his head. "The effect is similar in a way, but it seems to go beyond that. I'm not even sure there's a name for multi-spectrum interference like this. But, bottom line is, electronics are susceptible."

"Unless it's shielded like my camera," Julie added.

"I don't know. Sure as hell sounds like an EMP to me," Jacob replied. "I'm assuming that's why my engineer had to strip the nav systems down earlier to get us moving again." He shook his head. "Good thing this tub still has most of its original guts from the seventies."

"Pretty much." Derek leaned forward in his seat. "Far as we can tell, basic machinery has been unaffected."

Jacob narrowed his eyes. "You think this could be a weapon? Russians? Chinese maybe? Hell, I'd say the North Koreans, but I'm not sure any of their shit could make it this far."

Derek shrugged. "I'm not going to pretend to know much about counter-intelligence, except to say that testing something like that here in the Caribbean seems kind of risky."

"Never doubt the Russians to be ballsy. But I see your point. Hell, I'm just spitballing. For all I know, this could be a NATO project. It's not like they'd tell any of us first."

"Would they actually test something like that here," Julie asked, "where it could affect their own people?".

Derek glanced her way, however, Jacob merely smiled. "Oh, the stories I could tell you, lady. Too bad you're not a journalist anymore."

"Maybe you should write a book after you retire."

"And risk my pension or a bullet to the back of the head? No thanks."

"Regardless," Derek said, trying to steer them back on track. "We're not here to point fingers or shoot anyone in the head. Technically, with that thing out there now a floater, our job is done. We're happy to assist however we can, but you'll forgive me if we leave the international espionage to others."

"Fair enough. Shit, I'm happy to do the same, but the job is what it is." Jacob leaned back in his chair. "Getting back to our fine tentacled friend out there, you think its behavior was somehow tied to whatever else is going on?"

Mitchell nodded. "That's our assumption, for now anyway. But I'd say it's quite possible Mr. Tentacles there was minding his own business when something happened that drove him nuts."

Jacob tapped his fingers against the desk. "ZarroGreen."

"What about them?"

"This all started with them. What if they were out here testing some new type of, I dunno, fracking equipment and it went wrong?"

"Maybe," Derek replied. "Except for the fact that the Tortuga sunk."

"That's what bothers me about this theory. Unless maybe it was something automated. Something that they can't turn off now."

"That would be ... unfortunate," Derek said. "But also..."

"Outside your team's jurisdiction," Jacob finished. "I hear you there, buddy. It's outside mine as well. Taking out drug boats is one thing, but full on salvage..." He trailed off, a wistful look on his face, one Derek had seen before.

"What aren't you telling us?"

"Nothing important, especially if you're planning on packing up and shipping out..."

There came a knock at the door, interrupting them. A moment later one of Jacob's people popped his head in. "We've spotted another vessel on the horizon, sir. Catamaran from the look of it. Seems to be headed this way."

Jacob inclined his head toward Derek. "If that's who I think it is, I guess we'll both know what your marching orders are soon enough." He then turned to face the other agent. "Hail them if you can. If they're not one of ours, warn them off. Oh, and tell Mac it's time to cover our tracks. We need to sink that big bastard out there once and for all."

"About that, sir, there's one other thing."

"Yes?"

"That scientist, Reid. He's requesting Dr. Jenner and his team back aboard the Rogers Will-Do. Says he found something."

"What?"

"He didn't specify. He just said it's something they need to see."

Derek raised an eyebrow to which Jacob sighed. "We might as well all go see what's what in the good doctor's world. Wouldn't want any of us getting bored now, would we?"

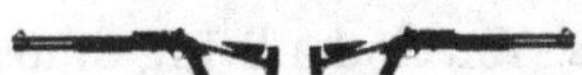

On the way up to the main deck Julie figured she'd try her luck, being that she had no idea when she'd get a chance to talk to their team's founder again.

"Would you mind if I asked you a question, Agent Caseman?"

"Can't promise you an answer, nature of the business, but you're free to ask. Oh, and it's Jake."

"Thanks. It's about what you said, about covering our tracks. You helped found this team, right?"

"Allegedly," he replied with a smirk.

"So, why the cover up? I mean, why keep these creatures from the world?"

Derek chuckled at her question. "Good luck on that. I've been asking him the same question for ten years now. It's always the same answer." His voice dropped an octave in mimicry of the other man. "You know I can't tell you that, Derek. It's need to know."

Jacob turned and raised an eyebrow at him. "I do not sound like that."

"Sure you do."

"Do not. And don't tell me you actually believed that bullshit."

"Wait. What bullshit?"

"What I just said. I was pulling your leg with that shit. Figured you knew that."

"Hold on. What do you mean, pulling my leg?"

"Exactly that. Thought it was funny. Hell, it's the same answer you get from the Shop if you ask where the fucking bathroom is."

"Are you serious?"

Jacob let out a chuckle. "Hell yeah. The only reason they keep this shit quiet is because mega-fauna would attract all the yahoos out there. You discover a new frog and nobody cares. You find a living dinosaur, though, and every redneck with a rifle will be out hunting for one, laws be damned. Saving endangered species is a hell of a lot easier when the poachers don't think they exist."

Derek stopped in his tracks, almost causing Julie to bump into him. "Are you telling me I had to listen to Frank's crackpot theories, day in and day out, all because of a stupid running joke?"

Jacob laughed again. "You have to admit, he did have some good ones." He nodded toward Julie. "Did you ever hear his theory about using squatches for slave labor, like this was *Planet of the Apes* or something?"

"Can't say that I have."

"It was a hoot. Damn, I miss the big man. He had some imagination on him." He glanced back at Derek. "You're serious? You didn't know I was joking?"

Derek shook his head and started walking again. "Let's just go see what Reid has to show us before I start wishing the octopus had won."

"You wanted to see us, Doctor?"

Derek noted that Llanzo looked a bit shaken as they gathered around him, probably not entirely surprising considering what they'd been through.

Llanzo nodded then turned to face Jacob. "Agent

Caseman, I'm glad you came, too. Your people were hesitant to allow it, but I wanted to ask your permission to film something."

"Why?"

"Because I'm not sure I trust my eyes. And even if the footage is destined for a vault somewhere, I think what I'm about to show you should be documented nevertheless."

"My minicam should still be on board," Julie offered.

Jacob appeared to mull it over for a few moments, but finally he nodded. "Fine. I'll allow it on the caveat that if I don't like what I see, we immediately erase it. Deal?"

Both of them nodded, and then Julie headed below to retrieve her gear.

Llanzo waited for her to return, which Derek could tell was straining his friend's tolerance. Back when Jake had been leading the DoCC, Derek remembered him mostly tuning out once a mission's active stage was finished. He was a doer, not really known for his patience when it came time to wrap things up.

After a few minutes, though, Julie returned, camera in hand.

"You want to say the Crypto-Hunter intro before we get started?" Mitchell remarked.

"I can always dub it in later," Derek replied with a smirk. "Doctor, if you would. I think you'll find us a captive audience. However, it might be best if you got straight to the point."

Llanzo nodded. "I'll be happy to. What I'm about to show you... Well, it's best if you observe it yourself."

He donned a pair of rubber gloves, opened a nearby ice chest, and removed a bowling ball sized hunk of flesh – a portion of the beast's tentacle.

"A sample of the creature," he confirmed. "While there hasn't been time to do anything close to a complete morphological analysis, I can confirm that while this appears on the surface to be an octopoid, there are some fundamental changes that render it unique compared to its smaller cousins. Not the least of which are the presence of serrated sucker ridges, most commonly found in squid species. I've also noted differences in the density of the collagen layers that I believe helps strengthen the underlying..."

"The point, doctor?" Jacob prodded.

"My apologies. The point is that my analysis is far from complete ... which is regrettably irrelevant to what I'm about to show you because I fear this new finding must take precedence."

"And that would be?"

"Watch. Ms. Wilhelm, if you would." Llanzo proceeded to place the specimen onto a nearby scale. He then gestured to the dial beneath it. "If you'll zoom in here, you'll note its weight is approximately nine point eight three kilos. As an aside, I will point out this tiny piece alone is heavier than the vast majority of octopi in these waters."

"Is that what you wanted to show us?" Jacob replied, sounding dubious. "Because I have a lot of work to..."

"I ask for a few moments of patience," the scientist interrupted. "Please. There's no doubt a pattern to the phenomena we've been experiencing. However, I haven't had much free time to study it."

"The phenomena?"

"Those EMP pulses which aren't EMPs," Derek offered.

"Precisely," Llanzo continued. "They seem to be happening intermittently, but that doesn't mean there isn't a pattern. I just haven't been able to..." He trailed off as the lights in the cabin began to flicker.

"Dr. Reid?"

"Now," he told Julie. "Zoom in again, quickly please.

There. Look at the reading now. Please note for the record, the scale's weight now reads nine point nine four kilograms. That's a slightly larger change than I noted earlier."

"Holy shit," Mitchell said. "That can't be right."

"What can't be right?" Jacob asked. "And why do we care about a quarter of a pound?"

Derek held up a hand. "Before we consider what this might or might not mean, Doctor, how do we know that whatever's happening isn't simply affecting the electronics of that scale?"

At this, Reid finally smiled. "That's what I thought, too, and its why I pulled this old model out of the forward storage compartment. It's purely mechanical, no electronic components inside."

"And you said there was a similar differential earlier?"

"Oh yes. I kept notes of it. Agent McAvee was here as my witness." He glanced again at the scale. "Ah. Look now. The phenomena must have passed because, as you can see here, the object is back to its original weight. As such, we must surmise..."

"Interesting. So how come none of us noticed it before?"

"That's simple," Mitchell interrupted. "Even scaling it up, we're talking about a pound or two difference. If we were sitting around on dry land doing nothing, we might notice that. But out here playing Captain Ahab? It'd be easy to dismiss as nothing more than the motion of the ocean."

Jacob stepped forward. "Okay, slow down a bit. I'm not sure why everyone's panties are in a bunch over a scale."

"It's because of what it implies," Mitchell said. "You're sure that scale isn't hinky or anything, right?"

Llanzo nodded. "I tested it several times. It may be old, but it's working perfectly."

"Then if this is right," the medic continued, "it could potentially go far beyond electronics, making whales go crazy, or anything we know of for that matter."

"How so?" Jacob asked.

"Gravity," Derek said. "If something is actually affecting the pull of gravity itself, then there's no way it can be a good thing."

"And why's that?"

"Because," Llanzo replied, "so far as I am aware, this is something no force on Earth should be able to do."

PART II

18

Derek had been somewhat dismayed to see Danni as she and Norah boarded the cutter from their vessel – a sailing yacht called the Sun Angel.

He'd never have admitted it aloud but the truth was he'd benched her, under the guise of wanting a team member to remain behind to monitor the situation.

He'd been protective of her ever since Bonanza Creek, having promised her parents he'd keep her safe in a job where safety often took a backseat. Though a part of him had regretted recruiting her into this life, he'd also gotten the sense that, had he not, she'd have simply gone off looking for answers on her own.

He knew she was there of her own free will and fully capable of making adult decisions, but he still couldn't help it. After all, she wasn't the only one haunted by memories of Harrison Kent's death.

With the creature they'd been sent to find dead, the mission was technically over. However, the strange phenomena they'd experienced seemed undaunted by that fact, which meant the potential danger remained.

153

How much of that would fall on his team's shoulders, though, was what they were now gathering to discuss.

"Are we waiting for anyone else?" Norah asked from the head of the briefing room table.

Despite this being Jacob's ship, the original mission had fallen under her jurisdiction – meaning she was in charge.

For now, anyway.

Derek was silently hoping the point of this meeting was to wrap up his team's involvement and discuss next steps. Whatever was going on went way beyond their charter, unless someone here was about to suggest that octopus was somehow bending the forces of nature from beyond the grave.

Yet, at the same time, something still nagged at the back of his head ... some unfinished task or unanswered question he couldn't quite put his finger on.

"Present and accounted for on my end," Jacob replied. "Unless we're waiting on that stowaway you have locked up on your boat."

"Stowaway?" Derek asked.

"Klipsch," Danni replied. "That photographer from earlier. And he's not a stowaway."

"So you brought him along, why?"

"Time was of the essence," Norah said, "and he was proving to be ... problematic. Relax. The Sun Angel is currently moored on the far side of this vessel, out of sight of that squid. The only thing he's going to see if he looks out the window is nothing but a whole lot of water."

"Octopus actually."

"Whatever, it's dead now. Good job, by the way."

Derek motioned toward Jacob. "It was a group effort. Bait and hook."

Norah glanced her ex-husbands way. "I appreciate the assist."

"Anytime."

Their tones were both neutral and professional, as Derek expected them to be. He would have been lying, however, if he said he wasn't curious to see how things would've played out with a smaller audience. From what he understood it had been a mostly amiable separation, but he'd known them both long enough to suspect there were things left unresolved, especially the way Jake had been talking earlier.

But they weren't here to discuss their feelings. At least not yet. First up was seeing how Norah handled the remaining six-hundred pound elephant in the room.

"Doctor Reid, would you mind bringing everyone up to speed on your findings?"

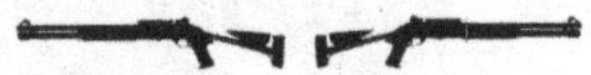

"It's nothing short of amazing. A preliminary analysis suggests a total length of between twenty and twenty-five meters, with a weight estimate of roughly five and a half metric tons..."

Dr. Reid was certainly an interesting fellow, Danni noted. It was like he wavered back and forth between trying to maintain a veneer of professionalism, with occasionally letting his excitement slip through. At the very least he was more lively than most of the professors she'd had, even if some of his presentation was a bit long-winded for her tastes.

Still, he was right. What a catch that creature had been – a veritable giant compared to the critters they normally hunted. Danni had caught sight of its corpse from the cutter's deck, submerged just below the waterline. Though a small part of her wouldn't have minded seeing such a fabulous beast alive, she'd also noted the damage it had done to the research vessel. The fact that he and her friends were all okay was probably a small miracle.

All that remained now was to wrap this up and hope for a few relaxing days in paradise – all while avoiding Klipsch. *Maybe Norah can keep him locked up a while longer in the...*

"Hold on, Dr. Reid," the aforementioned senior agent interrupted, dragging Danni back to the here and now. "Did you say gravity?"

Huh? She sat up, realizing she'd missed something important while she'd been daydreaming. *Not so different than my classes after all.*

"As hard as it may be to believe, Agent Caseman, I did. I ran several tests, both with the creature's remains as well as mundane items. All showed the same results. Agent Caseman ... the other one I mean, tried to independently verify this..."

"But the only scales we have are digital, meaning they're FUBAR," Norah's ex replied. "Just like everything else that isn't shielded. And silly us, nobody here thought to pack a gravimeter for the trip."

"We were going to try radioing back to the institute," Derek added, "to see if you could pull some stuff out of storage that might've been able to better withstand whatever's going on ... but, well, here you are instead."

"Excuse me for being worried about your asses," Norah replied dryly before turning back to the topic at hand. "The point remains, we're here now. Dr. Reid, in your estimation, how big of an immediate threat are these ... disturbances?"

In response, he looked like a deer in the headlights. "I

don't even know what they are. How can I possibly begin to answer that?"

"It's okay, Doctor," Derek said, jumping in. "Why don't we all start instead by looking at what we know? Shipboard communications, radar, sonar – anything with sensitive electronics. All of it seems prone to going haywire."

"Propulsion and navigation, too. Don't forget about that," Mitchell replied.

"Nothing we didn't already suspect," Norah remarked with a sigh. "Hence why we thought a sailboat might be our best bet to reach you."

"What if it's more than just ship-based?" Alvita asked, finally speaking up. "Let us not forget, there was that helicopter crash involving our employee, too."

Norah shook her head. "A regrettable accident, likely nothing more."

"With an experienced pilot at the stick. Am I wrong, Mr. Caseman?"

Jacob shook his head.

"So might I suggest this problem may be more urgent than perhaps we're willing to acknowledge."

"We don't know that for sure."

Derek opened his mouth, as if he were about to say something to that but, before he could offer whatever opinion he had, one of Jacob's team entered the room.

"What is it, Novak?"

"I think you should see this, sir." The agent handed him a slip of paper.

Jacob looked at it for a few moments, his eyes opening wide. "Oh my god."

"What's wrong?" Norah asked.

"Passenger jet, a 737. Went down just north of Nassau about an hour ago."

"What?! Are there any survivors? Is there a rescue effort?"

The man who'd delivered the news, Novak, shook his head. "Coms are still scrambled, ma'am. That's all we were able to pick up. Been nothing but static since."

"You were saying, Agent Caseman?" Alvita replied, her tone calm yet condescending.

He glared at her for a moment, but then took a deep breath. "This is tragic news, but we can't jump to conclusions. We don't know for certain its related."

"What about our flight down here?" Danni asked, the question popping out of her mouth before she even realized it.

"Excuse me, Agent Kent," Norah replied, her voice tight. "You have something to add?"

Oh crap. The spotlight was definitely on her now. She could either apologize and shut up, or... But what if there was a connection? "Remember what we told you about our flight in? It was terrible. Bumpy, up and down, seatbelt light on for most of it. Can we really afford to assume that's a coincidence, especially now?"

"Son of a bitch," Mitchell muttered as the rest of the room continued to stare at her.

"I ... apologize if I'm speaking out of turn," she said after a moment, feeling self-conscious.

"Don't be." Derek said, turning to Norah again. "She's right."

"Could have been a lot of reasons for that," Jacob replied.

"Could be, but maybe it would be best if we assumed there wasn't, that we might be dealing with a worst case scenario. Think about it. Mass equipment failure centered around one of the most heavily travelled vacation spots in the world. I don't even want to imagine what could happen if we're right."

Mitch leaned forward and added, "Or if this gets any worse."

Norah turned back toward Llanzo. "Your thoughts, Doctor?"

"I can't begin to speculate, except..."

"Except what?"

He shook his head. "Except that I've seen no indication that this phenomenon is slowing down in any appreciable way."

Silence descended in the room for several long minutes, the horror of the tragedy no doubt sinking in. Danni couldn't know what the others might be thinking, but she was already wondering how many more lives might be lost before this was over.

"Very well. I suggest we proceed under the assumption this is an issue that needs to be dealt with," Norah said at last. "Standard operating procedure will be to reroute flights while this is being investigated, but that won't last long if they think it's simply an accident."

So much for wrapping this one up quickly, Derek mused. "What's our next step?"

"Good question. Under normal circumstances, I'd say we radio this in and run it up the ladder."

"Easier said than done," Jacob replied.

"As I'm well aware."

"Even if we could, there's the international community to consider," he continued. "Assuming this isn't some natural phenomena, we don't know what we're dealing with here or how big a response is warranted. It's a fair bet we don't want to draw unwanted attention to these disturbances, especially if whatever's causing them can be harnessed."

"As a weapon," Mitchell replied, before adding, "don't look at me like that. I'm just saying what everyone here is thinking."

Derek couldn't help but grin tightly. His friend wasn't wrong, even if his gift for tact left a lot to be desired.

"Thank you for your insight as usual, Agent Harkness," Norah replied, before taking a deep breath. "All of that taken into consideration, I think we're left with two options. We can head back to port, however long that takes, or we commit to doing what we can to solve this." She turned to her ex. "This is your vessel. I'd like to hear your take."

"My official orders don't go any further than the rescue operation for the Tortuga. That said, and this is not to leave the room, I've done this long enough to know what's expected of me. We need to collect whatever intelligence we can on these so-called disturbances. Otherwise, they're simply going to send someone else to do the same thing and we'll have lost that much time figuring this out."

Norah nodded. "True, and, though this falls somewhat outside our usual charter, the DoCC aren't exactly strangers when it comes to dealing with the unexplained."

Derek made eye contact with his team one at a time. It seemed their die had been cast.

"And if you're wrong?" Llanzo asked.

"Then we've wasted no one else's time but our own," came the unsurprising answer.

"No offense," Julie said, speaking up, "but how are we supposed to investigate anything with most of our equipment on the fritz?"

"Most still leaves us with some," Jacob said. "And, it's not like we aren't prepared for a seaborne operation ... or undersea, if it comes to that."

"Oh?" Derek replied, raising an eyebrow.

"The people my team ... *deal* with, well, they're not

stupid. They see an unmarked ship closing and they're just as likely to dump their cargo and run as they are to fight. Our job is to be ready for both. There's a five man submersible in the hold, reinforced for salvage operations and rated for the depth of these waters." He paused a moment before adding, "Nothing designed for fighting super squids, mind you."

"And you call yourself prepared," Mitchell scoffed.

"This is all fascinating, I'm sure," Alvita said, rising from her seat. "However, my interest here ends with the fate of ZarroGreen's property. As the creature that sunk the Tortuga has been dealt with, I must request that I be returned to shore as soon as possible. We will, of course, be mindful of any restrictions put into place before we begin salvage operations."

Alvita's words sunk into Derek's mind like a hot dagger, finally acting as the glue to the puzzle pieces which had been bothering him ever since the battle with the octopus. "*The Tortuga.*"

Norah turned toward him. "Excuse me, Dr. Jenner?"

"I'm sorry, but I think there might be a major flaw in our logic here."

"And that would be?"

"We've been going on the assumption that this is the same creature that sunk the Tortuga. But what if it isn't?"

"I don't like where this is going," Jacob said with a sigh.

"Continue," Norah replied, her face unreadable.

"Something's been bugging me ever since that thing attacked us, but I didn't know what it was. Dr. Reid, you said the creature we killed was what, eighty feet long, maybe six tons? Do you think that's large enough to have sunk the Tortuga?"

"It came perilously close to sinking us."

"Us, yes," Derek replied, standing up. "But let's not

pretend the Rogers Will-Do is anywhere close to the size of a drillship, even an old one."

"It tried its damnedest to take us down, too, don't forget," Jacob added.

"That's exactly what I mean. It tried and failed. It latched onto this ship with everything it had. Yes, you were listing pretty hard, but at no point did it seem like it was close to succeeding." He glanced back at Alvita. "I did a little reading up before we came down here. Am I wrong in assuming that not only was the Tortuga significantly larger than this vessel, but the systems on a ship like that are specifically designed to compensate for any instability it encounters?"

"You're not incorrect," she said, a troubled look creasing her face.

"Then I submit, Agent Caseman, that we're still well within the DoCC's wheelhouse. Because if my theory is correct, we not only have another of these things out there somewhere, but it's a hell of a lot bigger, too."

19

The leviathan floated just below the surface, funneling chunk after chunk of rich blubber into its beak.

It was used to being an ambush predator, spending long periods of time lounging upon the ocean floor, waiting for prey to wander within its reach. But that was before it had been driven near mad by the thrumming which set its brain afire.

Now it was a creature of swift and deadly action. But such action came at a cost – energy which it needed to quickly replenish if it were to survive.

Fortunately, its newfound savagery had borne fruit. It had surfaced amid a pod of the squeaking things. First it had drowned the largest bull, using its mighty arms to compress the air from its foe's lungs. Then it had turned on the rest, tearing them apart and leaving the surrounding waters cloudy with viscera.

That had been some time ago. How long, it wasn't certain. But the rage, followed by the feeding frenzy, had managed to dull the pain enough that it had allowed itself

163

to float listlessly with the current, not knowing or caring where it was taken.

Now, though, the blissful haze of violence and flesh was finally beginning to pass. Another pulse raced through its body, lighting up its nerve endings and bringing it fully awake – causing the water around it to swirl and froth as it righted itself. The thrumming was weaker here, more distant, but still enough to torment it.

Its tentacles easily touched the sandy bottom, telling the beast it was far from its hunting ground. Its memory and sense of direction were both keen, though. This was a place it had been before, long ago, when it was still prey to many of the larger predators that roamed the sea.

It was close to the shallows where it had been born. Instinct had commanded it to leave once it had grown too large, but now here it was again. And though it knew these waters were no longer its home, it sensed movement and sound which drew its interest.

From its early days it remembered this as a dangerous place, the border between its world and that of the small screaming things. Its usual disposition toward them had once been mere curiosity, but these were far from normal times. The thought of the screaming things trespassing into its domain infuriated it as yet another invisible pulse wracked its body.

Distant or not, it would find no solace here from the damnable thrumming.

No solace except that which could be found in violence.

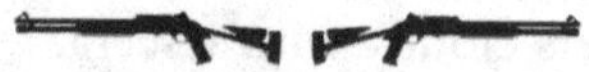

"Are you saying there's another of those goddamned things out there?"

"I don't think there's much doubt of that," Derek

replied to his old friend. "Unless anyone here thinks the creature we killed was a one-time aberration. The more important question is whether there's another that's been affected the same way our friend out there was. I'm just saying, maybe we shouldn't let our guard down, at least not yet."

"Makes sense to me," Mitchell said. "I mean, from the sound of things, we're all going on this ghost hunt anyway to find whatever's making gravity go crazy. So we might as well not get complacent while we're doing it."

Derek glanced sidelong at him. "In a nutshell, yes." He then turned toward Norah. "Or so I'm assuming."

She let out a resigned sigh. "You would assume correct, at least until such time as we're able to reestablish communications. As the senior agent here..."

"Senior agent for the Department of Agriculture," Jacob corrected. "I'll remind you, neither myself nor my team are under your jurisdiction. If we're going to do this, it'll be as a joint operation. Agreed?"

"Fair enough," she replied after several seconds, albeit through slightly gritted teeth.

Derek met Mitchell's eyes and he gave his friend a slight nod. There was no doubt in his mind that this was little more than a pissing match. However, considering his relationship to both, he decided it would be in his best interest to keep his mouth shut ... for now anyway.

He could only hope Mitch showed the same level of restraint.

"Ms. Guerrero," Norah said, turning to the rep. "In light of this new theory, you're welcome to remain aboard with us. Or, if you still wish to return to shore, I'll ensure one of the other vessels can accommodate you." She likewise inclined her head at Llanzo. "Same goes for you, Dr. Reid. While your assistance is highly appreciated, we'll all understand if you feel you've done your part."

Llanzo actually laughed, although Derek didn't sense a great deal of humor in it. If anything, the younger man was looking more stressed by the minute.

"I would like nothing more than to get back to the Institute and forget this whole mess," he said. "But the more I think about Dr. Jenner's theory, the less inclined I find myself toward wanting to be aboard either the Will-Do or that sailboat out there. Thank you, but I like my odds here better."

"As you wish, Doctor," Norah replied. "However, please understand this isn't a pleasure cruise. If you remain aboard, we'll expect your full cooperation."

He threw her a quick nod as if that were the least of his concerns.

Derek couldn't blame the man. None of them had expected to run across that first creature when they had. Who in their right mind would want to chance doing it a second time with no backup?

Hell, even he found himself hoping he was wrong. Perhaps there'd been an explosion aboard the Tortuga which had caused its demise or some other incident. Maybe the octopus's attack had been a coincidence, nothing more.

Yeah, hopefully that was the case, because the alternative was terrifying to consider.

Sadly, Derek had learned to trust his instincts over the years and they were telling him his theory was sound, which wasn't exactly doing wonders for his current stress levels.

Looking around the room, the same was likely true for the rest.

"If there are any doubts with regard to the Tortuga's sinking," Alvita said after a moment, her tone measured, "then my duty is clear." She let out a deep breath. "And, truth be told, I'm forced to agree with the doctor's assessment. Remaining aboard this vessel appears to be the sound choice, for now."

"Okay, so we're all present and accounted for," Julie said, speaking up again. "What now? How do we find a monster we don't even know exists?"

"Same way we found the last one," Mitchell offered. "We sit here and look appetizing."

"This isn't a fishing trip," Jacob replied. "And from the sound of things, these creatures aren't the cause of these disturbances so much as reacting to them." He nodded toward Derek. "That sound right to you?"

"I'm no expert, but I know sonar has been shown to mess with whales. We're dealing with an unknown here but, based on our individual observations, I'd say it's the most reasonable answer among unreasonable questions."

"That's really not comforting," Mitchell commented.

"It wasn't meant to be. The point is, I think we'd be best served focusing on finding the source of these disturbances instead of chumming for sea monsters."

"Just for the record, I agree," The medic said. "Solving one should hopefully solve the other."

"Sounds like a plan to me," Norah replied. "So how do we make that happen?"

She and Jacob both turned toward Llanzo, as Derek expected them to. Poor guy. He'd figured out the gravity thing, which was a great help, but now they assumed he was their resident expert, when in actuality he was in way over his head.

Albeit, it's not like any of the rest of them had much of a clue either.

They were, in a sense, floating dead in the water.

"Don't look at me," Llanzo finally snapped. "I'm a marine biologist, not an astrophysicist."

"In all fairness, Doc, even if you were I'm not sure it'd

help much," Jacob said. "Outside of that scale of yours, we're not exactly running in tiptop shape here."

"Wait! Maybe that's it," Danni blurted out.

"Maybe what's it?" Norah asked, her tone suggesting she wasn't hopeful.

"Most of our equipment isn't working right, but what if we could maybe use that to our advantage?"

"And how might we do that?"

"What if we could ... maybe figure out what direction is causing things to work even worse than they are? That could act sort of like a compass."

Out of the corner of his eye, Derek caught Jake rolling his eyes.

Before he could outright dismiss her, though, Mitch spoke up. "Hold on. Maybe she has a point there." Jacob moved to speak, but he held up his hand. "Hear me out. If it was just us, we'd probably be talking a turd hunt. But we have three ships at our disposal here. So why not use that? It seems reasonable to assume that these disturbances would hit us all at the same time, right? So if we spread out our small fleet a bit, maybe we can figure out which of us is getting hit slightly harder ... and then use that as our guide."

"Would that even work?" Norah asked.

"We'd need to eliminate as much chance as possible," he continued. "Use the same equipment, attuned to the exact same frequencies, and only report on measurable distortions, like the weight fluctuations Dr. Reid showed us earlier."

"How would we check our findings?" Julie asked. "I thought the radios were shot."

"Long range, yes," Jacob said, leaning forward. "But maybe at short range we could boost the signal to have a better shot. And we have plenty of portables on board. Who knows? Maybe those'll work better."

Mitchell nodded. "It's worth a shot."

"If I may remind you all," Alvita replied, "we were just discussing how much more vulnerable those other two vessels were."

"Noted," Norah said, her tone telling Derek she was probably open to at least trying this plan. "That's why all nonessential personnel will remain aboard this ship. The rest will be manned by skeleton crews of armed agents." She waited for any dissent before continuing. "Dr. Reid, you're the one who first measured this anomaly. I'm going to ask you to work with Agent Harkness to brainstorm and then coordinate this effort."

Llanzo seemed to think about it for a moment before nodding. Derek didn't even bother to glance Mitch's way. He knew his friend would be a kid in a candy store with an assignment like this.

It was a long shot at best, nothing more, but all at once the energy in the room changed. Where before there had been indecision, fear, even malaise, now there seemed to be purpose.

What they were planning was more than likely to fail, Derek didn't fool himself into thinking otherwise, but it was something to do – something other than crawling home with their tails between their legs, all the while knowing that more innocent lives were at stake because of whatever was going on.

"All right then," Norah said after several moments. "It sounds like we have a plan. Let's make it happen." She then glanced her ex-husband's way. "But first, let's take care of that oversized guppy floating alongside us."

20

Kerry Klipsch was certain he was going to die ...
or worse.

He'd heard tales of people being kidnapped
from the islands, never to be seen again – their families left
to wonder if they'd been murdered or sold into slavery.

However, he never in his wildest dreams imagined it
could happen to him.

Worse, it had been at the hands of that woman from
the airport, the one who'd claimed she had business with
the cast he'd been sent to photograph.

What did that mean? Were they in on this, or were
they too destined to become victims?

Kerry didn't know or really care, at least on that latter
part. All he knew was that woman had shown up at the
dock, somehow taken over the charter he'd paid for, and
then had her goons lock him below deck as they'd set sail
for god knows where.

She'd shown up at the door of his cabin sometime
later, spouting bullshit about the government and the need
for secrecy, but he hadn't been fooled for a second. He
knew she was trying to lull him into a false sense of secu-

rity, get him to drop his defenses. They'd even had the gall to offer him some sandwiches, as if he were stupid enough to accept them.

Sadly, his attempts to rebuff their efforts hadn't gained him much. All it had done was gotten him locked up again as they sailed further from shore.

Now, it seemed his fate was sealed. A while back the catamaran had pulled alongside a much larger vessel, and there he'd waited – trying to listen to the voices on deck but failing to pick up anything that could help him.

Kerry considered his surroundings. They'd taken his cameras but nothing else, leaving him locked in one of the yacht's pontoon staterooms. Ironically, it was the same one he'd scoped out in the hope of getting a few boudoir shots of that Kent chick, something his bosses would no doubt drool over.

But now photography was the furthest thing from his mind. He frantically searched the bedroom for anything he could use as a weapon. There were actually plenty of options – a lamp, a table ... hell, he could have taken off his shoelaces and used them as a garrote.

Kerry wasn't a fool, though. If this was a movie, he could have fought his way to freedom, taking his captors down one at a time, but this was reality. He knew full well he stood little chance against the people he'd seen, especially since all of them seemed to be armed.

The truth was, he was afraid and the only viable option he could see was maybe bribing his way out. But in order to make that possible, he needed a bargaining chip in his favor. And, heck, it's not like it would've taken much torture to make him spill his ATM pin.

But maybe they didn't know that. If he was able to act tough, convince them he meant business, then maybe they'd be willing to cut a deal – not knowing he'd have gladly given up anything to regain his freedom: his money, his car, even the private phone numbers of his more famous clients.

None of that mattered so long as he was able to walk away from...

All thoughts of escape scattered to the wind as there came the sound of a muffled explosion. A moment later, he felt the boat vibrate beneath his feet.

More blasts followed, hollow thuds that seemed to come from somewhere below.

What the hell?

Had there been an accident aboard the larger vessel?

Good! I hope it sinks to the bottom and takes them all with it.

His second thought was to think it might be the authorities. Maybe someone had witnessed his abduction and reported it. If so, rescue could be within his grasp ... assuming his abductors didn't decide to do away with the *evidence* first.

Oh, god, no!

There was no doubt in his mind they'd do it, too. What did one life mean to scumbags like these? What did it matter to them if he...?

There came a sound from right outside the closed door – voices.

This was it. They were here to make sure he'd never get to breathe the sweet smell of freedom again.

I have to do something!

Kerry Klipsch wasn't a brave man but, much like a cornered animal, he realized his only chance was to stand and fight.

He grabbed hold of the bedside lamp just as the door was unlocked, preparing to do whatever was needed to survive, even if it meant taking a life.

"If it wasn't dead before, it sure as hell is now." Jacob looked over the Nest's railing, noting the rapidly spreading chum slick below.

"Here we are, blowing up a giant octopus together," Derek said from his side, "and yet you claim to not miss this job."

"Maybe some parts," he replied with a chuckle. "Not really this, though. Think that'll do it?"

Derek nodded. "Hopefully. The blood should draw in the scavengers and they should take care of the rest."

"Even with the weirdness going on?"

"Never discount the appeal of a free meal. And if anything is left to wash up on shore, well, you know the drill."

"More shit for the internet nerds to argue over."

"Exactly."

Jacob grimaced, feeling his stomach tighten. Now that Reid had made them aware of those gravity fluctuations, he was questioning even the tiniest rumble of flatulence. "You feel that?"

"Yep," Derek confirmed. "Another of those disturbances."

"Fun stuff, eh?"

"Not really."

"Speaking of which, how are Mitch and that Reid fellow coming along?"

"We should be ready to start testing within the hour. Multi-function arrays on each boat, all calibrated identically. And I think your men are almost done shoring up the work Mitch did on the Will-Do's engines. With any luck, it'll be smooth sailing from here on..."

He was interrupted by the distant rumble of thunder. Both men turned to see clouds gathering to the south.

Jacob shook his head. "You just had to say it, didn't you?"

"C'mon. You didn't want this hunt to be boring, did you?"

"Trust me, buddy. With you around, I knew there was little chance of that happening."

Danni had little time to process anything other than the small desk lamp that went flying past her as she opened the door to Klipsch's room.

It missed by a country mile, crashing into the opposite wall where it clattered to the floor in pieces.

She turned back to find him staring wide-eyed, although whether it was at her or because of his lousy shot she wasn't certain.

"What the hell are you doing?"

"Are you one of them?" he cried.

"One of who?"

Apparently that was the wrong answer because he let out a bellow, lowered his head, and charged forward. "I knew it! I'll kill you, you ... OOF!"

Why did I have to get assigned to this clown? Danni spun and caught Klipsch dead center with a side kick that sent him tumbling ass over tea kettle onto the bed. She pulled the blow at the last second, not wishing to hurt the photographer, who was obviously scared out of his mind. However, she didn't pull it as much as she *could* have.

Oh well. Either way, it took the wind out of his sails.

"Are you done?"

Whatever bravado Klipsch had mustered immediately crumbled as his *war cry* turned into something more closely resembling pathetic begging.

"Please don't hurt me. I have ... money! Everything I have, it's yours. Here, take it!"

For one brief moment Danni was tempted to play

along, but then she shoved that thought out of her mind. She knew what it was to be a prisoner, to be terrified of what might happen.

Unlike her ordeal in the Pine Barrens, though, the photographer wasn't in any danger. If anything, he was being detained by the good guys. However, he either didn't realize that or didn't believe it.

Guess Norah must be rustier than she realizes. It didn't help that the senior agent practically radiated an aura of intimidation, at least in Danni's opinion. Derek, on the other hand, was as charismatic as he appeared on TV. It usually didn't take long for him to verbally disarm anyone. Now it was apparently time to see if any of it had rubbed off on her.

"Sorry about that. Reflexes. Are you okay?"

"Just let me go. I..."

"We can't. I mean, we're nowhere close to shore and not heading back just yet."

"W-what are you going to do with me?" Klipsch asked, sounding as if he were close to tears.

"That's an easy one. We're heading over to the other ship so you can sign some paperwork. Then, when we're done, we'll drop you off back at port and you can go your merry way."

"That's what that other woman said. You really expect me to believe..."

"Yes, I do, Kerry." She sat down next to him, feeling slightly guilty as he flinched away from her. "Because it's the truth."

"I don't..."

"The only reason you're here is because you gave Norah a hard time back at the dock. She was the one pushing you to walk away, remember? We only needed the boat, not you."

"The boat? Why? There's plenty of other boats on the island."

"Yeah, but it was kind of an emergency and I knew you had it packed and ready to go."

"So *you* did this?"

"Yes. And I'm sorry for that ... and for scaring you. But like I said, we were kind of in a rush. That's pretty much the ins and outs of it."

"Oh yeah? Well then why were you in such a rush? And what were those explosions a few minutes ago? And why did..."

"One question at a time," she said, holding up her hand. "For starters, we thought our friends were in trouble. Those explosions you heard were timed charges, by the way. Routine demolition work, nothing more."

"That..."

"Doesn't make much sense? I know. And I'm not really sure how much I'm allowed to tell you. Truth of the matter is, I'm not the one who usually handles these things. All I know for certain is we need you off this boat. We're going to be sailing into ... some rough seas, and you'll be safer aboard the other ship."

"How do I know this isn't a trick?"

She barely repressed the sigh that wanted to escape her lips. This always seemed so much easier when Derek did it. "You don't. But think about it. Nobody's hurt you since you came aboard. The only reason you were locked down here is because we didn't want you getting in the way." Danni put a hand on his shoulder. "Listen, I know it's scary to be shanghaied like this. Trust me, I do. But the only danger right now is staying where you are."

"Why?"

"It's hard to explain. And I'm not sure you'd believe me anyway." Danni considered this. She probably wasn't authorized to say much more, but the clock was ticking.

Soon, it was going to be a choice between him walking out or being dragged. "The things we hunt on our show ... they're real. That's why we're out here."

Kerry raised an eyebrow and then he burst out laughing, although it sounded far more manic than whimsical. "You expect me to believe this is all because we're searching for a sea monster?"

"No. Me and my team are searching for one. You just happened to be..."

"Let me guess. In the wrong place at the wrong time?"

Danni couldn't help the grim smile that played out over her lips as she nodded. Sadly, it was a situation she was far too familiar with.

21

"Isn't this great?"

"What?"

"I *said* ... isn't this great?!"

"Yeah, I guess."

Darren Henderson shook his head. There simply seemed to be no impressing his seventeen year old son.

After the divorce, he and Max had drifted apart. Part of it had been Max becoming a moody teenager, slipping full force into that time of life when one's parents were the furthest thing from cool.

The rest, though, had been Wendy being a spiteful cunt. There was no telling how long she'd been screwing around behind his back before slapping him with divorce papers, basically accusing him of being the worst person on the planet. All of it – the accusations, the crocodile tears, the lies – had been for one purpose, to bleed him dry. And for years she'd done a damned good job of it, too.

It was only recently that his luck had changed. He'd managed to pull himself back up by his bootstraps, securing a good paying job and putting a down payment on another house.

Wendy, on the other hand, had gotten charged with a DUI not long ago. Though she should've been thrown in jail, Darren had still been able to use the police report to renegotiate their settlement – convincing the judge to finally grant him joint custody.

Sadly, it hadn't gone as he'd hoped. Gone was the little boy who'd once wanted to do everything with his dad. In his place was a sullen teen who was more interested in his Xbox than his father.

Darren was nothing if not persistent, though – saving up, then jumping through every legal hoop imaginable, so he could take his son on this dream vacation.

That it was also a not-so-subtle slap to Wendy's face was simply icing on the cake. She'd always wanted to visit the Bahamas. Too bad she'd decided that sucking every dick in the neighborhood was more important than being a good wife. Her loss was their gain.

Or it would have been had Max not spent most of the trip complaining about being bored. Near wit's end, Darren had almost given up. But then he'd spied a pamphlet in the hotel lobby, advertising a parasailing adventure.

If that didn't excite his son, he didn't know what would.

It almost hadn't happened, though. First Darren had to hide Max's phone, not the easiest thing in the world as he would've almost sworn it was surgically grafted to the teen's hand. Then came news of that plane crash, prompting the government to issue a call to all capable vessels to aid in the search for survivors.

The only upside was it had happened north of one of the other islands, meaning there wasn't as much of an impact where they were staying.

Finally, as if his luck hadn't sucked enough, they'd arrived at the dock only to be told by the manager of the parasailing company that their trip was cancelled due to some bullshit small craft advisory that was in effect.

He'd been close to tears at the news, fearing that his last best chance was slipping between his fingers. So, without thinking, he'd offered to double their fee – in cash.

Much to his surprise, the manager had locked the door before turning back toward them.

"Cash up front. We take my private boat, along with one other man. You tip him well."

Part of him was sure that had been the man's strategy all along, hoping to milk some stupid American for all he could, but that didn't matter. The trip was back on.

Within the hour they were pushing off from the dock and heading out, the old speedboat's twin outboards propelling them onward.

It had been near perfect from there, as if they had the entire ocean to themselves, barely another boat in sight. The only issue had been after they'd strapped in and were waiting to fly, when the boat's engines had refused to turn over for a few minutes.

But then, true to their word, they'd gotten it going again and he and Max were suddenly airborne, rising higher with every passing moment. It was great. The sea was calm, the weather warm, and he was spending time with his son ... who, minus his phone, had little choice but to engage with his dear old dad.

Soon, they were floating three-hundred feet above the water in a double harness, the tether line leading far below to the tiny boat ... only for his son's enthusiasm to come down to, "Yeah, I guess."

"Come on, check it out!" Darren cried. "You can see for miles."

Max finally looked around, his head turning every which way, and then it happened ... a near miracle as far as Darren was concerned. The slightest hint of a smile appeared on his son's face.

"Think we'll see any whales?" he asked after another minute or so.

"I don't know. Maybe." Darren had heard about the recent beaching, so at least he knew they were in the area. Hopefully whatever had caused it hadn't spooked the rest away, albeit he had no idea if that was how things actually worked. His knowledge of whales was pretty much limited to them being big and wet.

That wasn't important compared to seeing an emotion resembling actual joy on Max. Fuck it. If his son wanted whales, he'd give him whales. If he could bribe the parasailing guy, certainly he could find another captain willing to take a few bucks for a whale watching tour. This trip was already expensive, but what were a few dollars compared to making up for all those lost...

"Hey, what's that?" Max asked, pointing below.

Darren looked down and realized there might be no need for further bribery. The water was more than clear enough for him to see a large shadow somewhere beneath the surface.

At first he was worried it might just be a reef, but he quickly dismissed that idea. Whatever was down there was moving and it seemed to not only be headed toward the boat, but rising as well.

The closer it got, the larger it became.

Definitely a whale, he thought, *hell, maybe a whole school of them.* "I think we're about to get a show, son."

He was right, albeit not in any way he ever wanted to be.

Whatever was beneath the waves surfaced right under the boat. Darren caught a quick glimpse of something massive and fleshy, and then the speedboat was sent careening, its two crewmates thrown overboard. A few seconds later, he and Max were jerked violently down as their towline was dragged by the out of control vessel.

"Jesus, fuck me!" Max cried as they were both spun around multiple times in midair.

Normally Darren would have scolded his son for that sort of language, but right then he was sure it was – if anything – an understatement. It was just his luck to have a bunch of dumb fuck whales ruin the best day of their trip so far.

He and Max spun around each other again, almost causing him to lose his lunch, then there came one more downward jerk and suddenly they stabilized, riding on an up-current.

Thank goodness that's over with. Now to hope the...

"Um, Dad," Max asked, pointing. "Where's the boat?"

Darren looked down, realizing they were considerably closer to the water than they'd been just moments earlier. But then, a second later, he understood that altitude wasn't their only issue.

The boat and its crew were nowhere to be seen, the towline disappearing into the blue water.

Once again he felt their line being violently jerked, pulling them down another several feet.

Oh god. It's sinking and it's dragging us with it.

He glanced at Max, saw the fear in his son's eyes, and tried to force himself to calm down. Panic wasn't going to do them any good. And hadn't the boat's owner given them a quick tutorial on how to unhook themselves should they hit the water?

Besides, they were both snuggly strapped into life vests. What was the worst that could happen? They could simply float around in the serene waters waiting for...

Waiting for what? There was virtually no other traffic

out on the water. Between the rescue effort and the advisory, they were quite literally on their own.

"Um, Dad..."

"It's okay, Max. We'll be fine. We just need to keep our wits..."

The words failed him as they were once again yanked downward. Then, all at once, they began moving again, picking up speed, even as they drew ever closer to the water.

"What the hell?!" Were the boat's engines somehow still propelling it along?

Amazingly, they continued to accelerate despite the parachute behind them doing its damnedest to slow them down.

Too fast! They were heading toward the water too fast. Whatever had a hold of them or had gotten entangled in the towline was heading deep, and it seemed intent on having them for company.

Both father and son hit the water hard enough to momentarily stun them both. Whatever small window of escape they might've had passed in an instant, and then the harness was pulled taut around their legs and they were both dragged under, their life jackets doing little to slow them.

Darren couldn't help the silent cry of surprise that escaped his lungs, despite knowing he was losing precious oxygen.

Then, a moment later, he caught a fleeting glimpse of what was dragging them through the crystal clear waters and let out a scream – emptying his lungs and causing him to pray they both lost consciousness before the massive beast turned and realized they were there.

22

"Turn northeast sixteen degrees."

"Aye, Doctor."

"Make that eighteen," Mitchell corrected, looking at the small device in his hands. "Yeah, that's more like it."

"Are you sure we should be...?"

"Look at the readings, Doctor. There's little room for doubt."

Jacob raised a curious eyebrow as Reid turned around and doublechecked the device before finally nodding in agreement.

"Trust me," the medic replied. "I'm surprised as all hell, too, but we work with what we got."

"And what exactly is it that you've *got*?" Jacob asked, stepping over to where the two continued to work.

Mitchell grinned and held it up for him to see. "EMF meter. Found a couple down in engineering that nobody was using. Turns out the fluctuations on this little puppy seem to be at least as accurate as the scale, while being a lot easier to keep an eye on." He let out a laugh. "Guess all those ghost hunters are on to something after all. What do you think, Jake? Should we lobby our producers to switch formats?"

"I think Derek would sooner shoot you."

"Yeah. You're probably right." He turned back toward Llanzo. "Oh well. Maybe next reality show."

It was actually working. Jacob could scarcely believe it, but so far so good. With the two smaller vessels running point, one to port and one off their starboard, they were not only making headway, but apparently getting closer too ... at least according to what his gut was telling him.

He stepped away from where the two continued their work – gathering readings from the other vessels, writing them down on a dry erase board they'd liberated from his office, and constantly comparing them to determine their course.

The bright day had clouded up since they'd started their journey. A misting rain was now drizzling down on them from the late afternoon sky. Fortunately, the storm wasn't predicted to get much worse, one of the few bits of luck in their favor.

Jacob smiled to himself, realizing he shouldn't have been surprised. Maybe he'd grown too used to intelligence reports, satellite feeds, and heavy recon – forgetting that in the early days of *cryptid containment* they'd worked entirely by the seat of their pants.

Doing a crazy job sometimes required crazy solutions, though, and if there was one man up for that task it was Mitch. The guy was one step away from being a mad scientist, but somehow he made it work.

They all did.

Derek had both a knack for recruiting the right people for the job, as well as the devil's luck when it came to finding them when he needed them most.

For instance, there was the night they'd met Mitch. It had been a squatch hunt gone wrong, back in the days before the suits had concocted the idea for that stupid TV show. They'd gone in looking for a rogue male, driven batty by mating season, and had instead wandered into the middle of a turf war between three of the horny sons-of-bitches.

He, Derek, and Chuck had taken down one of the brutes, but had gotten their asses pretty well kicked in the process, necessitating a hasty retreat.

They'd emerged from the woods at the side of an old country road and managed to flag down a car that just so happened to be owned by one Mitchell D Harkness.

Jacob had to give the man credit. Most folks would've floored it at the sight of three armed and bloody men emerging from the woods, two of whom were black. Not Mitchell, though. He'd stopped and immediately offered his help.

Mitch had been working as an EMT at the time and kept a med kit in his trunk. As he worked to patch them up on the side of the road, Derek had been the one to decide they should tell him the truth regarding what had really happened to them.

Anyone else would have likely judged them insane, then gotten their asses back in their car and driven to the nearest police station, but Mitch marched to his own tune. He'd instead started throwing out ideas for how they could bag the remaining two beasts, as if the story they'd told him had barely been the fourth or fifth craziest thing he'd heard that week.

Hell, it had been his idea to tranq one of the clan's females and use her pheromones to set a trap which had finally solved the issue once and for all.

Jacob had wanted to thank him, get him to sign the forms, and then move on. Derek, on the other hand, offered up the idea that their little three man operation could not only use a fourth, but someone with medical training, too.

Mitch could be a prick when it came to authority, but damn if Derek hadn't proven right in the end.

It wasn't his last time either.

Francis, Danni, and now that Wilhelm woman – all civilians caught in situations that should have broken them, and yet each rising to the occasion.

If anything, considering his own failed relationship, he was jealous of his friend's ability to pick winners from the crowd. It was a knack Jacob wished he'd had for his personal life.

He let out a sigh as he looked out the port window, spying the small form of the research vessel a ways off. *Knowing him, one day he'll be out in the woods and somehow manage to meet his soulmate, despite being covered head to toe in squatch shit. While I'll still be here, with my thumb up my...*

His stomach suddenly lurched, dragging him out of his darkening thoughts. It was almost as if a weight had dropped into his lower intestine. The intermittent discomfort had been growing steadily harder to ignore in the hours since they'd begun this operation. Either another of those damned distortions was hitting, or he needed to have someone check the expiration date on their MREs.

"What the fuck is that?"

Jacob turned at the sound of the expletive, finding Mitch and the doctor both staring out the front windshield.

"I see it," McAvee said. "Dead ahead!"

Jacob followed their gaze, at first spying nothing but lots of empty ocean. His stomach clenched again, although he wasn't sure whether it was the distortion or the anticipation of more goddamned tentacles erupting from the sea. But then he caught sight of what they were gawking at.

It was another ship, less than a quarter mile away. Big one, too, about their size. But how? There was no way it could have gotten this close without someone seeing it, even with the rain.

He was about to order an all stop so they could hail the other ship, when the weight lifted from his stomach. He blinked and suddenly found himself staring at nothing but open water again. The other ship had simply ... vanished. *What the hell?*

"It's not just me, is it?" Mitch asked. "You guys saw that, too, right?"

"Give me that," Jacob ordered, picking up a high powered walkie talkie from where it sat next to the medic. "Sun Angel and Rogers Will-Do, this is Nest. Do either of you have visual contact with the vessel about four hundred yards directly off our bow? I repeat, do either of you have contact? Over."

Silence descended on the bridge as the staticky replies came back, telling him that not only did the other crews have no visual on the ship they'd seen, but they had no idea what he was even talking about.

Yet it had been there in front of them, plain as day.

"Just keep your eyes peeled," he finally told them. "Over."

He waited on the bridge with the rest of the agents there, expecting to be radioed back at any second letting him know they'd caught sight of the unidentified vessel after all. But minutes passed and no such reply came.

It was pointless to ask if there was anything on the scope, as their systems were still mostly useless. Besides, there was no denying the fact there was nothing out there now. Aside from the other two ships, the sea was clear for what seemed to be miles ahead.

"Anyone else getting Mary Celeste vibes here?" Mitchell remarked.

"A mirage," Llanzo said after a few more moments. "It has to be."

Jacob turned to him. "Excuse me?"

"A trick of the light. That's all. You saw it. It looked like another cutter to me. Same shape, same color. It had to have been our reflection, somehow bouncing off the water."

"Or maybe from that distortion that just hit?" Mitch offered, albeit he sounded doubtful.

"Perhaps, but I'm certain that's what we saw. There's no other explanation."

Jacob looked around the bridge, seeing nervous expressions on the faces of his people. He was a pragmatic man, not quite willing to believe in ghost ships yet, and he realized his team needed to hear that. "You heard the doctor. Back to your stations. Show's over."

He handed Mitchell the radio. After a few more seconds, the medic hopped on and started asking for readings again, as if nothing interesting had just happened.

Nothing did, Jacob told himself. *You heard him. We were seeing things. Nothing more.*

And yet, somehow, as the medic barked out orders for them to slow their speed, he couldn't help but feel that someone had just walked over his grave.

"For the last time, Mr. Klipsch, if we wanted to do something to you, we would simply do it. There would be no need for affidavits or NDAs. I could simply have you dragged to the rail and tossed overboard."

Derek glanced sidelong at Danni. The look on her face – half amusement and half abject horror – matched his.

Though he wouldn't say anything in front of the increasingly terrified photographer, he made it a point to talk to Norah later about perhaps toning it down a notch.

"Not that anyone is going to do that," Derek quickly added. "Right, Agent Caseman?"

She narrowed her eyes at him, no doubt growing frustrated, but finally she nodded. "No. I was simply speaking metaphorically, of course."

"Of course," Derek replied.

After a pause, the photographer repeated the mantra he seemed to keep falling back on. "Please. I have money. I can..."

Again with this? "I don't doubt that you do, Mr. Klipsch," he replied. "But we don't want it. And, quite frankly, we don't want you." He pulled his badge out of his pocket and placed it on the table. "Take down my number. When we get to port, contact the U.S. Forest Service and give it to them. They'll be happy to confirm it."

"Why can't I do that now?"

"I already told you. We're experiencing some issues that are preventing ship to shore communications."

"No offense, but that's awfully convenient, don't you think?"

"Not for us," Norah groused.

She wasn't wrong, Derek considered, but now was not the time to give in to frustration, despite how tempting it might be. Hell, he should have been aboard one of the other vessels helping out. Instead he was in here dealing with a guy probably paranoid enough to believe the NSA was tapping his microwave.

"Let me put it for you as plainly as I can," Derek said, after taking a deep breath. He'd dealt with difficult types before, including angry hillbillies who distrusted anything even remotely government related, but he couldn't recall ever being stymied by someone this stubborn. "If you sign this paperwork, and yes you are free to read it first, then you'll be given free rein here. We'll tell you whatever you want to know. You can walk around the ship, hang out on deck, even dive overboard and make a swim for it if you want. I wouldn't recommend it, but we won't stop you."

"And if I refuse?"

"Then you'll be confined to quarters for the remainder of the voyage, after which you'll likely have everything in your life scrutinized by federal agents from here until the end of time." He leaned forward and looked the photographer in the eye. "All we want is your silence on this. That's it. We don't want your money, your life, or anything else. We're simply asking you to keep a secret."

Derek felt a hand on his arm, and he turned to find it was Danni. She had an inquisitive look on her face, as if seeking permission to speak. He glanced once at Norah, then nodded.

"You're not going to want to talk about this anyway," Danni said, speaking in a calm measured voice.

"Oh?" Kerry replied, sounding obstinate. He still seemed scared, but some of his obnoxious attitude was returning.

"Think about it," she continued. "What are you going to tell the authorities? That you were kidnapped by the TV show you were sent to photograph, and that they're part of a government coverup?" Danni stepped back and grinned. "Oh look. It's Danni Kent, co-host, swimsuit model, *and* government spook. How do you think that'll sound?"

Whatever smugness Klipsch was starting to show faded in an instant.

Derek, on the other hand, smiled. He'd used a similar line on Danni and her brother when they'd first met. *When in doubt, always go with the classics.*

These days, of course, it was easy to find folks willing to believe just about any conspiracy, some with a disturbing number of followers. Fortunately, mythical monsters tended to rate much lower priority with the conspiracy nuts than tragedies or politics.

So, while Klipsch might be able to find some sympathetic ears, Derek was fairly certain they wouldn't exactly be helpful to his cause.

There came a pause, no doubt their guest thinking over his options. Derek really hoped he made the sensible decision because he could tell from the look on Norah's face that she was about ready to seriously consider tossing him overboard.

Another hour of this and he might be tempted to join her.

"And if I sign, I'm free to go?" Kerry replied.

"Insofar as we're miles out to sea, yes."

The photographer looked down at the affidavits before him, all the spots requiring his signature marked with bright yellow sticky notes. Then he looked at Derek and Danni, then back at the papers again.

"And I can get copies of these?"

"As many as you like," Norah said, her teeth pressed so tightly together that she could've bitten someone's head off.

Klipsch took a deep breath then finally scribbled his name on the first form.

It's about fucking time.

The photographer then closed his eyes, as if bracing for something – probably whatever nonsense his imagination had conjured.

When nothing happened he opened his eyes again, gave a nervous smile, and continued signing.

"I will of course warn you of two things, Mr. Klipsch," Norah said. "One, these papers are legally binding. And two, you're in the middle of an active investigation."

Once more, the color drained from Kerry's face,

causing Derek to quickly jump in before they lost him to paranoia again. "Meaning please stay off the bridge and out of the way of any on duty personnel."

"Oh. I can do that."

"Glad to hear it," Norah replied, "because the last thing we need is…"

The door to the cabin opened before she could finish and Jacob stepped in.

"I knew it," Kerry cried, nearly falling out of his chair. "I knew you were tricking…"

"Oh shut the fuck up already," Norah snapped.

"Am I interrupting something?" Jacob asked, a grin breaking out across his face.

"Yes, but that's okay."

He turned to Derek. "Did you flash your badge yet?"

"You're about ten minutes too late for that."

"Damn. I love that part."

"Is there a point to this visit?" Norah asked tersely. "Or did you just pop in to heckle us?"

"Sorry. Wanted to tell you that we're here."

"Here?"

"The *spot* we've been trying to find." He glanced sidelong at the photographer. "Anyway, I need everyone up in the briefing room in ten. Please make sure Ms. Guerrero joins us as well."

"Why?"

"Because it looks like ZarroGreen's involvement in all of this might not be as done as we'd hoped."

23

"We've circled this area multiple times in an increasingly tighter radius, and there's no doubt about it," Llanzo said. "All of our readings point to the same thing. This is the proverbial ground zero."

Mitchell spun in his chair to face the rest of the attendees. "Or somewhere above it anyway."

Almost as if on cue, the lights in the briefing room flickered, the incandescent bulbs making a low humming sound before finally stabilizing again.

"You guys really ought to upgrade to LEDs," the medic added.

Derek raised an eyebrow. "Is that merely an assumption or do we have reason to believe it? I mean ground zero, not the light bulbs."

"You ruin all my punchlines."

Ignoring his commentary, Jacob stood and said, "Doctor, I believe you had some findings to share."

Llanzo nodded. "Sonar is, of course, unreliable at the moment, but we've attempted several scans of the bottom during the times between distortions. The process has been

194

arduous and prone to error. Whatever is happening seems to be having a cumulative effect on our equipment. However, despite all the anomalies, there seems to be some aspects that are consistent across soundings – leading us to believe there's something on the ocean floor."

"Something?" Derek asked.

"That's the best way I can describe it, sadly. There appears to be a depression in the sea bed below us, and within it some kind of large object."

"Like what? Are we talking a shipwreck here or something else?"

Jacob shook his head. "If it is a ship, it's nothing like the other one down there."

"Other one?" Norah asked.

"Yeah," Jacob replied, turning to face Alvita. "The Tortuga."

"Excuse me?"

"That's why we called you to this meeting, Ms. Guerrero. Turns out we've been chasing our tails this whole time. This is the exact spot where the Tortuga sank, and it just so happens to also be where those distortions seem to be originating from. That's quite the coincidence, wouldn't you agree?"

Derek turned a keen eye toward Alvita, as did Norah. What appeared to be genuine surprise, however, shown on the ZarroGreen rep's face. Either this was news to her or she was one cool cucumber.

"I don't see how that's possible," she replied after a moment. "Nevertheless, Agent Caseman, a coincidence is all this is. It has to be. Unless, that is, you're accusing my employer of somehow breaking the laws of nature via an old ship barely qualified for service."

"We're not accusing anyone of anything," Norah said. "We're simply asking if you have any knowledge that could help us here."

The older woman seemed to take a moment to compose her thoughts, as if debating what her next words might be. *Understandable*, Derek considered. Norah was baiting her, plain and simple. And this wasn't some mere vendor negotiation either. Though ZarroGreen wasn't a US-based business, there was little doubt the United States was a significant source of revenue for them.

"You have to understand," she said at last, "that I'm neither privy to every research project at my company, nor am I in a position to speak freely about them." Jacob opened his mouth, but Alvita held up a hand. "However, while I would certainly place my position in jeopardy if I were to speak to specifics, I can most certainly offer up my general opinion on matters."

"What does that even mean?" Llanzo asked. "You're talking about paperwork, when we're dealing with a phenomenon that could potentially..."

"That will be enough, Doctor," Norah interrupted. "You'll have your turn. Ms. Guerrero, if you'd be so kind to elaborate."

"Thank you, Agent Caseman. As I said, I can't speak to any proprietary technologies we have under development. But I can answer with full honesty to a few points. One, I am unaware of anything under development that is even remotely similar to what we are dealing with here. And two, if there was such a development being tested, I have full faith that it would be in a controlled environment, not anywhere that would potentially bring the ire of international superpowers down upon us."

It was, in Derek's opinion anyway, a measured and diplomatic answer. Sadly, it was a far cry from comforting. If she was telling the truth, that still left a gigantic unknown lying on the ocean floor, something that was causing issues far beyond an oversized octopus.

Judging by the looks on both Norah and Jake, they were having similar thoughts.

"I won't lie, Ms. Guerrero," Jacob said. "But I was really hoping for a different answer. Would make this mission a hell of a lot easier if we had nothing more than some errant experimental tech to clean up."

"How about a simpler question?" Norah replied to the rep. "Why here?"

"I'm not sure I understand."

"Why was the Tortuga drilling here?"

"It was an exploratory mission," she said.

"Meaning?"

Alvita appeared flustered for a moment, no more, but then finally she answered, "I trust that whatever is said here will remain in confidence."

"You have my word," Norah replied, throwing Llanzo a look that almost dared him to say otherwise. Fortunately, the young scientist seemed in no mood to risk her ire.

"Very well." Alvita stood up, smoothing her dress. "The Tortuga was sent to investigate a questionable find on one of our old seismic surveys."

"Define questionable."

"As proof of our intention to properly develop our drilling rights, we needed to show due diligence in exploring at least one site with potential impact. This was the site that was chosen."

"Hold on," Derek said. "So why was it questionable?"

Alvita let out a sigh. "The original surveys of this area were somewhat less than pristine. They show a pocket beneath the surface, gas likely, but give little insight into its composition." She shrugged. "Blame it on an extra dense sediment deposit atop it, or perhaps outdated technology. Either way, the site was considered low priority ... until recent needs dictated otherwise."

"So you sent them on a fishing expedition to a spot you thought was a dud," Julie surmised.

"In not so many words," Alvita said, sitting down again. "I'm sorry if that doesn't add any insight into what's going on, but it's the truth."

Silence descended on the briefing room for several moments as her words sunk in.

"So where does that leave us?" Norah asked.

Nobody answered until Mitchell chimed in with, "There is one ... *theory* nobody here seems to want to acknowledge."

Oh no.

Danni met Derek's gaze and it was all he could do to not roll his eyes. Still, he should have known this was coming.

"And that would be, Agent Harkness?"

"The Bermuda Triangle of course."

Muttering erupted around the table, most of it of the scoffing variety, which Derek really couldn't blame.

Mitch, however, waited for it to subside.

"This oughta be good," Jacob remarked, just as the room quieted down.

Mitchell stood up. "While I appreciate a good laugh as much as the next person, I'm being serious here. And before anyone starts spinning their finger against their forehead, I'll point out that most of us here have seen our share of weird-ass things. So if anyone should have an open mind it's the people in this room."

"Sorry," Jacob said. "Please continue."

"I doubt you are, but that's okay. It sounds crazy to me, too. But look at where we are and what's been happening. Unexplained instrument malfunctions, forces beyond our ken being manipulated in ways we can't begin to understand. And now we have this new development."

"What development?" Derek asked.

"What she said." He hooked a thumb toward Alvita. "A friggy seismic survey that shows something *questionable* at the bottom. And now we have sonar scans that, go figure, show the same thing. I mean, seriously, am I the only one putting two and two together here?" He held up a hand. "And yes, I'm well aware that ships, planes, and boats traverse this area all the time without a single hiccup. But what if that's a clue? All the strange sightings over the years, time vortexes, lights in the sky, et cetera, none of that stuff happens on cue. It's scattered at best, seeming to happen only once in a blue moon to the occasional unlucky sap."

"Which is pretty much the opposite of what's going on right now," Llanzo replied.

"Exactly! What if all those reports were actually sporadic events, discharges if you will, caused by ... I dunno ... something?"

"Something?"

"Best I've got for now."

"Assuming for a moment that's the case," Norah replied, sounding unconvinced, "what's changed?"

"I don't know. But maybe that something, whatever it is, is finally waking up."

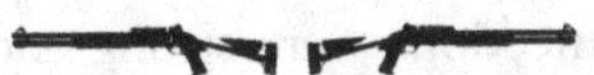

Kerry stood by the railing looking down at the water below. True to what he'd been told, he was now free to go wherever he pleased. Well, almost everywhere. Whatever hoity toity meeting was going on right now was off limits. He'd wanted to eavesdrop, make sure they weren't convening to talk about him, but the armed guard outside the door had quickly dissuaded that course of action.

He still wasn't sure what to think. After signing their forms, everyone seemed to lose interest in him, chattering on about ZarroGreen something or other.

Aren't they that oil company? Maybe they're planning on selling me to some horny Saudi prince.

Despite the drizzle raining down on him – chilly in spite of the warm temperature – he wasn't worried about getting wet. If anything, he'd get a whole lot wetter if he simply wised up and jumped overboard.

But then what?

Kerry could swim, but he was more of a pool kinda guy. And even if he had the endurance, he had no idea which way to go or how far. All he knew for certain was that the only objects in sight were the two other boats, including the one he'd chartered ... something that seemed so distant now as to be almost laughable.

As if to add insult to injury, his equipment was still aboard the yacht, assuming these gestapo assholes hadn't simply chucked it overboard. He wouldn't have put it past them. Despite their words, he didn't trust any of them as far as he could throw them.

At the very least, he made a vow to never turn his back on any so-called reality stars ever again. And it's not like he could even expose these people for what they were. Kerry was good at his job, but he didn't fool himself into thinking his connections were strong enough to fight the U.S. government, assuming that's who they actually worked for – something he still wasn't remotely convinced of.

So where does that leave me?

Kerry had seen the *Jason Bourne* films, but he didn't fool himself into thinking he could simply disappear, keeping his foes always a step or two behind him. How would he even survive? He had savings, but not enough to go on the run indefinitely. And what would that leave him as? Some dirty drifter, working at a greasy spoon just to afford a cockroach infested bed to sleep on?

Not happening.

He was a creature of comfort but at least he was self-aware about it.

All of that added up to him feeling scared and useless, able to run but with nowhere to go. All while the cast of that stupid show practically gloated over his...

Wait! The cast! Kerry couldn't have cared less about any of them, but he remembered that Wilhelm woman. Yeah, she was easy on the eyes, but there was more to it than that. She was also the show's camera operator.

Though he hadn't seen much in the way of film equipment since coming aboard, that didn't mean there wasn't any. He knew these showbiz types. He wouldn't put it past them to film a scene to mollify their egos while, just off camera, he was held captive at gunpoint.

But, if that was the case and he could find her stuff, then maybe he could do a little filming of his own, something that could give him leverage once they got back to shore.

It was a longshot, quite possibly as suicidal as jumping ship, but this was a danger he at least understood. Before moving on to more glamorous fare, he'd cut his teeth as one of the paparazzi. So, in a sense, he fully knew what it was to swim with the sharks, metaphorically speaking anyway.

He glanced down at his watch, unsure of how long it had been since they'd left him to his own devices. Then he looked back up at the sky, feeling confused. Even with the rain falling it still wasn't dark, yet he was fairly certain it should've been by then.

Oh well, it doesn't matter.

Despite knowing he was up against obstacles far more daunting than being punched out by a spoiled c-list celebrity, he set off below deck with renewed purpose.

Now to hope they all stayed busy in their meeting for a little while longer.

24

"Are you sure we're not going to get into trouble, Rena?"

Carol Sanford's wife, Serena, rolled her eyes before putting a comforting arm around her overly paranoid spouse's shoulders. None of this surprised her. Carol was an A-type personality in the law firm where she worked, but outside of office hours she tended to rely on the rules a bit too much. Serena thought it a side-effect of too many years spent prosecuting medical malpractice cases and seeing the penalties for those who messed up.

However, this was neither work nor a courtroom. They were on their honeymoon, at least technically. The reality was this trip was two years overdue thanks to the demands of both their careers, her a sculptress in the cut-throat New York art scene.

But finally here they were – three weeks of nothing but sand, surf, and each other, in a luxury resort complete with in-room hot tub.

Too bad they'd somehow managed to coincide their getaway with a plane crash and a dead whale, not to mention other weird shit going on.

Horrifying as it was to think what could have happened had they booked their flight a few days later, Serena refused to let it ruin their trip – dragging Carol out of their room and forcing her to focus on having fun.

Now, here they were on a glass bottomed boat, enjoying the incredible view beneath them. A mild storm front seemed to be heading in, casting a bit of a pall over the end of the day, but at least the sea was relatively calm.

Still, that they were even out there was reason to celebrate. Having caught wind that there was some kind of craft advisory in effect, she was certain they'd arrive at the dock only to find their scheduled sojourn cancelled.

Fortunately, their guide had happily laughed it off, telling them those were mostly for larger vessels heading out to open sea, nothing they needed to worry about as they were going no further than the reefs.

Carol hadn't been convinced, though, descending into her normal worrywart routine. She was certain they were out there illegally, as if at any second a police boat might pull up alongside them and arrest them like a bunch of drug runners.

"We're fine, Car. Nobody's going to care if we're looking at some fish. Ooh. Check that one out. It's like *Finding Nemo!*"

The fish swimming beneath them didn't actually look much like the titular Disney character, but Serena knew which of Carol's buttons to push. Since at least half their apartment was a virtual shrine to Disney classics, there was little doubt that wouldn't catch her wife's attention.

"Oh my god, look at all the colors," Carol finally replied, joining the voices of the other tourists gathered around the boat's glass bottom.

Serena was far more interested in getting back to a beach chair and a tropical drink, but even she was impressed.

It truly was better than any aquarium she'd ever visited. She was almost tempted to listen to their guide, who was busy talking over a staticky speaker, telling them what species they were currently looking at.

Carol, on the other hand, finally seemed to be getting into it, thumbing through the pamphlet they'd been handed upon boarding and checking off various species as they were pointed out.

"See? Isn't this fun?" Serena asked.

Carol looked up, a sheepish grin on her face, and nodded. "Yeah, it is pretty great."

"Exactly. So relax. Let's take in the sights, enjoy the fresh air, and then maybe we can catch dinner at Diego's later ... unless you're afraid that's off limits, too."

"After the amount you drank Tuesday night, it might be."

Serena playfully elbowed her in the side, glad they'd turned a corner and could get back to enjoying themselves.

With all the chatter on the island about the crash, the mood had been threatening to turn heavier than it should've been.

Though her heart went out to all those poor people who'd gone down on that doomed Pan-Caribbean flight, accidents happened from time to time, whether through bad luck or poor maintenance.

It was probably selfish of her to think that, but she didn't want it to ruin the rest of their vacation, not after everything they'd been through.

"Ooh, what's that one?" Carol asked, pointing toward the bottom.

"There are plenty of eel species in these waters," the guide droned. "From Conger to..."

"That's not an eel," another passenger said.

Serena pulled herself from her reverie to take a look,

seeing nothing but a long slimy object snaking along at the very edge of their field of vision below. It could have been an eel, a snake, or a discarded plastic bag for all she could tell.

Just as she was about to dismiss it, it began to rise, giving them a clearer view. Definitely not an eel. She could plainly see it was covered in...

"I see suckers," Carol said. "I think it's an octopus, or maybe a squid."

"It can't be," another passenger, a middle-aged man, replied. "Where's the rest of it?"

"Maybe it's a giant squid!" a woman with him, probably his wife, exclaimed.

"That's quite impossible," their guide replied, raising his voice to compensate for the lousy speaker system. "Giant squid are deep sea animals. However, there are plenty of indigenous species of... Oh my god!"

The tentacle, not that it could be anything else as far as Serena could tell, lashed forward past the range of their small viewing window, and then kept going – growing larger and wider as it snaked past them and continued to rise.

The boat shuddered as it came into contact with the hull, the massive appendage taking up nearly the entire width of the glass bottom.

With it came pandemonium.

"What the hell?"

"I told you it was a giant squid!"

"Someone do something!"

"Rena?" Carol asked uncertainly.

Serena had nothing to offer, though. Of all the things she could've imagined – engine failure, bad weather, even pirates – this hadn't been among them. Nor was there time to reconsider.

The boat slanted forward, the propeller coming out of

the water as the end of the massive tentacle rose up and wrapped itself around their bow.

Despite this, rational thought still held sway somewhere in the back of Serena's rapidly panicking mind. *That's one. How many arms do squids have again?*

A partial answer came in the form of the canopy above them being torn off and dragged beneath the surface by yet another impossibly long arm.

Half the passengers began to scream wildly, Carol among them, while the rest clambered and clawed at the crew, demanding they do something – as if they looked even remotely prepared.

It was her wife's hysterics which forced Serena back to her senses. It was almost a conditioned response by now. Carol would become upset at something and Serena would need to be the one with the cool head. Now was seemingly no different.

The boat lurched again, this time to the side, cold seawater spilling over the railing and drenching her legs.

Screw that. This is a lot different!

One thing wasn't, however – Carol.

Despite wanting to do nothing more than scream her throat hoarse as an enormous mound of reddish flesh began to rise from the sea just yards away, she grabbed Carol by the arm and yanked her back from the panicked masses.

As she tried to get her spouse's attention, the fleshy mass rolled and she caught sight of a massive malevolent eye which turned their way.

Serena had been a big reader in her youth, something which had gotten her endlessly mocked by the cool kids. All at once, her mind raced back to a collection of H.P. Lovecraft stories in which an ancient octopoid-like beast rose from the sea, driving men insane at the mere sight of it.

Feeling her own sanity start to fray, and fearing Carol's might have already been pushed beyond the tipping point, she stepped to the opposite side of the boat, dragging her wife with her.

Carol opened her mouth, probably to question her or cry out again, but Serena didn't wait for an answer. She silenced the unspoken words by shoving Carol overboard.

She glanced back once, only for a moment, then dove in herself.

Not today, Cthulhu!

It was madness itself, diving into the same water as that unthinkable leviathan. But it was the space of an instant for her to realize that their chances were no worse than those who remained aboard, still screaming in panic.

She surfaced next to Carol and forced her to look away, back toward the seemingly distant shore.

"Swim!" she ordered. "Don't look back. Just swim for your life."

As they both began to frantically paddle away, there came the sound of metal sheering and fiberglass shattering from behind them. It was followed by a heavy splash and then a pressure wave which helped propel them both a bit faster.

The screams behind them continued, fewer than before, but the ones that were left were more than making up for those who had fallen silent.

Serena paid them no heed, though, her entire being focused on the woman swimming beside her and the distant beach.

She had no idea whether they'd make it, dared not to think of what might even now be swimming up behind them.

But at least she was certain of one thing beyond a shadow of a doubt: next time there was a boating advisory, she was going to follow it.

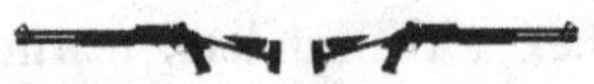

Though it instinctively knew the shallows left it vulnerable, the leviathan didn't care as it tore apart the fragile surface thing. It rent it into pieces, leaving almost nothing of it intact. Then it turned its attention to the screaming things that had been aboard.

Though some had already ceased their struggles, floating lifelessly in the water, it didn't matter to the great beast. It rained its anger and pain down upon all in its vicinity. Some it squeezed, using far more of its strength than necessary to break their fragile bodies. Others it tore to pieces. And a few it devoured, despite finding their taste repugnant.

The rage served to dull the pain that still tortured its mind even this far away from the source of the thrumming.

Some part of it screamed that it needed to keep running, that the pulses were weaker here and would continue to grow weaker the further it fled, even if it meant staking claim to new hunting grounds far from its home. It was an intelligent, adaptable creature. Such a thing was well within its abilities.

Yet another option was to retreat to its ancestral breeding grounds which lay inland – in deep holes filled with sea water, surrounded by rock and accessible only by underwater caves. Though its size suggested such a thing unlikely, it was capable of squeezing through openings far smaller than its bulk – much like its tiny cousins.

It contemplated these choices as the bloodlust settled down and once more it became a creature of thought and curiosity.

Sadly, that momentary peace was almost instantly shattered as another pulse wracked its body – dulled by distance, but still potent.

It began to flex and undulate, tearing up the seabed beneath it ... until it sensed it hadn't gotten all of the screaming things after all. Vibrations in the water alerted it that two were still alive.

It realized they were not only small and weak, but foolish, too. Did they actually hope to escape? With its size and speed it could be upon them in seconds.

It felt no hurry, though. Let them believe themselves safe for a few moments longer as it submerged and began to creep forward.

Soon the tips of its arms were beneath them, ready to grasp hold and drag them down where their screams would be silenced forever.

It prepared to take them both. After that, it would find others to sate its misery upon. It knew the shallows were full of the screaming things. They gathered, both in the water and up upon the sand where it couldn't survive for long. But its reach was long. It could remain safely in the water while its arms tore them apart by the multitude, painting the hot sand with their fluids.

The leviathan was within feet of snatching the two survivors when it paused.

Its senses were keen, able to detect prey, predators, and even rivals from long distances. The tide had brought with it something that caught its attention – blood. It was faint, only the barest trace of it detectable amidst the carnage it had wrought here. What caught the leviathan's attention, though, more than anything else, was that it recognized the scent – a rival, another of its species.

Almost immediately its instincts twisted around the rage already warping its mind.

Another of its kind was out there somewhere, most likely wounded, although that mattered little. It looked around, as if suddenly noticing just how far from its territory it had wandered, realizing it had left its personal hunting ground ripe for a rival to claim.

Though just minutes earlier it had been dead set on seeking out new territory to call its own, its instincts to protect what had already been claimed began to dictate a new course of action.

A part of it knew it was foolish to go back, that the thrumming was strongest there, but its abilities for higher reasoning – already under assault – gave way to rage.

It turned away, having already forgotten the two screaming things that continued feebly paddling toward the safety of the shore.

The leviathan had more significant prey to seek out this day.

25

Derek raised an amused eyebrow, noting this was the third time Mitchell had circled the submersible currently being prepped on deck.

The look on the medic's face was one of disbelief. "I can't believe you guys have this thing. I've been trying to get a replacement for our mobile lab for almost two years now and they keep giving me the freaking runaround. What else have you got down in the hold, a unicorn?"

"I think the Corps keeps those to themselves," Jacob replied with a grin. "And what can I say? The government apparently favors its war on drugs a bit more than its war on Bigfoot."

Mitchell turned to Derek. "That's it. Next squatch hunt we're bringing a kilo of coke with us."

"I'll be sure to note that in the logbook," Derek said as he stood alongside Norah, both of them watching as the ship's engineer worked to *downgrade* the minisub.

Norah glanced down at the clipboard in her hands, keeping tabs of what had been completed so far. "All right. That leaves us with propulsion, navigation, lights, and ballast. Hopefully that's all we need."

"We should probably remove the robot arm, too," Derek said. "We don't want that going haywire down below."

"The pneumatics have already been disabled," Jacob replied. "As has just about everything else that might be vulnerable … or useful."

Mitchell stopped pacing and turned toward them. "Yeah, much more and we might as well just grab a few upturned buckets and use them as diving bells."

"Think I'll pass on that," Derek said. "I guess the more important question is will it work?"

Jacob shrugged. "As far as we can tell from dealing with something that none of us even remotely understand, yes. Vakovsky's been running tests and so far so good. Everything is working within tolerance."

"And once we get down there?"

"Maybe take a really deep breath before you leave," Mitchell offered.

"Thanks. Not helping."

Jacob stepped in and clapped him on the shoulder. "Relax. Crazy as it sounds, we actually got lucky with this one. Whatever the hell's below us, it's sitting on a natural shelf right before the continental drop off. Just a bit further east and *boom*, the bottom drops to about four thousand feet. Believe me when I say we could be a lot more fucked than we are."

"I guess we should take what we can get." Derek glanced over to where Llanzo was looking over the side at the ocean. "Are you sure you're up for this, Doctor?"

Llanzo turned around, a look of uncertainty on his face. "No. Not really. But I believe it's my duty to go."

"Mitch can…"

"I think Mr. Harkness would be best served monitoring the distortions. He seems to have a much better handle on that than I do. Besides, I'm no stranger to dives.

The institute has two research submersibles at their disposal."

"Yeah, but we're not here to study the sea life."

"Aren't we? We don't know what's down there. Besides, I'm familiar with these waters, the composition of the bottom, and the local fauna." He paused for a moment. "At least *most* of the fauna." He paused to wipe his brow. "Believe me ... as much as I would prefer to remain here, I am forced to admit I'll serve us best by going."

"I won't argue, Doctor, and I'll be there right alongside you every step of the way."

"As will I," Norah said. Derek raised an eyebrow at her. "Call it senior agent prerogative. If there's something down there that's a threat to national security, I need to assess it."

"You mean *we* need to assess it," Jacob added. "You need a pilot and I've logged a lot of hours in this baby."

"But Agent McAvee..."

"Is an excellent field commander. She'll be taking charge in my absence."

"But..."

"As you said. Senior agent prerogative. Feel free to take it up with my superiors whenever the radios decide to clear."

Norah turned to Derek, no doubt seeking his support, but he held up his hands and backed away.

Truth be told, he was happy to have Jacob at the helm. The man was ex-Navy, a top notch operative, and one of the most capable men he'd ever met. The thing was, Norah knew all that, too.

And, though he wasn't about to say it, of the two, Jake was the more qualified for this mission since Norah had stepped away from field work a few years back.

Of course, she was also correct in that it was entirely her prerogative to join them.

"That makes four," Jacob said, no doubt sensing victory. "Room for one more ... maybe two with all the equipment we took out."

Derek looked around, noting Alvita's presence. She took a step forward, making him wonder if she was going to present a case for joining them, especially since they would be passing close to the Tortuga's wreckage. However, then her eyes settled onto the sub and her gaze, previously unflappable, became uncertain. A moment later, she turned and walked away.

Guess not. Oh well, probably for the best...

"I'll go."

Derek turned at the sound of Danni's voice, ready to shoot her down for no other reason than not wishing to see her exposed to more danger.

However, Norah beat him to the punch. "Looking to get your feet wet, Danni? Metaphorically speaking anyway,"

"No," she replied, heading toward them. "I mean, I think I can actually be of help down there."

"Oh?"

"Yeah, let's not forget I'm the team's tracker."

Derek shook his head. "This is a bit different."

"Is it?" she replied. "I'm trained to look for details others miss. Well, maybe once we get to the bottom that could be useful."

"Yes, but Dr. Reid will be there to..."

"To what?" Llanzo interrupted. "Have no idea what I'm looking for?"

"None of us do," Jacob said with a nod. "An extra set of eyes might be handy, especially trained ones. No objections here."

"Same," Norah said.

Derek narrowed his eyes, trying to think of some reason to object – maybe another crew member who would prove a better fit. But he quickly pushed those thoughts away. If anything, Danni was a better fit than Norah, yet he hadn't said a word against her joining them. No. This was nothing more than him trying to play surrogate father again.

After another moment, he nodded, albeit not without reservation. "All right. Sounds like we have our crew."

Jacob stood in his briefing room looking out the porthole, having just finished giving McAvee her orders.

"The institute won't like that, sir."

"Hang the institute. They can file a complaint with someone who gives a rat's ass. Bottom line is that sailboat is probably your best bet for reaching shore if you need to bug out. The Will-Do is already beaten half to hell. Won't take much to put her on the bottom if shit hits the fan. All I'm saying is don't waste time or personnel on her."

"Do you think Jenner's right, that there's another of those things out there?"

"I don't know about that, but I know the man. If he says to be worried, then we should be worried. Problem is we don't know jack shit about that one we sunk. It could've been an adult, hell, probably was, but..."

"You think it might've been a juvenile?" the other agent asked, disbelief coloring her voice.

"I'm not saying anything of the sort, Mac, but I've seen too much strange shit in my years to assume I know everything that's going on."

"No offense, sir, but I think you're underestimating yourself."

"I appreciate that, but I don't pretend to be a smart man. I just try to be a bit less dumb than whoever I'm up against." He let out a chuckle, but there wasn't much humor to it. "But let's face facts. I'm not really worried about some oversized squid here."

"You mean those phenomena?"

"I do. You've noticed it haven't you?"

"That they're getting stronger?" she replied. "Hard to miss."

"True enough. As soon as one hits, it feels like my pants are two sizes too small. My main worry, though, is wondering what else they're affecting."

"Beyond gravity?"

"Uh huh. Have you noticed the time, Mac?"

"Twenty thirty seven."

"Exactly. Now look at the sky. It's overcast but still light out."

"Not following, sir."

"Sundown was supposed to be at twenty twenty three."

"Are you sure?"

"If I'm lying I'm dying."

She stepped to the window. "How is that even possible?"

"I don't know. But whatever it is, I think we need to figure it out and stop it before it gets worse."

"How do we do that?"

"Not sure yet. I'm working on a few ideas, though." He handed her a slip of paper. "But just to be on the safe side, I need you to pack a few things for me before we leave."

Danni tried calling up Harrison's picture on her cell phone, hoping to take a few minutes to gather her thoughts before she was needed on deck. Sadly, the device, much like almost everything else, was malfunctioning –

the screen distorted, giving her brother an almost ghoulish appearance once she was finally able to open the photo app.

She put it down in frustration then closed her eyes and tried envisioning him instead. It took her several long moments to push the misshapen image from her head, but eventually she was able to *see* him in her mind's eye as he'd once been.

"Hey, Harrison," she said, forcing her voice to remain steady. "How's this for awesome? I'm going on a submarine. I can't help but think of that time we went to Disney with Mom and Dad. Remember *Finding Nemo*? I was terrified, thinking we were all going to drown, but you were there to hold my hand. And then I ended up pestering you to get back in line again. I know you wanted to ride the Matterhorn, but you still went with me. Well, this one might be more *20,000 Leagues Under the Sea*, but I like to think you're still here holding my hand."

She took several deep breaths, willing herself to take strength from his memory, until at last she was able to smile – finding herself more excited than scared.

They were heading into the unknown, true, but that wasn't so much a factor. She'd already survived the worst the unknown could throw at her. She'd survive this, too. Besides, this was a brand new adventure as far as she was concerned, far different than their normal missions spent traipsing through forests ... or muddy swamps full of traps set by...

No! Not now. Focus on what needs to be done. She took another breath, forcing the unpleasant memories back as she once again turned away from the past to what lay ahead of her.

Yes, they were descending seven hundred feet down in a cramped minisub as day gave way to night up above, but it wouldn't be into darkness. The sub was fitted with a powerful LED array that was almost certain to give her a view more spectacular than anything Disneyworld had to offer.

That was the hope she chose to hold onto as she prepared to head out, imagining her brother next to her, eager to join her on this...

So caught up was she in her pleasant reverie, that she almost ran into Julie as she stepped foot into the narrow hallway. "Oh crap! I'm sorry."

"No harm no foul," the other woman said with a grin, quickly sidestepping her. "Heading up?"

"Yeah." She fell into step with her teammate. "Almost time to leave. You coming to see us off?"

"Yep, but after that I need to take one of the launches over to the Rogers Will-Do."

"Oh? What for?"

"Thought I brought the minicam with me when we came on board, but now I can't find it. Figured I might try to get some time lapse footage."

"Cool."

"Not really." Julie shrugged. "It's just something to do while you guys are busy knocking on Davy Jones' locker."

"Don't tell me you're jealous."

Julie shook her head and laughed. "Are you kidding? I've already sworn off calamari for life. Think I'll quit while there's still some seafood left I can eat. Nope. This one's all yours."

"Thanks," Danni replied, although in the back of her mind Julie's words struck a chord, reminding her of Derek's theory.

Hopefully he was wrong, because if not then it was quite possible she hadn't seen the worst the unknown had to offer after all, in which case she'd need her brother's strength more than ever.

"So you're telling me you think this is some sort of pissing match between me and my ex-husband?"

Derek shook his head. He had a feeling this was the way the conversation was going to go. "I'm not saying anything of the sort. All I'm asking is whether you think it's wise to go down there with us?"

"I'm in charge. I need to assess the situation."

"Not arguing that, but let's face facts, Norah. You haven't been in the field since you took over the DoCC."

"So you think I can't handle myself?"

"I think you can handle yourself just fine. I'm simply voicing concern that we might be better served with you calling the shots from up here. If anything goes wrong down below..."

"Then I'll face it same as you."

"I don't doubt that you will, but that doesn't mean you *should*. Jake and I can..."

"Is that it?" she asked. "Is this some excuse so you two can relive your glory days together?"

"What? No!"

"Or are you afraid he and I will..."

"This isn't about Jake."

"You're right, it isn't," Norah replied, sitting down. "It's about you."

"*Me*? I'll admit this isn't exactly my specialty, but Dr. Reid can easily fill in any blanks that I don't..."

"This isn't about your knowledge," she said, lowering her voice. "It's about ... your leadership."

"My leadership? Now you've completely lost me."

"I wasn't going to say anything. Hell, I'm not *supposed* to say anything, but you ruffled a lot of feathers with that mess back in Jersey."

Derek took a seat. This talk seemed to be heading in a

far different direction than he'd envisioned. "Well aware, and I'd happily do it again."

"I know that," Norah said. "But you have to understand, Governor Yarlberg..."

"Ex-governor."

"Don't be pedantic, you know what I mean. The problem isn't his title, it's his friends, friends who were heavily embarrassed by all the muck you dredged up."

"Then they should've picked better friends."

"Which I will gladly tell them should I ever grow tired of being employed. However, it seems sidelining your team wasn't enough to placate them. There have been voices actively speaking out against you in D.C., demanding that someone more ... *compliant* to the chain of command be placed in charge of the team. They've been actively lobbying against you."

"Do you really think this job needs someone who goes by the book?"

"Of course not. That's what I'm here for, to dot the I's and cross the T's. But I'm telling you right now, it hasn't been easy. Hell, I even had a junior congressman threaten to go public with what you do."

Derek could only imagine the scene that would cause. "Can't say I wouldn't be curious to see that happen."

Norah waved him off. "It was obviously an idle threat, but the fact remains that feathers have been ruffled and I've been having a hell of a time unruffling them."

"So what then? You want my resignation?"

Norah shook her head. "No. In fact, that's the real reason I'm down here."

"And here I thought it was the surf-n-turf."

"I'll admit, the weather definitely beats being back home, but no. I'm to observe you in the field and then submit my observations as to your fitness for command."

And suddenly it all made sense. Derek had been

wondering if Norah's presence here was because of Jake's involvement, but now he understood that was merely a coincidence. "You could've just written a report from the hotel, y'know, telling everyone what an awesome job I did."

The look she gave him said it all. Her job was to observe him, but that didn't mean there might not be others observing her.

He shook his head. As always, the worst part of this job wasn't the creatures they hunted, it was the politicians – always on the lookout for ways to grease their own wheels.

There was a reason why D.C. was considered a shark tank.

Tempted as he was to simply tell the suits to stick his badge where the sun didn't shine, he knew he wouldn't. And it wasn't even for the sake of what they did or who they helped. He wouldn't quit because his team was counting on him. They had his back out in the field, so he made it a point to have theirs at all other times.

Sadly, that sometimes meant making compromises.

"Fine. So, how does this work?"

Norah leaned forward. "I go with you as planned. I meant what I said about assessing the situation."

"Fair enough."

"But outside of that, I'll also be there to observe you ... and Danni."

"That's why you let her tag along, isn't it? You can't assess my leadership skills if there's no one there for me to lead."

Norah was silent for a moment. "My advice is simple. Keep it by the book and let's all come back alive. Do that and maybe we'll all walk out of here with our jobs intact."

Derek let out a sigh. Following the book wasn't even a consideration in the vast majority of missions they undertook. Hell, there was no rulebook for being chased by an angry Sasquatch.

And now, out here, miles from shore and with something messing with the fundamental building blocks of nature, he had a feeling they were as far from the proverbial book as they could possibly get.

"My name is Kerry Klipsch. What you are about to see has not been doctored or altered in any way."

Kerry stood on the upper deck, trying to pretend he was doing nothing but casually observing. It wasn't all that difficult. The crew below all seemed preoccupied with the task at hand – whatever that was. It made hiding the minicam he'd swiped from that woman's bunk all the easier.

Bitch should have locked her door.

He'd gotten lucky, in that it was both charged and had a large capacity memory card in it. That last part was key. All he had to do was keep it from being found and he would have all the leverage he needed ... hopefully.

"I'm not sure what they're planning to do with that submersible," he whispered in a tone low enough to not be overheard, but enough for the camera's microphone to capture. "All I know for certain is these are the same people who kidnapped me, claiming to be government agents. And now they're out here preparing to dive. For what? I don't know. Drugs, sunken treasure, maybe a rendezvous with a hostile foreign power. Who can say for certain?"

Goddamn it all! Despite his words, so far he'd captured a whole lot of nothing, his testimony probably doing little more than making him sound like a loon as the crew worked below.

He needed more. He needed to catch them in the act of doing *something*.

About the only thing of note he'd seen so far had been them removing equipment from the sub – suspicious yes, but not exactly damning.

He briefly considered the possibility of trying to stow aboard, but quickly dismissed it. Not only was there zero chance of him remaining undiscovered in the cramped vehicle, but he dreaded what might happen once he was caught.

But that didn't mean he wouldn't keep filming in the hope of...

Hello?

Down below, a small group were heading toward the sub. He recognized Jenner along with that little blonde bitch who'd almost broken his ribs earlier. If the rest of the cast was joining them, though, he didn't see them, although he did recognize two of the other faces – including the mouthy cunt who'd kidnapped him in the first place.

The final member of the crew was someone Kerry didn't recognize, a thin guy with short dreadlocks and glasses. Judging by the look on his face, he didn't seem too enthused with whatever was going on.

All at once Kerry wondered if this man was like him – another victim, kidnapped from shore, lied to, and now being taken god-knows-where.

Was a similar fate in store for him?

Kerry didn't care to speculate on that, but he wasn't about to let this opportunity pass without comment, especially once the man stopped in his tracks and cried out – no doubt pleading for mercy, futile as it was.

Kerry wasn't brave enough to risk trying to help him, but he could at least document his fate for posterity.

"I'm not sure what we're seeing here, but I can only guess it's some form of human trafficking. I don't know the poor man being escorted inside that sub, but I believe him to be an unwilling passenger, about to set sail on a cruise bound for terror..."

"Wait!" Llanzo cried.

"What is it, Doctor?" Derek turned, wondering if the man was having second thoughts. If so, he'd have to recruit Mitch for the journey ... and then hope Norah didn't kill him in the cramped quarters.

Llanzo patted his pockets then let out a sigh of relief. "Never mind. I thought I left my Dramamine behind, but I have it." He smiled sheepishly. "Being on the water doesn't bother me, but diving tends to upset my equilibrium."

"If he pukes, I'm not cleaning it," Jacob said.

Derek was about to echo the sentiment, but then he saw Danni climbing up toward the hatch and remembered the conversation he'd had with Norah.

In some ways, he wished she'd kept her silence, because now he found himself second guessing everything about this mission. And that was even assuming anything he did made a difference. He wasn't worried about Norah. He trusted her to be fair. But it was more than possible this was all smoke and mirrors, his fate having already been sealed behind closed doors.

Derek wasn't afraid of being fired for his sake. However, he was deeply worried about what might happen to his team if they were left in the hands of a pencil pusher more concerned with political brownie points than safety.

If so, then...

He shook his head to clear it. None of that mattered right then. For the time being, he was still in charge of his team. Worrying about being handed his walking papers could wait until they were all back on dry land.

For now, the mission was the important part – keeping his people safe and figuring out the mystery of what was causing everything to go haywire.

At the same time, he couldn't help but feel they were about to step into something far bigger than any of them – something they weren't even remotely qualified to deal with.

Derek didn't know what was waiting for them below, but he had a bad feeling it went far beyond an oversized octopus with an attitude problem.

The leviathan was exhausted, confused, and in pain. But, above all else, it was angry as it once more approached the territory it had claimed as its own.

To swim so fast for so long was a dangerous thing, expending precious energy that a creature of its size needed. Normally it would've known better, but such logic was beyond it now – and growing further away with every mile of ocean it crossed.

The only reason it stopped was because it sensed its adversary was near, the water here thick with the scent of blood. There was little doubt its rival had already been vanquished, but it needed to be sure. So it dove deep in search of its remains, following the trail of blood and scattered flesh.

It encountered none of the expected scavengers as it swam – all of them having either been driven off or killed by the thrumming. Only the tiniest of creatures remained, their nervous systems too primitive for the pulses to affect ... not that the leviathan understood or cared about such things.

Down it went into the darkness, the stink of viscera thick enough to replace the rage inside it with growing hunger. Finally, it found the body. It had been torn apart, a strange smell coming from its many wounds, something alien, not of its world ... something from the surface.

The other leviathan was a juvenile, perhaps a third its length and not even close in mass – large compared to most who called the sea home, but little more than a joke to its larger brethren. Had it still been alive, it would have been easily driven off.

In the short spans between the thrumming, during those fleeting moments when it was able to think again, it realized that whatever had killed its would-be foe was the true rival to be dealt with.

Up above, it had been too consumed by rage to notice much more than the blood, but now it began to realize there were other scents in the water.

A surface thing, perhaps more than one. It recognized the faint but acrid scent as belonging to them, a dirty unappealing smell that could belong to nothing else.

The trail led off into the distance, in the direction of its hunting grounds, back to where the massive thing – the source of its misery – lay upon the ocean floor.

Caution and pain began to once more give way to blinding rage. They all needed to die – the massive thing and any surface things foolish enough to enter its territory.

However, one imperative was still stronger than the need to kill. It needed to feed, to refuel its massive body.

It began to tear apart the smaller leviathan, shoving the pieces into its beak and gorging itself upon them.

Once that was finished, then it would be time to finally unleash its wrath upon whatever dared claim what was rightfully its.

27

Jacob tapped the minisub's transponder twice, to try and signal to the cutter that all was well.

Nobody had been surprised when communications back to the Nest became garbled the second they were lowered into the water.

However, Danni would have been lying if she'd said it hadn't made her slightly nervous as the sub slipped beneath the ocean waves and began to descend.

They'd done all they could to downgrade the submersible's systems to a point where they would hopefully remain unaffected by the disturbances. None of that changed the fact that they were on their own for this mission.

If something went wrong, their only hope would be to drop their ballast and shoot back up to the surface. Fortunately, though much deeper than a person could safely dive, it wasn't like they were descending into the Marianas Trench.

There wasn't much to see at first, as day had finally given way to night up above. With the darkness had come a slight increase in the rain but it was still fairly mild, nothing the crew couldn't handle.

Jacob flipped a couple of switches, turning on the powerful outside lights and illuminating the waters around them.

"Passing twenty meters and seeing a whole lot of nothing," he remarked.

"Something is very wrong here," Llanzo said.

"You're just figuring that out now, Doc?"

"No. What I mean is there should be plenty of ocean life around us, but it's like we're submerging in the Dead Sea."

Danni shook her head. "Probably not the words I would have used."

"Sorry. First analogy that came to mind."

A moment later, the EMF detector Derek had brought at Mitch's insistence beeped to life. Danni felt a weight hit her stomach – as if she'd instantly put on ten pounds.

"Try to hold onto your cookies, folks," Jacob said in response. "It should hopefully pass quickly. All systems, those remaining anyway, appear nominal."

That was good for now, but Danni could feel the tension in the cramped chamber rising. The harsh reality was they had no way of predicting whether those distortions would grow stronger the deeper they got, or by how much.

Though she'd initially been excited for this trip, now she found herself worrying that they might suddenly all find themselves weighing a thousand pounds.

A few seconds later, though, the weight disappeared.

"I think that one's over and done with." Derek glanced down at the meter before turning Danni's way. "I just want to be clear on one thing before we go any further. No way are our producers allowed to learn that we're using this thing."

"Aw, no Crypto-Hunter Halloween special from the Stanley Hotel?" she replied.

"Only if someone spots a Sasquatch on the fourth floor."

"Can we please focus here?" Norah snapped.

However, her ex was quick to reply, "Oh, relax. They're just letting off some steam."

She turned his way, her eyes narrowed. "Did you just tell me to relax?"

All at once, Danni found herself wishing she'd stayed topside, and it had nothing to do with the danger they were facing.

"Yep," Jacob replied without missing a beat. "Far as I can tell, that's pretty much all we can do for now. That shelf's not too deep, but I'm taking it extra slow. Don't want to accidentally fall into a black hole or something."

"I see you've been talking to Mitch again," Derek remarked before Norah could speak up, probably hoping to head an argument off at the pass.

"Hell, no. You think I'd talk to that crazy bastard before coming on a mission like this?"

Norah turned her head to look out the side of the glass dome that made up the front of the sub, letting out an annoyed sigh as if accepting defeat.

"I wonder if this is what it's like to be in space," Llanzo said, likewise taking in the nothingness around them.

"I wouldn't doubt it," Jacob replied, keeping his attention on the controls. "Only one difference as far as I can tell."

Danni raised an eyebrow. "What's that?"

"In space, we'd weigh a lot less, not more."

Almost as if on cue, Derek's EMF meter lit up again and she once more felt the strange shift in her body weight, which – in the close confines of the sub – somehow made it that much worse.

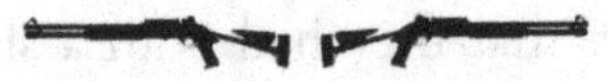

"Anything I can do to help?" Julie asked.

The agent at the helm of the research vessel, a rather short fellow with a solid build, shook his head. "I'm not even sure I'd know what to ask for, ma'am. I mean, heck, we're pretty much jerry-rigged with spit and bail wire here right now."

"Save the ma'am for my mother. I'm Julie."

"It's a pleasure," he replied, looking away from the equipment array, most of which seemed to be full of static and interference. "Name's Kyle."

"Nice to meet you, Kyle."

She'd finished going through the interior, looking for the missing camera and coming up empty. It was annoying but not that big of a deal, more something to do as she'd felt a bit superfluous ever since they'd managed to stop that sea monster. She'd been aboard a few boats in her life, but not enough to be of much use to the other team.

Though she wasn't particularly comfortable being on the smaller vessel, especially banged up as it was, the look on Kyle's face was more one of boredom than apprehension, making her feel a bit better as they waited for the sub crew to return.

"Mind if I ask you a question, ma' ... I mean Julie?"

"Sure. Go right ahead."

"What's it like?"

"What?"

"What you do. I mean, we were briefed, partially anyway. So I have some idea. Just not a lot."

Julie considered her answer. Technically they weren't supposed to talk freely with people about it, but this was a fellow government agent – almost certainly a senior one, unless he, too, had been recently recruited. Julie didn't have much insight into what Jacob's team did, but she supposed the fact that they had both a ship and a sub at their disposal meant it was pretty important.

What the hell? "I guess you could say it involves a lot of looking, then waiting, and then shooting depending on what happens next. Oh, and occasionally screaming, because as big as that fish was, don't think for a second an angry Bigfoot is any less terrifying."

"I meant the TV show," he replied. "What's it like being a celebrity?"

"Oh. Well, for starters I'm not sure I'd call us celebrities."

"Try telling that to my kid brother. He pretty much worships you guys. Speaking of which..."

"I'd be happy to give you an autograph for him."

"Aces! He'll go absolutely nuts. Thank you."

"No problem. Always happy to help out a fan."

"So tell me what it's like shooting an episode. Is it really by the seat of your pants?"

Julie shook her head. "Most of what makes it onto the TV is either filmed before or after the real stuff happens. And a good chunk of it is scripted. It's actually more about..." She trailed off as one of the screens he'd been monitoring caught her attention. It had been clear a moment earlier, but now there was a large reading clearly visible in one corner.

Kyle, no doubt noticing her gaze, glanced at it for no more than a moment before turning back toward her. "Just another ghost. They appear every time one of those damned ... whatever the hell they are hits." He let out a chuckle.

"Why's that funny?"

"I'm just thinking how lucky we are."

Julie raised an eyebrow. "Lucky?"

"In a sense. My father was in the navy during the Cuban missile crisis. If all of this had been happening then

... well, let's just say they'd have thought they were surrounded by Soviet subs and..."

"Boom?"

"Pretty much." Kyle shrugged. "Weird thing to laugh about, I know. But as strange as things are right now, we at least have the advantage of knowing the equipment's messed up. It could be a lot worse..."

There came the faint sound of roiling water, drawing their attention, then a light spray washed over them. But it wasn't from the sky, Julie noted. It had been seawater.

"What was that?"

"No idea," the agent replied, turning back toward the equipment. "Maybe the storm's finally getting worse."

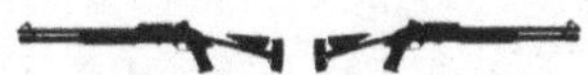

Andrea McAvee was not happy. She prided herself on being analytical, on making decisions based on good data. However, reliable intelligence was the last thing they had going for them right at that moment.

Sure, the cutter was old on the outside. But a good deal of the instrumentation had been upgraded to state of the art. Or at least it had before this assignment. Now, with the exception of the makeshift distortion monitoring station off to the side of the bridge, she might as well have been captaining a steam-powered barge.

She steadied herself as a weight dropped into the pit of her stomach, telling her another of those damned disruptions was hitting them.

Fucking things will probably give us brain cancer. The thought brought a grim smile to her face, as she'd heard it in her father's voice – one of his favorite excuses whenever he'd eschewed the idea of owning a cell phone.

Maybe you had a point after all, Dad. "Report."

"More of the same," Cortez replied from the sonar array. "Lots of contacts, all from out of nowhere."

She glanced over toward where that scientist from the USDA fiddled with his hodgepodge of equipment, looking happy as a clam despite everything. *Weirdo.* "Status report, Dr. Harkness."

"Mister," he replied.

"Excuse me?"

"It's Mister Harkness," he said, not bothering to look up, his tone a bit too casual for her liking. "Never had much interest in grad school. I swear, I'd have sooner swallowed paint chips than write a dissertation. But anyway, you can call me Mitch."

"If it's all the same, *Mr.* Harkness, I'd prefer to keep things professional."

"Whatever you say, Agent. Personally, though, protocol's not my thing either, especially with the weird shit my team is usually up to ... present times included, and I do mean time."

She was about to scold him for his language. Running a tight ship, so to speak, kept people from being sloppy in other aspects of their duties. However, then she registered the odd thing he'd just said. "What do you mean by that."

"Wish I knew for certain but, much as I hate to say it, we are definitely dealing with some Bermuda Triangle level weirdness here. Check it out." He held up two devices for her to see.

"It's a ... stopwatch?"

"Both of them technically are. The difference is one is digital and the other is my old analog wristwatch. Gift from an old friend. You know the drill. One of those takes a licking but keeps on ticking deals."

"And your point?"

"I've been noticing that things have been getting screwier. There was that weird-ass mirage earlier ... and then sunset came later than it should have, which by all accounts is impossible outside of Star Trek reruns."

Andrea nodded. "Agent Caseman and I were discussing that earlier."

"As crazy as this sounds, whatever is messing up our electronics and gravity seems to be having an effect on time as well, which is pretty insane if you ask me. That said, I wanted to see if it was measurable, mostly to make sure it wasn't just my imagination playing tricks on me or some sort of mega mirage. Any change in our perception of reality wouldn't exactly be good, don't get me wrong, but it's gotta be better than the alternative."

"And what did you find out?"

"Nothing promising, I'm afraid. Both of these devices, they're working exactly the same."

"And that's bad, why?"

"Because like I said, one is digital. So if something is going to go screwy, it'll be this one. Problem is, they both kept the exact same time when that last distortion hit. The screen went a bit wacky on the newer one, but at the end they both showed the same time had elapsed."

Andrea made a hurry up motion, still unsure where this was going.

"In addition to the watches I've been keeping count in my head. You know, one Mississippi, two Mississippi, that sort of thing."

"Not exactly scientific."

"Agreed, that's why I've done it several times over the last hour, as well as timed myself between distortions so as to get at least a reasonably accurate measure of things."

"Okay and...?"

"Since I started measuring this, each time a distortion hits my count ends up at least two seconds off from what these are both showing. And sometimes more."

She shook her head. "That doesn't prove anything."

"That's what I keep trying to tell myself. And why I'm going to ask you to take these and kindly do the same thing, so as to either prove my point or determine that I'm completely off my rocker."

"And that point is?"

"That things might be even more wrong than we originally thought. I think time itself is somehow being bent in this spot. That we're perceiving things the way we normally do, but that reality is slightly ... different." He stopped and held up a hand. "Now, I don't want to cause a panic or anything, as we're only talking a few seconds here and there right now ... but I also think it would be wise to remain vigilant."

"Vigilant for what?"

"That's the problem. I don't know. When this is all done, we might end up returning to shore an hour earlier than expected, or we might put in to port and discover we're about to reenact the plot from *The Final Countdown*, and I don't mean the song."

28

"**N**earing the shelf," Jacob announced after a slow careful descent that felt much longer than it was.

It had been dead silent aboard the tiny sub for the last several minutes, the banter from earlier having given way to a more somber note, and it had nothing to do with Norah's chastising.

Little by little the eerily empty sea had given way to something far worse. At first it had just been the occasional fish – hanging motionless in the water, almost as if stunned.

That itself had been strange.

But then they began to see more. Some were partially eaten, bites clearly taken out of them, but most were whole, as if a free meal simply wasn't enough to entice the predators that called this place home.

Used to call it home, Jacob noted, spying a barracuda floating upside down among a group of other fish.

Shortly afterward, the sub had encountered what could best be called resistance, the controls becoming – not unresponsive, but *less* responsive. All the readings, the ones that could be reliably taken anyway, appeared normal, but it was as if the thrusters were being forced to work harder than they should have.

"This shouldn't be possible," Llanzo had said. "Those fish are dead, but they shouldn't be hanging there like that."

"Don't goldfish usually float?" Danni had asked.

"Yes, but not all fish do. Those that don't, sink. They don't just hang there like..."

"Christmas ornaments?" Jacob offered.

That had caused Derek to chuckle from behind him. "You have some interesting ideas about the holidays."

That bit of forced levity had been the end of the discussion as they continued to descend. It gave Jacob a chance to try and figure out what was causing them to slow down. At first, he thought they might be fighting against some kind of undersea updraft or perhaps a thermal vent, but that didn't explain the fish just hanging there.

With no further input from either Derek or Reid, he'd been forced to conclude they were just as stymied as him. The only other theory he could come up with was that something was affecting the viscosity of the ocean water itself. Salt water was more viscous than fresh, and extreme examples, like the Dead Sea, were even more dense, but nothing like this.

It was almost like piloting the sub through pancake syrup, insane as it sounded. However, crazy or not, at least that kind of explained the macabre aquarium around them.

Jacob wasn't easily spooked. He'd stared down men who would have slit their own grandmothers' throats for shits and giggles. And, though it had been a while, he'd also faced creatures that time itself had forgotten.

Yet, at the same time, he was looking forward to this

mission being over. Drug runners, Sasquatches, even sea monsters – those were tangible threats. As the saying went, if it bled they could kill it. But this was freaky deaky voodoo shit as far as he was concerned. DARPA or maybe NASA should be the ones handling this crap, not him. But getting them out here required him figuring out how to get their equipment working correctly again – a bit of a catch 22 for the time being.

Thankfully, despite the increased drag, the batteries were holding up. He checked the rest of the equipment, all green. So long as the syrup didn't turn to concrete, they'd be fine. This was only a reconnaissance mission after all, unless they ran into something which...

"Watch out!"

Jacob's thoughts scattered to the wind as something massive rose up directly in front of them, like the skeletal fingers of an ancient sea god reaching up to punish those who dared disturb its rest.

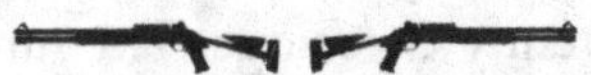

"What exactly do you think you're doing?"

Oh shit! Kerry turned to find a middle aged woman in an almost disturbingly crisp suit staring up at him. He didn't know her name, but her face was familiar. He'd caught a brief glimpse of her back at the dock, just as that other woman's thugs had led him aboard.

"Listen ... um, Agent..."

"It's just miss, thank you very much," she replied with a Hispanic lilt to her voice. "I'm aboard as an unaffiliated observer."

"Unaffiliated..."

"Meaning I'm not with them."

"Oh." Once again, Kerry was forced to consider who he was up against. If she wasn't one of these so-called agents, then who was she? All sorts of unpleasant thoughts ran through his mind in the space of a second – drug cartel, hostile foreign government, buyer for some shadowy human trafficker.

She held out her hand. "Alvita Guerrero. I represent ZarroGreen's interests here."

He glanced down at it as if she were a snake ready to strike. "ZarroGreen? You mean the oil company?"

"Yes, although you'll excuse me if I respectfully decline to say more. You're that photographer aren't you? Mr. ... Klipsch, correct?"

"Y-yeah. Pleased to meet you."

"Likewise. Now, back to the point. You didn't answer my question."

Kerry tried to shuffle the camera behind his back although, judging by the way her eyes shifted to follow, she wasn't fooled for a second. "Pretty sure it's the same answer you just gave me. I respectfully decline to..."

"In that case, perhaps I should alert Agent McAvee. I believe she's currently in charge. I'm sure she'll be interested to know one of her *guests* is sneaking around with ... what is that behind your back?"

Bitch! "It's not like that," Kerry said, debating how he might get out of this one. He quickly glanced around, noting it was dark, drizzling, and there was nobody else in sight.

The sailboat wasn't too far away, but it was barely visible in the spray, meaning it was likely nobody there could see them.

It would be so easy...

Kerry shook his head, trying to push that thought away. A part of him wanted to believe the story he'd been given, that this was all some government operation he'd unwittingly stumbled upon – and that he'd be let go once they reached port.

But the rest of him refused to accept it, insisted that things didn't add up. And now, here was this woman claiming to be, not a government spook, but some secretary or something from a freaking oil company of all things.

Did these people truly think he was that stupid?

"Not like what?" the Guerrero woman asked, if that was even her name. "You're not acting suspicious or no you don't have a camera behind your back? Interesting, since I seem to recall Agent Caseman making mention of having confiscated your gear."

Smug cunt. He felt like a cornered animal – fear coloring his thoughts. A part of him wanted to fight, but what good would that do? This whole ship was one giant steel trap and he was nothing more than a rat. "F-Fine. You got me." He showed her the camera. "What now?"

"Thank you for your honesty." Alvita looked down at the camera as if it were barely worth her notice. "Now ... nothing. What you do with it is your business, Mr. Klipsch."

"What?!"

"But," she continued, her eyes hard as steel, "I must insist on reviewing your footage."

Oh no! "Why?"

"To ensure there is no mention of my employer. That is the price of my ... disinterest, if you will."

"I ... I don't understand."

"It's very simple. Though my employer's involvement here is ... circumstantial at best, there exists the possibility for public embarrassment. Needless to say, that could cost us a great deal of money, something I would care to avoid." She took hold of his hand and closed it over the minicam. "My interests in whatever you choose to do with your little documentary end there. The rest is, as they say, none of my concern."

Kerry was caught off guard, expecting for this woman to scream for help or alert the crew at any moment. But she continued to meet his gaze, her expression giving away nothing he could discern. "Why should I believe you?"

"Because it's the truth. I wish to avoid undue scrutiny for ZarroGreen, nothing more. However, I'm not blind to the state of the world either. Perhaps there's merit in the international community being made aware of what's happening here ... so long as discretion is maintained."

"What's happening here?"

"Yes. I assume you're aware, otherwise why let you roam freely?"

What the fuck is she talking about? "Um, yeah. Of course I am. And ... I one-hundred percent agree. The world needs to know."

"So then, can I assume we have a deal?"

A part of Kerry wanted to relax, but something about this so-called deal niggled at the back of his head. "S-sure. Why not?"

"Excellent." Alvita nodded then turned away. "Shall we?"

"Shall we what?"

"Go back to my cabin of course, so we can review your footage. Unless, that is, you'd care to go..."

She was interrupted by the brief sound of rushing water from over the side. Kerry turned to glance that way, seeing a wake and momentarily spotting what appeared to be movement beneath the surface. He had far more pressing concerns, though. *Probably another stupid whale.*

He turned back toward Alvita, but her attention was firmly focused on the water below them.

"Um, you were saying?" he asked, curious as to what had caught her eye.

"Nothing, Mr. Klipsch." Gone was the faux friendly

attitude, and in its place something more primal. "Come along. We have to go see the captain."

Shit! I knew it! "The captain? Why?"

"Because this is something she needs to know about."

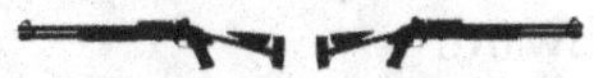

"What a mess."

"What a tragedy," Danni added.

"That, too," Norah replied as they stared out at the twisted remains of the San Cristóbal Tortuga's derrick, the sub's powerful light array illuminating the length of it.

From Danni's perspective, the broken ship looked like it had dropped off a mountain than simply sunk to the bottom of the ocean. Though she didn't know enough to speculate on the last minutes of its doomed voyage, it sure as hell looked like something big had gone to town on it.

Up above it had been easy to hope that Derek's theory about a second creature was wrong. Down here, though, seeing the size of the drillship and the amount of damage done to it, it was a whole different story. It was hard not to imagine the creature from that old painting – the kraken – a beast large enough to drag down even the mightiest of sailing ships.

As they neared the hull of the Tortuga, lying upon its side, Danni could almost visualize what had happened, as if it was...

"What's that?" Norah asked, leaning forward.

"It's ... a body," Derek whispered.

Danni quickly saw he was right, her breath catching at the sight of the lifeless corpse floating just to their port. Whoever this poor soul was, however, they sadly weren't alone. As the sub moved further along, they saw more – people, most appearing to have drowned, but a few much worse off. All of them were like the fish they'd seen above, hanging suspended in the water as if held there by invisible strings.

"Oh my god!" she gasped.

They were navigating through a literal sea of the dead, scores of lifeless eyes staring at them almost accusingly as they continued onward.

"All right, that's enough," Norah finally said. "Bring us up a bit, put some distance between us and these poor bastards."

"But..."

"Now!"

Jacob looked like he wanted to argue with her, but he simply nodded, easing the thrusters back and angling them higher over the wreck and its nightmare audience.

Sadly, that only made the view that much worse as the powerful light array illuminated more of the ship and the unfortunate souls who'd crewed her.

"The hull looks mostly intact below the waterline," Jacob said, his voice hitching for only the barest of seconds before taking on a businesslike tone. "I'd need to see the side she landed on, but from here it looks like she might have simply capsized and gone down. A big enough wave could have done that."

"True," Derek replied, not sounding even remotely convinced.

"There doesn't seem to be much else of note along the..."

Danni's eyes opened wide. "Nothing else of note?"

"I meant the wreckage, not ... the rest," he replied before continuing. "Old ship. Plenty of corrosion along the bottom. Signs of metal fatigue on the... Whoa!"

Danni felt it in her gut in the same instant Derek's EMF reader went haywire. More importantly, they *saw* it, or something anyway, as a pressure wave seemed to undulate the water around them, causing the corpses below to twitch as if some twisted puppeteer were pulling their strings.

"You all saw that, right?" Jacob asked, his neutral tone instantly gone.

"Kind of wishing I hadn't," Norah said.

Derek nodded. "Me, too. Any ideas, Doctor?"

"Other than thinking I should've stayed at the surface, no." He took a moment to seemingly collect his thoughts, then added, "But I don't think that came from the Tortuga. The angle was all wrong. If so, it would have hit us from directly beneath."

"I guess that's one good thing about this," Danni said, causing both Derek and Norah to turn toward her questioningly. "I'm serious. What's worse — something new and undiscovered, or knowing that some oil company is testing out a device that can bend the very forces of nature? I mean, they're not exactly known for their altruism."

"You've got a point there," Derek replied.

"Personally, I'd say a lot depends on what that undiscovered thing turns out to be," Jacob said, angling the thrusters once again. "So why don't we see about discovering it and finding out just how screwed we really are?"

29

They didn't have to go far.

Clearing the wreckage of the Tortuga, the distortions only seemed to grow worse, rattling the frame of the submersible as if they were a physical thing.

"Seems like we're getting closer," Derek remarked.

Jacob glanced back at him. "Ya think, Captain Obvious?"

"Stop promoting my team members," Norah chided. "At best he's Lieutenant Obvious."

Derek chuckled but there was little humor behind it. Typically Norah was all business. If she was cracking jokes, then she must've been seriously nervous.

The thing was, none of them knew what lay in wait for them as Jacob once again angled the sub toward the bottom, but Derek couldn't pretend that seeing his boss lose her cool, even slightly, didn't cause a chain reaction of unease in his own gut.

"That doesn't look right," Danni said, pointing past him. "The bottom I mean. That section right there. It looks all torn up."

"She's right," Llanzo added. "Look at the silt off to either side. That looks normal, but that swatch there, it's all disturbed. You can see the under layer."

"Good eyes, folks." Derek leaned forward, seeing what appeared to be huge mounds of heaped sand at the far edge of their vision. "Maybe bring us up a bit, Jake."

"You want to pilot this tub?"

"You offering? Because I always wanted to..."

"No." He did as suggested, taking them up again as they neared a ridge that, on closer inspection, appeared to be a small mountain comprised of bottom silt.

Llanzo leaned forward as well, crowding the already cramped space. "Whatever happened here, it's had time to settle. Otherwise we'd be sailing through a cloud of mud."

"What could cause this?" Danni asked. "An underwater eruption maybe?"

"If that were the case, we'd already be boiled alive," the scientist said, although he sounded far from certain. "Perhaps a localized undersea current."

"Would have to be a hell of a current."

As the sub rose to clear the sand hill, Derek saw something in the darkness ahead, an object of some sort jutting up in the water in front of them.

The sub's search lights illuminated it a moment later. Whatever it was, it was long, thin, and metallic in appearance, appearing to reach up from the bottom – which was still obscured at their current angle.

"What the hell is that?" Jacob asked. "Some kind of frigged up telephone pole?"

"Not unless the phone company got their cross streets seriously wrong."

Danni pointed at it. "Look at the top. It's all jagged, like part of it was broken off."

"Um, guys," Derek said as they passed the rise and the

bottom beyond became visible, "I have a feeling an undersea telephone pole is the least of our worries."

The leviathan circled the surface things, taking stock of them. There were three in total, and though only one rivaled it in size its instincts warned it to be wary of pack predators. It had been a long time since it had felt threatened by the squeaking things, but it still remembered hiding in its youth as pods of them patrolled near the surface. Working together, smaller things were able to mimic the power of much larger beasts, allowing them to take down prey they'd have no chance against individually.

Back in its claimed territory it should have felt secure, yet the thrumming was now worse than ever. It could sense the pulses affecting the very water around it in ways it did not understand, only knowing that this place – once its home – now felt very wrong.

Worse, was how empty the sea around it felt – the leviathan being one of the few creatures strong enough to continue functioning in this place, despite being driven near mad.

It considered its options during the brief moments when it could think, debating which of the surface things it should attack first. The smaller ones would be easiest to kill, but that would potentially leave it vulnerable to the large one. Attacking the largest one, though, might allow it to be surrounded.

Just then, however, its keen senses detected something else near the surface – blood. It knew the surface things didn't bleed, at least not like most life it knew. Keeping well beneath them, it swam to investigate, reaching up one long tentacle to probe the tiny object it had noticed.

Grasping hold, it realized it had found one of the

screaming things. This one was dead, though, albeit recently as it was still leaking its foul tasting fluids.

The leviathan was confused. It was the apex predator here. It was the one who tore the screaming things to pieces or drowned them in the deep. Were the surface things responsible for this?

Or was it a trap?

In the space between the maddening pulses, its mind was still keen. It knew from experience that the squeaking things were intelligent hunters. Perhaps something similar was at play here. Maybe the surface things were trying to lure it up, using the dead screaming thing as bait.

If so, it wouldn't work. It...

Its body shuddered as another pulse passed through it, causing its limbs to momentarily seize up.

As the wave of pain passed, it noticed something new, something it had missed before – a faint hum of sound, similar to what the surface things made. But this was coming from below, from the direction of the massive thing responsible for its misery.

Some of the surface things had spawn that were capable of traversing the depths. It knew as much, had seen them before. Most were slow and clumsy or lit up like they were a part of the surface itself, making them easy to avoid. Though the noises they made could be irritating, the ocean was a big place and they were easily given a wide berth – at least under normal circumstances.

Now, though, enraged by the constant assault upon its senses, it came to one conclusion – the subsurface thing was working with its podmates. They were boxing the leviathan in, hoping to use their numbers advantage to either kill it or drive it off.

The leviathan had been closing on the smallest of the trio, intent on drowning it before the others could act, but now it veered off. The one below was perhaps the most dangerous because it could venture into places where the others could not. However, it was also the most vulnerable, able to be attacked while its fellows were incapable of reaching it to help.

Releasing a cloud of ink to hopefully confuse the surface things, it began to speed toward the depths, the dead screaming thing still stuck to one of its arms.

The massive thing was down there, along with the pain it caused. But if it could hurt the leviathan, then it had almost certainly hurt the subsurface thing as well, leaving it crippled and ripe to be finished off.

Julie looked out from the deck of the Rogers Will-Do, not that there was much to see in the darkness. "Do the spotlights on this thing still work?"

"Hopefully," Kyle replied. "Hold on a sec and we'll see."

He flipped a switch and the area around the research vessel was illuminated, revealing little more than light rain and a mostly calm sea.

A few moments later, the radio clipped to his waist crackled to life with static. He quickly plucked it from its holster. "Come again."

There came a response, barely understandable, as Julie continued to scan the water, seeing no swells that could account for the splash that had just soaked them.

"We're just checking something out, over," Kyle said into the radio, eliciting more static. "I said we're fine, over." The response was a garbled mess, to which he angrily jammed it back into its holster. "Piece of shit. Um, sorry for the language."

Julie chuckled. "Do I look like some kind of Puritan to you?"

"One can never be too sure. Excuse me for a second." He stepped past her to the stern, where he cupped his hands together and shouted, "I said we're fine!" Then he turned back and laughed. "Figure that'll work as well as anything else."

Kyle leaned against the railing next to her, but then quickly stepped back again. "Ugh. Guess they didn't clean this thing as well as they should have."

"What is it?"

The agent held up his hands, now covered in some thick black gunk. "It's all over the railing."

Julie raised an eyebrow then looked around the deck itself, noticing dark spots here and there. She glanced down at herself, realizing her pants and jacket were dotted with those same stains. "Hold on a second. This stuff wasn't here earlier."

"Yuck. Ocean crud. Even worse."

Julie ran her finger across the railing, finding it smeared with dark ichor. "What is this?"

Kyle shook his head. "Oil maybe? Don't forget, that ship went down around here."

Julie considered this for a moment, but then shook her head. "It was a drillship, not a tanker. And from the report, it sounded like they were mostly drilling test holes."

"Maybe they hit pay dirt."

"Possible ... but wouldn't we have seen an oil slick when we arrived? Or back when you picked up that survivor?"

"I guess so. But if it's not oil, than what is it?"

Julie considered this for a moment, remembering the battle from earlier in the day. The thing was, she distinctly remembered Jacob ordering his crew to hose off the smaller vessel before they set sail again, so as to remove any evidence.

Either someone did a lousy job with the cleanup or...

"Kill those lights and pull us alongside the cutter."

"Why?"

"I need to get back aboard and see if we can raise the sub on the radio."

What the hell?

Derek blinked several times to make sure his eyes weren't playing tricks on him, and still had no idea what he was seeing. There were only two concrete facts he was willing to commit to so far: whatever this was, it was massive, easily dwarfing both the Nest and the sunken drillship; and that telephone pole thing was poking out of the top of it, a dim light visible where it met the ... *hull* ... rest of it.

"Duckling to Nest, I ... think we found something," Jacob said into the radio, receiving nothing but a crackle in return. "No response, trying text communications."

"Duckling?" Derek replied.

"No comments from the reality show peanut gallery."

As Jacob typed in his message, Llanzo stared wide-eyed. "That's no rock formation."

"I'm no scientist," Norah said, "and even I could've told you that."

"So is that thing sticking out some sort of antenna or something?" Jacob asked.

Silence greeted him as they tried to take in what they were seeing. It was like some sort of massive undersea excavation had taken place. Mounds of silt and debris were piled all around the partially unburied ... *thing*. What was visible, though, was covered in a smooth dull-grey surface.

Derek was no mineralogist, but he would've bet good

money it was some sort of metal. And, judging by the amount of debris piled up, it had been buried deep – meaning it had been down here a *lot* longer than the Tortuga. At the same time, there appeared to be no sign of corrosion. There were no barnacles attached to it, no coral growth, no indication that the myriad forms of sea life in the area had attempted to make it into a home – as they did with nearly everything that came to rest in their domain. Hell, it even appeared mostly clean of dirt, as if whatever had unearthed it had taken a polishing cloth to it surface.

The water beneath them seemed to pulse, just as Derek's EMF reader went off, the needle burying itself in the same instant his body felt heavy, as if he'd put on an instant thirty pounds.

Or maybe the dirt was simply knocked off of it.

The sub's frame groaned around them as it shifted in the water, indicating this was no optical illusion.

This close, whatever was happening was powerful enough to have an actual physical effect on the very space around it.

"We're all gonna get brain cancer, aren't we?" Jacob remarked.

Derek clapped him on the shoulder. "One could argue you'd need a brain first."

It was gallows humor, meant to lighten the mood, but there was little mirth to be had in light of the massive artifact jutting from the ancient silt.

"What is it?" Llanzo asked. "An aircraft carrier maybe?"

"No aircraft carrier that ever sailed in Uncle Sam's Navy," Jacob replied. "I can tell you that much."

Derek was forced to concur. Though the top of the object appeared mostly flat, there was a slight curvature to it. And from there, the similarities to naval vessels ended.

The edge of it was likely curved as well – the section leading down below appearing to continue in that shape, at least until it was lost in the sand beneath it. In some ways, the part he could see reminded him a bit of a massive river worn stone, the same kind he used to skip across ponds as a child.

As he continued to take in the sight, he realized it wasn't as smooth as he'd first thought. Shallow squarish indents covered it, each one several times larger than their sub and too regularly spaced to be anything natural.

There were no markings or numberings visible. The part of the object they could see, though, appeared to be uniformly designed with the exception of the ... *mast* sticking out from the top, light continuing to leak from the spot where it met the...

Wait a second.

"Bring us closer to that thing. To where the antenna thingamabob is attached."

Llanzo turned, looking at him incredulously. "You actually want to get closer?"

"This is a fact finding mission is it not?" Norah replied.

"True," Jacob said from the pilot seat, "but those facts are kinda telling me this is way above our pay grade."

Before Derek could reply, Danni turned to him, her eyes sparkling. "You see it, too, don't you?"

He nodded, to which Norah asked, "Care to bring the rest of us up to speed, Doctor Jenner? Or should we wait for the Q&A?"

"I wish it were that easy," he said. "Let's be clear about one thing. I have no idea what this is or what it's doing down here. But I think I might have one small bit of insight."

"And that is?"

"That thing sticking out of it. At first glance, I thought

it was an antenna or some kind of protrusion, but look more closely. I think that's the drill from the Tortuga. Alvita was right. This isn't some new tech from her company. But I think she may have been very wrong in assuming they weren't the cause of this."

30

"I have a feeling Mitch is going to be full of 'I told you so's' when we get back."

"How so?" Jacob asked.

"Remember what he was telling us earlier? About something letting out hiccups of weirdness over the years ... except now it seems to be waking up."

"Please don't tell me you think that thing is alive."

"God I hope not," Derek replied. "I mean in the general sense. For instance, look at all the dirt heaped around it. Whatever this thing is, it was buried pretty deep. Who knows how long it's been down here? Do you concur, Doctor?"

Llanzo held up his hands. "I don't even want to begin to speculate. This is so far outside my realm of study, it might as well be ancient Sanskrit."

"Fair enough."

"Buried," Danni remarked, taking up that line of thought, "until the Tortuga sunk a diamond-headed drill bit into the top of it. That would be a rude awakening for anything."

Derek nodded. "Call it what you will. Woke it up,

pissed it off, or accidentally hit the on switch. Whatever way you look at it, I get the impression the Tortuga was simply poking around in the worst place possible."

"Guess now we know why those seismic surveys of theirs were a bit iffy," Norah said.

"Pretty much."

"That doesn't explain how it got dug up," Jacob said. "Unless you're going to tell me their drill did all of that, too."

"Like I said, I had *one* thought on this. The rest ... your guess is as good as mine. Who knows? Maybe it was some kind of reaction to being damaged, an explosion or a..."

"No," Llanzo interrupted, continuing to stare at the massive thing below them. "I don't think so."

"I'm forced to concur with the good Doctor," Jacob added. "This doesn't look like any form of concussive force I've ever seen. The dispersal pattern is ... all wrong. And if that were the case, why didn't it uncover the whole thing? I mean, look at it. It's partially excavated at most."

The sub rattled again as another pulse passed, causing Derek's meter to once again let out a high pitched beep in his hands.

"I think you can shut that off now," Norah snapped.

"Good point." He adjusted the volume and put it down. "Unless, that is, anyone here thinks for one second that thing isn't the source of those disturbances."

"Nobody's going to say it, are they?" Danni replied. "That we're looking at an actual UF..."

"No," Norah said. "We are specifically *not* going to say that, not until we have a better idea what it is."

"Okay. So what now?" Jacob asked. "I can take us in closer, so we can..."

"*Now*, we get the hell out of here." Norah let out a huff of breath. "And then we get those ships moving again until we get a clear enough signal to run this up the flag-pole." She turned to Derek. "Do you agree?"

"Well, actually ... not really."

He didn't think she would have looked more surprised had he pulled out a gun and shot her. "What do you mean, not really?"

"Most of that, yes. But since we're already down here, I agree with Jake. We should take a closer look."

"I didn't say I wanted to. I said we could." As Norah glared at him, he elaborated. "The Duckling's holding together fine and battery levels look good. Vakovsky did a hell of a job stripping her down to a pressurized tin can."

"Still a dopey name."

"Nobody asked you."

Derek turned back to face Norah. "I think it behooves us to gather as much information as we can, so when we're finally able to make contact we have a little more to report than finding some big scary thing at the bottom of the ocean."

Norah narrowed her eyes, making him wonder if he shouldn't have phrased that slightly different, but after a moment she nodded. "You probably have a point. The more data we have, the better it'll be for everyone. Any response from the surface?"

Jacob shook his head. "Crickets. We might as well be the last people left on Earth."

"Let's hope not. Are we at least recording this?"

"As far as I can tell. Vakovsky said the hard drive should be shielded well enough, but I'm not placing any bets right now."

"All right." Norah looked at them each in turn. "Let the record state I take full responsibility for this decision. Bring us in closer. But the second you see any red lights, I want us on the surface."

"You don't have to tell me twice."

Jacob angled the thrusters and the sub began to once more descend. As it did, the enormity of the object below them was driven home as it continued to fill their field of vision.

"Big son of a bitch, ain't it?"

"Pretty sure that's exactly what Frank would have said," Derek replied.

"Probably with a few more expletives."

"Depending on how the next few minutes go, we might be able to make up for that."

"Focus, gentlemen," Norah warned. "We're doing something potentially momentous here. I'd prefer the transcript be filled with something other than one-liners."

"One small step for a woman," Danni said softly, a nervous grin on her face.

"Exactly, Agent Kent. This should be a time for ... oh, what the hell is that?"

"So much for the transcript," Jacob muttered as the indentation nearest them on the massive hull suddenly lit up brilliant green, illuminating the water around them.

One second it was a dull grey metallic, seemingly no more translucent than a sheet of steel, the next it was glowing brightly as if it were one giant LED.

"Um, anyone else seen *Independence Day*?" Derek asked as the interior of the sub was illuminated by the bright beam coming from the – *oh enough of this crap, call the damned thing what it is* – vessel.

It was no mere flash of light, though. The green hue seemed to creep through the cabin's interior, washing over Jacob first, then down his back, where it shouldn't have been able to reach.

He and Norah were next, his skin tingling as the light washed over him, as if a million ants were crawling over his body. Then it moved passed him toward the others before finally hitting the rear of the small sub.

And just like that it faded away – leaving nothing but spots in his eyes – as the glow faded from the indent and it once again became an opaque square of metal.

"Did anyone else feel that?" Llanzo asked, sounding as if he were rapidly reaching the end of his already frayed nerves.

"What the fuck?" Jacob replied.

"I ... I think it scanned us," Danni said.

Derek glanced toward her, his eyebrow raised.

"What? You guys have seen Star Trek, right?"

"What I've seen is enough," Norah stated. "I don't know what the hell that thing did to us, but I don't care to give it a second chance."

"Same," Jacob replied. "Say the word and we're outta here."

"Take us home."

"You got it. Dropping ballast plates in three ... two... Ugh!"

The sub lurched hard to the side, catching them all by surprise and throwing Derek into both Llanzo and Danni.

"What the hell?" Jacob cried.

"Are you two okay?" Derek asked as the sub righted itself again.

"We're fine," Danni replied, peeling herself from between the two men. "What just happened?"

"Jacob began checking his instrument cluster. "All I know is it wasn't me."

"Was it the UFO?" After a moment, she added, "Come on, seriously? Does anyone think it's anything else?"

"The only thing I think is that we need to be else-where. *Now*," Norah barked. "Forget the ballast. Just move us away from that thing."

"Hold on. I'm making sure the thrusters didn't take a hit. Then we can... What in Sam Hill is that?"

There came a grinding sound from outside their little vessel, as if fingernails were being dragged across their hull.

And then something dropped into their field of vision from above.

At first, Derek wasn't certain whether he was hallucinating or his mind had simply come unglued.

"Oh my god!"

But then, as gasps of surprise and terror filled the cabin, he realized the awful truth of what they were seeing.

A woman, her eyes open but glazed over in death, stared sightlessly at them from outside, dangling from something long and fleshy wrapped around her waist, as if she were being held in place like a marionette.

And then he looked up and saw them ... rows upon rows of hooked suckers, impossibly large and so close that he was certain there could be no chance of escape.

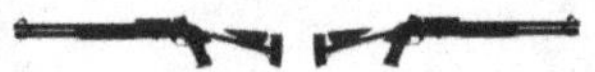

Andrea McAvee was used to chaos. It was part of her job, her life. But that was usually chaos that could at least be understood.

For instance, some people could be little better than wild animals – unpredictable and savage. However, in accepting that, one could understand them as well as make educated guesses to overcome them.

The forces of nature were no different. There were rules. It was how things worked.

Yet, regardless of all that, she found herself trying to manage something that was beyond explanation.

"Try raising the sub again," she ordered.

"Nothing but static on the transponder and the text link is showing garbage," the agent at comms, Novak, replied.

"Well keep trying." Andrea stood up, suddenly feeling

like her pockets were full of lead. *Great! They're getting worse.* "Harkness, got anything for me?"

"Nothing good," Mitchell said, continuing to monitor his station. "Although, if anyone here was thinking of switching careers to sumo wrestler, now's probably the time."

"Not funny."

"Wasn't really trying to be." He turned toward another of the readings he was monitoring. "Oh crap."

"What *now?*" Andrea had a degree in computer science with a master's in advanced cryptography. She was neither stranger to man nor their machines, yet right at that moment she was wishing she'd taken a minor in quantum mechanics. Even then, she had a feeling it might not have helped them much.

"I don't know what they're doing down there, but I'm getting some seriously strange readings off the gyro compass now."

"Define strange."

"As in Santa must've relocated his workshop down to Rio."

Before she could answer, the chaos inside the bridge was interrupted as one of Mitchell's teammates, that camerawoman, barged in like she owned the place.

Too bad now was really not a good time.

Andrea opened her mouth to say as much, but the other woman was faster on the draw.

"I think Derek and the others are in trouble."

"No offense, Jules," Mitchell replied. "But they might want to take a number. Because..."

"Excuse me, Ms. Wilhelm," Andrea interrupted, "but we have a situation developing here. You're welcome to stay as a courtesy, but we don't have time for..."

"That's the problem," Julie snapped. "*They* don't have

time." She held up her hand to show it covered in some drippy black runoff.

"What is that?"

"I think it's octopus ink, which means they aren't alone down there."

So intent was the leviathan on destroying the subsurface thing, that it threw caution to the wind, advancing without heed despite its target being close to the massive thing it had failed to kill earlier.

It sped down through the depths, its territory now nearly unrecognizable from what it had known. Everything had changed. Gone were the myriad prey that had once inhabited it, leaving nothing but the dead behind.

Even the water itself was different – the once comforting currents somehow now disturbingly still. Worse, it was hard to both swim and breathe in this place, as the water had become more akin to a living mucus.

None of that stopped the leviathan, though, its tortured brain insisting it achieve the momentary release from pain that killing afforded it.

However, in its haste to ambush the subsurface thing, it raced too quickly into the strange undersea necropolis its home had become. As it neared its prey, preparing to strike, a bright light had emerged from the massive thing – almost like the lure of a gigantic predator.

The leviathan had stopped at the sight of this new occurrence, its natural curiosity taking hold for a moment.

Its hesitation had been a costly one.

Just as it was about to attack, intent on squeezing the subsurface thing until its inedible shell cracked, another thrumming pulse had struck it. It found itself momentarily paralyzed as its nerve endings lit up, leaving it little better than the other victims left to float in the dead waters surrounding the massive thing.

Far worse was knowing that it was mere feet away from its enemy – an enemy it realized was likely now aware of its presence.

The element of surprise had been lost.

No matter. The subsurface thing was nothing compared to the leviathan's might. It was outmatched in every conceivable way. If it tried to run, it would be caught. If it tried to fight, it would lose. And if it tried to play dead, the leviathan would make sure of it before turning its attention back to the enemies still waiting at the surface.

And then, once the interlopers were finally all dead, it would turn its attention back toward the massive thing, so as to finally cease its thrumming cries once and for all.

31

Oh my god. It's Alvita! But how?

There was no doubt about it. Though he hadn't spent much time with the ZarroGreen rep, Jacob had always been good with faces. It helped in his line of work. Split second decisions were often required of him, decisions he needed to be right about. It was also a handy virtue to have for less onerous assignments, like being stuck in a conference room full of suits.

However, right then he wished his recall was somewhat less perfect because all it left were questions as to how this woman had met her gruesome fate – and what it meant for the rest they'd left behind at the surface.

Sadly, there wasn't much time to ponder her death, as their own was likely seconds away at most.

"Wait. Why isn't it attacking?" Llanzo asked, pulling his eyes away from the macabre image hanging directly before them.

Sure enough, the creature was close enough to snare the sub. That much was obvious from their vantage point. *Goddamn, that thing is big.*

"Hold on. The scavengers!" Derek cried.

Jacob glanced over his shoulder at his friend. "Pretty sure that thing ain't no hyena, buddy."

"You don't say. I'm talking about what we saw on the way down here. All the dead fish."

Danni nodded. "The disruptions. We saw it with the whales. Whatever this is, it affects sea life. And it's stronger than ever here."

"Strong enough to stop that thing?" Norah asked, sounding as if she couldn't bring herself to believe it.

"No idea. Maybe for a few seconds anyway."

"That's not good for us," Jacob replied.

"Why not?"

"Because those distortions don't last long, meaning we just wasted those precious seconds arguing when we should've been running." Another flash of light from outside caught his attention, just as he was starting to angle the thrusters away from both the object below and the monstrosity hanging above them. "Oh, what now?"

"It's opening up," Norah said, her voice barely a whisper.

Sure enough, she appeared to be right. A four-way seam had appeared in the surface of the same spot that had *scanned* them. As he watched, it split the squarish indentation into four quarters, each retracting into the rest of the hull to reveal what appeared to be an interior chamber bathed in a soft red light.

Jacob couldn't see much detail aside from that, nor was he really sure he cared to.

"What do we do?" Llanzo cried.

"We get the fuck out of here, that's what."

Jacob didn't particularly like their odds, but it wasn't the first time he'd had to run for his life. He immediately began formulating strategies for escape – rejecting some and refining others, even as he gave the propulsion system power.

They had zero chance against that thing in the open water, and it was too far a shot to the surface, even with their ballast dropped. He'd seen how quick that first octopus had moved. If this one was half as fast, they'd be shit out of luck.

What he wouldn't have given for some countermeasures right at that point. Too bad the minisub was designed for covert operations and recovery, not combat.

No. Their best bet was to hug the bottom. Maybe he could use the loose mountains of sand and dirt surrounding the half-buried vessel to kick up enough debris to cover their escape. It was a longshot but, as far as he could see, it was all they had.

"Say goodbye to E.T., folks, because we are getting out of…"

His words were lost as something hit the stern of the ship from the starboard side, sending the small sub into a spin. Red lights began flashing on the instrument panel as he fought to both maintain control and keep his lunch.

The fuck?!

He needn't have bothered wondering. It was painfully obvious what had hit them. The only plus in their favor was that it had been a glancing blow by a tentacle. Judging from the size of the beast out there, taking up nearly the entire field of vision above them, a direct hit would have split them open like an egg.

Jacob had a feeling they wouldn't get so lucky a second time, a fact which Derek confirmed a moment later.

"I think it's waking up."

Sure enough, the beast's tentacles were starting to thrash about, their sheer size enough to pummel the small sub with shockwaves of displaced water.

Jacob made the mistake of glancing up, catching sight of a wicked beak that looked sharp enough to puncture steel plate.

Turn off the lights, stupid!

Heeding his inner voice, Jacob killed the LED array, which had no doubt been serving as little more than a fishing lure to the creature.

With the lights off, the octopus disappeared from sight, but he didn't pretend to hope it was gone. Another shudder from the sub confirmed as much.

"Jake..."

"Not now, Norah," he growled.

With the exterior array off, the only illumination came from the massive craft beneath them – the glow from the open chamber lighting up the sea around it an eerie red. A fitting portent for the hell they found themselves in.

That was fine, though. He didn't plan on sticking around long enough to appreciate it.

This next part's gonna be tricky. With the sub stripped of most of its instrumentation, he was going to have to play this by ear, hoping his memory of the surrounding area was good enough to...

"Oof!"

Another hit sent their craft reeling, this one a bit more than a glancing blow as sparks began to fly from elsewhere in the cabin.

"That's not good," Danni said.

"No shit." Jacob grasped the control stick and tried to steer them hard to port, only to be met with an anemic lurch. Glancing down, he saw why. Some of those warning lights were from the sub's thrusters.

Fuck! They were down to half power on the starboard side, meaning if they wanted to get out of there, it would be at a fast limp at best.

"Why aren't we moving?" Llanzo asked, sounding close to tears.

"Calm yourself, Doctor," Norah replied.

"Why should I calm myself when we're about to...?"

"It's because we can't," Jacob snapped, his frustration boiling over. "Goddamned monster damaged our thrusters. Steering is compromised, too."

"That thing will tear us to…"

"I know, goddamn it!"

"What about in there?" Danni pointed past him toward the vessel at the bottom, the strange reddish portal still open, as if beckoning them.

Jacob dared a glance back at her even as the ocean around them swirled, the whitish underside of a massive tentacle visible as it closed on them. "Are you insane? We have no idea what's in there."

"Yeah," Derek replied, his voice calm enough to make Jacob want to deck him. "But we already know what's out here. Our odds can't be much worse."

"You're fucking nuts, man."

"Then count me as crazy, too," Norah said. "Do it."

"But…"

"Don't make me order you, mister."

Every instinct within him screamed that he should tell them to go to hell, but he also knew he needed to make a decision and fast.

Damn it all!

Pushing his doubt to the side, he put everything he could into the thrusters, then angled them downward toward the opening. He always knew he was likely to be killed on the job. This was not the time to get squirrelly about it. Even so, he found himself at odds with his own actions, knowing there was a good chance they'd die inside that thing, leaving their bodies lost forever as the sands of time once again slowly consumed it.

That said, an empty grave wasn't a hard choice compared to ending up as a lump of squid shit.

The sub limped toward the opening, the water around them taking on the hue of the hellish illumination spilling out. Freaky as it was, it was still better than the thing just off their port, a tentacle covered in suckers the size of a dinner plate.

Jacob didn't dare look to their other side, knowing what he'd see there was probably equally as bad if not worse.

Come on!

The sub's engines whined as he gave them everything he could, even as more warning lights flashed, telling him he was expending precious battery power on the damaged thrusters.

At least there was no chance of this being a tight squeeze, the opening ahead easily three times as wide as their craft.

Therein lay another problem, though. If the opening turned out to be too shallow, what was to stop that monster from simply reaching in and dragging their asses back out?

"We're not going to make it," Derek said from over his shoulder. "Brace yourselves!"

Out of the corner of his eye, Jacob saw the tentacle closing in around them. In another few moments, no more, they were going to be caught. Once that happened they were as good as dead. There was nothing on the little sub capable of fending off such a monstrosity. Hell, even had the hydraulic arm not been disabled, it would've been little more than a matchstick against...

What the...?

The water seemed to ripple directly in front of them. In that same instant, Jacob felt as if a twenty pound burrito had just dropped straight into his lower intestine – this disruption easily the worst he'd felt since starting this crazy journey.

All at once, the octopus's massive arm began to twitch in place, barely a yard away, as the beast was stunned just as surely as all their equipment topside had been.

"It's another distortion!" Danni cried. "Get us inside, quick."

"The hell with that," Jacob replied, reversing direction. "I'm getting us out of here before that thing wakes up."

Rather than change direction, the engines began to whine in protest as the minisub increased its speed toward the strange portal ahead of them, as if they were being dragged along by the hand of some invisible giant.

You've gotta be fucking kidding me! Before any of their systems could burn out, leaving them stranded or worse, Jacob eased up on the controls.

"What's happening?" Norah asked. "I thought you just said..."

"Something's got us," he replied with a defeated sigh. "A current maybe, or something else. Could be a fucking tractor beam for all I know. Either way, we're going in whether we want to or not."

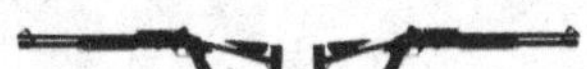

Derek took a deep breath as the reddish glow grew closer and their speed increased. Much as he wanted to panic, he forced himself to stay calm. He'd faced death before, had gotten out of near-impossible situations more times than he cared to remember. If this was to be his fate then he'd accept it, knowing he'd likely been living on borrowed time for a while now and this was simply destiny collecting its due.

He'd never been a religious man, preferring science to give him the answers he needed. Despite that, he found himself saying a silent prayer anyway – not for himself, but for Danni and her family. If he had one regret about dying in such a way, it was bringing her along. Her parents had already lost one child to the unknown – her brother killed by an enraged Sasquatch driven mad with disease.

Now it seemed they were destined to relive their heartache, and once again it was all his fault. It was a heavy burden to bear, made that much worse by all the others he'd failed over the years – the ones he'd been unable to save.

But there were also those who'd made it, those who'd lived to tell the tale thanks to the actions of his team.

It didn't erase the many mistakes he'd made. But hopefully it was enough to balance the scales for whatever awaited them afterward.

Guess we'll find out soon enough, he pondered, as the sub entered the craft and the hellish red light within swallowed them whole.

PART III

32

Kerry nearly jumped out of his skin as two crewmen threw out a polite hello.

He readied himself, not sure what he might actually do if confronted, but they continued on their way as if he wasn't worth their time.

Kerry didn't fool himself, though. He had no doubt they were on to him. He knew modern technology. This entire ship was probably covered with hidden cameras and microphones.

It was only a matter of time before they realized what had happened to that Guerrero woman.

She'd turned her back on him, smug in her betrayal, ready to turn him in, and he'd ... hesitated. He simply couldn't do it. Hell, he'd been sick to his stomach that he'd even considered it.

However, where his resolve had faltered, destiny had chosen to step in and intervene.

In her haste, she'd slipped on the slick deck, her shoes expensive but a poor choice for being up on deck during a rainstorm.

Unable to catch herself in time, she'd hit her head on

the rail, stumbling to remain upright and clearly dazed from the accident.

Kerry had moved in, meaning to help her, but some primal instinct had kicked in and taken over, making him almost feel like a stranger in his own body. He'd been reaching out to steady her, but had ended up shoving her instead, sending her tumbling overboard into the sea.

His first instinct had been to shout for help, but even he could tell it was too late. She'd surfaced for a moment, no more, and then disappeared beneath the waves. After that, there'd been no sign of her. She'd either drowned or been swept away into the vast unyielding darkness.

There was nothing to be seen or heard – no cries for help, no frantic splashing. She was simply gone.

The thing was, he knew he should've been horrified, but he wasn't. This entire incident had left him feeling small and weak. He'd been captured, locked up, and the one time he'd tried to assert himself he'd gotten his ass handed to him by a girl half his size.

He'd felt powerless, the stolen camera the only thing left to reassure him that he had some say in his fate. And that woman had wanted to take it away from him ... leaving him no choice but to stop her.

He slowly began to realize that maybe he wasn't as powerless as he thought. If he could have this one victory, who was to say there couldn't be more? The problem was, he was still outnumbered. And it was only a matter of time before they grew wise to what he'd done.

If he was going to do anything, though, it would have to be soon. He was well aware that his window of opportunity was short. His captors were currently spread thin between the three boats and the sub, but that wouldn't last forever. Eventually someone would notice that Guerrero woman was missing.

Kerry needed to figure out a way to either be gone by

then or thin out their ranks enough so that he stood a fighting chance. He had no real idea how to do any of that, but two of the three ships had nothing but skeleton crews on them. He'd overheard as much.

If he could find some way to exploit that, then maybe he could sail back to port and inform the authorities. All of these fake agents would be hunted down and arrested. Hell, there might be interviews afterward, perhaps even a book deal.

He'd be hailed as a hero.

But first he had to come up with a plan to get aboard one of those other boats.

"What do you mean, you have no way of contacting them?"

"I need you to calm down, Ms. Wilhelm."

Julie was not in the mood for this patronizing shit. "Don't tell me to calm down, and its *Agent* Wilhelm, as you fully well know."

"Fine. But if you don't lower your voice, I will have you removed from my bridge, *Agent* Wilhelm."

"If you think for one second..."

"She's right you know," Mitchell interrupted, looking up from his cobbled together instrument cluster.

"Excuse me?" the agent in charge, McAvee, replied.

"Not to be anal about it, but if there is another monster octopus out there, then technically that makes this our jurisdiction again."

"Yes, and you're on our vessel."

"Okay, so more of a joint operation," the medic replied. "Look, I'm not trying to mutiny or whatever the kids call it these days. I'm just saying we're all in this together. And if we can't play nice, well, it's that much extra paperwork for everybody. And I, for one, get writer's cramp really easy."

Agent McAvee took a deep breath, looking to Julie as if she'd have happily thrown Mitch overboard, paperwork be damned. However, after another moment she said, "Very well. You can stay, Agent Wilhelm, so long as you don't disrupt the operation of this bridge."

That seemed an easy enough thing, being that there didn't look to be a lot going on at the moment – mostly people sitting at stations with perplexed looks on their faces.

McAvee stepped to the far corner of the bridge, beckoning her and Mitch to follow. "I'm not the enemy here. We all want the same thing."

Julie nodded. "I realize that. I'm ... sorry for my outburst."

"Okay, now that we're all happy campers again," Mitchell said blithely, "did you actually see this other octopus?"

"No," she replied. "We didn't see anything, me and Kyle that is ... I didn't get his last name. It was too dark, but there was a splash and the next thing I knew the deck was covered in this black gunk."

"There's a lot of gunk in the ocean."

"You think I don't know that? I grew up in Jersey."

"Fair enough."

"Is there a way to figure out what that is?" McAvee asked.

"Of course," the medic replied. "Problem is, most of the equipment I'd need would probably explode right now ... figuratively ... maybe. Best I can probably do on short notice is hope Reid remembered to pack a decent microscope. Octopus ink is mostly melanin and mucus, so I should be able to at least determine if it has a cell structure or not."

Julie grimaced. "Mucus?"

Mitchell grinned in response. "Bet you're wishing you'd washed your hands before coming over."

"The real question is," McAvee replied, "how much time will that take, and can you spare it?"

"Shouldn't take long. Shit's been getting weirder and weirder, but I'm pretty sure it won't matter much if I step away from the switch for a bit."

"What about the sub?" Julie asked.

"I already told you..."

"It's not that easy," Mitchell interrupted. "We've got a transponder in the water and we're scanning multiple channels. But even with that, we've been getting zilch since they passed about the halfway mark to the bottom." He held up a hand. "Now before you panic, that doesn't mean anything. I wouldn't be surprised if the interference gets exponentially worse the closer you get to whatever is causing it ... no different than how a WiFi signal will be stronger in the same room than two floors away. Bottom line is, we'd probably have just as much luck being heard by shouting at the water."

Julie shook her head. "But if something went wrong..."

"We accounted for that," McAvee said. "The ballast plates have redundant failsafes. They'll also automatically detach in case of catastrophic power loss. If that happens, boom, they shoot back to the surface."

"But..."

Mitchell put a hand on Julie's shoulder. "Trust Derek and Jake. They both know what they're doing. Believe me, neither of them has a death wish. Besides, we have no other choice for now. Communications are dead and sonar is buggy enough that we can't tell if the water is clear or if we're surrounded by..."

"Ghosts?" she replied. "Yeah, I know. Same thing

happened earlier. You were there, too, Mitch. We both know the problem with ghosts are..."

"What if one of them is more real than the rest?" McAvee finished.

Silence followed, no doubt all of them remembering back to the last battle they'd fought and just barely won – wondering if it happened again whether they'd be as lucky this time. Especially if Derek's theory held true and there was something out there far worse than what they'd already encountered.

33

Derek felt Danni's hand entwine with his as they waited to see what would happen next, the interior of the sub awash in eerie red light. He gave her hand what he hoped was a reassuring squeeze as the seconds played out.

He'd made his peace and was ready for whatever awaited them.

They didn't have to wait long.

The sub jolted violently around them, sending sparks flying from the instrument panel.

"Shit!" Jacob cried as they began to be dragged backward. "I think that thing's got us!"

It was a good try, Derek thought. Ultimately, though, it had been too little and too late against a foe they were hopelessly outmatched against.

But then, just as quickly as the sub started shaking, the shuddering subsided and all became still.

"What the hell is that?" Norah asked.

A dark substance was clouding the water around them, slightly dimming the reddish light.

"What have you people dragged me into?" Llanzo cried.

Derek opened his mouth, trying to think of something comforting to say, but he quickly realized any words would be wasted as their ordeal was seemingly far from over.

"Oh for fuck's sake, what now?" Jacob swore as the water began to swirl and bubble around the sub, but in a different way from moments earlier. Several long seconds later there came a *clang* from beneath them as the minisub settled onto the floor of wherever they were.

"Did you do that?" Derek asked.

"Nope."

The reason for them setting down, however, became apparent as they all watched the water level outside the sub begin to rapidly drop – the red light simultaneously dimming by several degrees of intensity.

Finally, the last of the water drained away, leaving them in what appeared to be a featureless chamber made of that same dull grey metal that covered the outside of the vessel.

At least that was one thing Derek was beyond arguing about. At this point it seemed the height of obstinance to pretend this was anything but some kind of ship – although of what origin, he dared not speculate.

Guess there's something to that Bermuda Triangle crap after all.

Finally, Jacob spoke up. "I hate to say this. I mean, I *really* hate to say this, but I think we're in some sort of airlock."

"So what do we do about it?" Norah asked.

"That's a good question," Derek replied, kind of amazed to find they were still alive. Even he hadn't been willing to bet on that one. "We don't know what's out there or if the air's even breathable."

"I don't suppose we have anything to test the O2 levels with," Danni said.

Jacob glanced back toward her. "We probably did ... before we stripped this thing down to a bath toy."

Norah leaned forward, ignoring them. "Look at the floor. What is that stuff?"

The surface upon which they sat was still wet from the seawater, but mixed in were blotches of darker liquid.

Derek took a look, realizing he'd seen something similar only a few short hours earlier. "I think I know why that thing let us go."

"Are you gonna share, or do we need to play charades?" Jacob asked with a huff.

"Well, we probably have time. Doesn't look like we're going anywhere."

"Derek," Norah warned.

"Sorry. Forgot. Still under observation, I know."

"What's under observation?" Danni asked.

"I'll tell you later."

"No, you will not," Norah stated flatly.

This was getting them nowhere quick. They might be safe for the moment, but the sub had limited supplies of both oxygen and power. And there was no telling how much damage they'd suffered.

"Okay, let's focus here." He leaned forward. "We should probably shut down anything we don't need so we can..."

"Way ahead of you," Jake said, already working the controls. "Good thing is, most of the non-essential stuff was already disconnected."

"I guess that's a plus in our favor." Derek inclined his head toward Norah. "Back to your question, I'd be willing to bet that's blood. Would you concur, Doctor?" He turned to find a blank stare plastered on Llanzo's face. The poor guy was obviously the least prepared among them for whatever was happening. "Doctor?"

"Huh?" he replied. "Oh yeah. I suppose."

"Thank you. If I had to guess, I'd say there's a hunk of that thing behind us, right inside the closed door."

"Closed? I didn't hear anything," Jacob said.

"Nor did we hear anything when it opened, or when this room drained," Derek countered. "I'm thinking this place, whatever it is, gives new meaning to the phrase silent service. Regardless, I don't doubt our *friend* is waiting outside, probably angrier than ever. The bigger question is..."

"Let me guess," Danni said. "Whether this ship is from another planet or the future?" Jacob and Norah both raised eyebrows at her. "What? Didn't any of you ever see *Sphere*?"

"Pretty sure it was a book first, kid," Jacob replied. "But either way, I usually leave the sci-fi to the... Oh goddamn it, what now?"

As he spoke, the lighting outside their tiny craft changed, shifting from reddish in hue to a more natural illumination, mimicking that which was inside the sub.

"Why the hell did it do that?"

"Maybe it heard what you said and realized this was better light for reading," Derek replied.

Jacob shook his head. "I swear, man, as looney as that sounds, at this point I'm just about ready to suspend my disbelief."

"How can you two banter at a time like this?" Llanzo finally snapped. "We're trapped at the bottom of the ocean inside this ... thing!"

Norah let out a breath. "Please calm yourself, Doctor. Panicking is going to do nothing but eat up our remaining oxygen."

"But..."

"I believe I speak for everyone else here when I say this is simply how we're coping with the unknown. Speaking of which, it's time to put our thinking hats on, people. I want to hear fewer one-liners and more ideas for getting out of here and making contact with the Nest."

Silence greeted her as the severity of the situation began to sink in. Yes, they were safe for the moment, but that was an illusion, nothing more. Derek sighed inwardly. Far as he could tell, their current options seemed limited to smothering slowly as their air ran out, or suffocating quickly if the atmosphere outside turned out to be unbreathable.

Neither really held much appeal. Having made his peace only to survive, Derek found himself in no real rush to make peace with death again anytime soon.

Sadly, they were between a rock and a hard place – and right outside that hard place was a giant pissed off cephalopod that was probably waiting to finish the job it started.

"Hey," Danni said, interrupting his train of thought, "has anyone felt anything weird since we got in here?"

"You mean besides fear and confusion?" Jacob asked.

"Not that. I mean physically. Those disturbances seemed to get worse the closer we got to this thing, but now I don't feel anything odd. I just feel ... normal."

"Interesting choice of words," Norah replied. "Derek?"

"On it." He switched on the EMF meter again, realizing Danni was right. He hadn't felt any of those weight fluctuations in a while. He'd just been too preoccupied to notice it.

It was possible that, whatever this place was, it was somehow shielded from the effects of...

The EMF meter buzzed loudly, the needle burying itself in the far side of the scale.

So much for that theory.

"I don't suppose it's too much to hope that cheap-ass thing is busted," Jacob said.

"Are you saying I should have brought a scale as backup?"

Norah shook her head. "I think the bigger question is what does it mean?"

Derek shut off the device, having no ready answer to give her.

"W-what if we're thinking about this the wrong way?" Llanzo asked after a minute or two, still sounding squirrelly but apparently trying to rally himself.

"How so, Doctor?"

"What if we just think we're not experiencing those disturbances ... because they're actually ongoing in this place, whatever it might be?"

"Not following."

"The readings on that device, this ... vessel." He took a deep breath to steady himself. "What if it's not shielding us from the effects so much as *regulating* them?"

Derek glanced at the others, then back toward Reid. "But if that's the case then how...?"

"I don't pretend to know how it works," he continued, already sounding better. Having a problem to focus on seemed to be helping him keep it together ... for now anyway. "Maybe inside this place, these forces are somehow in balance, or canceling each other out. I can't even begin to guess which one it might be. But what I'm saying is, maybe what's going on outside is the result of these ... *energies* escaping little by little."

"That's ... a disturbing thought," Jacob replied.

Derek nodded. "Especially since we now know Zarro-Green unwittingly drilled right through the top of this thing." He shook his head. "I don't suppose anybody brought any duct tape."

"Even if we did, we'd still need to pop the hatch,"

Danni replied, before adding, "So ... maybe we should do it already and get it over with."

Norah fixed her with a questioning stare. "Excuse me?"

"We can't just sit here. Jake even said ... sorry, I meant Agent Caseman."

"Jake is fine," he replied. "I think we can dispense with the formality while we're playing Jonah in this whale. Continue."

Danni nodded. "You said you thought this might be an airlock. And we all saw how it only opened after that light show outside. Remember what I said about us being scanned? Well, maybe it determined we were worth opening the door for. If so, it could have also made note of the atmosphere in here, too."

"That's a big if," Derek said.

"Yeah, but it's our only if. We can either sit here and hope something happens before the air runs out, or we can take a leap of faith."

"And if you're wrong?" Norah asked.

"Then we're just as dead as we will be later, only a bit sooner."

Derek chuckled. It wasn't too far off from what he'd been thinking. "She's not wrong, you know."

Jacob joined him. "Goddamn, man. Kid's got guts. You really know how to pick 'em."

"I think it's more like she picked me."

"This is all fascinating," Norah said, "but maybe we should save the hug-fest for later, assuming we survive."

"I agree," Derek replied. "So what's it going to be? Stay or go?"

"What do you mean?"

"You're the agent in charge. This is your call."

Norah met his gaze and held it. "No, it isn't. It's *your* decision."

"Have you all gone crazy?" Llanzo cried, once again near panic.

Norah, however, opted to ignore the scientist. "You're the DoCC's top man in the field. Others ... may doubt you, but I don't. I trust your gut. And in this situation I'm forced to concede I trust it a lot more than my own."

"Me, too," Danni said.

"Same here, buddy," Jacob added. "So hurry up and figure out how you're going to kill our asses."

"Well, when you put it that way..." Derek turned and gave Danni's arm a gentle clap. "I trust my instincts, but that also means trusting my team, too. Want to crack this tin can open and see what's waiting outside?"

She nodded. "Let's do this."

"Before you do," Norah said. "It's been a pleasure serving with you, Doctor Jenner."

"Likewise, Agent Caseman."

"Don't look at me," Jacob remarked after they were done. "My money's on us surviving the next five minutes. Save the sap for another day."

Norah looked like she wanted to say something to him, but after a moment she simply nodded and turned back toward Derek. "If you'd kindly do the honors, Doctor."

"My pleasure." Derek reached up toward the hatch, noting that Llanzo had started reciting a prayer.

I'll take whatever help we can get at this point.

Hoping he was making the right choice, the Crypto-Hunter turned the hand crank and popped the seal.

Pain, rage, confusion!

All of that and more warred for dominance inside the

leviathan's tortured mind as the sea around it filled with the scent of its own blood.

It had been seconds away from destroying the subsurface thing when another of those damnable thrums had wracked its body. Then, in the next moment, sheer outrage had spurred it back into action as it spied the massive thing attempting to devour its prey.

It had reached inside the massive thing's gullet, had even managed to grasp hold of its prize, only to have it swallowed whole, along with the tip of its arm.

It wasn't a bad wound. It had suffered worse in its life. But even minor pain was too much to bear heaped atop the agony it had already suffered. It wasn't used to feeling this helpless. Even in its younger days, when it had been smaller, more vulnerable, it had seldom felt as it did now. Being a thinking animal had always meant there were options to explore.

But what choice did it have now? The massive thing was too large to crush the life out of, especially while it continued to thrum — its cries powerful enough to stun even as great a beast as itself.

It began to circle the massive thing, considering whether it should try unearthing more of it in the hopes of finding a soft spot, some way to pay it back for all it had done.

On some level, it realized the massive thing wasn't alive, the same way it understood the surface things weren't. Such distinctions meant nothing, though, after all the torture this thing had inflicted. An enemy was an enemy, and this one needed to die in as much...

Something caught its eye as it circled.

It noticed a faint glow from atop the massive thing, where some antenna or proboscis protruded from its body. The leviathan swam closer to investigate, noting the way oddly colored light appeared to be leaking from that spot.

There was only one conclusion to be made – its seemingly unkillable foe was wounded after all.

It was a tiny breach, unlikely to be fatal, but the leviathan didn't care. With a powerful jet of water, it descended upon the protuberance and wrapped its arms around it,

Unlike the rest of the massive thing, it turned out to be far more fragile – deforming as the angry beast increased the pressure, until finally the leviathan ripped the strange proboscis out of the massive thing's body.

It had hoped to see its enemy bleed. What happened instead, though, was the small fissure of light atop its foe grew far brighter as more of its insides were exposed to the cold seawater.

The leviathan approached the injury, hoping to reach inside and cause the massive thing even more harm. Just then, however, the light pulsed brightly, sending a fresh wave of agony through the beast – far greater than anything it had experienced before.

This went beyond mere pain, as all along its body tiny cuts opened up, as if it had swum full bore through razor sharp coral, filling the water with the stink of its own blood.

Terror welled up inside its mind, forcing back the rage. Its fight or flight response screamed that it should flee, but it refused. Its battle with the massive thing needed to end. And there could be only one victor.

The leviathan released its ink into the water, hoping to blind its enemy. Then it attacked without mercy the strange glowing laceration in the massive thing's shell – neither understanding nor caring what it was about to unleash upon the world.

34

"I can't explain it," Cortez said. "It's like the scope just decided to start working again."

"That's a good thing, right?"

"It would be, except the readings from the doppler are going absolutely nuts."

In the next instant, Mitchell called out, "Holy crap. Barometer's going haywire, too."

"All right, everyone, calm down," Andrea commanded. "We all know the equipment is malfunctioning and..."

"Not like this," the DoCC medic interrupted, seeming to not care that he was risking getting bawled out. "The barometer's been working fine. It's old school. But what it's showing me here..."

"Mr. Harkness, if you would please..."

"You ever see the movie *Twister*?"

That caught Andrea by surprise. "Come again."

"All at once the reading dropped below eight hundred millibars, which is ... needless to say, somewhere south of good."

"You mean a tornado?"

"Pretty much. Or maybe a category 8 hurricane."

"There is no category 8," Julie replied from the corner, where she'd been waiting for word from the sub.

"I'm being facetious."

Andrea was tempted to dress him down in front of the rest of the bridge crew. Hell, judging from the expressions a few of them wore, they were expecting it. Protocol needed to be maintained, otherwise respect went out the window, especially for a female holding command. At the same time, this was worrisome even by the standards they'd already established.

Knowing she was risking losing face, she turned back to Cortez. "What's the wind speed?"

"Holding steady at twelve knots."

Not quite hurricane level. "And the doppler?"

Cortez hesitated, as if realizing what he was about to say didn't make any sense. "Um ... it sorta agrees with the barometer. According to what I'm looking at, there's a major event developing and we're sitting right beneath it."

"The distortions maybe?"

"Negative on that," Mitchell said. "I'm not seeing any weight fluctuations or extraneous EMF."

"A residual effect perhaps?" Andrea asked, just as the prow of the ship and the sea beyond lit up through the forward windscreen, giving them a momentary view of the sky above.

Great. Now we've got lightning.

A second passed and there came the rumble of thunder. Yet still nothing but a gentle rain fell.

"Did you see that?" Julie asked from behind her.

"It's just a storm. It's... Hey! Where are you going?"

"Mitch, I need your eyes," Julie replied, heading out the door as more lightning flashed from above.

"Just as long as I get them back." The medic left his post and followed her.

"Return to your station, Mr..."

"Yeah, about that," he called back through the doorway, his head craned upward. "You might want to take a break and come see this."

Andrea gritted her teeth and blew out a frustrated breath. Discipline was rapidly going to hell, and she'd be damned if she was going to let that happen.

"Oh, yeah. You *really* want to see this."

Feeling the eyes of the other crewman turn her way, she strode after Mitchell. Whatever he had to show her had better be damned good, otherwise she was going to chew him so many new assholes that he'd be shitting...

That thought came to a grinding halt as she stepped into the light rain and looked up.

Andrea had expected to see nothing in the night sky but rain and more rain, so she was surprised and, truth be told, somewhat horrified at what she beheld instead. Lightning flashed high above, arcing from cloud to cloud – lighting up the grey sky and revealing something that should have been impossible.

Thunder boomed, drowning out the sound of the bridge crew behind her, but she was far more mesmerized by the clouds above. They were swirling in a clockwise direction – as if this were the eye of some localized hurricane. Yet the weather remained mostly benign, the wind and rain mild at best. More importantly, the ocean was still calm as far as she could tell.

Whatever was going on high above them shouldn't have been possible, not for what could best be described as a light summer storm.

Yet there was no doubt about it. And their equipment – whatever was still working anyway – seemed to back up what her eyes were telling her.

Andrea didn't know what was going on, but her gut screamed that something had recently changed – somehow making an already bad situation infinitely worse.

How? She had no idea, but she wasn't about to stand there doing nothing about it.

Mitchell pulled his gaze away from the spectacle to face her. "See what I mean?"

"Unfortunately, I do." She headed back into the bridge, turning to Novak at comms. "Contact the other ships. Send up smoke signals if you have to. Get them back over here. Moor them to the side if you can, abandon them if that isn't practical, but I want all personnel back on board. *Now.*"

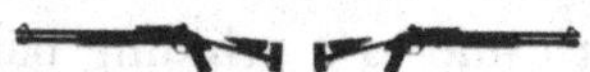

Serena Sanford wasn't a paranoid woman by nature, but she was pretty sure she could feel the eyes of the orderlies following her as she stepped out of Carol's room to grab a cup of coffee.

The doctors had wanted to keep them both for observation following their frantic swim to shore, but Serena had declined. Though still freaked out by their encounter at sea, she'd stepped from the warm ocean relatively unscathed, physically anyway. Carol, on the other hand, had managed to swallow a decent amount of seawater.

That wouldn't have been an issue except that, despite Serena's ardent warning to the contrary, Carol had told the authorities the truth about what had happened.

As awful as she felt about those who'd been far less fortunate than them, Serena was practical at heart. She knew what she'd seen, but she also understood their story was laughable at best – likely to draw the unwanted attention of psychiatric services.

And lo and behold, Carol's otherwise brief stay was now in danger of being extended as they treated her for shock and evaluated her mental state. Serena knew they had a lot to work out in the coming days and months regarding the attack, but she was also wary of the fact that they were both outside the U.S. and fifteen hundred miles from home.

Their honeymoon was over. That much was obvious, but they didn't need the added stress of dealing with a legal and medical system neither of them was familiar with. The only thing Serena wanted at this point was to go home. There they were safe and could deal with this in their own way.

But now that was in jeopardy. After checking herself out, she'd gone straight to Carol's side. By then it had been too late. Ever since, she'd been trying to convince her wife to – not lie, that would be wrong – but to *modify* her story a bit.

Sadly, Carol could be stubborn as a mule when it came to the facts. She saw what she saw, and that was the story she was going to tell.

Serena wasn't optimistic about what would come next. The authorities would either decide she was crazy, ordering more tests, or they would begin to suspect she and Carol had something to do with the sinking.

That was ridiculous, of course, but it could still keep them from going home.

Sadly, the police had been mute on whether any bodies had been recovered. If just one showed signs of being mauled by an ocean predator then maybe this could all be put behind them.

Unfortunately, she'd seen that thing up close. The fact that they'd survived was miracle enough. To hope it had left behind any evidence that would exonerate them, well, that was probably a bit much to expect from the universe.

She stopped outside Carol's room and took a sip from her cup, the bland liquid inside barely qualifying as coffee. So long as it gave her a much needed caffeine boost, though, she'd...

The soft beeping that had been coming from inside the room suddenly grew shrill and became a steady note, sending a wave of terror through Serena.

Oh no. Not that. It has to be coming from another...

At the nearby nursing station, the hospital staff immediately bolted into action, grabbing a crash cart and heading her way.

Despite knowing she should step aside, Serena raced into the room, spilling her forgotten drink.

She only stopped when she saw Carol sitting up, a quizzical look on her face.

"Oh hey, hon," Carol said. "This thing just started going nuts."

The hospital staff were hot on her heels, entering the room just as the lights blinked twice and then went out altogether, along with seemingly all the power in the building.

That wasn't a good sign, but Serena couldn't have cared less in that moment. She stepped to the bed, even as the doctors and nurses scrambled behind her – some racing off to no doubt check on other patients.

She hugged her wife hard, ignoring a nurse who was trying to order her out of the room.

"Don't do that to me, jerk," she whispered in Carol's ear before adding, "Next time, we're going to Scotland like I wanted. No arguments."

Kerry wasn't sure what was going on, other than the weather had turned strange and people were scrambling about on deck.

At first, he was certain they must be after him, but several of the so-called agents passed by without giving him so much as a second look. That was probably fortunate for them, since he'd swapped the minicam for a filet knife he'd found in the unlocked galley.

He'd been contemplating places to hide, knowing his options were limited. His best bet was either down in the hold or maybe the engine room. Problem was, that also put him the furthest from escape once the time came to make his move – whatever that might be.

Something new seemed to be happening, although Kerry didn't know what. Maybe it had to do with those freaky clouds circling overhead. After all, he'd heard that the weather could be strange out at sea.

Regardless, something had these people in a tizzy. It seemed the entire crew was hard at work unloading the two other ships, both of which had been moored alongside them for whatever reason.

Kerry knew a chance when he saw it. The only problem was figuring out how to take advantage of the situation.

He couldn't sail for shit, but he'd been aboard enough powerboats in his time to have a basic idea of how the controls worked. Hell, it wasn't much different than driving a car. He didn't even need to get it perfect. All he needed was to get close enough to shore to radio for help.

True, he had no idea which way shore was, but that's what compasses were for. He wasn't some outdoor survivalist whack job, but he was certain of his ability to figure out which way was north and go from there. Hell, he just needed to get far enough away to radio in an S.O.S.

But first he had to figure out how to get aboard that other vessel, the one that looked like it might've been a fishing boat at some point, without causing...

"Hey, buddy," someone said from behind him, almost causing him to lash out with the knife concealed in his hand.

Fortunately for Kerry, he just barely managed to keep his cool. "Huh? You talking to me?"

"Sorry to startle you. Orders from the boss. We need to unload the institute's boat stat. You mind giving us a hand?"

Kerry grinned back at the man. Despite being wet, scared, and desperate, he realized things might be finally going his way.

35

"I knew it!" Danni cried, taking a deep breath.

The air was cool and crisp, with a slight metallic aftertaste – kind of like what an old air conditioner smelled like after being stored away all winter. So far, though, it seemed more than breathable.

"It doesn't make any sense," Llanzo said, staring up at the open hatch. "Something this old, buried this deep..."

"It's like I told you. Whatever this thing is, it scanned us." Danni found herself glad for all those old science fiction movies Harrison used to make her watch when they were kids. The thought brought a smile with it and, for a moment anyway, it was almost like he was there.

"You know what," Jacob said. "At this point I'm willing to believe just about anything, so long as I'm alive to believe it. Yo, Derek, you going to stand up there sightseeing all day, or let the rest of us out?"

"Hold your horses," he called back. "I'm just making sure breathing isn't the only thing we need to worry about." After a moment, he added, "Oh yeah. There's definitely a piece of our friend in here with us, Doctor. You're going to want to see this."

"You're all crazy to go out there, you know," he retorted, sounding only slightly calmer than he had moments earlier. "We don't know what kind of pathogens could be in the air, or…"

Norah let out a sigh. "That will be enough, Doctor."

"Yeah," Derek said, climbing out. "Besides, if there are, we're already exposed. Speaking of which… Hey, Jake, any chance the Nest has a quarantine protocol in place for situations like this?"

"Situations like this? Not exactly, but we'll figure something out. Worst case, we'll lock ourselves up in that yacht for the trip back and quarantine in style."

"That's the spirit."

"How's it look out there?"

"Come see for yourself. I'm not sure yet whether to be overwhelmed or the opposite."

Jacob was next to climb out of the sub, standing atop it for a moment before making room. "Holy shit. That's one big sucker, ain't it?"

Danni glanced expectantly at Norah, hoping now wasn't the time for her to draw guard duty.

"Go on," the senior agent said. "I can see by the look on your face you're waiting for this. And honestly, if things go south at this point, I doubt being in here will be any safer." She then glanced at Llanzo. "You next, Doctor. I'll bring up the rear."

Danni didn't say anything, but she thought she understood why that was. Dr. Reid was obviously at his wit's end. Leaving him behind would potentially be a mistake, especially if he freaked out and decided to lock himself in.

She hated to see the poor man further traumatized, as he obviously hadn't signed up for anything like this. But there was a small selfish part of her that realized she'd like it a lot less if they got stranded due to leaving him to his own devices.

That said, she kinda wished they'd brought Mitch along instead. He might not have had the fancy credentials, but he wouldn't have blinked twice at the situation around them if it meant a chance to geek out.

Danni climbed out then nimbly slid down the side of the sub to where Derek waited, her shoes making no sound as they alighted on the floor beneath them.

The chamber they were in was cube-shaped, roughly thirty feet on all sides. The walls were a smooth dull grey, similar to how the exterior of the ship had appeared. But there was something strange about them, almost as if...

"Notice the lights?" Derek asked, grinning.

She looked up, not seeing any bulbs or other sources of the illumination keeping the room lit. "I don't see any."

"Exactly. No shadows either. Now take a closer look at the walls, all of them, even the floor."

Danni did as he told her, realizing after a minute or so that they were all the same consistent brightness, even the floor beneath her feet ... dimly illuminating the bluish blood pooling there.

"All of it," Derek confirmed. "Somehow these walls are semi-translucent. The light's coming from everywhere at once, but so uniform that if you look at any one spot it seems opaque."

She watched as he knelt and put his hand just above the floor, seeing just a tiny bit of light around the edges as it was illuminated from below.

"I'm going to assume they don't sell this stuff at IKEA," she replied, unable to help the smile that had crept onto her face. "You realize what this kind of technology implies..."

"I'm trying not to realize anything yet," he was quick to reply. "There's no way I'm ready to jump to any conclusion other than about what tried to yank us out of here."

Danni followed his gaze toward the back of the sub,

where a twenty foot long section of tentacle lay. She took a step toward it, but Derek grabbed her arm.

"Be careful. It's still twitching. Wouldn't want to get too close and have it reflexively wrap around you like an anaconda." He looked up to where Jacob was guiding Llanzo out of the minisub. "No Sir Mix-a-Lot jokes from the peanut gallery."

"I'm not commenting on your buns," the other agent replied, next helping Norah from the craft.

"Glad to hear it," she said, easing herself down the side where Danni waited to help her. "Thank you, Agent Kent."

"My pleasure."

"Incredible," Llanzo said, moving to examine the tentacle fragment despite Derek's warning.

Guess there's a bit of Mitch in him after all, Danni thought, glad to see his panic subsumed by curiosity, at least for the moment. How long that would last, well, that would probably depend on...

The floor suddenly rumbled beneath them, enough to rattle the minisub. Then it went dark, the illumination around them cutting out all at once.

Talk about weird. Normally when the lights in a house went out there was that moment when the bulbs dimmed. But here, Danni noted, it was instantaneous – illumination from all around, then nothing but pitch blackness.

Fortunately, it didn't last. The walls flashed bright red for a second or two, before once again settling down to a uniform grey.

Danni waited a moment to see if it would happen again. "Did we do that?"

"If we did," Jacob said. "Don't do it again."

"I don't think that was us," Derek replied. "I mean, I've put on a few pounds over the years, but not enough to shake the rafters here." He looked around, as if thinking it over. "No. Don't forget, our friend is probably still out there. And considering this place took a chunk out of him, I doubt he's in a good mood."

"I-I'm forced to concur," Llanzo said. "It's too early for conclusions, but based on both this sample and what we saw out there, there's little doubt in my mind that this creature dwarfs the specimen we caught earlier."

Jacob turned to his friend. "Is this the part where you say I told you so?"

"Maybe we'll save it for the afterparty," Derek replied, just as the floor shuddered beneath them again, once more causing the lighting to briefly flash red.

For a split second, Danni felt her feet leave the floor, her stomach lurching as she lifted up perhaps half an inch before hitting the ground again. Her landing was echoed by a heavy *thunk* as the sub settled as well. "What the hell was that?"

Derek looked at her wide-eyed, an expression of confusion on his face that she hadn't often seen. "Is it just me, or did the gravity turn off for a second there?"

"How does gravity just turn off?" Norah asked.

"Wish I knew, but at least we can rest easy knowing this place is *definitely* ground zero. Wait. Hold on a sec." Derek scrambled back up the side of the sub and into the opening, reappearing several seconds later with two objects in his hand. One was the EMF detector he'd left behind. The other appeared to be a flashlight. "Hope you don't mind me borrowing this," he said to Jacob. "We might need it if the lights go out again."

"Just remember, you break it, your department bought it."

Derek ignored the comment as he started fiddling with the detector. Danni stepped in to look over his shoulder as it started to whine, the needle burying itself in the red.

"So now we're trapped *and* you're trying to annoy us to death," Jacob remarked.

Norah, however, was far more to the point. "What are you doing?"

"Just give it a few," Derek replied, turning the volume down. The needle, however, stayed buried. "Readings holding steady just like in the sub. Whatever's going on in here, there's a lot of it."

"Isn't it unhealthy to be bathed in that much EMF?" Danni asked.

Derek nodded. "Yeah, but I doubt it's any less healthy than the other effects we noticed up top. Just be thankful none of us have ended up weighing five tons."

"What if that's not an accident? If this place can control gravity, then maybe that's part of what it scanned us for."

"You do realize we have no proof that's what actually..."

The room shuddered again, leaving little doubt in Danni's mind that the massive creature outside was continuing to vent its displeasure. Once more, the lighting dimmed and she felt disturbingly light on her feet.

Before she could voice as much, though, Derek cried, "Look!"

She followed the beam of his flashlight to where it shone on the meter, the readings on the device dropping off to barely anything. "Holy shit. Um ... sorry."

"Forget it. Took the words right out of my mouth."

A few moments later, normalcy resumed – if such a thing could be said of this strange place. As it did, the needle on the detector once more shot to the far edge of the screen.

"What does it mean?"

"I have no freaking idea," Derek replied. "But I have a feeling it's not good."

Norah shook her head. "Please feel free to share. It's not like our day can get much worse."

"You forget who you're talking to here," Jake commented.

Derek explained what they'd observed during the ... *outage,* for lack of a better term, the confusion on the faces of all present more than evident. When he was done, the room lapsed into silence, until he broke it by saying, "You know, the more I think about it, the more Dr. Reid's theory makes sense."

"My theory?" the scientist replied. "I didn't..."

"Call it a guess then. I mean what you said about this place and how it's maybe meant to contain all of that stuff that's been going on. The high but consistent readings since we got here seem to bear that out, as well as the fact that we haven't felt any distortions."

"Are we talking about the same thing here?" Jake asked. "Because didn't your transistor radio there go haywire about the same time my ass decided it wanted to fly?"

"That's the not good part," Derek replied. "I have a feeling something changed in the last few minutes, and I'm willing to bet our large friend outside is responsible."

Norah raised an eyebrow. "You think it might have damaged this place?"

"More like damaged it worse than it already was, but yeah ... maybe. It's too soon to know for sure. For now, the readings are back to, well, what seems to be normal for this place."

"Interesting choice of words."

"Best I can do on short notice. The point is, whatever's *regulating* this place seems to be functioning again. The problem is when the lights start blinking..."

"And everything goes crazy," Danni added.

"For us, yes. But I'm worried that's only half the problem."

"What?" Jacob replied. "Are you afraid we're going to float away and not come back down?"

"Maybe. Who knows? I meant what's going on out there. We didn't feel the distortions in here at first, but we know they're going on outside. Now that's changed, and it makes me wonder..."

"That maybe this place had a slow leak when we found it," Norah surmised, "that's now a much larger leak?"

"Something like that."

"Hold on," Jacob said. "Are you saying things might be even worse out there now?"

"I'm not sure there's much doubt of that," Derek replied. "Even if I'm wrong about all of this stuff, there's still a hell of an octopus problem. Am I right, Doctor?"

Llanzo seemed hesitant to answer for a moment, still staring at the tentacle fragment at the rear of the sub. "I-I'm forced to concur. The creature that attacked the Rogers Will-Do was a magnificent specimen ... terrifying as well, if we're being honest. But I'm convinced it's nothing compared to what's out there now."

Derek nodded, although he didn't seem happy to be right.

"So what do we do about it?" Norah asked.

Derek paused as if he were about to say something he knew the others wouldn't like.

Danni, however, had a feeling what that was, and she couldn't help but feel a smidgeon of excitement at the prospect.

"We need to figure out a way to escape and make contact with the surface," he finally said. "Which means it's time for us to get off our asses and do some exploring."

36

It was near perfect. Kerry helped unload some piece of equipment, a box with a screen on it. After that, it was almost like he became invisible among the small contingent of people unloading the research vessel.

They were so busy scrambling that nobody questioned when he headed below deck, pretending to look for some non-existent piece of junk in need of moving. He kept at the ruse, searching through drawers and cupboards, making his way further in, even as the stream of workers slowed.

Once the trickle finally slowed to nothing, Kerry hunkered down as deep as he could go – a storage locker near the front, two levels below deck, as he listened for the sweet sound of silence.

He clutched the stolen knife tightly as he waited, hoping against hope that nobody put two and two together. If so, he'd be as good as dead.

As the minutes stretched on, though, another fear began to settle into his gut. He had no idea why they'd been in such a rush to transfer all that equipment off this ship. Hell, he wasn't even sure what most of it was for. What if they'd been stripping it for parts, leaving it unusable?

Worse, what if it was done with the intention of scuttling it for whatever reason? Kerry wasn't sure why they'd do such a thing, but trying to think like a criminal was still new to him. Who was to say what their diabolical motivations were?

What if they purposely lured me on board?

The idea sounded ludicrous, even to his panicked mind. They were in the middle of the ocean. If they wanted him dead, they could have tied him to an anchor and simply tossed him overboard, certain that he'd never be found.

However, logic had no home in the mind of one certain of his own conspiracy theories.

The fear of finding himself on a sinking ship, trapped with no escape, was too much. Claustrophobia set in and soon he could barely breathe, certain that any moment he'd be underwater with no hope of survival.

Unable to take it anymore, Kerry slid out of the locker and looked around. All seemed to be dark and quiet aboard the vessel, save for the lap of water against the side. Maybe it wasn't too late.

He began to feel his way back toward the stairs, passing recently emptied rows of shelves as he...

The darkness of the cabin was erased for a moment as a flash of lightning shone through the portholes, nearly causing Kerry to cry out before he was able to clamp a hand over his mouth.

Thunder rumbled outside and he admonished himself for almost stupidly giving away his location. But then, a mere moment later, he paused again, certain he'd heard a sound from above.

Probably just the weather.

As Kerry opened the swinging doors leading to the upper cabin, though, a beam of light landed upon him from the darkness ahead.

"Who's there?" a harsh voice barked.

Oh shit! Think fast! "Um, it's just me. I was looking for the..." *What's something they have on a boat?* "The last piece of the ... sonar."

Kerry was certain he'd be called on his obvious lie, but instead the flashlight beam was lowered to the ground.

"Sorry. You scared me for a second. Thought everyone had gotten off. I was just doing one more sweep to make sure everything was clear."

"No worries," Kerry replied, feigning calmness as he took a step forward.

"Find what you were looking for?"

"It wasn't down there. I was coming up to take one more look around. It shouldn't take more than a few..."

"Don't worry about it," the man replied. "I think we got all the important stuff. If Vakovsky doesn't like it, he can come look for it himself."

"Are you sure, Mr. ... I mean, Agent..."

"Kyle."

"Nice to ... um ... meet you," Kerry said. "But the person on the bridge..." *What was her name?!*

"McAvee?"

"Yeah, that's her. She told me she needed it."

"Must be old orders. Things are getting strange topside. Last I heard, she wanted all hands back aboard the Nest."

Damn it! Kerry realized his window of opportunity was slipping. "Just two more minutes. I'm pretty sure it's around here somewhere."

Kyle, whether that was his first name or last, let out a sigh and for a moment Kerry was certain he'd be called out, but then he said, "Fine. Two minutes. I'll help you look."

"It's really not a big..."

"Come on," he said, leading the way and leaving his back turned. "I think I saw some boxes just past the galley."

The next few moments were a blur. Kerry wasn't even sure what he was going to do until he acted. Before the rational part of his mind could persuade him otherwise, he pounced, plunging the knife into the other man's back again and again, refusing to stop until the air stank with the smell of spilled blood and ruptured viscera.

"Report."

"Almost finished securing the other vessels, ma'am."

"Good," Andrea replied. "I want a full headcount once that's done. Make sure everyone is accounted for."

"Roger that."

She took a moment to catch her breath, surveying the bridge. It was the best she could hope for, keeping everyone busy for now.

"Well, this is weird," an annoyingly familiar voice opined.

So much for hoping for the best. She turned to where Mitchell was still busy taking readings from his jerry-rigged station. "We've been living at the corner of weird and abnormal for the last day. I hate to ask, but what now?"

"I'm not really sure, but ever since the cyclone o'doom started forming above us I've..."

"Can we not call it that?"

"Fine. Ever since the cyclone of happiness and unicorns appeared, I've been keeping an even closer eye on things. Not to be a negative Nancy, but I figured it was a sign that stuff was about to go even more cray cray."

"And your findings?" Andrea replied with barely contained annoyance, certain her day was about to get even worse than it already was.

"Zilch. And I do mean nothing. In fact, nearest I can tell, there hasn't been a disruption since the sky started getting all swirly." He picked up his EMF reader and showed her the screen. "See? Nothing. No abnormalities, no fluctuations in weight, and time seems to be working again."

"Okay, so that's a good thing, right? Maybe they found the issue down below and fixed it."

"I don't think we're dealing with a leaky pipe here." Michell turned toward one of the other stations. "Hey, Cortez. How's radar looking?"

The agent glanced once at Andrea as if seeking her approval. When she nodded he replied, "Good but not good. I mean, the scope seems to be working, but I've never seen anything like what's on it."

"Sonar?" she asked.

"Tracking a pretty big ghost right now," the agent monitoring it replied.

"Guess it's not *that* normal."

"Hold on," Mitchell said. "Has there been any chatter on the radio?"

"If you mean the sub..."

"No. I mean ship to shore, civilian chatter."

"Nothing but white noise," Novak replied.

"Hmm. Actually, maybe that's not too surprising."

"And why's that?" Andrea asked him.

"I don't know. Call it a hunch. Things have suddenly started working for us again, but I have to think whatever's above us is doing *something* ... and my gut says that something isn't good. Maybe it's like a..."

"Like a what?"

"Hold that thought. Let me try something first." Mitchell pulled a backpack from beneath his station and started rooting through it. "All right, where is it?"

"Where is what?" Andrea's patience was wearing thin. "We don't have time for games..."

"Ah, here we go!" The medic pulled out a satnav phone and turned it on. "We're only supposed to use this for official business, but since my boss is twenty thousand leagues under the sea..."

"I'm not sure I see the point here."

"And ... I actually have a signal." He met her gaze. "When I last tried it a couple hours ago, I got nothing. Zero bars. It was like we were trapped in a faraday cage. But now, check it out. Maybe we can actually find out what's going on in the outside world."

Andrea was about to tell him to get to the goddamned point, but as he tuned in to a staticky news report, she hesitated. "Turn that up, please."

"Widespread power outages throughout the Keys and as far north as Miami..."

"A second passenger plane has gone down, this time in the Gulf headed toward New Orleans, and reports are coming in that a third has gone missing from radar..."

"Officials in Cuba are blaming the U.S. for what they're calling electronic warfare..."

"We're receiving reports that cell service is down across the southeastern United States for all major carriers..."

"Witnesses described a series of lights in the sky..."

After several long minutes, Mitchell finally put the phone down, turning off the seemingly nonstop litany of strange occurrences throughout the Gulf region. "It's as I thought."

Whatever annoyance Andrea felt at him had melted

away upon hearing the news, so she merely replied, "What is?"

"That thing above us. I think it's some kind of storm, but not the wind and rain variety. We're right beneath it, stuck in the eye so to speak, which I think means we have a limited space here where stuff is almost back to normal. Outside of that, though..."

"How bad is it?"

"No idea, but the pessimist in me says that anyone who steps foot from our small oasis here is gonna get hammered by all the weirdness we experienced earlier, except a lot worse."

"How much worse?"

"I can't begin to..." The medic's eyes suddenly opened wide. "Shit!" He turned from her and marched over to the sonar array. "Quick. Show me."

Andrea normally would have chewed him out, but what she'd heard had left her shaken. He had to be wrong, had to be. However, she found herself joining him at the sonar nevertheless. "You heard the man, Novak. What's going on?"

"It's still out of whack," he replied, pointing toward a massive reading on the screen. "No sign of the sub. I've just been looking at the same ghost for the last hour."

"The last hour," Mitchell repeated. "As in..."

"When that storm started forming above us," Andrea finished.

"That's not good." The medic turned to face her. "I don't want to cause a panic. But I think we should consider the very real possibility that we're not looking at a ghost here."

Julie stared out over the ocean. The rain had finally stopped, but that didn't make her feel any better as yet another bolt of lightning streaked across the sky, momentarily illuminating everything as far as the eye could see.

"Where the hell are you?" she muttered to herself, continuing to make her way around the deck, an M4 slung over her back.

Though Julie was certain it was mostly to get her out of her hair, McAvee had finally relented and assigned some of her agents to keep watch for signs of anything strange in the water.

Six in total, one at both the prow and stern, and two spread out on both sides, all while Julie acted as a floater – walking the perimeter and checking in with them all.

It was nice to have something to do, something to focus on, even if so far they'd seen a whole lot of nothing.

It actually wasn't all that much different than filming the show. Bottom line – night stakeouts could really suck. Hours upon hours of searching and waiting, with no guarantee that anything would happen. She remembered one such hunt about two months back. As the junior member of the team, she'd pulled *nest duty*. They'd found a spot where the rogue Sasquatch they'd been searching for had recently bedded down. She'd sprayed herself with descenting agent then settled into the cold muddy hollow for six long hours of nothing.

It could be boring as hell, but it was also necessary. The second you lowered your guard something bad could, and likely would, happen. That's why she kept checking on the people McAvee had assigned her, to make sure they continued taking this seriously.

For a while, it was chaos on deck as the vast majority of the crew scrambled to secure the other two ships. But now that was finished, and those agents had all gone below deck — some to other duties and some no doubt seeking a bit of downtime.

There would be no rest for her, though, at least not until the minisub returned. Her gut was telling her something was out there. She'd learned to trust it as a reporter, and her work with the team these last few months had helped hone that instinct even further.

That still didn't make *nest duty* any more exciting.

"Anything going on?" she asked the next agent in the rotation, a tall dark-skinned woman by the name of Simmons.

"Just a lot of ocean. That freaky lightning isn't helping things. I'm surprised we're not all jumping at shadows."

"I hear you," Julie replied. "I'll check in with the bridge to see when you guys can get some relief."

"They'll probably find you first."

"Oh?"

"Mac's taking a headcount, making sure everyone is here who should be. Sent Caldwell to do it."

"I'll keep an eye out for him," Julie said as she continued walking the deck.

She neared the spot where the Rogers Will-Do was moored to the side, slowing down for a moment and taking in the damage still visible on the stern of the ship.

It wasn't the most terrified she'd ever been in her life. No, that honor still fell to those damned Lesterfields. However, this assignment made her consider that it might be a while before she complained about dark forests again. There was something about being on the water that made her feel a lot more vulnerable, as if she was trespassing upon a place she didn't belong.

Too bad I can't grow a set of gills. Julie started walking again just as another flash of lightning lit up the surrounding waters.

She blinked for a moment, certain she'd seen movement aboard the other vessel, near the pilot house. Julie was about to shine her flashlight in that direction, but as the darkness reasserted itself she remembered what Simmons had said about jumping at shadows.

I'll probably be seeing mermaids and two-headed sharks before this night is over.

Thunder boomed from above as she continued making her circuit, sounding loud and menacing, even if the current weather was still mild.

On and on it went, booming as if some great giant were preparing for battle. After several long seconds, though, Julie realized what she was hearing was no longer thunder. It was the rumble of powerful engines revving up.

She turned back and, sure enough, it was coming from the Rogers Will-Do. Her eyes hadn't been playing tricks at all. There was definitely someone on board.

Still, her response was more curiosity than suspicion. McAvee had probably just sent someone aboard to run the bilge pumps or something.

There came another flash from above, confirming movement near the wheelhouse. But that wasn't the only thing that caught Julie's eye in the brief moment of illumination. Lifting her flashlight, she shone it toward the side of the other vessel.

What the hell happened to the mooring lines?

Before she could question what she was seeing, the Will-Do's engines roared to life at full power. A wake kicked up behind the science vessel as whoever was aboard began to steer it away from the Nest.

Julie's first instinct was to launch herself over the cutter's side and onto the smaller ship, to see what was going on.

In the next instant, though, she was glad she hadn't. That was the sort of thing that only worked in the movies.

All she'd have done was likely landed herself in the drink, assuming she didn't crack her skull first.

Instead, she turned back toward the bridge. Hopefully McAvee would simply tell her this was part of some new strategy she'd come up with. But deep in her gut, Julie didn't think that was the case.

Glancing back over her shoulder at where the Rogers Will-Do was starting to pick up speed, something about this just didn't feel right.

Hell, nothing about this mission period felt right.

37

Vernon Vasquez was no stranger to night fishing. He enjoyed the peace of lighting up a cigarette and relaxing as he cast out a line. Though his grandson had warned him they weren't supposed to venture out onto the water, he'd paid it little heed. His trusty sixteen foot outboard was well maintained. He wasn't going far, and the weather called for nothing more than light rain. Worst case, he had a paddle on board and the exercise would do his heart good.

He'd brought his radio along, hoping to listen to some music as he fished, but he soon turned it off. The local stations were mostly static tonight, and the few bits he was able to pick up were all news reports. He'd heard about that plane crash earlier, so that's likely what they were all still chattering about, but Vernon had no interest in bringing his mood down. That was fifty miles to the west and of no concern to him.

He was far more focused on coming home with a few sea bass for tomorrow's dinner. Vernon wasn't shy of telling anyone who asked that his wife Cecilia was the best cook on the island, having run a small seaside bistro for the last twenty years. What she served to her customers, though, was nothing compared to what she could do for family.

It was no wonder he'd put on at least thirty pounds over the course of their marriage, despite remaining active well into his sixties.

Vernon cast out his line then lit a smoke, knowing he might be there for a while but not caring much. He leaned back and looked up at the sky. The rain had finally slaked, but there wasn't much to see. He sometimes liked to pass the hours star-gazing, but on a night like this such a thing was...

Huh?

The sky above briefly became visible as what appeared to be a bolt of purplish lightning flashed through the clouds.

He'd seen a lot of strange things during his years, most of them while out at sea — a water spout, a tiger shark longer than his boat, and even one time what he was sure must've been a giant squid. Purple lightning was a new one, though.

He sat up, hoping to see it again, and was taken aback to find that a low fog had set in at some point during the last few minutes. Not only that, but there was a strange smell in the air, the clean ocean scent replaced by something more brackish.

Vernon glanced down at his wristwatch, thinking he'd accidentally nodded off. Wouldn't be the first time the tide had lulled him to sleep and probably wouldn't be the last. Of course, that meant Cecilia would likely be waiting up to tan his hide good when he...

Son of a... That was strange. His watch had stopped. He knew for a fact he'd wound it before coming out. It was part of his routine. The watch itself was old but still reliable, a Timex he'd been gifted the year his son Miguel had been born.

He was distraught to find it broken after so many years, but hopefully it was something minor that could be easily...

There came a splash from somewhere off the bow. Then the float on his line submerged. Forgetting the time-piece for the moment, he grabbed hold of his fishing rod just as the reel began to spin, the line racing out far faster than it should have.

Oh great. Another one.

About four years back, a sailfish had snagged his bait, nearly capsizing his boat before he'd decided to cut his losses and the line with it. It had made a run similar to what he was seeing now.

He waited for it to slow down, so as to nudge it to the surface and know for certain, but the line kept going. No way was this a sea bass.

All right, pendejo. You want a fight?

He braced his feet, preparing to put his back into it, but then let out a cry as he found himself whipped forward, the rod dragged out of his hands and right over the side ... almost taking him with it.

Vernon let out a nervous laugh as he pushed himself back up. That had been his favorite rod, but it thankfully wasn't his only one. And he'd sooner have lost it than find himself pulled overboard in the strange fog that had descended. It was odd, rising no more than a foot above the water, making it seem as if he were fishing atop a cloud – more like something he'd expect to see in a swamp than out on the water on a night like this.

As far as the eye could see, it was like he was adrift in a sea of cotton – the moonlight illuminating the strange mist, making it seem almost...

Wait, moonlight?

Gazing upward again, Vernon's breath caught in his throat. Gone were the clouds, giving him a full view of the night sky and the stars above, along with the nearly full moon hanging low on the horizon.

That wasn't possible, though. The moon was currently waning, a quarter crescent at best. It wasn't supposed to be this full for weeks. There was no way it could...

Another splash, this one from off the port side, caught his attention. Vernon turned his head just as something breached the water, catching a quick glimpse of something before it submerged again.

Whatever it was, it had been massive, dwarfing his small boat – which was feeling smaller by the second. Big as it was, it had been like no whale he'd ever seen in these waters – with some kind of serrated frill running along its back. Disturbingly enough, it reminded him of those *Jurassic Park* movies his grandchildren had insisted he watch with them.

Vernon could only remember being spooked a handful of times while out on the water, but nothing like this. Terror leapt into his heart as he abandoned all thoughts of fishing and moved to start his outboard motor ... just as there came the sound of more splashing from around him.

The fight with the fish had turned the small boat around, so he looked down at his compass to get his bearings, finding the arrow spinning uncontrollably.

Madre de Dios, what's going on?

Suppressing the fear that wanted to take hold, he turned his head skyward. If his compass didn't want to work, there were always the stars.

Regardless, as the boat began to move through the misty waters, Vernon had a bad feeling in his gut. Though he was calling it an early night, he was somehow certain the journey back home would prove to be far longer than he could ever imagine.

Goddamn it! Knew I should have waited.

Maureen Hennesy had made this run dozens of times, some of it in far worse weather. But this was the first time she'd gotten a warning midair that flights were being grounded. She was too far out from Turks and Caicos to turn around, so the tower had informed her that, rather than let her finish her run to Orlando, she was being rerouted to Grand Bahamas Airport.

"What a pain in the ass," she'd muttered once she'd acknowledged the new route, which had taken her at least three tries due to all the goddamned static.

She was a modestly successful real estate agent during the week, but on the weekends she indulged her passion – flying – earning some extra cash giving island tours. It was a near perfect setup as far as she was concerned. And, with a down housing market as well as having recently broken up with her longtime partner, she now had extra time to devote to it.

Hell, she was even considering packing up her day job and moving down to the islands full time. She'd already made plenty of contacts down there, and it didn't hurt that she'd befriended a great mechanic – helping set up his daughter with a sweet deal on a condo over in Fort Lauderdale. That alone had made sure she could skip the line whenever her Cessna needed maintenance.

Maureen tried radioing the tower again, despite knowing it was pointless to argue. The decision had been made. They weren't going to rethink it simply because she wanted to sleep in her own bed tonight. Nor did she expect them to.

Two commercial plane crashes in one day was definitely something to be concerned about. It was just her luck the second had happened while she was already in the air. Though the reports from earlier had pointed toward mechanical failure, an unfortunate accident, there was little doubt that speculation would shift now that another had gone down.

Though she personally doubted that any terrorist groups had suddenly decided to target the Caribbean, she knew that flights would likely be grounded until they could rule such a thing out.

That almost certainly meant she was looking at more than a couple hour layover, not ideal as she was supposed to be showing houses tomorrow to an elderly couple looking to retire. She could always reschedule, but not if she didn't know how long she was going to be stranded. And being grounded, it's not like she could make up the lost revenue in tours.

Rather than connect to the tower, the radio began to whine – uncomfortably loud, until she cut it off.

"What the hell?"

The answer to her rhetorical question came not from the radio, but from the air around her as the plane started to shudder – right as a bolt of lightning flashed from somewhere ahead of her, lighting up the ominous sky.

That can't be right. She'd been flying through light cloud cover just minutes earlier, but now there was a thick blanket of thunderheads forming around her.

Warning lights lit up on her console and she looked down to find her instruments going crazy.

The fuck?!

The altimeter alone was fluctuating wildly. One minute it was telling her she was thirteen thousand feet in the air. The next, it was reading below sea level.

Maybe Diego isn't such a hot mechanic after all.

Before she could make any sense of this, the clouds in front of her began to swirl, almost forming a tunnel in the air, one lined with pure electricity.

Shit! "Mayday!" she cried into the radio. "This is Cessna N74955. Repeat this is Cessna N74955. I'm flying blind, en route to Grand Bahamas. Please respond."

Nothing but more harsh static met her entreaties, and then that too disappeared as the lights in the cabin all went out at once.

Oh no.

A moment later the engine stalled as well.

Panic reared its ugly head but Maureen forced it back down. That was the last thing she needed. Panic got people killed in situations like these.

She'd suffered a midair stall once before, but it hadn't been like this. She wasn't getting a response from any of her systems. It was like the battery died, along with everything else, taking all backup systems with it, including navigation.

Though she began mentally calculating how far out she was from the airport, trying to figure out if she could glide the rest of the way, a part of her realized that was simply busy work to keep her mind occupied as the plane began to nose downward, buffeted by the freak storm around her.

Dark clouds and strange colored lightning were all she saw as the plane began an uncontrolled descent.

Maureen desperately worked the controls, trying to get some power, anything back into the system, but it was more like flying a bathtub than an airplane. The yoke might as well have been encased in concrete for all the response she got from it.

The plane broke through the cloud cover, somehow managing to not get struck by the freak lightning, and then she was in freefall. One last bolt from above illuminated the air around her, giving her at least an idea how long she had until she slammed into the water. As far as Maureen could tell, she'd eaten up at least half her altitude and was rapidly running out of options.

Then, just as she was about to make peace with the fact that she wouldn't be making her appointment with the Feinbergs tomorrow or ever, her console lit up again and the propeller roared back to life.

Maureen didn't question how or why. There wasn't time. Not daring to look at the altimeter in case it told her it was a futile effort, she pulled back on the yoke, adjusted her flight speed, and said a quick prayer.

The plane's engine whined from the strain, threatening to stall again, but finally she began to pull up from the dive.

"Come on. Hold together for mama."

There came a crackle in her ear, then she heard, "Unidentified aircraft, please respond."

"This is Cessna N74955. Mayday! I'm having engine problems. I just pulled out of a stall. Power is back on, but everything unexpectedly cut off ... and I mean everything!"

"Cessna N74955?" There came a pause. "We don't have you on our flight logs. You were supposed to be rerouted to Grand Bahamas."

"That's where I'm headed."

"Cessna N74955, this is the tower at Miami International. We have you on our scope ten miles out and closing."

What?! "That isn't possible, Miami. I'm still eighty miles from Andros."

"Negative, Cessna N74955. We have you on our scope ... now anyway."

"What do you mean by that?"

"You ... I can't believe I'm saying this ... but you just appeared out of nowhere. Maintain course and heading."

"But..."

"You're our bird now. Lock your transponder to..."

Maureen followed the tower's orders, her hands working almost separately from her mind as she tried to process this.

She checked the clock to make sure she hadn't gone crazy, but it seemed to confirm what her senses were telling her. Somehow she'd overshot her mark by almost a hundred and fifty miles, all in the space of a few minutes.

There was little doubt there were going to be a lot of questions waiting for her once she got to Miami, probably not a few of them from the air marshals.

It was likewise going to take some time before she even remotely came to grips on what had just happened.

On the upside, she considered, though she might not make it back to her own bed this night, she at least had a chance of making her appointment tomorrow.

Emilia Carnesworth sat in the small rental cabin in Big Pine Key, grading papers next to a desk lamp, the sole source of light in the room.

Though she was technically on vacation, using up a few weeks of the accumulated PTO she'd acquired over the years as a vice principal in rural Pennsylvania, she wasn't spending the time idly.

She knew herself too well for that. Though she could easily occupy her days hiking, canoeing, or exploring the numerous trails that crisscrossed the area, she preferred the safety of the indoors once the sun went down. However, she'd never been one for TV, and had finished the latest

Nora Roberts book while still waiting at the airport for her flight.

Fortunately, she'd made plenty of contacts over the years, calling in a favor to secure a short term TA project for an online university. She didn't really need the money, but it kept her mind fresh and made the nighttime hours seem to pass by more quickly.

Noting the time, she took a quick break to glance over at the Ruger Super Blackhawk sitting next to her laptop, reassuring herself it was within reach. It was a large gun, almost comically so compared to her four foot nine frame, but it was also a welcome friend these days.

Though she was an academic by trade, she'd grown up in a household of hunters. Her father had taken her four older brothers out hunting ever since they'd been old enough to carry a rifle, and he'd seen no reason to break that tradition once she came along. She'd been a crack shot most of her life, even if the students she saw day in and day out hadn't realized it – at least until recently.

That had all changed the prior summer when her beloved town had nearly been overrun by... She shook her head and pushed the unpleasant memory away, lest it bring even worse thoughts. That was the real problem, as well as the reason she'd finally given in to the school board's pressure to use up some of her accumulated vacation.

Though she clearly remembered the rogue biker gang riding in to town, hellbent on causing chaos, it was always different in her dreams. She'd relive the siege, clear as day in her mind's eye, but bikers weren't the cause. It was always the same, impossible as it sounded – dark beasts, possessing fangs and claws, tearing her fellow townsfolk to shreds as she fired off shot after shot trying to stop them.

Regardless of dream or reality, she'd done what she could that night to defend her home.

Emelia had long known about the nickname the kids used whenever they thought she wasn't listening – Carnivoreworth, but in the months since the attack there had been an undercurrent of respect to their voices, something she still wasn't sure whether to appreciate or nip in the...

The desk lamp next to her went dark, pulling her from her reverie. A moment later, her laptop chirped, letting her know it was now running off battery power.

Hmm.

The light switch next to the door proved equally dead, so Emilia next stepped to the window. Further down the lake, she spied a few flashlight beams, but no other lights in any of the other cabins.

"Great. Guess the power's out."

She shrugged and turned back toward the desk, trying to convince herself it was no big deal. She had at least three hours' worth of charge on the laptop, more than she needed to finish. Worst case, she could drive into town tomorrow and find a place with working WiFi to load it up to the shared drive.

But as she sat down again, her laptop screen did something she'd never seen before. It began to flicker, the picture growing distorted and wavy, almost like an old cathode ray TV with a bad signal.

"What now?"

Had one of the students uploaded a virus along with their work? She was pretty obsessive about that sort of thing, but she also knew not to underestimate the stupidity of kids, even college aged ones.

A flash from outside caught her attention. Emilia's first thought was the power must be coming back on. Her second was that maybe one of the other campers was coming to check on her. Regardless, she felt her hand creeping toward her weapon as other, less pleasant thoughts filled her head. She saw another flash of light and let out the breath she wasn't aware she'd been holding. It was nothing more than lightning, even though she hadn't seen mention of any storms in the forecast.

Oh well, this is Florida after all.

A boom of thunder sounded from above, rumbling through the small cabin for a few seconds. But, as it dissipated another sound could be heard, one far more alien than mere bad weather.

What the?

Grabbing hold of the Ruger, she stepped to the cabin door and opened it, letting in the damp night air. The humidity was quickly forgotten, though, as the sounds intensified – hoots, hollers, and screams – like something out of a nightmare zoo. All of them seeming to come from the surrounding woods.

Her rational mind insisted it had to be someone having a laugh, but deep down a part of her knew better. Whatever was out there didn't sound human, a crazy thought if ever there was one.

Then another sound caught her ear, the hollow echo of wood knocking against wood from all around, growing louder as long minutes passed, almost as if the strange lightning had awoken something deep in the swampy woodlands – something that now seemed to be headed her way.

The hairs on the back of her neck stood on end as her fight or flight response spurred to life. She could almost feel it in the air – a heaviness that hadn't been there earlier, as if the lightning were electrifying the night sky.

A part of her insisted that she should leave, hop into her rented Jeep and bug out, but she quickly silenced that voice. It would be too slow going in the dark, through narrow roads boxed in by forest on either side – no big deal if she was wrong. But if her instincts were right...

She turned and headed back into the cabin. There was

a high powered flashlight in the kitchen and a full box of ammo waiting in her suitcase.

Whatever was coming, she intended to stand her ground and meet it head on, just as she'd done once before – while defending her home, the small town of High Moon.

38

Well, that was easy.

Derek hadn't been even remotely certain how to proceed. Despite his big words about finding a way to make contact with the surface, he was well aware they were stuck in the equivalent of a locked bank vault. Sure, it had let them in, but there had been no obvious signs as to how to make it let them out again.

Nevertheless, it was painfully obvious that this room represented a tiny fraction of the massive vessel they were now inside. Yes, it was possible the rest was flooded or in some other ways inaccessible, but he found himself unwilling to believe that. Though there was no way of knowing how long this thing had sat at the bottom of the ocean, the fact that this chamber seemed to be working told him more of it had to be.

The problem was figuring out how to access it, as the strange light emitting walls around them all seemed solid.

Derek had been prepared for a lot of poking, prodding, and experimentation. He'd been less prepared when Danni had checked the wall opposite the one they'd entered from, only for a four-way seam to suddenly appear in it. A moment later, that section of wall retracted into the rest, creating an opening roughly four feet wide by eight feet high.

"Um, I meant to do that," she said, stepping back.

Beyond lay a hallway of roughly the same dimensions. It trailed off into the darkness, perhaps the first forty feet or so lit by that strange uniform illumination before becoming pitch black.

"Is that going to light up as we walk toward it, or would that be too cliché to hope for?" Danni asked.

"I'm more interested in whether or not the size of this doorway is representative of whatever called this place home."

"You can't possibly be thinking of going out there," Llanzo said, pulling himself away from his examination of the tentacle fragment.

"I'm not sure we have much choice, Doctor," Derek replied, before turning to their other companions. "Norah?"

She sighed and gave her head a shake. "Knew I should've stayed in my office. This is officially your expedition now. Lead the way."

"Stow that thought," Jacob said. "It may be his expedition, but it's not *yours*."

"Excuse me?"

"Just give me a minute." He scrambled up the side of the sub and disappeared into the hatch.

"I really hope he's not popping in there for a pee break," Derek remarked, drawing a snicker from Danni, "because we still need it to get back home."

"Better to be pissed off than pissed on," Jacob called back, climbing out a minute or so later. He had a heavy looking backpack with him. "A little something I had stashed in the hold. Pays to be prepared."

"I'm assuming that's not an overnight bag," Norah said.

"You bet your sweet ass," he replied, drawing a glare from her. "That's going into your report when we get back, isn't it?"

"Still to be determined. So what exactly did you mean about this not being our expedition?"

"I said you, as in singular. I think you should stay put, keep a handle on things. We can use this room as our home base."

"I don't know what kind of macho bullshit this is, but..."

"Now that's definitely going in *my* report," he replied, before quickly holding his hands up. "Relax. It's nothing of the sort, Nor. We need somewhere we can regroup and, if necessary, bug out quickly. This is as good a place as any, especially since that sub ain't fitting through the door. But we also need someone here to coordinate while the rest of us try to figure this shit out."

"I'm staying," Llanzo said, likely to the surprise of no one present.

"As I fully expected, Doctor," Jacob replied. "We need you to figure out everything you can about the thing that tried to give us the last handshake of our lives. There's no one here more qualified."

Derek saw Danni give him a glance and he subtly nodded in return. Reid was capable, but he was also just barely holding it together. Under normal circumstances, leaving one person behind to man basecamp made sense, but in this case it was probably wise not to leave him alone. And, though she might not like it, Norah made the most sense to hold down this fort.

"I concur," Derek said, backing up his friend. "You're our rock when we're out in the field, Norah. We need you to be that now."

He could tell by the look on her face she knew he was right, but she also wasn't about to give up so easily. "Fine, but how exactly am I supposed to coordinate anything from here?"

"Taken care of." Jacob opened up one of the side pouches in his pack, pulled two radios out, and handed one to her.

"Look at you going all boy scout," Derek said.

"Oh, that's not all." He next opened the main flap and produced two holstered sidearms, offering one to Derek. "Unless, that is, you're going to tell me you brought your own party favors."

"On a pressurized minisub?"

"Look at you acting like a responsible adult," Jacob said with a laugh, strapping his on.

"Got one for me?" Danni asked.

"Sorry. Only so much room in my pack of many things."

"Still looks pretty full to me," Derek replied. "What other surprises have you got?"

Jacob, however, was quick to close it up. "For that, you'll either have to wait until Christmas or you have a need to know, whichever comes first."

"Cute." Norah sounded less than amused. She flipped on her radio and depressed the talk switch, causing a squeal of sound to come out. "How do we know these will work once you're out there?"

"Simple. We don't."

"Actually," Danni said, "I might have an idea. If it doesn't work, try waiting until the gravity goes all weird, assuming we're not bouncing off the ceiling." At Derek's raised eyebrow, she explained, "What you showed us earlier. There's a lot less EMF when things are going screwy, so maybe that means a better chance of a radio signal punching through."

He nodded. "Good enough for..."

Before he could say more, though, the lights in the room dimmed, almost as if mocking their discussion. Within seconds, Derek felt his stomach lurch, like he'd just lost an instant twenty pounds.

When it had finally passed and the lights stabilized again, he continued. "As I was saying, that's as good a plan as anything I can come up with." He then turned toward the hallway, noting the disturbing uniformity of everything in front of him. "I think a better question is how are we going to find our way back, assuming this isn't one big straightaway? Call me cynical, but it's probably too much to hope for room numbers."

"Hold on," Jacob replied. "Think I have an idea. Should be a tool kit near the back of the sub, assuming Vakovsky didn't filch it."

He headed back inside once again, leaving the rest where they were.

"How much stuff did he bring on this trip?" Derek asked idly.

"Don't look at me," Norah replied. "He never did pick up after himself."

"I heard that!" Jacob emerged holding a roll of electrical tape and another flashlight. He then handed both to Danni. "Not quite a gun, but probably just as handy."

She looked at the tape, pursed her lips, then walked to the door where she tore off two pieces and marked an X on the wall just outside.

"Yeah, this'll work." She turned back toward them and grinned. "Come on. I think this is as close to an engraved invitation as we're getting down here."

Danni was happy to see she was right on two counts. It was cliché, something straight out of a bad movie, but the hallways appeared to light up for them as needed – at least when the lights weren't busy going all wonky. Sadly, it seemed as if those moments were beginning to occur more frequently, complete with messed up gravity.

The upside was that their radios were at least minimally functional whenever that happened, allowing them to check in with Norah. So far, all seemed to be well, even if she sounded unhappy to have pulled babysitting duty.

From their end, it had been a lot of the same. Aside from a slight downward incline to the passageway, likely a result of how this ship had come to rest on the ocean floor, it was all hallways and junctions leading to more hallways, all of which looked mostly alike. It was only broken up by the occasional *door* unexpectedly opening as they passed, although so far they'd revealed nothing except more dull square rooms. Regardless, each time they came upon a turn or hidden doorway, she'd mark the spot with an arrow, pointing the way back toward basecamp.

Despite the sameness of it all, she couldn't help but feel excited, as if some great truth were lurking around every corner, instead of just more hallways.

"How far have we come?" Jacob asked after a while.

"Hard to tell," Derek said. "But I'd guess maybe around a quarter mile."

"All that and nothing but empty rooms. This can't be it. It feels like the E.T. version of one of those self-storage places."

"Who said anything about it being extraterrestrial?"

"I did," Jacob replied. "Fuck skepticism. Until I see a sign reading *Made in China*, I'm calling it like I see it." He let out a sigh. "And the way I see it, it's time to start mixing things up a bit."

"You mean split up," Danni said, to which he nodded.

Derek didn't seem happy about that, which didn't surprise her much. He'd been tiptoeing for the last six months, making sure she was never alone on a mission, probably thinking she hadn't noticed. The thing was, he had to know that wasn't a luxury they could afford down here, not with their limited resources.

Before he could say anything, she took the bull by the horns and began unraveling several long strips of tape. "Okay, here's how I think it should work then. We'll split off at the next room or junction we come across. Mark everything you can, so we don't waste our time in case someone else comes across it. And keep going until you run out of tape or find something significant."

"Define significant," Jacob said.

Derek let out a breath. "Anything that could kill us, save us, or blast us to another galaxy."

Danni inclined her head at him. "Yeah. That probably works."

Jacob stared at her for a moment before nodding. "Goddamn, Derek. You better watch this one. She'll be taking your job before you know it. By the way, I call dibs on first divergence point."

"Fair enough," Derek said. "Second."

Danni had expected as much, so she didn't argue ... for now.

"Why don't I take the radio?"

"How about you take both." Derek held out the gun, too, as they stood at the junction – Jacob having headed off on his own several minutes earlier.

"I'm not playing this game."

"Neither am I. That's an order."

Danni glared at him. "Seriously? So you're just going

to head off on your own with no way to either defend yourself or contact us? That's stupid. Mitch would say it's stupid and Julie would back him up."

"Good thing they're not here then."

"Well I am, so I'm telling you for them. Listen, Derek, I know you're looking out for me, especially after Jersey, and I really do appreciate it. But I'm a part of this team. I know the risks and accept them."

He shook his head. "Well, maybe that's part of the problem. You shouldn't have to. Maybe this job, this life, it isn't..."

"Don't. Just don't. I'm here because I want to be and you know it. Now, if you want to write me up when we get back, that's your prerogative. But right now, the only way this is going to work is if you trust me to shoulder some of the burden." She considered things for a moment. "Or you could march me back at gunpoint, but that would only waste time."

After holding her gaze for a moment, he finally grinned. "That probably wouldn't work anyway."

"Why not?"

"Because you're taking the gun." She opened her mouth to reply, to which he said, "End of discussion. I'll take the radio if it'll make you happy, okay?" He held the weapon out again and this time she took it. "Just don't shoot me the second my back is turned."

"And waste bullets when there could be aliens around? No way."

"Yeah, well, I'm personally hoping for more Yoda and less Klingon empire."

"Says you," she replied. "I always thought that puppet was kind of creepy."

"Me, too." After another moment, his tone turned businesslike again. "All right. I'll see you soon. Be careful."

"Always am."

He took the left turn at the junction and started heading away from her, the walls lighting up as he progressed.

"Oh and Danni?" he called back.

"Yeah?"

"Thanks for occasionally reminding me when I'm being a horse's ass."

"You're welcome. Thanks for watching out for me."

"Always am."

Danni turned away. Then, after marking the junction with some tape, she too started walking.

It wasn't long before the corridor turned again and he was out of sight, leaving her alone in that strange place, feeling almost like a trespasser. *Probably the first human one anyway.*

The lights once more began to dim and she braced herself for whatever followed ... this outage different than the last few, making her feel like she'd put on an instant thirty or forty pounds.

Ugh! Guess gravity swings both ways here. Definitely not cool.

Far more unpleasant, however, was when the lights went out entirely, leaving her in complete and utter darkness. In the space of a second, she realized that not only had she retrieved her flashlight, but she'd drawn the gun as well.

Don't waste the battery. It'll pass. You can do this.

She wasn't entirely sure she could, though. Despite her earlier bravado, a cold sweat broke out on her forehead. In the dark it was far too easy to remember. Though she knew he was dead, her reptilian brain insisted that Noah Lesterfield, the Jersey Devil, was somewhere close by, waiting for her.

Despite the nearly absolute silence, she could've sworn she almost heard his whispering, wheezing voice calling out, calling her his *Sarah*. And with this place weighing her down, what chance did she have of outrunning him this time?

I beat him. I won.

Sadly, such things were only easily believed in the light of day. But here, away from everything she knew, everyone she cared for, safety was an illusion, nothing more.

Her breathing began to speed up as the suffocating fear became almost cloying.

How long is this goddamned distortion going to last?

There was little doubt things were getting worse, although it was hard to tell how much time had actually passed, despite it feeling like an eternity.

Finally, she had enough – the terror too much to bear. Her finger moved to switch on the flashlight. But before she could call forth the blessed illumination, the sagging weight lifted from her shoulders and the lights flickered back on.

Thank God!

Danni took several deep breaths, trying to force all thoughts of Noah Lesterfield away. Only when he'd finally retreated back to the dark corners of her memory did she dare to start moving again. However, she'd barely taken a single step before she once more froze in place.

The sounds she'd thought she'd imagined in the dark were somehow still audible, coming from up ahead. Impossibly enough, they sounded like hushed voices, calling out in whispers from the corridors of what should have been a long dead ship.

There was no way she could have gotten turned around or circled back to where the others were yet, which meant the impossible had to be true.

Somehow, they weren't alone.

39

The leviathan sped toward the surface, its rage rivaled only by its torment.

It had hurt the massive thing, there was no doubt of that, even if it bled sickly colored light instead of blood. Despite its best efforts, though, the great beast had failed to kill it – leaving the strange radiance atop the massive thing to pulse brighter than ever.

In a battle witnessed by none save the floating dead, it had waged war against the massive thing. Again and again it had attacked, even as its foe let loose with more thrumming cries. Each one ignited the leviathan's nervous system with stinging agony, bursting blood vessels in its brain and ganglia – dulling its intelligence and slowly killing its ability to reason.

None of that had mattered, though, as the mighty beast had finally managed to ram one arm into the wound it had caused, hoping to tear the massive thing apart from the inside.

Groping blindly, it had felt something inside its enemy's body. Thinking it had found a vital organ, it grabbed hold, intending to bring its monstrous strength to bear.

An instant later, fire had raced up its arm, bringing with it a pain it had never known before. The leviathan pulled away too late – the last thirty feet of its arm ablaze in horrific white fire that even the cold seawater seemed unable to quench.

In that moment, the fear finally overwhelmed the rage, leaving it with no other course of action than to flee from the massive thing as fast as it could.

However, as it ascended, it began to realize it had at least achieved a partial victory. For, though the light inside the massive thing continued to pulse, the thrumming waves of pain seemed to grow faint as it neared the surface.

Soon enough, it remembered there were other intruders within its domain – the surface things. Despite its burning arm continuing to send waves of fresh agony throughout its body, the rage began to assert itself once more.

It knew what needed to be done.

The massive thing was wounded and the subsurface thing devoured. That left the pod at the surface, their presence having been tolerated for far too long already.

The leviathan continued to rise, a strange beacon in the darkness as the substance coating its tortured arm continued to burn.

The pain was nearly unbearable, but it took comfort in knowing it would soon be shared.

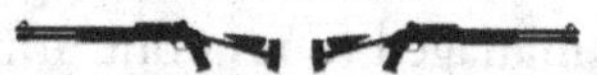

"Anything?"

"Hold on," Mitchell said, dialing the satnav again. "And ... another busy signal."

Andrea shook her head. So much for reaching any

backup. It seemed their window to the outside world was intermittent at best. They were able to receive the occasional news report, but their attempts to make contact with the outside were seemingly hampered by the fact that, when they were able to punch through, which wasn't often, they found the phone lines overwhelmed – no doubt thanks to the madness going on above them.

Thankfully, Caldwell picked that moment to distract her by handing over the headcount report she'd asked for. She glanced down at it, hoping to see no discrepancies, and was quickly disappointed to see there were three names unaccounted for.

She let out a muted sigh. *Of course two of them are civilians.*

The third was odd, though – Kyle Bastino. He was a good man. Well liked, competent, didn't slack at his job.

"Bastino was assigned to the Will-Do, wasn't he?" she asked Caldwell, figuring she'd tackle the low hanging fruit first.

He nodded. "Affirmative. I think he was heading up the unloading effort after you ordered them back."

"And then?"

The agent shook his head.

Goddamn it! It wasn't like him to wander off and disappear. As for the civilians, for all she knew they'd snuck off for a quickie, thinking this a chance for a cheap thrill.

A cabin by cabin search could wait, though, especially since the news from the Caribbean and southern United States seemed to be getting worse every time they managed to get a signal. And that wasn't even counting the rumblings coming out of Cuba.

She was pulled from those unpleasant thoughts as the door to the bridge opened and that Wilhelm woman came stalking in again like she owned the place.

"What's going on with the Rogers Will-Do?"

"Excuse me?"

"The research vessel," Julie clarified. "It just pulled away at high speed."

"What? It's supposed to be moored to the..."

"Sonar contact rapidly closing," Cortez interrupted.

"Is it another ghost or..."

Sadly, the answer came in the form of automatic weapons fire from out on deck.

Shit! She met Julie's gaze, the other woman's eyes echoing what she was thinking. All at once she was glad she'd assigned those agents to keep watch on deck. It had seemed like busy work at the time, but now...

"Holy pig balls!" Mitchell cried, dragging her attention back to the bridge crew.

At least in this case, she didn't need to ask what had caused the outburst as it was plainly and terrifyingly evident.

A massive tentacle rose from the ocean directly to their port. That alone was bad enough, but the fact that it was on fire – glowing white hot as if it were covered in burning phosphorus – well, that certainly changed the game a bit, especially once it became obvious which way it was headed.

"Everyone take cover!"

The monstrous appendage slammed down directly in front of the bridge, shattering the windscreen, before sweeping toward them like the finger of God itself.

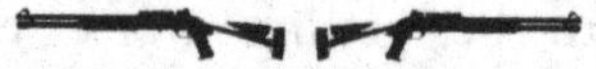

Jacob paused to mark the doorway that had just opened up on the far wall of the room he'd been investigating – revealing yet another hallway beyond.

"Knew there was more to this place," he said to

himself, starting down it. Though he wasn't sure if there was any meaning to what he saw, the walls of this passage were a noticeably lighter shade than the one he'd come from.

It was quite possible the different color was less a marker and more a technical glitch, but Jacob's gut told him he'd found something significant. At the very least it was a change of pace, maybe leading to something that might be *interesting* enough to warrant attention.

While he was certain he didn't have close to all the answers he needed, he was slowly starting to work things out. After all, he'd brought a good team down with him. Each of them had been quick to figure out some piece of the puzzle, giving him enough to start painting a larger picture.

That ZarroGreen ship hadn't been up to anything more nefarious than being the unluckiest motherfuckers on the planet. They'd struck oil all right, proverbially speaking anyway. It just hadn't been the type they'd been looking for.

Go figure that they'd done so right next to the lair of a real life sea monster. Had that not happened, the situation might've been containable, even salvageable.

But the chips had fallen where they had. There was no changing that. Just as there was no way of keeping this under wraps long enough for his superiors to take proper advantage. Much as he wanted to believe Derek was wrong about things now being even worse on the outside, his instincts told him otherwise.

Sadly, with one plane already down and God knows what else going on, this situation was bound to draw attention. The last thing they needed were Russian frigates crawling all over the place, poking around for salvage rights. The location alone put the United States' interests in a precarious position.

It was partly why Jacob had packed his special bag of tricks. Though he'd had no idea what they'd discover down here, he'd made it a point to come prepared as best he could, at least without drawing undue attention.

The truth was, much as he'd wanted to see her again, this operation would've been a lot simpler had Norah not shown up. He knew Derek. The man was one of the best he'd ever worked with, but he stayed out of politics. Had Jacob pulled rank and convinced him this operation was now outside his team's jurisdiction, he doubted his friend would have argued much. They were here for a big fish, not this craziness.

At least he'd caught a bit of a break with the Guerrero woman's death. She'd been the wildcard in this. They had enough leverage to lean on both Reid and that photographer. If either of them were stupid enough to talk, they'd be lucky to find jobs as cabana boys going forward. Zarro-Green wasn't going to be so easy to intimidate, though. But now that problem had seemingly solved itself.

That left two major loose ends to deal with. The first was that creature outside, but he hoped that by taking care of the second issue that maybe it would go back to whatever it had been doing before this shit started.

The challenge now, he considered, was finding the proper place to plant the bricks of C-4 in his backpack, and then making it out before sending this ship back to whatever hell it had come from.

Derek had long ago opted for career over family. Hell, he hadn't even had a pet since rehoming his beloved cockatoo Maurice, back when it became obvious his schedule was going to be too erratic to properly care for the bird.

Yet right at that moment he felt like a proud papa. He

was still worried about Danni, there was no doubt about that. But the fact that she'd stood up for herself, laying it out straight to his face, secretly delighted him.

From the moment they'd met, he'd seen her potential. She was smart, brave, and cool under fire, all necessary virtues for a good agent. She also cared about others, making her an ideal choice for what his team stood for.

Though he hadn't made it official, he already considered her the team's second in command. Yeah, Mitch technically had far more superiority, but he knew his friend. The man was a force of nature in the lab, but he was happy to cede authority while on a hunt.

A small part of him still hoped Danni might choose a less dangerous career path, but the rest of him would've been happy to see her take over as team leader one day.

He had no doubt she'd make him proud.

But that was for another time and place, hopefully a long ways off. Derek still had plenty of adventure left in him. So long as he felt a sense of wonder and satisfaction at his job, he planned to keep forging ahead.

Of course, that all assumed he didn't end up being fired the second they got back to shore.

If that happened, well, maybe he'd try to channel his minor celebrity status toward something positive, like a charity aimed at conservation. That would be nice, although a lot depended on how quickly he'd end up bored out of his skull.

One thing was certain, though. He wasn't bored at that moment – quite the opposite actually. After all, how often did even a cryptozoologist get to explore something built by hands not of this Earth?

Crazy as it was, little by little he was beginning to become more comfortable with that explanation.

What he wasn't comfortable with, though, was the eerie silence. Derek didn't actually expect to find anything alive on this vessel, but so far everything they'd seen had been mostly devoid of ... well, just about anything. That alone struck him as odd.

Though he doubted he'd find anything recognizable by human terms, there should have been some signs of habitation aboard to tell him whether...

A sharp hissing sound caught his attention, causing Derek to stop and listen. He was wondering what it might be when a portion of the wall next to him retracted, in much the same way the other doorways they'd found had.

Another room. Now to hope this one isn't as...

Those thoughts fled as his eyes opened wide. It was like providence had heard his complaints and decided an answer was called for — one in the shape of a room not nearly as empty as the rest had been.

40

Danni wasn't sure if she was going insane, or if maybe the strange energies of this place were finally starting to affect her.

Hugging the wall and adopting a shooter's stance, she crept forward toward the source of the sounds. The closer she became, the more she was convinced she was not only hearing human voices, but they were speaking English, too. And they seemed to be coming from the junction right up ahead.

The walls of this place weren't great for carrying sound, but she guessed it to be two males conversing in low tones.

Maybe Star Trek had been right after all and alien life was nothing more than people with ridged foreheads who all spoke the same language. Whatever the case, she intended to get answers.

Danni inched along toward the junction ... until a section of wall unexpectedly opened next to her.

Son of a...

It didn't make much noise, just a quick *whoosh* as the metal plates retracted, but it was enough. The voices immediately quieted, as if listening – assuming they hadn't merely been in her head to begin with.

A part of her was certain she'd round the corner and find nothing, her mind playing tricks on her like this was something out of that horror movie her brother had made her watch once – the one with Laurence Fishburne and Sam Neill.

Not exactly a comforting thought.

Of course, ghosts were ultimately less a problem than actual physical threats. So, until the walls started bleeding, she intended to handle this as she'd been trained to.

Go on, she told herself. *And if whatever's there has more than one head, shoot them both.*

She crept to the corner, holding her breath and keeping as quiet as possible. Then, in a flash of movement, she sprung.

Sadly, she wasn't the only one.

So much for ghosts, she thought, as a figure slid around the corner of the junction, likewise holding a weapon.

Less than a split second later, though, Danni found herself far less willing to dismiss the supernatural.

Her eyes opened wide as she considered the very real possibility that her mind had finally unraveled.

There were two men in front of her, both armed. The first she recognized immediately as her team's medic Mitchell.

How the hell did he get down here?

However, all hope of a rational answer fled as she took in the other face, one she still saw in her dreams but had never dared hope she would ever see again in person.

"Harrison?"

Stay focused and do your job. There are scientists out there who would sell their own mothers for a chance to study a specimen like this.

Llanzo considered himself a man of science. Becoming a researcher had been his passion ever since childhood. It had been a dream his family, most of them humble fisherman, had come together to make happen.

He'd been the first in his family to earn a Ph.D., devoting his life to the pursuit of science. It had been everything he'd ever hoped for.

Yet here now, confronted with not one, but possibly two of the greatest scientific discoveries of his time, he found it hard to focus.

Things had spiraled out of control so quickly. This was supposed to have been nothing more than a quick fact-finding mission. Now, less than a day later, he was stranded at the bottom of the ocean, examining a tentacle *fragment* that alone rivaled the largest colossal squid ever found.

Had they been back at the institute, he would've likely set alarms to remind himself to eat, sleep, and shower. Here, though, in this undersea madhouse – one that was likely to become their tomb – it was hard to be excited by the find of the century.

Part of it was the company.

Llanzo liked science, but he wasn't lacking in common sense. He was well aware that the only reason Norah Caseman had stayed behind was to keep an eye on him. The others no doubt feared he'd try to do something stupid.

It was an insult of the highest order yet, at the same time, it was hard to blame them for their concern. His conduct so far had been lacking. He couldn't help it, though. He was terrified beyond anything he ever thought possible, especially since he'd expected his week to involve little more than updating the institute's current model on coral reef decay.

"Need a hand, Dr. Reid?" Norah asked, sounding bored.

"No thank you. I have this," he replied, albeit there wasn't much to have. All of his equipment was up at the surface. The best he was able to do was take measurements and try to estimate the full size of the animal. Other than that, there wasn't much he could do, other than maybe seeing if there was a hacksaw in the tool kit so he could preserve part of the specimen for the trip back home.

Assuming there's a way back.

Llanzo was trying desperately to shake that thought from his mind – the very real possibility that he might never see his family again – when the lighting in the room abruptly changed.

First it dimmed, as it had done before, causing him to pause in his examination. But then, rather than go back to normal, the walls lit up bright green, similar to the hue they'd seen when they'd first approached this vessel.

"Derek, Jacob? Do you copy?" Norah said into her radio, her voice maddeningly calm. "I think we may have a situation here."

There came a garbled response, barely intelligible. Just then, the green light began to flicker. Llanzo suddenly felt much lighter on his feet than he should have, his stomach doing flipflops at the weight change.

"...found something, Norah," Jenner's voice squawked from the radio, the static clearing enough to be understood. "...you need to see this."

The walls stopped glowing that eerie green color, returning to their normal hue just as Norah tried hailing him back. "Come again? What do I need to see?"

The response was nothing but more static.

In the next moment, however, the radio seemed like

the least of their worries as sections of the walls began to shift and move.

To the right of where the door had opened, a platform slid out about three feet off the ground, continuing to expand until it was roughly four feet deep. More sections slid out on the wall adjacent it, at varying heights and depths, running the length of the room.

"What's it doing?" Llanzo asked, watching the room seemingly reconfigure itself at will.

"I wish I knew."

Unlike the walls themselves, the tops of the various surfaces were unlit, a stark contrast now that he could see it.

On one of the sections, a pedestal roughly four feet high, the top retracted into itself, revealing a hexagonal shaped hole. Llanzo, curious despite his terror, stepped forward to investigate, noticing something appeared to be rising out of it.

"Careful, Doctor."

"Believe me, Agent Caseman, I have no intention of being anything but."

What was pushed out, though, seemed somewhat less than a threat – a harmless lump of greenish brown vegetation, almost as if the device were some sort of advanced dumbwaiter.

"Why don't I have a good feeling about this?" Norah remarked.

Llanzo, however, actually grinned as he took a closer look, breaking out into the first bit of real laughter he'd had since they'd descended into this nightmare.

"Something funny, Doctor?"

"Yes. The fact that my first instinct was to assume this to be some kind of threat, when I believe it's the exact opposite."

"Care to clue me in? Now's not the time to play coy."

He nodded. "If I'm not mistaken, this is just ... seaweed. In fact, I'm fairly certain it's a variant common to these waters."

"Seaweed?"

"Yes, it's quite popular in salads."

"And?"

"That's it. Unless you count snagging the lines of fishermen."

She stepped over and looked down at it. "And do you have any idea why this room suddenly decided to hand us a pile?"

"Maybe." He shrugged. "Although, I don't think I'm in much position to speculate."

"Take a guess. Nobody will hold you to it."

"Very well. There's only one conclusion that comes to mind, as absurd as it may sound."

"And that is?"

"I think we were just served dinner."

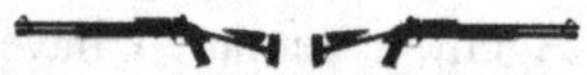

Though the media liked to dismiss him as nothing more than a crank, Derek had once been an accomplished zoologist, at least before life had taken a left turn and led him to become the Crypto-Hunter.

There was no doubt some of his skills were rusty, as research had oftentimes taken a backseat to other aspects of the job. The upside, however, was being one of the world's foremost authorities on extant megafauna – hell, one of the *only* authorities on the subject. As such, Derek's depth of knowledge might not have been as deep as others, but his breadth more than made up for it.

Regardless, he found himself absolutely flabbergasted by the skeletal remains littering the floor in front of him. Derek didn't fool himself into thinking he could positively identify every creature on Earth by its remains, but there were some rules that all vertebrates followed – first and foremost being that they tended to only have *one* spine, unlike whatever he was looking at.

It was like something one might expect to find at a turn of the century sideshow. Too bad there was no PT Barnum in sight to charge him a nickel.

He continued to stare slack jawed at the find. To say that he'd finally found something interesting was the understatement of the century. The quick hiss of air followed by a delay before the door opened should have clued him in that something about this place was different. The others hadn't done anything like...

The radio clipped to his belt suddenly blared to life, forcing him to push his awe to the side for a moment. "Derek ... Jacob? Do you co..." The rest of the message was too garbled to understand.

"You always did have impeccable timing," he replied into the receiver, hoping his message got through. Before he could say more, though, the lights began to flicker, giving the macabre scene before him a nightmarish quality.

A few of the bones in front of him toppled over, causing him to cry out in surprise.

It's just the change in gravity, Derek told himself. *Don't freak out ... at least more than you already are.* Then, remembering what they'd discussed earlier, he raised the radio to his lips again, hoping it worked now. "I found something, Norah. I'm not sure what, but you definitely need to see this. Over."

As he finished, the lighting stopped flickering and he felt his feet settle firmly onto the floor. Not surprisingly, the response he got from the radio was once again little more than static.

Despite everything, a strange excitement began to take

over – the researcher in him coming to the forefront. Much as he considered *little green men* to be outside his area of expertise, the impossible was staring him in the face. It was perhaps an opportunity unequaled by any in history.

But where to start? The only thing he was certain of was that these remains were old. The air was free from any smell of decay and the bones themselves were fully calcified – if that term even applied. Hopefully that also meant any contagions these things might've carried were also long dead, although Derek was fully aware that the normal rules of biology had likely been tossed out the window the moment they'd stepped from the sub.

Sadly, he was also aware that he couldn't spare this room much time, as – fascinating as it was – nothing here appeared to be a solution for any of their problems. Still, a few minutes probably wouldn't hurt.

He once again spoke into the radio.

"I don't know if you can hear this or not, Norah, but I'm going to document it anyway, as I think saying it out loud is the only way I can keep from losing my mind."

Derek moved further into the room and continued speaking.

"There appear to be the remains of three individuals. Though it's impossible to determine exact details based on the advanced state of decay, I estimate them to be between four and six feet in length. And, crazy as this may sound, their method of locomotion seems to have been tripedal. The first individual appears to have died leaning up against the far wall, while its nearest fellow is..."

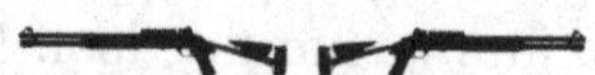

Danni leveled her gun at the thing slash hallucination slash robot that was wearing her dead brother's face.

Whatever was down here playing with her mind had gotten it right enough to be recognizable, but had messed up some of the details. Harrison's hair had been a shade lighter than this imposter's and he'd always worn it shorter. Most telling was the scar which snaked down the left side of this faker's face, from his lower cheek down his neck and disappearing into his shirt.

"Drop it," she warned.

"I don't know what the fuck you are," he replied, "but you've got a lot of fucking nerve. Understand that I will not hesitate to put a bullet in you if you don't drop the act."

"If *I* don't drop the act?" She tightened her grip on the weapon. "Nice try, whatever you are. That's not even a real handgun. Everyone knows Glocks don't have safeties."

"Since when?"

"Am I the only one here who thinks this is getting really fucking weird?" the fake Mitchell asked, raising his hands.

"Nice try," she said to him, not taking her eyes off the bastard wearing her brother's face. "But you're not real. Mitch is up on the ship."

"Um, no," the faux medic countered. "Frank and Alison stayed with the ship. We..."

"Seriously?" the Harrison thing snapped. "Why don't you just tell her our weapon capabilities and social security numbers while you're at it."

"It probably doesn't even know what a social security number is."

"Of course I know what that is," Danni growled. "Don't play head games with me. We don't mean you any harm, but I am warning you. If you don't drop the act, I will open fire. My brother's dead. He died a year and a half ago at Bonanza Creek when..."

"Wrong! That's where Daniela died. Something you

probably already know if you scanned my mind for her face." The faker gritted his teeth, his eyes flashing dangerously. "So once again, I'm warning you..."

"Guess you're the one with the faulty brain scan. Harrison never called me Daniela. He called me..."

"Danni."

"Okay, everyone calm down for a second." The Mitchell lookalike took a slow step forward. He put a hand atop the barrel of Harrison's gun and gently pushed it down.

"What the hell are you doing?"

"Trying to make sense of the nonsensical." He then turned toward Danni. "Please don't shoot, or melt our faces, but I can assure you we come in peace."

Danni backed up a step, making sure she was outside their reach, then took her finger off the trigger.

"Okay, that's good. Save the shooting for the angry squatches I always say. But I'm afraid my friend here is right. The girl whose face you're impersonating died some time ago."

"You didn't even get her hair right," Harrison snapped.

"I cut it after Bonanza Creek, moron," she replied. "It was easier to work in the woods this way."

"You never left Bonanza Creek."

She was sorely tempted to shoot them both. If this was some kind of crazed way of pushing her sanity to the brink, well, kudos to whoever was bastard enough to think of it. "Wrong. You ... fell trying to save me and Derek. Allie died that day, too. And you know damned well Frank was killed by those bastards in New Jersey."

"Huh," Mitchell replied with an amused huff. "He's not going to be happy to hear that."

"Close but no cigar," Harrison said, ignoring the fake medic. "Frank's got some nerve damage in his left arm, but he's otherwise fit as a fiddle. As for Allie, well, I'm pretty sure I'd know if my fiancée was a zombie."

"Fiancée?! When the hell did that happen?"

"After Derek recruited them, obviously," Mitchell said, the freer talking of the two, almost like the real one. "Or Harrison anyway. She sort of tagged along and ... well, it wasn't long before they were sharing a tent."

Harrison gave him some serious side-eye, finally holstering his weapon. "Do you mind?"

"Just filling in the blanks for contextual purposes."

This is insane. Danni backed up another step, lowering her gun to her side. It was like she was peering into some twisted mirror. She could almost fathom alien technology scanning her mind and pulling both Harrison and Frank out of her subconscious. Neither were far from her thoughts as of late. But Alison?

Alison Chan had been her friend, roommate, and romantic rival – if she was being entirely honest – at South Dakota State, where they'd both vied for the attention of a boy who, in the end, hadn't been worth the effort. Danni wasn't exactly proud of it, but the truth was it had been some time since she'd thought of Allie, or the others who'd lost their lives that day, the memory of Bonanza Creek simply too painful to relive.

So then why her? Why not Rob, her brother's roommate, or Greg, or – god forbid – even Phil?

An uncomfortable feeling began to settle in the pit of Danni's stomach, even as the lights flickered and her legs suddenly felt like they were made of lead.

"Oh crap," Mitchell said. "Gravity's shitting the bed again."

"Forget about that," Harrison replied. "We need to phone this in."

"Yeah, good point." He unclipped the walkie talkie

from his side and showed it to her. "This is called a radio. It's not a weapon. It's something we use to..."

"I know what the fuck a radio is."

"Relax. Just checking." He lifted it to his lips. "Mitch to Norah. Come in. We've got ... a bit of a situation here. Over."

"What kind of situation?" Norah's voice replied, or at least something that sounded like her.

"The *Night of the Living Dead* kind," Mitchell replied.

A moment later, however, the radio crackled to life again. "Who the hell is on this channel?" It too sounded like Norah, but the inflection was different, more suspicious. "Derek, did you catch that? Over."

The two ... whatever they were, both glanced at the radio and then at each other, just as the lights stopped flickering and gravity returned to normal.

"Um, Derek's still on the boat," Harrison said, looking confused.

"Survey says..." Danni made a buzzing sound with her lips. "He's a few hallways over, back that way. All I have to do is scream ... or shoot."

"Likely story." Harrison inclined his head toward the fake Mitchell. "We should take this thing back to the sub. Maybe you can dissect it and figure out what it is."

"Ixnay that idea. I'm still trying to process why there were two Norahs on the squawk box." After a moment, though, his eyes opened wide. "Oh god."

"What is it?" Danni and Harrison both replied.

The medic glanced between them both for a moment. "That's not going to stop being weird anytime soon."

"What's wrong?" Harrison asked. "Are you okay? Did this thing do something to..."

"Don't call me a thing!" Danni snapped.

The fake Mitchell nodded. "Yeah ... maybe don't do that."

Harrison narrowed his eyes. "What do you mean?"

The medic looked between them for a moment, finally focusing on Harrison. "I'm about to postulate something that ... probably won't sound sane, and I need you to keep an open mind." He then glanced toward Danni. "You, too."

"I'm standing here in what is, in all likelihood, an alien spacecraft, talking to my dead sister. Pretty sure we left sane behind a couple hours ago."

"What he said," Danni added.

"Okay, so, ever since this mission started, we've been wondering exactly what's been going on," Mitchell replied. "We know electronics work like shit, gravity is messed up, and even time seems to be screwy. Well, what if that's just the tip of the iceberg?"

A part of Danni screamed that she should open fire, that these two must be some kind of trick meant to cause her to drop her guard. But she realized that same part was also terrified about what he was about to say next, because of what it might mean. "How so?"

"We know space travel is a bitch," he continued, "because even if you could somehow travel at the speed of light, it would still take years to get anywhere meaningful. But that's where quantum mechanics steps in and says that science fiction might not be so fictional after all. The trick isn't going faster so much as creating shortcuts from point A to point B."

"Wormholes," Harrison said.

"Exactly. The thing is, wormholes have the potential to go far beyond just getting to Alpha Centauri before lunch, stuff we don't even begin to understand yet. And some of the theories out there postulate they could also potentially be doorways to a parallel universe ... one in which, say, Danni Kent survived instead of you."

"Or," he continued, turning toward her, "in your case, the exact opposite."

41

Julie had thought their earlier battle was likely to cause her to wake up in a cold sweat for a long time to come.

She now realized it was a pleasant daydream compared to the monster currently attempting to drag them under – and doing a hell of a job of it.

Automatic and semiautomatic gunfire erupted from all around. Hell, it would've been coming from her, too, but she'd already emptied one magazine and was in the process of reloading.

They might as well have been throwing paper airplanes at it, though, for all the good it seemed to do. Even the 50's appeared to be little more than gnat stings to the beast, drawing lines of bluish blood but seeming to do little to stop it.

It was like something out of a bad movie. The bow of the ship was currently ablaze, along with one of the octopus's tentacles – looking like little more than a burnt tree branch at this point. Unfortunately, the damage had been done – despite a small crew desperately working to put out the fire even as their fellows battled the creature.

Sadly, this monster had far more than one tentacle to call upon. The bulk of the beast had surfaced on the port side, a small mountain of flesh rising out of the ocean, made nightmarish by the freak lightning that continued to arc above them.

Though it was hard to tell in the chaos, she estimated it to be nearly as long as the cutter itself, maybe even longer.

Every which way she turned, there were tentacles reaching and grasping, each of them covered in suckers the size of her head or larger. Thankfully, the bridge had been evacuated just in time, right before being crushed like a house of cards, even if that left them, quite literally, up shit creek without a paddle.

That was a problem for later, though.

Julie was currently fighting with a four person team, two firing on the creature while two reloaded. They were trying to dislodge a tentacle that had come up from beneath them on the starboard side and snaked its way around one of the upper deck's support struts.

Julie had just finished reloading when one of their fighters, a man by the name of Cortez, was ordered elsewhere. "Keep it busy. They need me up front."

Good luck, Julie thought as he took off. She lined up her shot, staying low as the boat lurched from side to side, and then began to fire off rounds – hoping against hope to find a weak spot.

Although it could have simply been a trick of the light or the stress of battle, already the water line seemed to be much closer than it should've been. The smaller kraken – because what the fuck else was she going to call these things – had been a joke, comparatively speaking. She had no problem envisioning this new beast dragging that ZarroGreen ship below the waves, a fate it currently seemed likely they'd share if they couldn't fight it off.

She wasn't sure how long they could keep it up, though. Already, screams filled the air. They'd rise in pitch, then abruptly be cut off, only to start again elsewhere.

"Watch out!" Simmons, another of the defenders, cried at her.

Lightning flashed high overhead, yet Julie was still left in shadows as the bolt lit up the air above them.

What the hell? She turned to see another impossibly long tentacle reaching up from the sea, easily as thick as a tree trunk. In the next second, it descended toward her like the fist of an angry giant.

"Move!" Simmons yelled, plowing into Julie and shoving her out of the way.

Sadly, she was a bit too slow.

The titanic appendage crashed down onto the hapless agent with enough force to bend the deck plates beneath them. Julie screamed as she landed on her side, her left leg partially caught beneath Simmons as the poor woman's body was crushed to pulp.

Pain exploded up through her leg as she felt her tibia snap like a matchstick.

As agonizing as that was, it was the splash of warmth across her face that horrified her far more. Forcing herself to look, she found Simmons's lifeless body staring sightlessly toward her, the poor woman's eyes bulging from their sockets due to the pressure that had snuffed her life out.

There was no time, sadly, to mourn the loss of this brave woman as the next instant brought with it more searing agony. The tentacle pulled free of the deck, relieving the pressure from Julie's leg enough for her nerves to fully fire, sending a shockwave of pain up her body.

Simmons was yanked away, caught on the creature's sucker teeth. For a split second she hung in the air, like some ancient sea curse brought to life, before the beast dragged its tentacle back into the sea, taking its gruesome prize with it and leaving Julie lying in its wake, desperately trying to hold onto consciousness.

It was as if the battle had been raging for hours, although Andrea knew only minutes had passed since she and her people had been forced to abandon the bridge. It wasn't her first time in a firefight, but it was her first time against an enemy that couldn't fire back, yet somehow maintained every advantage.

From her vantage point just behind the smashed remains of the bridge, she'd already seen at least five of her team dragged overboard by that thing, all of them good agents. Once again lightning flashed, momentarily illuminating the great beast – its alien eyes seeming to stare at her like some Lovecraftian nightmare.

Next to her, Mitchell worked to patch up Agent Kori. He normally assisted down in engineering, but had gotten slammed into a support strut as he battled alongside them. As much as she needed people down below to ensure the pumps kept working, there was little doubt this was an all-hands emergency.

Too bad the octopus had arms to spare. Its size and strength were incredible. They were fighting just the one foe, yet somehow it still felt like they were badly outnumbered. She had no doubts whatsoever that this was the creature responsible for the Tortuga's demise. The only question now was whether they'd share its fate.

"You'll be fine," the medic told Kori. "Minor contusions and maybe a bruised rib."

"Get that man below deck," Andrea ordered.

"Um, I'm not sure that's such a good idea," Mitchell

countered. "I'm not saying for sure that thing's gonna sink us, but if it decides to put in the old college try, the lower decks are probably the last place you want the injured."

Damn it all! He was right. If this beast got the better of them, something which was looking likelier by the minute, then sending her people below could be a death sentence. The problem was, it wasn't much better up there. Hell, there was likely no place aboard that could be called safe at the moment, especially as the groan of tortured metal was almost as loud as the peel of weapons fire.

"Any sign of the Rogers Will-Do?" she called to Agent Lin, who normally acted as a sniper for their team but was currently helping to direct the offensive.

"Negative."

What the fuck had happened to the other ship? Though she didn't fool herself that they could pull off the same gambit twice, using the research vessel as a diversion could have bought them some much needed time to regroup.

They still had the Sun Angel, but she doubted it would be effective, the Will-Do's engines being far more powerful. The mystery of its theft would have to wait, though. She needed a workable strategy now, one that didn't rely on hoping for a last minute save.

Andrea glanced at the medic and considered her options. She wasn't normally a petty person, but she had to admit her feathers had been ruffled when the other Agent Caseman had asserted authority over this operation. Once the submersible had descended, she hadn't been shy about reminding the others about who was in charge.

The thing was, she and her people were trained to deal with monsters of a whole other kind – the type a bullet would dissuade. Whenever they had to deal with animals, it was usually more of the guard dog variety.

A monster the size of a destroyer, on the other hand, was so far out of their league that she could barely fathom the idea even as they fought it. However, the same wasn't necessarily true of Harkness and his teammate, wherever she'd gotten off to in the chaos.

She motioned to Lin. "Go get Patel. I want the wounded moved to the helipad as well as enough launches to hold them. Bring Kori with you and keep that space secure for as long as you can."

"On it."

Lin helped the other agent to his feet and they began to make their way toward the stern, perhaps the only area of the ship still under their control – especially with the bow now a hell of smoke and burning metal.

Andrea then turned to Mitchell and took a deep breath. "I need your help."

"You got it."

"No, I mean *really* need your help. How do we beat this thing?"

"Um, briefcase nuke maybe... Oh shit!"

Both of them ducked for cover as a tentacle rose from the sea in front of them, the tip of it missing but the rest still massive in size. It began to snake its way up the side of the ship toward the conning tower.

"I'm serious!" Andrea snapped.

"And you think I'm not?" He shook his head. "Sorry. Force of habit. I tend to ramble whenever I'm fighting things capable of tearing me into bite sized chunks."

She was only partly listening, though, her attention focused elsewhere. If that tentacle managed to get a solid hold onto the conning tower, that could very well give it the leverage it needed to capsize them. "Take out that arm!" she cried, raising her own weapon. The base of the tentacle was nearly the width of a car, an easy shot. Too bad their weapons seemed to barely annoy the beast.

Still preferable to going quietly into the void.

"No!" Mitchell shouted.

"What do you mean, *no*? If that thing wraps around…"

"I know how it works. I mean ignore the arm. We're not going to do dick against it with what we have."

"Please tell me you have a better idea, then."

"Maybe." She gestured for him to hurry it along. "Okay … um … we need flares and any spotlights we have. The fact that we're dealing with something this big that nobody's seen before tells me it's a deep sea animal. If so, we might be able to disorient it with enough light."

"And then what?"

"We put everything we have right between its eyes."

"And that'll kill it?"

"Or at least give it a splitting headache. Octopus anatomy," he said, pointing to his own forehead. "Their brains are located right here, up front and center. Small arms probably aren't going to puncture its skin far enough, but if we point the 50s there and hit it with everything we've got…"

She didn't wait for him to finish, already barking orders to her people even as the ship began to list even more from the creature's hold on the tower.

It wasn't much, but it was hope, and right then even the smallest spark was like a shining beacon in this madness. So much that she barely realized it when she blurted out, "If this works, I owe you dinner when we get back to shore."

Mitchell blinked at her a few times, obviously caught off guard as the men scrambled around them to carry out her orders. But then he nodded.

"It's a date. Just don't be surprised when I recommend anything but seafood."

Kerry screamed as the lightning lit up the deck, illuminating the face of the dead agent – his unseeing eyes open and staring, as if aware of what had been done to him.

After another moment, he took a deep breath and tried to laugh it off, looking around even though no one else was there. Despite the watery isolation, it felt like he was being watched, but that was probably nothing more than the strange weather overhead – the lightning bright enough so that, if he squinted, he could still make out the silhouette of the other ship in the distance.

Or at least he thought he did. It could have simply been his eyes playing tricks on him.

That brought with it a new surge of paranoia. He'd made it a point to get away as quickly as possible, but what if he hadn't been fast enough? What if they were giving chase? Kerry was fairly sure the old trawler could outrun the much larger vessel, but he was far outside his expertise on this one – for more than one reason.

Case in point the body he was trying to dispose of. It was stupid. He should've waited until he was further away, but he couldn't stand it any longer. Kerry wasn't a superstitious man, but every time the lightning flashed, revealing the swirling clouds overhead, he found himself spinning in the pilot's seat, expecting to discover the man had been playing possum. Finally he'd had enough, stopping the boat so as to dump the body.

Now, with it hanging off the edge of the deck waiting for one last push, he wondered if maybe he should find something to weight it down with first.

Though the chances of it being spotted in the dark were slim, Kerry knew how his luck had been as of late. And, looking at the body, there would be no doubt of what had happened. The man had quite clearly been murdered.

It was self-defense! But even as Kerry tried to convince himself of that, he knew he had no way of proving it if they caught him.

Indecision caused him to hesitate just as faint popping sounds caught his ear from off in the distance. He turned his head in the direction where he'd last spied the other ship, certain he could see tiny pinpricks of light flaring up in the distance.

Again he heard the popping noises, just barely audible above the sound of the idling engines.

Were they firing at him?

Kerry instinctively ducked, despite there being no evidence he was being targeted. He'd been running with nothing more than the lights from the instrument panel, but apparently that hadn't been good enough.

There was no time to lose, but he realized it was now more imperative than ever to make sure the body was never found. That was no guarantee they wouldn't immediately execute him anyway, but he needed to stack the deck in his favor any way he could.

Leaving the corpse dangling over the railing, he raced below deck, hoping to find a spare anchor or something else heavy enough to ensure the man, whatever his name had been, was never found.

Sadly, in his haste, he forgot that the reason he'd been able to slip onto the vessel in the first place was because he'd helped unload it. He hadn't realized at the time just how thorough of a job they'd done.

Pretty much the only items of substance left were the cushions on the chairs and a few empty glass beakers on a shelf.

He was about to try his luck deeper in the hold, hoping maybe something had been left in one of the storage compartments, but then he remembered the winch at the back of the boat. Maybe there was some spare cable he could use.

Kerry headed back up, hurrying so as to not waste more time than he already had. However, halfway to the crane he stopped dead in his tracks, noticing something amiss.

Where the fuck is the body?

Kerry's paranoia switched into overdrive as he began searching for signs of movement from the shadows around him. Unsurprisingly, he saw nothing except the gentle swell of the sea around him, as well as the occasional flash of...

There!

The lightning illuminated something floating in the water about twenty feet away.

All at once Kerry felt like a fool, one who deserved whatever fate had in store for him. Not only had he squandered his time, but it had been for nothing as the damned body had simply fallen overboard, likely a result of nothing more than the rocking of the boat.

It was too far away now. Using the lightning to find it was a hit and miss proposition at best and he didn't want to risk turning on the boat's exterior lights – assuming he could even figure out how to.

And it's not like the lack of a corpse would exonerate him if they caught him now, there still being a thick trail of blood leading from the cabin across the deck.

He'd need to clean that up, but first he had to put some more distance between him and the other ship. If they were firing wildly into the night, hoping to hit him, he wanted to be certain they were nowhere in sight before stopping again to clean up the evidence.

As for the dead man, well, Kerry could only hope – as he hopped back into the captain's chair – that the sea claimed him as its own.

He set the throttle to full and once more sped off into the night, hoping that when next he stopped it would be to better fortunes.

42

Danni backed away, shaking her head. She didn't want to believe what this man, this doppelganger, had just told her, didn't *dare* to believe it.

It was absolutely batshit insane. The thing was, could she truly claim it was crazier than anything else that sprung to mind? She was well aware that high EMF was known to cause hallucinations, and from the readings she'd seen earlier that probably couldn't be ruled out. Hell, if they all came out of this without brain damage it would be a miracle. The two men in front of her, however, seemed pretty damned solid to be nothing more than delusions.

Her other thought – that these were aliens in disguise – well, that wasn't much saner than Mitchell's theory, considering how long this ship had likely been at the bottom of the ocean. She supposed suspended animation could be a thing, but then why impersonate her dead brother when they could have easily appeared as one of her other teammates already down here?

"Occam's razor, guys," Mitchell said. "Unless, that is,

anyone thinks shape-shifting robots makes more sense. If so, then please let me state for the record that my name isn't John Connor."

Danni barely heard him, hope warring inside her mind with the realization she'd be utterly crushed if this turned out to be some sort of trick. But then the reptilian part of her brain, the part that had somehow given her the strength to survive the Lesterfields, spoke up, telling her she wouldn't be the only victim if this was nothing more than a deception.

She blinked back the tears threatening to fall and steeled her voice. "When I arrived for our trip, before ... Bonanza Creek. What's the first thing I said to you?"

Harrison narrowed his eyes. "That was a long time ago, but I remember every moment of that goddamned weekend like it was yesterday. You told me you were glad to see your favorite brother, and I reminded you that I was your only brother."

Danni's breath caught in her throat. *Oh my god!*

"My turn. That guy you brought with you, Wild Feather..."

"I'll stop you right there," she replied, forcing her voice to remain calm. "His real name was Phil. You ended up decking him after he freaked out. They found his body in Paula's room, naked, but..."

"They kept that information from her and Rob's parents," Harrison finished, his mouth dropping open. "And ... just for the record, that's not the only reason I punched him. Didn't like how he was gaslighting my little sister."

He grinned at her and that's what did her in, because it was *his* smile, that easygoing smirk he always seemed to wear even during the worst of times. Hell, he'd even had it at Bonanza Creek when everything had gone to hell, as if to tell her it was going to be all right. He'd been wrong that day, but right then all of that seemed so unimportant.

On some level Danni understood, assuming Mitchell was correct, that this wasn't her Harrison. But did that really even matter? If what she was hearing was true, then there was a world out there where he'd survived that awful night.

An awkward, but not entirely awful silence descended in the hallway, until Mitch finally said, "I'm going to scout down this way a bit, give you guys a few minutes to decide if you still want to kill each other or not."

He started walking away, but then Danni called out, "If you see any electrical tape on the walls, that's from my team."

"Electrical tape?" He pulled out a roll of silver duct tape. "I see I'm dealing with a universe of heathens here."

She turned back toward Harrison. "He's taking this well."

"It's Mitch. If the world blew up around him, he'd spend his last few seconds collecting soil samples."

"All while talking smack to whoever's in charge."

Harrison smiled in return. "I see your Mitch is alive and well."

"Yeah. He's topside. Derek wanted someone up there to monitor all the weirdness and maybe figure out what to do about it."

"Ah, makes sense. That's why ours insisted on coming down. We have a local scientist up top helping out with that stuff."

"Reid?"

"No. His name's Anderson."

Danni nodded, her heart thumping in her chest even as she tried to play it cool. "Okay, so I guess there's some differences. That kinda makes sense in a butterfly effect sort of way."

"I ... I'm sorry I almost shot you."

"That's okay. I would've shot you first anyway."

"Think so?"

"I know so."

More silence, then the lights began to blink again. In that same instant, Danni felt light on her feet, albeit she wasn't entirely sure it was the gravity.

"I-I missed you, Danni."

That did it. Whatever dam had been inside her burst. At those four simple words, tears began to stream from her eyes, a few of them floating in the air in front of her – something that would have amazed her at any other time.

She launched herself forward, seeming to cross the distance between them in one step as she threw her arms around her brother and buried her face in his shoulder.

"I thought I would never see you again."

"Same here," he choked back. "Who would've ever thought a giant octopus would be responsible for a miracle?"

The more *occupied* rooms Derek found, the less he liked the things he saw – and he saw many strange things.

There was a disturbing uniformity to it all – most of the chambers identical to the one they'd docked in. By the third, he began to detect a pattern. If a door opened immediately, the room would be empty. If there was a hiss of sound, it would be ... *less empty*. What the hiss meant, he wasn't sure, only that it seemed to herald a scene designed to rattle his sanity.

He couldn't even claim to be discovering new life forms. Such a thing would imply that he found anything alive, which wasn't the case. Skeletonized bodies were all that were left – except in one instance where the word skeleton was being generous, the remains there being more akin to vulcanized rubber than anything else.

Now, in the fourth such room he'd found since breaking off from Danni, he stopped to consider things. Whatever the creatures here had been, they were, so far anyway, the closest analogies to Earth-based lifeforms – bipedal and roughly the size of large cows, minus their long tails and oddly shaped skulls.

The skeletons were intact, like all the others had been. Whatever these things had died from, it didn't appear to have been violent. Derek didn't care to speculate, but his instincts told him they likely hadn't died when this ship crashed – assuming it even had crashed.

What was curious was that the decomposition process appeared to have occurred naturally. The bones were stripped clean, not mummified – which he would have expected had this been an airless space.

Unless that means this place has had power and atmosphere this entire time.

That was probably more a question for the top minds on Earth, but he found it curious nevertheless.

Aside from the skeletons, the room itself appeared clean, with no dust, debris, or old droppings in sight. He supposed it was possible that these creatures had all starved to death, but what Norah had told him when last he'd checked in seemed to cast that in doubt.

I guess if we end up trapped here, we should get used to seaweed salads.

Sadly, there was no way of telling if these creatures had been intelligent or not. The best he could conclude was that they were all vastly different species, perhaps with vastly different origins if the strange rubbery remains in the previous room were any indication.

Derek turned to leave just as the lights flickered again and gravity began its weird flip flop. It reminded him it had been a while since he'd last checked in. He unclipped the radio from his belt and lifted it up.

"Norah, this is Derek. Come in."

No sound met his entreaties, worrisome for a moment, but then he glanced at the radio and shook his head. In his haste to put it away last time, after making his first discovery, he must've accidentally turned the volume down.

He quickly took care of that and was about to apologize, in case she'd been trying to reach him, when her voice squawked out from the radio.

"For the last time. Who is this and what have you done with Doctor Jenner?"

Done with? That was odd. Derek was about to speak, but then Norah replied again. "Doctor Jenner isn't on this mission, which you would know if you weren't a fake. This is your last warning. Identify yourself or we will be forced to conclude you have hostile intent."

He stared at the radio for several seconds, wondering if perhaps the air down here was more toxic than they'd originally assumed. "Norah, are you okay?"

"How the hell are you on this line?" she replied. "Please tell me you found some way to punch through the interference, because otherwise..."

"Don't listen to her," Norah interrupted, speaking over ... herself? "We need to assume there's something strange going on down here and that we can't trust our..."

"All right, enough of this shit," a third voice cut in, equally as familiar yet impossible all the same way down here.

"Mitch?"

"Yeah, it's me, man," the voice of his friend replied. "But I'm not your Mitch ... not that you could ever afford me."

"What?"

"Sorry. Force of habit. What I meant to say is..."

Norah, or the competing Norahs anyway, both began to babble, throwing out accusations, until Mitchell finally shouted them down. "Okay enough!" There came a pause and then he continued. "I apologize for breaking protocol, the chain of command, and whatever else, but we don't have time for this. So, you'll excuse me if I tell you all to kindly shut the fuck up so I can explain what's going on down here."

Before either Norah could reply, Derek decided to take the bull by the horns. "Okay, not my Mitch, you have our undivided attention."

Jacob was definitely making progress, although he wasn't certain it was good progress. The floor of this section of hallway was covered by roughly a foot of freezing cold water. Daring a quick taste test so as to prove a theory, he'd confirmed it was seawater before spitting it back out again.

That likely meant he was either close to the breach made by the Tortuga's drill, or some other rupture they hadn't seen from the outside. Either way it told him to be careful, especially in a place that played fast and loose with gravity.

So far his exploration had been interesting, if not particularly fruitful. He'd found more chambers, a few of them considerably larger than the one the minisub was in. They hadn't all been empty either. One had been filled with large humming cylinders ten feet across, which rose from floor to ceiling. Another had been covered with rocks and dirt at one end. At first he'd thought maybe a section of wall had collapsed, allowing the undersea sediment in, but he quickly saw that probably wasn't the case, as the room had been dry as a bone.

There'd been something screwy about the sediment as

well – sand and dirt of multiple different hues and consistency mingled together. Same with the rocks lying about. Jacob was no geologist, but he knew enough to tell vastly different terrain apart.

He was no goddamned engineer either. So he had no idea what either the dirt room or the cylinder room might have been for. He'd been aboard ships, inside nuclear facilities, and even infiltrated presidential palaces – yet, for all he knew, that cylinder room could've been an engineering bay or this place's septic system. Nevertheless, he'd stopped to plant a few bricks of C-4 among them on the off chance it was important.

Now, tromping through the cold water, he couldn't help but feel he was on the verge of a significant discovery, not that it would ever make the light of day. This vessel was simply too dangerous. If he found a specimen that could easily be carried out, so be it – a gift to the eggheads, something to keep them busy for the rest of their lives. The rest of this place needed to go, though, before anyone else came snooping.

He just hoped he had enough explosives to make a difference. But if he could find that breach in the hull and blow it wide, hopefully without drowning himself in the process, well, that might very well be the key to taking this place down.

Jacob didn't know what purpose this ship had once served, how long it had been here, or even what the damned translucent walls were made of. But he was certain of one thing – the Tortuga's drill had damaged it in some way that the energies contained within were spilling out. That meant the only options left were to fix it – something so unlikely as to be laughable – or cause enough catastrophic damage to shut it down for good.

There was no doubt the hull was tough. The fact that it was lying in seven hundred feet of water with nary a scratch was testament to that. He had friends at NASA, though, and had listened enough to know that rockets were like turtles in a way – tough on the outside, but soft on the inside. This place was obviously way above even their pay grade, but if that same logic held true then any chance he had at sinking this ship would be from within.

He continued onward, the slosh of water loud in the quiet corridor, when the lights in the hallway ahead of him turned on, illuminating what appeared to be a four way junction about thirty feet away, but that wasn't all. He paused as he tried to make sense of the sight before him. The junction itself was nothing new, but the wall of swirling water directly past it was most certainly different.

"What the fuck?"

Jacob approached slowly, trying to figure out if this was real or some kind of fucked up optical illusion.

Just past the junction the entire corridor appeared to be filled with seawater, but apparently that wasn't all. Something was glowing past that point, too, intermittently lighting up the submerged hall – kind of like the fountain show he and Norah had caught in Vegas back during their honeymoon. Jacob made out a doorway on the left, about fifteen feet past where the water began – this one open. Whatever was causing the underwater light show was in there, beyond where he could see it.

For the moment, though, the multihued flashes were far less interesting than the static wall of water just standing there, as if behind a pane of glass so clear as to be invisible.

How in hell? Jacob continued walking until he was standing directly in front of the watery barrier.

Despite knowing he was on a timetable he reached out, fully expecting to touch something solid. To his surprise, however, his hand easily passed through into the frigid water, prompting him to quickly pull it back.

"The fuck?"

He once again considered the strange light show coming from the open door ahead, immediately cursing himself for being an idiot. What if that had been the spark from an open electrical conduit? His curiosity would have done nothing more than gotten him fried like a Thanksgiving turkey.

Would have served him right, too, if he'd been...

The lighting in the hall around him began to flicker.

Oh great. Another of those goddamned...

And then he was knocked off his feet as the wall of water suddenly surged forward and slammed into him, dragging him under and knocking the breath from his lungs

He slammed into the far corner of the junction, bruising his back, then was swept the way he came, unable to find any purchase to stop his progress. There was no doubt in his mind that this was the end – that he and the rest of his team were destined to drown in this underwater rat maze where their bodies would never be...

His own body was his more immediate concern, though, as he hit the floor just as the torrent slaked, allowing his head to break the surface.

Jacob sat up, coughing salt water out of his lungs, desperately trying to catch his breath as he looked around to see if he could figure out what the hell had just happened. The water he was sitting in now was only slightly deeper than what he'd been wading through just moments before. He turned his gaze back toward the junction only to find that the wall of water had seemingly reestablished itself, holding back the deluge just as it had when he'd first approached it.

As he pulled himself to his feet, still coughing, he noticed that the lights in the hall were back to normal as well.

"S-shit. Guess ... the ... gravity isn't the only thing that stops working when the power flips out."

If so, that made it more imperative than ever to speed things up. In the grand scheme of things, considering the probable size of this ship, it was likely little more than a slow leak. But there was no doubt in Jacob's mind, as he once again stood at the junction, that sooner or later this ship was going to fill with water. More importantly, this section was going to flood first. He was now more certain than ever that if he was going to end this nightmare, he was close to where it needed to be done.

Jacob quickly considered his options, left or right. Each looked the same from where he was standing. For now, he pulled off a strip of tape and stuck it to the wall, where it promptly fell off.

Great. Got it wet. Guess I need to have a word with Vakovsky about packing waterproof tape in the goddamned sub.

He balled up some more and tried again before discarding the rest, annoyed but not dissuaded. Despite what he'd agreed to with Derek and Danni, there was no way he was turning back now. Not when...

"Son of a..."

What the fuck?! Jacob flattened himself against the wall as the sound of the muffled curse reached his ears. It had come from somewhere down the left-hand passage. He was sure of it. But how? Had one of his teammates gotten ahead of him? Couldn't have been Danni. No way had that voice been hers, not unless she'd packed a few cartons of menthols with her and decided to smoke them all. Derek maybe? If so, he'd need to play this cool.

But if not them, then who?

Yeah, he'd just gotten bitch-slapped by a wall of water, one that was now behaving nicely behind its ... force field again. So it was entirely possible he wasn't in his right mind. Yet, he was pretty certain of what he'd heard.

Either way, he intended to find out. Drawing his sidearm and staying close to the wall, he began to creep down the left corridor – keeping his eyes peeled for anything that moved, alien or not.

43

The leviathan could taste victory. It had gravely injured the large surface thing, as well as killed several of the screaming things aboard it.

Now it intended to finish the job, pulling it under and dragging it to the depths where it would sink and drown, much as it had done to the other surface thing not too long ago – the one that had been here when its misery first started.

The pain it had felt below seemed to be all but gone now, its senses clearing up, although the rage remained. It wasn't aware that the damage already done to its sensitive nervous system was irreparable.

Even had it known, though, it was unlikely to have cared.

There was still plenty left to deal with. Its arm had finally stopped burning, but the tip of it was now little more than useless gristle. Equally as annoying were the screaming things. They were putting up a fight, peppering it with tiny attacks that were slowly starting to add up, fueling its desperate anger.

Wherever it grabbed hold of them, enjoying the feel of

their fragile bodies breaking beneath its power, it seemed two more would appear to make noise and hurt it from afar. The louder the noises, the more pain they caused, even if the wounds were ultimately superficial.

Now, with the thrumming having subsided, it found it could think again – albeit not nearly as well as before. A haze had settled upon its mind, making it hard to focus on anything that didn't have to do with killing. Fortunately, killing was exactly what it wanted. It remembered how it had drowned the other surface thing, wrapping its arms around the highest part and pulling until it finally gave way and tipped over.

It would kill this one the same way.

Even as the screaming things made their noises and tried to hurt it, it had lifted one of its arms from the water, up toward the highest spot it could find. There it entwined itself in an unbreakable grip and prepared to pull.

Before it could bring its strength to bear, though, the screaming things did something new, something that caught it by surprise. Bright light flashed in its eyes, much like the light of the surface during the day. In its youth it had hunted in the shallows and been used to such brightness. As it grew, it had retreated to the depths, gradually growing accustomed to the darkness.

The powerful lights dazzled it, causing it to hesitate. It was of minor concern, though, and it quickly began to shake off the effects so it could continue its...

Intense pain erupted through the front of its head as the screaming things suddenly redoubled their efforts, lancing the delicate flesh and what lay beneath with their attacks.

It tried to pull away, but in its haste its arm became caught where it had entwined with the surface thing, holding it in place.

Then came sheer blinding agony as one of its eyes

exploded from the onslaught. Pain, as bad as anything the massive thing had caused, wracked its body as they continued their assault.

For the very first time since this had begun, the leviathan felt fear at facing the tiny screaming things. It was a feeling it did not like, but it heeded it all the same. Pulling with all its might, it yanked its arm free, smashing through whatever had ensnared it.

The leviathan spat a great wad of ink at the surface thing then dove beneath the waves, the torment of its defeat leaving it disoriented.

Such a thing should not have been possible. To lose to the screaming things was unthinkable. They were small, weak, reliant on the surface things to keep them from drowning.

It began to circle the area, staying well below the surface as it warred with itself, unsure whether it should flee or attack again. Just as its rage threatened to fully consume it, though, its keen senses noticed something new.

One of the surface things was missing. Only a pair remained now – the large one and a smaller one that seemed to be drifting lifelessly behind it. Where was the third?

For a moment it wondered whether, in its confusion, it had killed it and sent it to the depths, but then it heard a faint buzz vibrating through the water. It was distant, but sound traveled far in the ocean. That could only mean one thing: the other surface thing had run, abandoning its fellows.

That meant it was out there alone ... easy prey.

The leviathan considered its options. The large surface thing had injured it, but hadn't escaped unscathed. It was crippled, vulnerable, but obviously still capable of fighting back. The fleeing one, however...

Pursuing the smaller surface thing was an easy choice — a chance to lick its wounds while still sating the rage inside. It would find the fleeing thing and drown it, then it would return, having regained its strength, and finish what it had started.

With a jet of water, the leviathan broke from its course and took off in pursuit, the pain of its injuries slowly feeding its ever growing anger.

"We're never getting this shit off of us, are we?" Mitchell asked.

Andrea glanced sidelong at the medic, dripping head to toe with thick dark mucus — as was she and seemingly everything else in sight — not sure if she wanted to hug him or punch him in the face.

Maybe both were called for, but that could wait. His plan had worked. Their communications array had been smashed in the process, and most of the ship seemed to be a mess of twisted or burning metal, but they'd managed to actually drive the damned thing off.

The fact that they were quite literally covered in its ink was a small price to pay, but it was also one of many problems that needed to be dealt with. Andrea started barking out orders to her closest people. They needed three things ASAP as far as she was concerned — a casualty list, a damage report, and to have their weapons and ammo inventoried ... and cleaned.

Sadly, with their survival on the line, she knew she might need to rethink the priority in which those happened. "Do you think we got it?"

Mitchell chuckled, although there wasn't much mirth behind it. "On Team Crypto-Hunter we pretty much go with horror movie logic for these things. If there's no body, we assume it's not dead. The good news is I'm pretty certain we hurt it. The bad is we've probably pissed it off right and proper, too. This is my first giant octopus, but experience has taught me that doesn't exactly lead to a live and let live attitude."

"Wonderful."

"I never claimed to be a bearer of good news. Now, if you'll excuse me. I have a teammate to find and wounded to look after." He turned away, but then glanced back over his shoulder. "By the way, how do cheesesteaks sound?"

"Awful."

"You wound me greatly. But I suppose this means our relationship has nowhere to go from here but up."

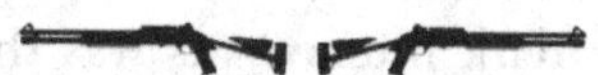

"This is going to hurt, a lot."

The medic, one Agent Patel, wasn't shitting her either. Despite an injection of local anesthetic, Julie still had to wonder how she managed to not bite her own tongue in two.

The ship's helipad had been converted into a triage area, despite there being a perfectly serviceable medical bay below deck. However, considering everything that had happened, it was easy to guess the cutter's modest accommodations would quickly be overwhelmed.

That said, the fact they were still alive was probably a small miracle unto itself.

For some reason she still wasn't privy to, the octopus had broken off its attack while she'd been semi-conscious. The pain of being moved, though, had jolted her fully awake again. Now she found herself with the other wounded, as agents scrambled back and forth on various tasks no doubt meant to stabilize their severely compromised situation.

On that matter there was little question. Julie couldn't see much from where she was currently lying, but she could easily discern the haunted expressions of those who were still able to work, their training probably the only thing standing between them and a complete breakdown.

The triage area itself wasn't nearly as full as Julie would have guessed it might be — the bulk of the patients appearing to suffer from burns or smoke inhalation. But then she remembered what happened to poor Simmons and was no longer surprised.

The creature which attacked them had been massive, far larger than even she had been prepared to accept. Surviving even a glancing blow from something of that size would require the devil's luck. Hell, the fact that they were still afloat was, quite frankly, nothing short of astonishing.

She pushed herself to a sitting position, doing her damnedest to move her leg as little as possible, then noticed the nearby launches. Their presence seemed to explain a lot. It was quite possible McAvee — assuming she'd survived — was already considering the possibility of abandoning ship, knowing they were unlikely to survive another attack.

As lightning continued to arc overhead, she was able to see more now that she was sitting up. The conning tower had been crushed as if it were nothing more than a cheap aluminum can. Beyond it, smoke was still rising from the bow.

It didn't exactly paint a rosy picture for their survival. Hell, the swirling miasma of clouds above them didn't paint a good picture period. If anything, it seemed to be getting worse. Who knew what effect it was having on the outside world even as they battled to stay afloat?

"Hey you!"

Julie looked over to see a familiar face heading her way.

For a moment her heart leapt into her throat as she thought he might've been badly burned, but then she realized he was simply drenched in something that looked like motor oil but probably wasn't.

"What are you smiling at?" Mitchell greeted as he approached, his tone light but concern etched across his face.

"I'm imagining all the showers you're going to need."

"Hilarious. Well, while you're undressing me with your eyes, let me take a look." He knelt down and began to examine her. "Goddamn. That thing really did a number on you ... unless, that is, you're going to tell me you tripped and fell down the stairs."

"No such luck." The image of Simmons being dragged overboard played in her memory, causing her to grimace. "Could have been a lot worse, though. How are things looking?"

"Same. It's not good, but we're still here. We got lucky, managed to hurt it enough to make it think twice. Oh, and I think I got a date for when we get back."

"Go you." She sighed, turning serious once again. "That octopus, kraken, whatever it is ... it's going to come back, isn't it?"

She could tell by the look on his face that he wanted to lie, but thankfully he didn't. "Yeah. No doubt about it."

"Any sign of...?"

He shook his head, turning away. "No."

"So what do we do now?"

"*You* don't do anything for the moment. Andrea has her people working to get this place back up and running."

"And you?"

"I'm going to head down and check out the med bay. This is an active ops team, so they're pretty well stocked.

With any luck, I'll be able to find a walking boot and a pair of crutches for you. And then..."

"Then what?"

He grinned down at her. "There'll be no time to lose, so we'd best get *kraken*."

"I so hate you right now."

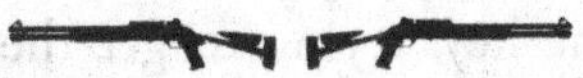

Kerry felt much better having put more distance between himself and his former captors. The other ship was no longer in sight from what he could tell, and the only sounds he heard were the roar of the boat's engine and the occasional rumble of thunder from overhead.

He'd managed to convince himself that the chances of anyone finding the body were a million to one. All that blood would surely attract sharks, barracudas, or whatever the hell else was in these waters.

It was time to move on from that as he still wasn't entirely home free. He'd noticed a hose coiled on one side of the deck, one of the few items that hadn't been unloaded. His plan was simple: keep running until first light, then stop to clean both the cabin and the deck of any blood stains. After that, he could set his sights on...

His thoughts were interrupted by the abrupt sound of silence as the engines suddenly died. They didn't sputter or cough, they simply went dead – along with all the lights on the instrument panel.

Within seconds he found himself in pitch blackness, the surface tension of the water quickly erasing the boat's momentum. With no stars overhead, he could barely see his hand in front of his face.

He didn't even have a flashlight on him. All he had was his watch and whatever meager illumination it provided. Just enough to tell him his arm was still attached.

Kerry was fairly certain he wasn't out of gas. He wasn't an accomplished mariner by any means, but he knew enough to have checked the fuel gauge. Lightning flashed overhead, giving him just enough time to double check that the tank was at least a quarter full.

He turned the key, trying to get the engines to turn over, but there wasn't even a sputter from it. Thunder rumbled overhead, but when it quieted all that was left was the sound of water lapping against the boat.

Repeated tries produced the same effect. Somehow the goddamned boat had just broken down completely for no apparent reason. Maybe that was why they'd been in such a rush to unload it – they knew what a piece of shit it was.

Kerry glanced down at his watch, hoping to figure out how much time he had until the sun came up.

"What the fuck?"

Rather than give him the time, though, his watch was doing nothing but displaying a jumble of seemingly random numbers.

Then, as if mocking him, the watch too fell dark, leaving him feeling very alone, as if he were truly the last man on Earth.

44

Derek thought he surely must be hallucinating.

When he'd left Danni, she'd been by herself. He never imagined that when he saw her next it would be with her brother. Derek had been there when he'd died, had watched his face turn from triumph to terror as his life was snuffed out. He'd seen death before and since, but watching the light go out of the poor kid's eyes had haunted him, especially since Harrison had died saving his life.

Tragedy went hand in hand in this business. There was no doubt of that. And every life lost was regrettable, but some stood out among the rest. Over the years, Derek had run into just about every flavor of humanity he could think of. Though he was happy to say the vast majority had been positive, it was still rare to find those exceptional people who were willing to put others before themselves in times of danger.

Harrison had been one such person. Hell, Derek still vividly remembered their first meeting. The team had been stalking a rabid Bigfoot that, in turn, had been hunting

397

the Kent siblings and their friends – finally trapping them in an old dilapidated ranger station deep in the woods.

The squatch had managed to drag one of their group outside, where it would've certainly killed him had Harrison not leapt into action – racing up to the murderous beast and unloading a can of bear spray into its face.

It was one of the damnedest things Derek had ever seen, and he'd seen a lot. Suicidal and crazy as fuck, yes, but brave beyond compare.

So seeing him now, long after he'd had to look his parents in their eyes and tell them their son wouldn't be coming home again, was ... nothing short of mind blowing. He couldn't even imagine what Danni was going through, but the look on her face as they approached spoke volumes.

She'd somehow been given that miracle of miracles, a second chance with a loved one. He could tell she'd been crying, but they were good tears – the same which now filled his eyes.

Harrison smiled as he caught sight of Derek, but by then the Crypto-Hunter was on the move, stepping forward and grabbing hold of the young man. "It's damn good to see you, son."

Harrison actually laughed. "Been hearing that a lot lately. Although, no offense, but I saw you less than two hours ago."

"So I've been told."

Harrison pulled back after another moment. "Just for the record, I like your hair better this way."

"What way?"

"Long story," the other Mitchell said, also approaching. Interestingly enough, Derek noted, though Harrison looked different than he remembered, this Mitchell appeared almost identical to his doppelganger up on the surface. "Nice to meet you by the way, boss man."

"This is weird."

"You're telling me," Danni said. "But ... it's a good weird."

"I bet it is."

"For both of us," Harrison added.

"Yep," Mitchell replied. "Now all we have to do is figure out which universe we're in right now, how to get everyone else back to their respective dimension, and then a way to make it to the surface alive and not as octopus chow."

"Now you sound like my Mitch."

The medic grinned. "Bet he's an awesome guy. Would love to meet him."

"Maybe later," Derek said, turning serious. As happy as he was to see Harrison again, he had to admit he was glad as hell to have Mitch, or at least some version of him, down here, too. The second the sub's lights had shone them what lay at the bottom of the ocean, he'd regretted the decision to leave him up top, knowing he'd have likely been their best bet at figuring out what the hell this thing was.

He turned and hooked a thumb the way he'd come – having doubled back to meet Danni and her newfound friends. "Hate to say it," he told her, "but you're not the only one who found something. Although my discovery might be a bit less on the happy side."

Jacob crept forward as quietly as he could, weapon drawn as he dragged his feet through the cold water pooling around his legs. Since he'd heard the voice there'd been another outage, for lack of a better term. Fortunately, away from the wall of water, the result had been far less dramatic, allowing him to brace himself as a small wave washed around him, barely coming up past his knees.

That wouldn't be the case for long, though. Soon enough, he'd probably end up having to swim back. Once that happened, their window for exploration would rapidly close, meaning Jacob would be forced to consider his *options*.

Had he known what they'd find here, he'd have had a far more forceful say in the team that had come down. What was done was done, though. There was no taking that back. And if it came down to it, Norah, Derek, and that Kent girl were all federal agents. They knew the risks. As for Reid, well, sometimes duty required sacrifice.

Despite knowing he needed to focus, his thoughts turned back to Norah. Though it hadn't been an acrimonious divorce, it wasn't a welcome one either. He'd wanted to work things out, but her demands had put his back against the wall. He was a field agent not a desk jockey. He'd been sidelined a few times due to injury and the inactivity had nearly driven him nuts.

Sure, he intended to retire someday – maybe even look into opening his own combat arts dojo – but that was still far off. For now, he was happiest while in the thick of things and, not to toot his own horn, he was damned good at his job. He loved Norah, but deep in his heart he'd known he'd be consigning himself to growing old before his time if he'd done as she'd asked.

So there he was at forty-six, single and forced to start all over again. A pettier man might've welcomed the opportunity to put their ex in the line of danger, but the truth was it hurt his heart that Norah had insisted on coming. Why the hell had the suits picked this mission in particular to lean on her? It wasn't like any of Derek's other assignments tended to be safe, but this ... this was a whole other level of crazy.

Jacob forced himself back to the present as a faint sound caught his ears from up ahead. It wasn't much, just a brief splash, but then it was followed by another, and then another, as if someone or something were walking.

He listened to the cadence then continued onward, making sure his steps matched those of whoever was ahead of him, keeping his senses focused in case they stopped.

It was dreadfully slow going this way, allowing the cold to creep up his legs, but it was necessary. He had every intention of catching them by surprise. If it turned out to be Derek or one of the other expedition members, he'd apologize. If not...

Jacob didn't see much ahead of him, at least in the parts of the corridor still lit. However, there was an open doorway on the right. The water that way seemed a bit deeper than where he stood, but that probably made sense. Judging by the way he'd come, he was likely now moving parallel to where that weird-ass wall of water had been – which he was willing to bet was somewhere close to where that drill had punched through.

He stopped as the lights began to flicker around him. Jacob braced himself, although it was made more difficult as he suddenly felt very light on his feet. He glanced down to see water droplets rising in the air around his legs as...

"Oh fuck me. Not again!"

There was no doubt about it. The voice he'd just heard had sounded human, damned familiar too, although that had to be a trick of the acoustics. Whoever or whatever its owner happened to be was a question he intended to answer. And if they understood English, all the better to have a nice long chat at gunpoint.

He held the weapon out in front of him as a rush of water swirled around his legs. Sure enough, it seemed to be coming from both directions now – the expected wave from behind him, but also one from the open doorway, both of them serving to raise the level in the hall by a couple of inches.

Definitely running out of time here.

Jacob slid forward as another series of invectives was uttered from within. Whoever was in there sounded good and annoyed, which was a plus for him because it meant they were likely preoccupied.

He made it to the door and pressed himself up against the side, steadying his breathing and waiting for the right moment.

"What the hell are you?" came from within.

Jacob wasn't sure if the voice was addressing him or something else, but it was as if all the hairs on the back of his neck suddenly stood on end – something that hadn't happened in a long time. There was that unnerving sense of familiarity again at the sound of it, enough to spook him.

The hell with this.

Jacob spun, aiming his gun inside the doorway.

The room beyond was different than the others. One of the walls appeared to be some sort of display, with symbols flashing upon it that he couldn't begin to understand. He'd also been right about the water. There was a sizeable breach in the wall opposite him, beyond which the chamber seemed to be flooded, yet the water was somehow held at bay.

All of that was secondary, though, compared to the man standing within. His back was to Jacob, and though he couldn't make out a face he saw dark skin and salt and pepper hair over a well-built frame. The man was wearing fatigues, a black sweatshirt, and a flak jacket. From one hand hung a backpack not dissimilar to his own.

Whoever he was, he appeared to be staring at the hole

in the wall and the water beyond, intermittently lighting up with different hues – similar to what he'd seen back at the water wall junction.

Noting the holstered weapon at the man's side, Jacob decided not to take any chances as he slid into the room, quiet as he could, and approached. "Hands up. Turn around real slow."

He could tell by the way the stranger's muscles tensed that he was considering his options. Time to nip that one in the bud. "Don't even think about it."

"Relax," the man replied, his tone measured. "Wasn't going to."

Jacob's eyes opened wide with surprise. With no walls to distort the sound, the other man's voice sounded disturbingly familiar to his own. Come to think of it, his size, build, and look were nearly all identical to his own. They said everyone had a twin in this world, but who could've ever guessed he'd meet his down here?

"So which is it?" the man asked, slowly starting to turn, his hands in the air. "Cuban? Russian? Or do you work for that oil... What in the name of hell?!"

The sentiment echoed Jacob's surprise at seeing his own face staring back at him from the stranger's body. *The fuck?* But then, the man dropped his arms, although whether out of surprise or making a move, Jacob wasn't sure. Either way, his training kicked in. "I said don't move!"

"Who or what the hell are...?"

Jacob squeezed the trigger before the ... *other him* could finished speaking, firing off a single round. It was all he needed.

The doppelganger fell, a bullet hole nestled neatly between his eyes.

Derek would have preferred they all regroup at basecamp, but what he'd found warranted a second scientific opinion. And if this Mitch was anything like his, he'd get that in spades.

"This is amazing," Mitchell said, donning rubber gloves and placing bone fragments into sample bags. "I could set up a lab and live down here for the next twenty years and I don't think I'd ever get bored."

"Am I going to have to tranq you to get you out of here?" Harrison asked from just outside the doorway, where he and Danni stood.

"Probably."

"This is just the first," Derek said. "I found three others like it. Completely different species, as in not even close to the same morphology. Similar levels of desiccation. No signs of violence."

"I need to see those, too."

"Figured you'd say that."

He glanced back toward the door, where Danni motioned for Harrison to step away with her. No doubt they wanted to catch up. Considering none of them had any idea how much time they had down here, he wasn't about to get in their way. Let them get to know each other again, maybe find some closure. So long as it didn't affect their chances of getting back home, he wasn't about to say anything.

"I'm no paleobiologist," Mitchell said, drawing his attention back, "but I'd be willing to bet my next three paychecks that these aren't terrestrial remains."

Derek nodded. "That was my conclusion, too."

"I'm just amazed they breathed the same atmosphere as us. Maybe there's something to be said about all life in the universe being carbon based."

Derek raised an eyebrow, remembering something from earlier. "I don't care to speculate on that second one, especially since the guys in the next room over look like they're made out of spare tires. But I may have noticed something odd when I first came across these remains."

"You mean odder than the fact that these things have three legs and a double backbone?"

"Okay, maybe not that odd. But all the other doors we've encountered have opened right away. With these, however, there was a slight delay, along with a hiss."

"Like a snake?"

The realization hit him even as he spoke. "Kinda, but probably more like ... gas."

Mitchell zipped up the samples in his pack and stood up. "So you think maybe ... they were breathing something else?"

"Not anytime recently, but now that you mention it, could be. Quick question. Did you get scanned before being brought in, assuming that's even what it was. I mean, a flashing green light that seemed to go over every square inch of..."

Mitchell waved him off. "Yeah. Harrison thought that's what was happening, too. Guess it pays to watch Sci-Fi from time to time."

"I always said you needed to get out more."

"Now you sound like my Derek."

"Bet he's a fascinating guy."

"He's a legend in his own..." Mitchell trailed off as the lights began to flicker. "Here we go again."

"Hope you didn't eat a big lunch."

Outside, Danni called to them from some distance away, "Hey guys, is the floor supposed to be wet?"

Mitchell let out a sigh. "That's not good."

"Define not good," Derek said just as the lighting returned to normal.

"We saw signs of moisture earlier. Jake broke off to check it out. He's the..."

"I know who he is."

Mitchell nodded, but then the lighting in the room changed before he could say anything else on the subject, turning bright green this time. "Hold on. Is it supposed to do that?"

"I was hoping you knew."

Before either of them could say much more, the door leading out closed shut – the four corners coming together to once again form a seamless wall.

After a moment, Mitchell said, "I blame you for this, you know."

"Me?"

"You're the one who had to mention the green scanner thing," he said, just as the room began to shift around them.

The sections of floor beneath the three skeletons separated from the rest and began to lower down, as if they were some kind of piecemeal elevator, almost catching Mitchell, too, before he backed up in time.

As the remains disappeared into the floor, new panels slid in from the sides to replace those that were gone. Within seconds, it was as if the bodies had never been there at all.

"It's like being in a giant Rubik's Cube," Mitchell said.

"I was thinking more the puzzle box from *Hellraiser*."

"The what?"

"Are you honestly telling me you don't have that movie in your world?"

"No idea. Like you said. I need to get out more."

Speaking of getting out, Derek stepped to the wall where the door had been, at least once he was certain the floor wasn't going to sink beneath him. However, the doorway remained closed.

He stepped back then approached it again, causing

nothing to happen. Next he touched the wall, and then finally gave it a bang with his fist.

"Oh yeah. That's great," Mitchell said, just as more of the room began to shift.

Two sections of wall slid out to form platforms about four feet deep and about the same height. Then a hexagonal section on the surface of one opened up as a pile of greenish brown plants rose up from within.

"More seaweed?"

"What do you mean, more?" Mitchell asked.

As he continued to test the wall, Derek quickly relayed what Norah, his Norah anyway, told him had happened in the berth where their sub was docked. Once done, he continued tapping on the wall to no avail.

"You want to help me out here or should we...?" When Derek turned around, though, he found Mitch sitting on one of the platforms, bent over with his head in one hand. "I know that look. What's wrong?"

"Hard to say. Maybe a lot."

"Spill."

"You're not the boss of me."

"Don't make me fire my Mitch to prove a point."

The medic smiled, but there was little humor behind it. "You said Norah made a joke about being served lunch, right?"

"Yeah, so?"

"Well, what if that's actually the case?"

"Not following."

"You found four compartments all with a similar M.O. – multiple non-terrestrial species, vastly different, cause of death didn't appear violent. And then there's that green scanner thing and the fact that we seem to be able to breathe without our lungs exploding."

"We found a bunch of empty rooms, too, don't forget."

"Same here. All of them a uniform size and shape. But who's to say how many more are currently *occupied?*" He held up his fingers in quotes. "And now there's our own seaweed dinner to take into account, as well as the fact that we seem to be locked in."

"Dinner?" Derek raised an eyebrow, starting to catch on. "You think the seaweed is deliberate, don't you?"

"Maybe. I mean, it kind of makes sense. If this ship scanned us to figure out what we could breathe, then why not what we could digest too? And it's something easily obtainable from the local environment no less." He stood up and started to pace. "Four samples does not a conclusion make, but it has me thinking it's sorta pointing toward one possible theory."

"And that is?"

"What if this ship was designed to capture life from the worlds it visited? Capture them and keep them alive?"

"Like some sort of Noah's Ark?"

"I was thinking more like a giant space zoo, but same general gist. At least until, for whatever reason, it crashed here?"

"Considering that everything's dead, I'd say it didn't do a very good job."

"Except what if it did?" Mitchell countered. "You said it yourself. The bodies showed no signs of violence."

Derek considered his own thoughts from earlier. "No broken bones or anything to indicate that they died in a crash."

"Exactly. What if they all simply passed away from old age, after years of the ship feeding and caring for them?"

"That's ... not exactly a pleasant thought."

"Tell me about it. Especially if what I'm thinking is true."

"And that would be?"

"That this *zoo* now thinks we're its latest attraction. And its expecting us to stick around for the long haul."

45

D anni had wanted to spend some time with her brother, catching up on what his life had become since fate had torn them apart – even turning down the radio still strapped to her belt, so as to have a few uninterrupted minutes with him. However, that was tempered by her being the team's tracker, meaning her job revolved around noticing stuff.

As such, the puddle in the distance, at the far edge of where the light reached, had caught her eye and she'd gestured for Harrison to follow.

"Good eye," he said, walking alongside her.

"That's what they pay me for."

"Heh. Pretty sure they just keep me around to give the show some sex appeal."

Danni rounded on him, poking a finger in his chest. "Don't even get me started on that."

"Do I want to ask?"

"That depends. Has anyone from the production team ever asked you to drape yourself over a statue of Ogopogo while in a bikini?"

"Um, not that I recall."

"Then don't ask."

"Hey, at least you don't have to worry about me wanting an autographed copy."

She cringed at the thought. "Ugh! I already had two of our cousins ask."

Harrison chuckled. "Why doesn't that surprise me?"

It was an old joke between them, that the gene pool didn't run particularly deep for some of their relatives back east. All at once, a deep sadness settled into her chest, making her realize how much she'd missed talking to him like this.

Sure, in the months leading up to Bonanza Creek, they hadn't spoken much, both of them busy with college. But it was more the knowledge that they'd never speak this way again which really made her heart hurt.

Except now she was doing the impossible, actually having such a conversation with a brother she'd never met, yet somehow knew all the same. "Hey, Harrison."

"Yeah?"

"I'm really glad I didn't shoot you."

"Me, too."

"What I mean is…"

"I know what you mean." He put a hand around her shoulder. "It's … incredible isn't it? I mean think about it. Who gets a chance like this? A chance to say…"

"Goodbye?"

He actually let out a laugh. "The funny thing is, that's all I've wanted ever since it happened – one last chance to say goodbye. But now, I'm not sure I actually want to."

"Oh? You planning on kidnapping me back to your world?"

"No. Believe me, I watched enough bad TV over Rob's shoulder to know that screwing with the space-time continuum never ends well. Much as I hate to say it, we both need to go back to our respective homes. But what I meant is, now I know there's a Danni out there who survived Bonanza Creek, who's living life by her own rules..."

"Or the government's rules anyway."

"You know what I mean. The fact that I know you're out there somewhere, even if it's a whole universe away, well, I think that makes me ... really happy. Unless, that is, you're about to tell me you're engaged to your version of Mitch, because that would be weird as fuck."

She shook her head. "No worries there. Nice guy. Super smart. Not even remotely my type. Unlike you, I'm currently single. Last prospective boyfriend I had ended up being, well, killed by toxic Jersey hillbillies."

"Jersey, eh?" he replied, glossing over the toxic hillbilly part as only a DoCC member could. "There's been some chatter about sending us there next. Something about people disappearing in the Pine Barrens."

Danni stopped for a moment and considered this. Harrison's world apparently didn't mirror hers point for point. But if so, did that mean the same thing was waiting for him as had been for her team?

"Listen. I have to tell you about New Jersey, but I'm not sure if there are, I dunno, rules about saying something that might affect..."

Harrison shook his head. "You're talking about time travel, which is a totally different issue." He glanced past her. "But maybe we should table that for now. I think it's getting worse."

She turned her attention back to the puddle on the floor, seeing a trail of water leading away. "Worse?"

He nodded then pointed up ahead, to the spot where the lit part of the hallway ended. Sure enough, there was a duct tape arrow on the wall. "We came past that junction a while back and I'm pretty sure the water wasn't at this point yet." He shook his head. "Sorry. I probably should have led with that, but it's kind of been one surprise after another down here."

"No shit."

"It pains me to see the potty mouth my baby sister has developed."

She smacked him on the arm. "Baby this, genius."

He chuckled, but then quickly turned serious again. "We saw some signs earlier that this place wasn't as high and dry as we hoped. I don't know if you guys noticed it or not, or if it even happened in your world, but there's a hole in the hull up top. We think..."

"An oil company accidentally did it? Yeah, been there, done that."

"Okay, good. Saves me the explanation. Anyway, Mitch was thinking it might've happened somewhere close by, which would account for the water. Jake went to investigate, see if he could figure out how bad it was and whether it could be fixed."

"How do you fix an alien ship?"

Harrison paused as if considering this. "That ... is a good question. Jake seemed pretty confident, but now that you mention it, he didn't exactly get into specifics."

"Let me guess. And it's not like you could force the question without getting chewed out?"

He nodded. "Awesome as this job is, it still sucks to be at the bottom of the food chain."

"Quite literally some days." She turned away, not wanting to get back on the clock but knowing they needed to. "We should probably tell the others about this."

"Agreed. Hey, guys!" He paused as they both looked back. "Is it me, or was there a door there just a minute ago?"

"I didn't get all of that, Derek. Come again."

Llanzo was sitting on one of the platforms, munching on a bit of seaweed and listening as the garbled response came in. He'd done what analysis he could with the tools at his disposal, as well as taken what samples he could manage. Now he was trying to fathom the blockbuster news they'd received a short while ago.

It sounded impossible. Surely there was a more probable answer, like the air going bad. He could believe in a gigantic cephalopod, one with morphological changes not found in any related subspecies. That was what science was all about, discovering the unknown. But there were limits to what he was willing to believe without proof.

The problem was, he'd heard their voices – that medic's and the other Norah's. Yes, voices could be faked, mimicked. They could be dealing with some sort of AI for all he knew. Nevertheless, Llanzo felt now, more than ever, that he was in way over his head.

So, in a bid to keep from losing his mind, he'd instead tried to focus on the parts he could more easily understand.

Jenner had also told them of finding the remains of what he claimed were extraterrestrial life. Llanzo considered that it could have simply been a case of misidentification, however, Norah had vouched for the man's credentials. That, and the very existence of this vessel, forced him to at least accept the possibility. But if so, what did it all mean?

Llanzo looked down at the seaweed in his hand. It tasted fine, nice and fresh. More importantly it was what some considered a superfood, providing all the nutrition a body needed. He thought about it for a moment. What if that wasn't a coincidence? What if this place was actually feeding them what it thought they needed?

He remembered what that Kent girl had said about

them being scanned. Looking around, he noted that not only had they been given food they could eat, but the spot he was sitting on was just about the right height, width, and length to act as either a seat or bed. Another coincidence or not?

And how did that play into the bodies Jenner claimed to have found?

This was a problem Llanzo could at least wrap his head around. As insane as it was, it was still more grounded than the idea of doppelgangers from an alternate reality.

He glanced around, wondering if bathroom facilities would be the next thing to appear from out of the seemingly modular walls. *Maybe I should go pee in the corner and see what happens.*

He silently chuckled at the idea of defecating on an alien craft in the name of science, but then he looked down at the seaweed and once again tried to focus.

If this place is purposely feeding us food meant to sustain our needs, then that implies long term. But if that's the case...

Norah's radio crackled to life again. "We ... locked in."

"Come again, Derek. I didn't get all of that," she replied.

"...door shut ... can't open it."

Long term! Llanzo's eyes opened wide as he listened to Jenner's words. When last they'd heard from him, he'd been investigating one of the rooms with alien remains. But what if it wasn't simply another room so much as ... a holding pen?

Oh my goodness!

He glanced at the door, still open, then stood and ran for the sub.

"Doctor? What are you doing?"

"No time to explain," he called back, climbing up the side toward the hatch as horrific realization set in.

Just because nothing had happened yet, didn't mean it

wouldn't. And here he'd been idly sitting around, potentially letting their time run out.

How long ago was that last outage?

Sadly, he hadn't been timing them, more concerned with making sure he didn't puke when the gravity went haywire.

He clambered down into the sub and began scanning the controls, ignoring that Norah was outside yelling his name.

Thankfully he'd co-piloted a few dives before, and had made it a point to pay attention and ask lots of questions while on them.

Where's the damned ballast release?

"Doctor, I'm going to have to ask you to remove yourself from the sub ... *now*."

It was that last part that got his attention, and he looked up to find Norah pointing a weapon at him through the front bubble.

But where did she get...? He saw the answer almost immediately, though, a small shoulder holster beneath her now open jacket.

"Dr. Jenner may have had reservations about bringing his sidearm onto the sub, but I can assure you I did not," she said, her voice cold as steel.

Though he had doubts the bullet would be powerful enough to puncture the heavily reinforced acrylic, he really didn't care to test that theory. But, before he could stand up, a thought hit him.

"Are you really going to shoot me?" He looked away from her, back down at the controls. *Come on. Where is it?*

"I will remind you, Agent Caseman, that shooting me might not affect your chances of escape, but shooting this sub will."

She narrowed her eyes at him, then lowered the weapon.

"Thank you," he replied. "I assure you I'm not trying to run. Where would I even go?"

"Then what the hell are you doing?"

There! That must be it. "This."

He operated the controls for the plates, hoping he got it right and was only releasing a portion of their ballast. If and when they figured out how to open the outer doors again, they were going to need at least some of the weight to maneuver out of this prison.

In the next instant, he heard the heavy *clunk* of steel hitting the floor.

Reid hopped from the pilot's seat and climbed out of the hatch.

"You realize I could just shoot you now, right?" Norah remarked, although she'd thankfully holstered her weapon.

"If you feel you must, please wait until after I'm finished. I believe you'll thank me for it."

"Finished with what?"

Llanzo dropped to the ground and eyed the plate he'd let go. Heavy steel, designed for the depths. Fortunately, the ballast was in small sections so as to more evenly distribute the weight. He quickly grabbed hold of it, almost wrenching his back as he began dragging it toward the door.

"What are you...?"

Just then, the lights began to dim again.

"Either help me or shut up!"

She stepped aside, eyeing him suspiciously – probably his owned damned fault, but there was quite possibly no time for him to explain.

He considered their situation. Yes, the door leading out had opened for them, but it had only done so *after* the outages had started. What if that wasn't a coincidence either? What if they'd simply gotten lucky that this damned place was picking now to glitch out?

The gravity began to shift. Thankfully it was in his favor this time as the heavy metal plate felt ever so slightly lighter as he dragged it across the floor, making an ungodly scraping noise as he went.

Just a little more.

He was nearly there when the lighting resumed its normal illumination, along with the iron becoming a lot heavier again. However, this time the lights didn't stay steady. A few moments later, the room lit up bright green. Llanzo could have almost sworn he felt it as it crawled over his skin.

Off in the corner, where the seaweed had originally appeared, another hunk of vegetation began rising out of the platform.

Reid stepped through the doorway and dropped the plate dead center in the space between room and hallway ... just as the door began to slide shut.

If this didn't work, then it was entirely possible Norah would be stuck in there, while he'd be locked outside, alone in this horrid place and with no hope for escape.

It wasn't the first time Jacob had ever killed a man, but it was the first time he'd ever shot someone who looked like his mirror image. A chill ran down his spine, as if someone had just walked over his grave.

Yeah. And that someone is me.

He knelt down and checked for a pulse, despite knowing it was unlikely he'd find one. It had been a clean kill shot, dead center, bullet to the brain.

Yet seeing this ... *body double*, for lack of a better term, staring up at him was coming close to unraveling his nerves.

Dead as the body seemed, he kept his gun handy in

case this ... *thing* was faking. He'd seen that John Carpenter movie several years back and wasn't about to fall for the same shit. Nevertheless, he ran his hand down the doppelganger's face, closing its eyelids.

That at least made it a little bit better, albeit not much.

Much as a part of him wanted to run screaming from the room, he forced himself to focus on the mission. This was just another enemy combatant. What kind, he didn't know. But what did it really matter in the end?

Rather than continue staring at the corpse, he compartmentalized the weirdness for later, then set to work searching the body.

It was the handgun which convinced him this guy was some sort of replicant. Though to a layperson it would likely look authentic, it was no make or model he'd ever seen before. Moving to the imposter's backpack, he dug through it to find the contents disturbingly similar to the one he'd brought – including a small load of high yield explosives and detonators.

That gave him pause.

There was also a radio. It too was an unfamiliar model, albeit seemingly a step up from the ones he'd brought, complete with high gain antenna.

Jacob checked it out, noting it was set to a different channel than his team had been using. Turning it on, it immediately squawked to life.

"Come in, Jake. Do you read me? Over."

"Norah?" he replied, wondering why she was scanning channels looking for him when she knew damned well they only had the one pair of radios down here.

"Oh thank goodness. You had me worried there, hon."

Hon? "I'm fine. You're coming in loud and clear by the way," he said, throwing a nod toward the body on the floor. At least whatever that imposter had been, he'd packed well.

Norah paused before replying, "Where the hell have you been? No, don't tell me. Let me guess. You got caught up in the mission and forgot to turn the damned thing on? I swear, when we get home we're getting your memory checked, mister."

"No thanks. I'm not letting Mitch..."

"I'm not talking about Mitch. I mean after this is all finished and we get back to the house. And don't you even think of trying to sweet talk me out of it." There came another pause. "All right, enough of that. Good thing the others aren't listening on this channel."

"Yeah, when you say house, do you mean...?"

"Listen to me, Jake. While you've been playing around, there's been a bit of a ... development."

He glanced down at the explosives, wondering if he'd wasted precious time. But then his eyes slid back to the corpse. "Same here. I ... came across the damnedest thing."

"In a sec. You need to hear this. I know it's going to sound crazy, but if you see Derek or the girl who's with him, don't shoot them."

"Why would I shoot Derek?"

"Because I know you, and when you're in mission mode you tend to get tunnel vision."

"That still doesn't tell me why you think I'm gonna shoot him. Yeah, he's a pain in the ass at times, but..."

"Just shut up and listen, please."

Jacob did as asked, listening with growing horror as Norah relayed how Mitch and Harrison – *who the fuck is that* – had made contact with *other* members of their team, including someone who shouldn't be alive. She explained how Mitchell was convinced that whatever was powering this ship and causing the disturbances above had somehow punched a hole through reality, allowing an alternate group of DoCC operatives to somehow be in the same place they were.

A sheen of sweat broke out across Jacob's brow as his eyes once more glanced down at the dead man wearing his face.

It's not possible.

He remembered back to that weird mirage they'd spied on the bridge – a ship just like theirs, plain as day but then gone in the next instant.

What if it hadn't been a mirage?

"Believe me," Norah said from the other end, "I thought the exact same thing you probably are. This is some crazy stuff. But Mitch seems convinced it's real. I don't know if they crossed over into our world, we crossed into theirs, or this vessel is acting as some sort of bridge, but either way we're tromping through some deep shit here. Jake, honey, are you still there?"

"Uh, yeah. I'm here," he numbly replied, beginning to realize the Norah he was speaking to wasn't the one he knew.

This had to be some kind of trick. Maybe the air had gone bad, or maybe whatever was glowing in the next chamber was causing him to grow brain tumors.

The alternative was unthinkable – that he'd actually murdered himself in cold blood.

That was bad enough, but if he was reading between the lines correctly, listening to what the woman on the other end was saying, things between her and her Jacob had turned out differently.

There was only one way to be sure.

He shook his head, making sure his voice didn't falter as he spoke. "Yeah, that's crazy shit all right. Listen, babe, I'm sorry for dragging you down here. How about when we get home I make it up to you? A nice dinner followed by a soak in the tub?"

"None of that," she replied tersely, causing him to let out a sigh of relief ... until she added, "This is an unsecured line, don't forget. Save the sweet talk for when you can do it in person. Now why don't you switch to channel three so you can get caught up. We have other heads down here working with us now. Might as well put them to use."

"Um ... will do," he replied. "Just give me a minute. Finishing up some ... recon work on my end."

He didn't wait for her reply, once again shutting off the radio.

Staring down at the body – *his body* – Jacob's mind railed against what he'd been told. It was so much easier to believe he was going crazy or had maybe gotten zapped with an alien mind-fuck ray. Because if it was true, then he'd not only ended his own life in that other world, but he'd destroyed the happiness that this man and his Norah had found, the happiness he'd screwed up.

He glanced around, once again noticing the hole in the wall, the one where the water was held back by an invisible force. Jacob stepped up to it and touched the cold seawater, noting that, as before, his hand was able to easily pass through.

Then he backed up again and turned his attention to the body, as he began to get an idea of what needed to be done next.

46

Julie was impressed. There was no doubt about it. Mitchell was damned good at what he did, not to mention he really knew his drugs.

Her leg still hurt like hell, and she didn't dare put much weight on it, even with the military grade walking cast. But with the crutches he'd found, at least she was mobile again, which was more than she'd been hoping for.

"Try not to get that wet," the medic said.

"Excuse me?"

"That was a joke. You know, because we're..."

"On a boat. I get it."

He shrugged. "I was actually going to say likely to be sunk by a sea monster, but yours sounds more optimistic."

"Is it that bad?" she asked, lowering her voice and following him away from the rest of the triage unit.

"It's not great. Don't get me wrong, I'm not ready to start discussing whether the two of us could fit on one door yet, but..."

"We totally could. I've seen the reenactments. Rose was a selfish bitch."

423

"Glad I'm not the only one who thinks that. But things right now are both better and worse. Better as in the hull is still in one piece."

"And worse?"

"Our tentacled friend was just as busy below the water line as he was above. The rudder's been bent back into the propulsion system."

"Meaning?"

"It screwed up our screws so we're thoroughly screwed." Mitchell raised his hands apologetically. "Sorry. I just really wanted to say that. But bottom line is we couldn't run if we tried."

"Great. Has there been any word on the Will-Do?"

"Not a peep, not that we have much chance of contacting anyone with the communication array twisted into a pretzel."

"So we're up shit creek without a paddle *or* a radio."

"More or less. There is one other thing, though."

What now? Julie thought, wondering whether they'd inadvertently pissed off some kind of sea god in their travels.

He stepped in and lowered his voice. "Keep this on the sly. I don't think Andrea wants the crew to know yet."

"When did she become Andrea?"

He shrugged. "Getting inked together is a bonding experience."

"No doubt. So what did she say?"

"She thinks she knows who took the Rogers Will-Do. Aside from the sub crew, three people were unaccounted for before that thing decided to clip our fins. That Klipsch guy, Alvita Guerrero, and one of her agents ... some guy named Kyle."

"Kyle?" Julie replied. "I talked to him for a bit earlier. Didn't strike me as a runner."

"Maybe he got freaked out."

"Could be, but if so he could have made a run for it at any time. Why wait for those two?"

Mitchell raised an eyebrow. "You think something fishy is going on?"

"I swear, if you make one more ocean pun, I'm going to shove this crutch up your ass."

"I can't apologize for who I am."

Julie turned away, staring out over what should have been the dark ocean. However, the lightning above was now flashing so frequently as to make the darkness more the exception. She didn't need to look up to know it was getting worse. If Derek didn't surface soon...

She pushed that thought away. There was nothing she could do about it anyway. "You think maybe they kidnapped him? Kerry and Alvita I mean. Seems a stretch. I had the displeasure of spending a chunk of the day with Klipsch, and, well, he didn't really strike me as a criminal mastermind."

"Yeah. I wouldn't doubt she was the brains of the outfit."

"It still doesn't make any sense. Norah offered to send her home but she didn't think the Will-Do was safe. Why the change of heart?"

"Who can say? People do stupid things when they're scared."

"Maybe. None of that helps us, though."

"Us or Derek."

"Do you think they...?"

"I don't know," he interrupted. "I'm pretty sure *something* happened down there, since it all went crazy afterward. But beyond that..." He took a deep breath. "Listen. They have a good crew and a solid little sub, even if we did strip it down to the bare essentials. They've got at least ten hours of battery so long as they don't go crazy, and plenty of air. And if they get in trouble, the ballast controls are triple redundant with a mechanical failsafe. All they have to do is pull a couple of levers and woosh, up to the surface like an oversized rubber duck."

"If you say so."

"I know so. Derek's got a small army of guardian angels looking over his shoulder. I've never seen anyone walk out of so many no-win situations as he has."

"I hope you're right."

"Me, too. But for now, we need to focus on worrying about us, and making sure there's still a ship here when they get back. Speaking of which, I should probably go see how things are going."

"What do you need me to do?"

Mitchell smirked. "Can I assume it's pointless to tell you to sit this one out?"

"One-hundred and ten percent."

"Then do what Team Crypto-Hunter does best. See if you can come up with any ideas on how to nail this thing once it shows its slimy face again."

Julie nodded than turned back toward the sea, letting her mind wander to the problem at hand.

Mitch was right. She needed to put her thinking cap on.

This ship and its crew were outfitted to fight human enemies. It was time to remember their foe was anything but.

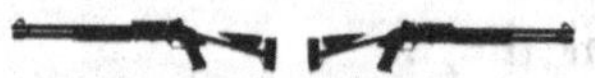

Things were not looking good as far as Andrea was concerned. She'd been forced to move her command deck down to the briefing room, but it was in name only. The bridge was smashed, beyond their capacity to repair. The engines were still operational along with the pumps, but propulsion was gone, too. And, most importantly, half their crew was on the casualty list, adding to the hopelessness of it all.

Communications were completely offline and their helicopter had crashed the day before, leaving them with no...

This isn't helping.

She needed to consider her assets, not their deficits.

"We're still afloat," she said to herself.

One of her people stepped in and dropped a clipboard on the desk, adding to the growing pile. "Agent Vakovsky reports that the fire on the bow has been contained."

That's two plusses. "Any idea what caused it?"

"He's taking samples now. Best he has so far was it seemed to burn like some kind of magnesium, except hotter."

"Hotter?"

"Enough to have buckled most of the steel plates on the forward deck. He advises keeping the crew away from that section of the ship."

She thanked the agent and dismissed her, looking down at the report. *So much for good news.* If that thing attacked them again, it was going to make defending the ship that much harder.

Enough of that, Drea. Back to your assets.

Though the Will-Do was gone and almost certainly not coming back, the Sun Angel had sustained negligible damage during the attack. She'd already dispatched two agents to it to monitor the radio and see if they could hail anyone.

She'd briefly considered sending a full crew and having them sail back to port. However, that would further deplete their defenders, as well as potentially leave both ships vulnerable.

There was also the fact that in a worst case scenario,

the Sun Angel would make a far better lifeboat than their launches.

"Knock knock."

She looked up to find Mitchell standing at the door. Though he was weird, quirky, and at times annoying as hell, she found the medic growing on her. Despite his oddities, he'd proven cool under fire, not to mention his earlier plan had likely saved their bacon. She waved him in, oddly glad to have the company.

"Too soon to talk about cuisine?" He quickly held up his hands. "Kidding. Thought I'd see if you needed any help brainstorming."

"How are the wounded doing?"

"Patel's got a handle on it."

"And Agent Wilhelm?"

"She won't be running the Boston Marathon anytime soon, but she's hobbling about, already trying to figure out how to get back into the fight."

"I can admire her spirit."

"That's how we roll in the Department of Cryptid Containment. We keep picking ourselves up until the monster stops moving ... or we do."

"You need a better slogan."

He nodded. "Yeah, well, that's why we're on the Adventure Channel and not HBO. But seriously, what can I do to help?"

She was about to tell him she had it under control, but the truth was she didn't. None of them did. So, rather than fall back on her pride, she decided to take the helping hand that was offered. "I was just making a list of assets at our disposal."

"Oh? So what do you have?"

"I didn't get far. We're still afloat, not on fire, and..."

"Oh yeah. Have your people save me a sample of that

plasma residue, if you don't mind. Would love to get it under a spectrometer."

"Plasma?"

He nodded. "Just speculating. Go on."

"That's it. Oh, and we still have the Sun Angel."

"All right, that's a start. So let's keep going with this. I'm hearing a lot about things that float but not much about things that go boom, which right now are probably the bath toys we should care about most."

Andrea let out a sigh. "We have plenty of ammo left for the rifles and sidearms, but we expended most of the fifty cals during the last fight."

"Grenades?"

"A handful for the launchers, but we used up almost all of the swimmers blowing up that first octopus."

"Too bad."

She shook her head. "Tell me about it. What I wouldn't give for a cache of good old fashioned depth charges right now."

"If wishes were horses."

"What about what we did last time? Think that might work again?"

Mitchell took a seat opposite her and leaned back, tenting his hands behind his head as he stared up at the ceiling. "Possible. Octopi are highly intelligent, but wounded animals tend to do irrational things ... which I will caution doesn't always work in our favor." He met her eyes. "So, is that it? What else do we have?"

She laughed. "Enough C-4 to blow that thing and probably five of its cousins sky high. Too bad I doubt it'll stand still long enough to let us attach a bunch of charges to its body."

"I'm not much of a betting man, mostly because I can't play Texas hold 'em to save my life, but you're probably right."

"Remind me to invite you to our weekly poker night."

"Ah, you wound me so. But..."

The medic was interrupted as another agent popped his head in the door.

"Sorry to barge in, but that..." he paused as he saw Mitchell sitting there. "um ... DoCC agent is barking orders and I wanted to check..."

"Barking orders about what?" Andrea asked.

"Setting up a defense for when that thing comes back."

She glanced at Mitchell who gave her a single nod. "So long as she's not advocating using anyone as live bait, follow her lead. This is their wheelhouse, not ours."

"Understood," he replied, sounding somewhat dubious before stepping out.

Andrea turned to the medic again. "She was right earlier about keeping our eyes open. Just wish we'd kept them open wider."

"Better late than never."

"True. At least we managed to drive it off before it tore us a new asshole."

At that, Mitchell's eyes opened wide. "Wait. Maybe that's it. Not the asshole part. What you said earlier."

"Which part?"

"About not being able to tie C-4 to that thing."

"Yeah, so...?"

"But maybe we don't have to."

"Not following."

Mitchell leaned forward, locking eyes with her. "You may want to sit back for this one, because I have a plan that might work. There's just one small problem."

"And that is?"

"You *really* aren't going to like it."

Kerry leaned over the side and vomited again. It wasn't the motion of the ocean, so much as it felt like his stomach kept flip-flopping. One moment he felt all heavy, almost to the point where he couldn't move, the next it was as if his feet wanted to leave the deck.

It was the weirdest sensation, almost like that time last summer when he and that blonde he'd been dating – *what was her name again?* – decided to spice up a night of tequila shooters with some X. Too bad there was nobody around now to suck his dick. It would've helped to keep him grounded.

Far as he could tell, though, his only company was the sound of thunder overhead along with the constant lap of water against the boat. At least that crazy lightning was now consistent enough that he could kinda see what he was doing.

The engine was still dead along with the batteries. Hell, even his watch had finally given up the ghost after failing to make up its mind about what time it was.

When he was done puking, he filled up the bucket he'd found below deck with more seawater and went back to the task of trying to scrub out the bloodstains. It was slow going, but with no power the hose was effectively useless. And with this piece of shit boat dead in the water, he figured it was time better spent than sitting around with his thumb up his ass.

Though he hadn't seen so much as the lights from a passing boat, the possibility still remained that he'd be found. And if that happened, the last thing he needed were uncomfortable questions.

He paused as he looked toward the door leading into the cabin. He was mostly finished up here. What remained was inside. But, even with the constant lightning, the thought of being in the dark cabin unnerved him.

With the strange flip-flopping in his stomach coupled

with the paranoia still eating away at him every time he turned around, it made going below feel claustrophobic. It was bad enough that he'd opted to piss overboard a short while back rather than go inside and use the head.

Still, it wasn't like he could avoid it. That's where the majority of the mess lay. it was foolish to assume anyone rescuing him wouldn't think to check down there.

There came a splash behind him, whipping up a bit of spray that chilled his backside, but Kerry was too busy focusing on his fear to care.

Might as well get this over and done with.

Maybe he'd get supremely lucky and find an unclaimed joint in one of the cabinets. A good toke would've gone over really well right about then.

For now, he headed inside the cabin, letting the intermittent lightning guide his steps as he descended into the quiet, almost tomb-like interior.

Killing – *murdering* – that man had seemed like a good idea at the time. And it's not like the dumb fuck had given him much choice. It was his own goddamned fault for doing a last minute check for stuff they'd missed.

Regardless, now Kerry wished he'd at least waited until they were in the main cabin to do the deed. The windows there were wide and plentiful. Down below there were few portholes, letting in, at best, anemic amounts of light from the strange storm raging above.

Unsurprisingly, he stumbled on the last step, miscounting them, as water from the pail sloshed out all over his shoes.

Goddamn it!

Oh well. It wasn't like this was dry work to begin with. Kerry got down on his hands and knees, dipped some rags he'd managed to find into the water, then waited for the next flash so he knew where to begin.

It came soon enough, revealing the mess – a thick

congealed puddle of blood covering the floor. *Goddamn.* There seemed to be a lot more than he remembered, the smell of copper thick in the air, nearly turning his stomach again.

Keep it together, he ordered himself. Though Kerry doubted he had much left in his stomach, the last thing he needed was to add to the mess already there.

Just as the darkness reasserted itself, he felt the boat list to the side. Or maybe it was his equilibrium shitting the bed again. It was hard to tell … at least until the bucket tipped over, sloshing water all over.

"Fuck me!"

Kerry stood up, then just as quickly fell back down again as the ship lurched violently around him. He smacked his head against something, feeling wetness drip down his cheek that he was fairly sure wasn't water.

Once again the boat listed, actually shuddering this time. The sound of fiberglass creaking, as if under great strain, could easily be heard.

Kerry had no idea what was happening. Had the storm outside suddenly gotten worse in the space of a few short minutes? Or was this maybe all connected to how sick he'd felt the last hour?

He wondered if maybe he'd been poisoned by those assholes back on the other ship. But poison wouldn't have accounted for what he heard next, a sound that made his heart leap into his throat – wood and fiberglass shattering as if someone had driven a truck through the side of the boat.

Lightning flashed again, lighting up the cabin enough for him to see the room around him deformed, as if it were being compressed from outside.

For a moment he wondered if he was maybe hallucinating, but then a spray of cold seawater hit him in the chest, followed by more sounds of destruction.

What the fuck?

Kerry scrambled to his feet. Whatever the hell was going on, it sure as shit didn't feel like some head trip brought on by food poisoning. No, something was happening to the ship – as if a giant hand had reached up from below and was now squeezing it like a paper bag.

He tried to feel his way back to the stairs as the water quickly rose around him, going from ankle deep to waist level in the space of seconds.

The ship lurched again, this time to the rear, as if the stern were being dragged down. Kerry fell forward against the steps, submerging in the cold water and splitting his lip as his face met the hard wood.

Fighting against the shock of both the pain and the cold, he tried to push himself back up as the orientation of the vessel changed again, this time listing to the front. However, the now perilously deep water kept him from being thrown forward. Kerry found his footing and stood up best he could in the watery darkness, only to find he was still submerged.

Oh God!

Realizing he was in imminent danger of drowning, he kicked off from the floor only to hit the ceiling. He desperately craned his neck, finding perhaps a two inch pocket of air left at the top, enough for him to take a breath but no more. The rest of the cabin was completely flooded, and in the darkness he had no idea which way was out.

That was the least of his worries, though, as the splintering of wood grew ever louder in the black hell, just as he was forced back underwater. Too late, he realized the entire cabin was being crushed around him. His legs were pushed up and his head forced down as the sides began to collapse in on him.

Lightning flashed overhead, briefly illuminating the

water and giving Kerry a momentary glimpse of something just outside his prison. It was massive, fleshy, and covered in nightmare-sized suckers. Something had found him adrift after all, but it wasn't the rescue he'd been hoping for.

He had a brief moment of stark naked terror in which he was certain that the sea was claiming vengeance for the lives he'd taken, then the walls caved in forcing the last of the air out of his lungs.

It's not fair! I got away. It's not...

Kerry's silent protests came to an abrupt end as the thing outside gave one more monstrous squeeze – instantly pulverizing his body and filling the water with the stink of hot blood.

The leviathan realized its mistake as the thrumming once again wracked its body. But by then it was too close to its quarry to break off. Somehow, despite the thrumming having grown silent near the large surface thing, here, just a short distance away, it was now worse than ever.

It had begun to sense the changes as it moved away from the large surface thing in pursuit of its smaller podmate. It was as if the water itself were somehow charged. But then the first of the pulses had struck it, causing its body to spasm with familiar pain, but also somehow different than before.

For a moment it seemed as if it had been slowed, moving through the water yet making no progress. When the next pulse hit, though, it was as if the leviathan had been propelled forward at speeds even it had never known.

With each thrum it felt its body mass shift, one moment struggling to keep from sinking, the next compelled up to the surface despite its efforts to stay submerged.

Though half-blinded, its one remaining eye was still keen. Yet at one point as it peered down at itself, its arms seemed to blur and then double. It only lasted for a moment, but it sent the beast into a frothing fury, thinking perhaps another of its kind was nearby – only to find itself alone mere seconds later.

By then it was tempted to turn back, to return to where the thrumming had ceased. But it sensed the smaller surface thing was near. Though its prey now sat in the water as if dead, the leviathan wasn't fooled.

The pulses torturing its body once again gave way to rage. Though on some level it understood that turning around could end the torment, its mind was too far gone to heed such reason.

It attacked the surface thing without mercy, coming up beneath it and entwining its arms around its fragile body. It had then squeezed with everything it had, crumpling the surface thing's shell and dirtying the water with the scent of the screaming thing that had been seeking shelter within.

The attack had been over in minutes, the surface thing now nothing more than a ruptured, battered corpse – a testament to the leviathan's superiority.

The fight, however, hadn't eased any of its pain – leaving it still boiling over with rage.

It may have won, yet the large surface thing and the massive thing at the bottom of the sea both still remained, each having forced it to retreat.

In agony and with its cognitive abilities in heavy decline, it turned away from the already forgotten husk still sinking to the bottom, and began swimming back the way it had come.

It was time to end this and prove to all the intruders within its domain that it and it alone reigned supreme.

47

Danni pulled out her radio just as she and Harrison reached the wall where the doorway had been, quickly turning the volume up – just in time for it to squawk to life.

"Danni, if you can hear me, do not go in any of the specimen rooms. We think they're like some sort of..."

The door opened in front of her, revealing both Derek and Mitchell, the latter of which had his radio up to his mouth.

"...holding pens," he finished, before blinking in confusion at them. "Well, that was ... ridiculously easy."

"And you're complaining?" Derek replied.

"Not really."

"What are you guys doing?" Harrison asked.

"Didn't you hear us banging on the wall?"

"No. We came back when we noticed the door was shut."

"Yeah," Danni added, moving to step in. "So why'd you close..."

"Wait!" Derek held up a hand. "Whatever you do, do not come in here."

"Yeah. guys," Mitchell replied. "Just back up a few steps, okay."

Danni and Harrison both did so, just as the lights began to dim again.

"Oh fuck," Mitchell said. "Let's go!"

Derek was already on the move, though. "Don't have to tell me twice."

As Danni and her brother stepped aside, the two men joined them in the hallway. As usual, there came the strange fluctuation in gravity. When it had finally passed, she looked back to see that the water in the hallway had seemingly inched up a bit.

"So what exactly was that about?" Harrison asked.

"It locked us in after that last distortion ... or outage," Mitchell said. "Still not sure what to call them."

"We can save the English lesson for later," Derek replied. "I think the better question is why didn't it lock us in earlier? And why did it open up for them and not us?"

"Beauty before age?" Harrison offered with a grin.

Mitchell raised an eyebrow. "This is why they don't give you more dialogue on the show."

"All right, enough," Derek said. "Let's be serious here. If your theory about this being an intergalactic petting zoo is right, then we almost became permanent residents."

Mitchell let out a chuckle. "Maybe they thought we were a mated pair." Then he quickly sobered up. "Okay, so that aside, I might actually have a theory as to why it locked us in."

"Guys," Danni warned, glancing at the water.

"Just a moment," Derek replied. "I want to hear him out."

She bristled a little at that, but held her tongue. At the end of the day, Mitchell had seniority, even if he was from a different universe.

"We don't know how long this ship has been down

here or the last time it brought anything aboard," the medic began. "But I think one thing is certain. Whether it's old age, crash damage, or that drill, this place isn't in tiptop shape. That's the reason its lying here and not blasting us off to Jupiter. And that's why I think it decided to lock us in now and not earlier. It's going all friggy."

"Either that or it's still booting up," Danni added, the idea popping into her head. "Like when you first turn your laptop on in the morning and it sometimes takes a few minutes for everything to work. Well, maybe it works the same here. We could have woke some parts when we came aboard, and now the rest is catching up."

Harrison shook his head. "Neither explains why we were able to open the door but they weren't."

"Sure it does," Mitchell replied. "If this place is going all wonky, then maybe it doesn't recognize the difference between who's allowed to roam the halls and the intergalactic cattle. It could be as simple as you guys being on the right side of the door and us being on the wrong side."

Derek nodded. "Makes as much sense as anything else I suppose. The door only shut after it scanned us, but it only started doing that fairly recently. So it could be both for all we know."

"Yeah. So until we know better, my suggestion is for at least one person to stay outside while we explore."

"About that last part," Danni said. "That might be a problem."

"Why?"

"Because I think the ship is flooding."

"What?!" Derek replied. "Why didn't you..."

"I tried to."

He let out a sigh and nodded. "Yeah, I guess you did. Sorry. Next time I say to wait a moment, you have my full permission to tell me to stuff it."

"Can I get that in writing?"

"Definitely, but first I think we need to start focusing on how to get the hell out of here once and for all."

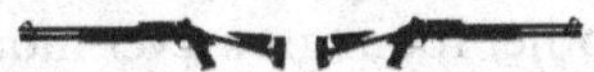

Jacob gave the corpse a shove, sending his body double floating away into the flooded room. Whatever was in there, the chamber itself appeared massive, larger than the others he'd seen. He considered how far past that wall of water he'd come, concluding it was likely several times the size of the other rooms he'd found. More important, though, was that something kept flashing inside, every so often sending out a pulse of light that lit up the seawater within. Sadly, whatever it was, it wasn't close enough for him to see, at least not without climbing in there and taking a swim.

He'd turned off the radio again. Hearing the other Norah had proven too much for him. He'd been through a lot in his life, had been captured and even tortured, but learning there was a place where he'd made different choices, well, it was more than he could bear. It reminded him of the poor decisions he'd made versus the life he could've had. He'd never been a fan of *It's a Wonderful Life*, and now finally understood why.

The lights began to dim, dragging him from his thoughts as he watched the other Jacob drift away.

"Shit!"

He quickly stepped to the side as whatever force held the water at bay faltered along with the gravity, causing a deluge to spray into his room, as if a floodgate had just been opened.

There was little question as to what the other Jacob had probably been cursing about. The poor fool had likely been caught the same way he'd been earlier — sent tumbling onto his ass as a small tidal wave punched him in the face.

He at least knew better now as he stood off on one side, waiting for the outage to pass, even as the pulsing lights inside the other room grew ever more frantic.

And then it was over. The water ceased pouring out as the integrity of the force field, for lack of a better term, was reestablished. Once again, the resulting outage had caused the water to rise, bringing it almost up to his knees. Yeah, there was no doubt about it. Soon enough this section would be flooded. It would then be only a matter of time before the entire ship filled up. After that? Well, they needed to be long gone before that happened, which meant he needed to stop dicking around and get back to work.

He turned to find his own pack had been pushed out into the hallway by the jet of seawater. No matter. It was waterproof

Jacob turned to grab his doppelganger's pack. He'd initially dismissed its contents as fake, but now knew better. Besides, the extra munitions meant a greater chance of getting the job done. The detonators within might be of a different design than he was used to, but the general idea was familiar enough that he was certain he could figure it...

The lighting in the room abruptly changed, catching him off guard, turning bright green as it had done when they'd first approached the ship.

"What now?"

But then it began to blink, as if whatever was going on wasn't working quite right, an easy conclusion to come to, considering the big freaking hole in the wall less than ten feet away. A hole through which something was obviously reacting badly to the seawater within.

None of that was his problem, though. It was time to plant his charges and get the hell out of...

Before he could so much as stand up straight, the doorway leading out closed.

Jacob stepped to the wall, now a solid panel with not so much as a crack in sight. He pushed against it, then banged his fist on it, producing nothing more than a hollow thud.

"Son of a..."

He wasn't sure whether it was a glitch or some sort of half-assed defense mechanism, but either way he appeared to be locked in tight.

That wasn't good. He needed to find a way out and soon. With the door shut, he estimated it wouldn't be long before this room filled completely with water.

Jacob eyed the bag of explosives still with him. It was possible he could blast his way out, but with little shelter to be had, he had an equal or better chance of blowing himself to bits as well, especially if he accidentally set off the charges in the pack lying right outside, too.

He stood there for a moment, considering all the assignments he'd taken over the years, all the risks that had come with them. He'd performed his duty proudly each and every time, all in the name of freedom. And if he had met his end during any of them, he would have done so honorably.

This was no different.

Duty first. Then I'll see about saving my own ass.

And if he couldn't, then so be it.

He glanced down at the other Jacob's pack, remembering what else was in it.

He would do his duty and possibly meet his maker, if that was to be his fate, but maybe he didn't have to do it alone.

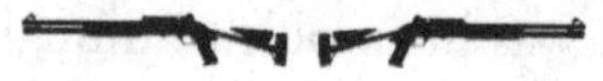

"Anything?" Derek asked.

"Nope." Mitchell clipped the walkie talkie to his belt. "Still getting the radio silence treatment from our Norah. I'm guessing either her battery's dead or she's on another channel."

The other team's equipment had proven far more effective at punching through the interference, although apparently it still couldn't account for the human factor.

"Why would she be on another channel?"

The medic shrugged. "Um, because she doesn't appreciate my effervescent personality?"

Derek shook his head but decided not to comment. "Regardless, we still need to find Jake ... both of them."

"We will," Danni said. "Harrison and I can go check down this..."

"No chance. We're not splitting up, at least not that way."

Though Derek wanted to give her as much time with her brother as she could get, he also understood too well that, with the ship going haywire around them, the last thing they needed was to split their limited resources in a way that practically ensured they'd have to search for each other again.

"I agree," Mitchell said. "I don't mean to cut this family reunion short, but let's save the trans-dimensional incursions for *Ghostbusters*. If we have to split up, it needs to be with our own teammates. No arguments." After a beat, he glanced Derek's way. "Goddamn. I sound like you now."

"Leadership tends to do that."

"Fine," Harrison replied. "Then we'll all stick together."

"Listen, kid..."

Harrison cut him off, though. "Don't give me that crap. We've already run into enough strange shit down here. Four heads are better than two."

Mitchell opened his mouth to say something, but Derek held up a hand. "He's right ... for now. We'd have probably gotten stuck in that room eating seaweed until the end of time if they hadn't been there. That said, we'll play this by ear. If at any point I decide things look too dicey, then that's it. We are to go back to our respective subs and get the hell out of here. Agreed?"

He held each of their gazes in turn. Mitchell was quick to nod, Danni and Harrison were a little slower, but each eventually agreed.

"Good."

"Just one small problem, boss man," Mitchell replied after a moment. "We still don't know how to get out. So far it seems like Earthlings check in but they don't..."

"I think I liked your zoo analogy better."

"Same difference."

"I have an idea," Harrison offered. "Let's head back to Norah. Doesn't matter which one. Yours is fine. That way we can brainstorm this together without getting locked up or worrying about the radios going crazy again. Maybe Mitch and that doctor you guys brought can figure something out. Once we have a plan, then we'll go find the two Jakes and get the fuck out of Dodge."

"Maybe we should head to your Norah," Derek countered. "The fact that she isn't answering..."

"Means nothing." Mitchell shook his head. "Well, it probably means something, but not what you're thinking."

"Not following."

Mitchell sighed. "Okay fine, you got me. I'm pretty sure the reason she's not answering is the same reason you – our version anyway – got stuck with ship duty."

"How so?"

"Earlier, I may have ... eavesdropped on the three of them arguing. Our Derek didn't sound happy."

"Let me guess. There are folks in D.C. who aren't exactly pleased with my – *his* – leadership."

"Not unless I need to get my hearing checked. From the sound of things, *he* was the one ticked off with what was going on. I heard him say something about another mission, something they were keeping him out of the loop of."

"What other mission?"

"No idea," Mitchell said. "They cut him off, pulled rank before he could get it out of them. That's when he was assigned boat duty. Trust me. I wasn't happy with it either. He should've been down here running things, just like you are."

"For the record, I'm glad he isn't," Derek replied. "Not that I wouldn't mind meeting him, but it allowed us to all be here. And, quite frankly, I think we work best as a team." He turned to the other two. "That means all of us. So let's head back and get to brainstorming."

"Okay," Danni said, "But shouldn't we try to find Jake first, not after..."

Derek shook his head. "This might sound cold-blooded, but logically we'd be better served trying to figure a way out of here first, versus the other way around."

"Agreed," Mitchell replied. "Besides, for all we know, they're both headed back on their own already. At least that's what we agreed on."

"Same here, assuming ours doesn't have a secondary objective as well. Probably a big assumption, unless..."

"Unless what?"

A grim smile crossed Derek's lips. "One Norah might be uncrackable, but maybe between the two of them there's enough differences to get one to spill what they know ... especially since all our lives could depend on it."

48

"You want to blow up my ship?!"

"Want is a really strong term," Mitchell replied. "More like I think this is our best shot at killing that thing."

"And if it fails?" Andrea snapped.

"We're fucked. But," he quickly added, "we aren't going to withstand another all-out assault, especially with most of our heavy ordinance depleted, and we both know it. So we're equally fucked either way."

Andrea put her head in her hands. "You know, I really don't like that kind of language on my bridge."

"Court martial me later then, or sue me for sexual harassment. Whatever floats your boat."

"Sexual harassment?"

"Well, I could try ... if you wanted me to."

She narrowed her eyes at him, but found herself chuckling nevertheless. "You know, you suck at flirting even more than you do choosing dinner."

"Hence why Derek gets the bulk of the marriage proposals from our fans."

Andrea was about to reply when another agent popped

447

in to hand her a status report, reminding her they were on the clock.

It was from Vakovsky stating what she already knew – repairs to propulsion were highly unlikely in any reasonable timeframe.

"Anything good?"

"Nope." She tossed the clipboard onto the table in front of her, already littered with similar updates. "So run this idea of yours past me again."

"Simple. You have plenty of C-4 but no way to get our buddy out there to sit still long enough to use it. So we do the next best thing. We wire the ship, turn it into a massive bomb. Then we evacuate most of the crew to the Sun Angel, where they sit very still and very quiet so as to not attract attention."

"And then?"

"We blow it to hell."

She massaged her temples. "And who's to say it doesn't go after the Sun Angel instead?"

"No one," Mitchell replied. "But, it came after us last time it attacked. Also, its smaller cousin broke off from the Rogers Will-Do when you showed up."

"So?"

"So, I don't pretend to be a marine biologist, but my guess is there's some fight or flight response going on here. I read up on cephalopods a bit before this mission. Octopi aren't considered territorial per se, but they do tend to have preferred hunting grounds. We have no idea if this applies to their giant cousin out there, except that this thing has had ample time to wander off and go elsewhere. But instead it sunk the Tortuga, and then did its damnedest to try and sink us. So I'm guessing that, in its confused state, it might see us as rivals or intruders, picking the biggest threat to take out first ... which is probably still better than it confusing us for a potential mate."

She raised an eyebrow. "Has something like that ever happened?"

Mitchell shrugged. "Once, about three years back during Sasquatch mating season. Young male, way too horny, and not overly picky."

She held up a hand. "Spare me the details. Getting back to this plan, you said most of the crew."

"That's the other part you're not going to like. We need someone here to set off the charges."

"We have remote..."

"I know. But think about everything that's been going on. It seems like we're in the eye of this storm, but can we really afford to take that chance? I don't know about you, but the last thing I would want to do is flip the switch and see a whole lot of nothing happen. No. If we want to be certain this works, everything needs to be hard wired. And that means one unlucky contestant stays for a front row seat to the fireworks."

Andrea sat back in her chair. He was right. She didn't like it. Rather than tackle that one head on, though, she asked, "And if that doesn't kill it?"

Mitchell nodded. "Always a possibility when dealing with something new, but I think it'll work. That thing is big and strong, but it's also relatively soft. If we send a couple tons of shrapnel flying into it at the speed of sound, that's definitely gonna mess up its day. Worst case, it'll be badly injured, almost certainly enough to drive it off. If so, the Sun Angel makes a run for it and hopes for the best. And by that I mean, hopefully doesn't pull into port and find it's now an alternate timeline where Hitler won."

"I really do enjoy your optimism."

"That's why I'm here, to help blow up your ship and

talk about *The Man in the High Castle*. But as interesting as the latter is, I think we need to discuss what you think of this."

"I'm going to be frank with you, Mitch. I hate it. It makes me want to vomit." She held up a hand. "But I also think we're backed in a corner and the only way out is to either hope for a miracle or grab the bull by the balls and make one happen. No offense if you're into praying, but I'm not."

"Hey, I'm all for squeezing bovine nut sacks, figuratively speaking. That said, we should talk about who gets to..."

"No, we shouldn't," she stated flatly. "*I* need to figure that out. This is my command, my decision."

"But..."

Andrea stood up and put a hand on Mitchell's shoulder, something she would normally have never done while on duty. "Listen. You've been a big help. I'm sorry if I came across as cold earlier. You didn't deserve that ... some of it anyway. I should've respected you and your team. But now I need to take care of this part." Mitchell opened his mouth to speak again, but she talked over him, assuming an authoritative tone that she hoped he knew better than to argue with. "I'm putting you in charge of the evacuation effort. Get the wounded and all support personnel onto the Sun Angel."

The medic hesitated for a moment, but then finally he nodded. "I can do that."

"Good. Double time it then. The clock is ticking and I'd hate for that thing to come back before we're ready."

"Got it." He turned and started heading toward the door.

"Maybe afterward," she said softly, not even sure he could hear her, "we can talk about those cheesesteaks."

He did, though, looking back over his shoulder. "Why

does that sound like the words of someone who has no intention of ever eating a cheesesteak?"

"As you were, mister."

He nodded. "Aye aye, Captain."

Then he turned and left, leaving her alone with her darkening thoughts.

Danni stood with Harrison outside the airlock. The room now faintly resembled crude living quarters, following the changes that had occurred in their absence. It gave somber credence to Mitchell's earlier theory. Inside, Derek was bringing Norah up to speed, while Dr. Reid assisted Mitch in studying the wall leading back outside.

That left she and her brother as the official door holders, which was fine with her.

To Llanzo's credit, he'd come up with the idea of using one of their ballast plates as a doorstop. It looked solid enough, even if the door itself hadn't made any attempt to close during the last two outages. That said, she could appreciate his foresight.

However, much as their current *assignment* probably made sense, she also had a feeling it was Derek's attempt to give her a bit more time with her brother before they were inevitably forced to go their separate ways.

Almost as if echoing those thoughts, Harrison said, "It's crazy ... trying to share a lifetime of memories in a few hours that is.."

She nodded. "Yeah, but how many crashed spaceships can we reasonably expect to find, even in this job?"

"Tell me about it. So ... how's Mom doing?"

"She and Dad were both pretty crushed when ... you know. But they've been doing their best." She let out a chuckle. "Dad even has a new hobby, trolling Twitter for anyone making crude comments about me and giving them a piece of his mind."

"Really? Heh. Definitely sounds like Dad." He turned away and sniffled. "God, I miss him."

"Wait, miss him? Why?"

He turned back, his eyes glistening. "Car crash last year, not too long after ... you know. He was coming home late. The roads were wet and an eighteen wheeler lost control in the opposite lane."

"Oh my god! I'm so sorry. I..." She didn't even know how to respond to that. It was so ... surreal, especially since she'd spoken to both her parents shortly before hopping on the plane down to the Bahamas.

"It's okay," he said, wiping his eyes. "I'm actually glad you told me. I think it's kind of like with you. Knowing the old man is out there, even if it's not in my world, well, it kind of makes it ... better."

Knowing she was stepping on eggshells, she replied, "How's Mom holding up in your world?"

"Probably better than me," he said with a small laugh. "You remember Mr. Pendelston?"

"The postman?"

"Yeah. He asked her out for coffee and she said yes."

"No way."

"I'm one hundred percent serious."

Danni cracked a grin. "Do you think I should tell Dad to keep an eye out for him?"

Harrison shrugged. "I dunno. Maybe." Then, he shook his head. "Goddamn. There's simply too much to say and not enough time."

"I know."

"But how about this," he offered. "If you ever feel a tingle in the back of your head, like someone is looking over your shoulder, well, that'll be me thinking about you."

"Same, big brother." She stepped in and hugged him. "And, just for the record, you can expect to feel a lot of tingles."

"Just make sure it's not when Allie and I are getting busy."

"Eww, gross." She stepped back and smacked him on the arm.

"I'll tell her you said hi, though."

"And that I miss her."

"Definitely." He reached into his pocket and pulled out a phone. "Hey. Before I forget, can I get a selfie?"

Danni nodded, suddenly regretting she'd left hers behind. "You know they're not going to let you keep that – evidence of a, what did Mitch call it, a trans-dimensional incursion or something."

"I know. But maybe I can find a WiFi printer before that happens."

"Screw it." She moved to stand next to him. "Some rules are made to be broken."

Just as he snapped the photo, though, she heard Mitchell call out.

"That's it! I'm at a loss. There's no buttons, panels, handles, or even a freaking divot. Hell, I can't even find a scanner to tell the damned door I'm standing in front of it."

"Which is probably a good thing," Derek replied, "considering we're all outside the sub."

"The scientific method doesn't care if your shoes get wet."

"It's more the rest of me I'm worried about."

Mitchell looked like he had more to say to that, but his universe's Norah interrupted, picking that moment to finally check in.

"Mitch, are you there? I need a status report. Over."

However, before he could respond, their Norah, the one present in the room, said, "I've got this."

She moved to unclip her radio, but the medic handed his over instead. "Use mine. I had an inkling we might be stepping into shit, so I upgraded the antennas before we left."

"Appreciated," she replied before raising it to her lips. "This is Agent Norah Caseman. Is everything okay on your end? We've been trying to reach you."

Danni turned to Harrison as this was going on, but he said, "Go and see what they're talking about. I'll wait here and play door man."

"Are you sure?"

"Yeah. It's cool. Although, if you get trapped in there with Mitch, I can't promise I'll save you."

She grinned back then walked in to join the others who were now gathered around Norah, listening as she spoke to her other self.

God, this is weird. But if they were going to brainstorm a way out of this mess, this was their best bet – to bring all their minds together.

"Sorry for causing any concern," the other Norah replied after a few seconds. "I was on another channel."

From the look on Mitch's face, this wasn't a surprise.

"And why is that?"

"If you're the same person I am," came the reply, "then you know I can't say."

Derek glared hard at Norah. "Do you have any idea what she's talking about?"

"No. Of course not."

"I'm serious, Norah. This is not the time to play games."

"I agree," she replied. "Believe me, I had no idea what we'd find down here, and I can say with certainty that I have nothing even remotely approaching orders on what to do in case of alien contact. It's not like there's a standing protocol for this stuff."

Derek hesitated for a moment then held out his hand. "Mind if I run the show for a few?"

"Go right ahead. Talking to myself is weird as hell."

He took it and pressed the receiver. "Norah, this is Derek. We've been discussing theories on what this ship might be, and there's a few precautions we think you should take."

"You mean the door?" she replied. "It's secured. Dr. Anderson here figured it out before we could get locked in."

"Good to hear. Saves us some time. Now for the bad news. This place is starting to fill with water. I don't know how long we've got, but we need to make figuring a way out our priority."

"I agree. That's certainly one of our priorities," she replied, causing Danni to raise an eyebrow. "We haven't made much progress on how to get the outside doors open again, though. If you have any suggestions, I'm open to hearing them."

Mitchell nodded at Derek, who depressed the talk button again.

"That's kinda the problem," the medic said. "We're here putting our heads together, hoping some idea presents itself. But if there's a mechanism or sequence that triggers the outside doors, I have no idea what it is."

"So where does that leave us?"

"In deep shit?"

"Thank you for your professional opinion, Agent Harkness. How about the rest of you?"

"Nice to know some things are the same regardless of universe," their Norah muttered.

"Hold on. We know the hull isn't invulnerable," Danni offered.

"That's a good point," Derek replied. "That drill ripped right through it."

"Interesting as that is," the Norah on the other end of the radio said, "I'm going to assume you didn't think to bring an industrial-sized drill bit with you either."

"Sadly, no. But it does open up possibilities."

"*Such as?*" both Norahs replied.

"I'm just spitballing here," Derek said. "But maybe with enough concussive force..."

Mitchell inclined his head. "You mean blow it open?"

"In a nutshell."

"And how do we do that?"

"No idea yet."

"Maybe if we could find something in the ship, a power source or something," Harrison called from the open door.

"Possible," Mitchell said. "But you're talking about finding and identifying something like that on an alien spaceship that's gotta be at least twice the size of an aircraft carrier. Not saying it can't happen, but so far the only thing we've seen that's been portable has been seaweed."

"Before anyone asks," Llanzo added. "No, it does not explode."

Danni smiled even though their situation was grim. It was good to see the doctor had seemingly overcome his earlier shock.

Over the radio, the other Norah let out a heavy sigh.

Before they could move on, though, their Norah grabbed the walkie talkie back from Derek. "I know that sound because I make it myself. What aren't you telling us?"

"What?" Derek asked, but she waved him off.

"You can fool the others but you can't fool yourself," she said into the radio. "And before you try any bullshit, we both know my security clearance is the same as yours. Spill."

There came a slight pause and then her double replied, "And we both know there are some things bigger than ourselves."

"Like that octopus?" Mitchell asked.

"No," Derek spat. "She's talking about state secrets, things our government wouldn't want getting out there." He glared at Norah. "Isn't she?"

"What does that have to do with a sea monster?" Danni asked.

He shook his head. "Nothing, except we're not just dealing with a sea monster, not now anyway, and we're not the only agency involved here."

"I can assure you," Norah replied, "Nobody aboard the Nest had any idea what we were going to find down here, least of all me."

"Same," her counterpart said.

"And as for protecting the interests of the... Son of a bitch." Norah narrowed her eyes as she lifted the radio back to her lips. "It's Jake, isn't it? In the event of a radio blackout, he must have standing orders to neutralize anything he or his people conclude is a potential threat to our government's stability. That's it, isn't it?"

"I find it hard to believe you didn't know. I did."

"We ... don't exactly talk much these days."

When next the other Norah spoke again, there was a tinge of regret in her voice. "I'm ... sorry to hear that."

"Not as sorry as I'm going to be if I end up entombed in this place because your man decided to blow it up. So enough with the games. Did your Jacob bring munitions with him? Yes or no?"

Derek put a hand over hers, a look of horror dawning on his face. "It wasn't just the other Jake." He glanced at Danni. "That backpack of his. It wasn't a coincidence that it just happened to be aboard the sub." Then he turned back to Norah. "And this is exactly why I hate playing politics."

"We can table that discussion for a later time." She depressed the button again. "So, would I be incorrect in assuming we probably have two Jakes running around this vessel, both of them carrying high explosives?"

Another pause, then, "I can't speak for yours, but I can't rule out the possibility either."

"What?" Llanzo cried. "That's insane. He can't..."

"Not now, Doctor," Norah snapped. "Believe me, I'm as upset about this as you."

"I highly doubt that."

"Oh trust me, she is," Mitchell said. "You can tell by that vein in her forehead ... and shutting up now."

"What are his standing orders for a situation like this?" Norah asked into the radio after throwing a glare the medic's way.

"There's never been a situation like this," the other Norah replied. "But we talked about it. Whatever effect this ship is having, it seems to be spreading. I don't know how far it's going to go, but we can neither afford the possibility of the Gulf region being compromised nor allow another nation to attempt a salvage effort."

"You know how crazy that sounds, right? Especially if he thinks he has enough C-4 to put a dent in something this size..."

"He doesn't need to," the other Norah interrupted. "And I'm pretty sure you know that."

"What does she mean?" Llanzo asked.

"Demolitions 101, Doctor," their Norah replied, looking none too pleased. "You attack the weak spots, causing a chain reaction ... which tells me why our Jake isn't back yet. He's out there looking for a spot where he can maximize the destruction, crippling this place..."

"And killing us all in the process," Danni muttered.

She expected to be met with disapproving looks from her superiors, but the glance Derek gave her was entirely sympathetic.

"Maybe not," Norah said before speaking into the radio again. "I'm going to assume both of our Jakes are working toward the same goal, searching for the same weak points."

"A fair assumption," came the reply.

"Then is it also a fair assumption to make that if one of our Jacobs gets the job done and we can convince the other of that fact…"

"Then that could leave us with some spare charges to try and blow the doors," her double finished for her. "It's a longshot, but it could work."

"How do we know we can trust this woman?" Llanzo asked.

Norah raised an eyebrow at him. "Because, Doctor, that other woman is me. And, while I have always been proud to serve Uncle Sam, I've never had a death wish about it. And if I'm hearing myself correctly, I doubt she does either."

"Thank you," came the reply. "And no, I most certainly do not."

"Wait," Danni said. "There's one problem we're forgetting. How do we even know which universe's ship we're trying to blow up? What if we destroy one, but the other is left to…?"

Mitchell held up a hand. "That's a good question, one we'd probably have zero chance of answering even with a boatload of quantum physicists here with us. So, instead I say we hope for the best. And yes, I know how that sounds. But, and this is a big but, if both ships are connected via however the hell it works, then maybe knocking out one will take out both."

"Are you willing to stake your life on that, Mitch?" his Norah asked.

"If we live, definitely. If not, then there won't be anyone left to call me on it."

Derek nodded. "It beats doing nothing. Norahs?"

"Count me in," the one present replied.

A moment later the other said, "So long as we cripple this ship in the process, I'm amenable."

"Good. Then kindly inform your Jacob of the plan."

There came a pause from the other end. "That could be a problem."

"Define problem."

"I haven't been able to raise him in several minutes. I don't know if it's interference or something else. But you may need to contact yours instead."

"Easier said than done," Derek replied. "We have his radio."

Norah shook her head. "Well, that's just great."

"Just means we need to find them first," Harrison called from the door.

"Exactly." Derek nodded his way. "Earlier, we decided that searching for Jake could wait until we figured out how to open the doors. Now, it seems that finding him is our only hope for making that happen."

"Say the word," Danni replied.

"The word is given. Crypto-Hunters, it's time to start hunting."

49

The Leviathan found itself increasingly confused. After sinking the surface thing, it had turned back to once again confront its larger brethren, the one that still dared sit atop the waters of its hunting ground.

The large surface thing was still where it had left it, along with its smaller podmate. However, it hadn't expected to find that other, even smaller surface things had joined them at some point, racing along the top of the water between the other two.

Perhaps they were calves, much the same way as the clicking things kept their young nestled between the adults.

If so, it didn't matter. These new smaller things were puny, not much larger than the screaming things themselves. Despite their size, however, they made a lot of noise, enough to irritate the leviathan.

As before, the thrumming was gone in this place, allowing the pain to subside. Its mood was not improved, though. It was hard to think, to distinguish between foes worthy of its wrath and those not. Though its instincts told it the smaller ones were no threat, its thoughts were too muddy to make sense of it.

The only thing that made sense was killing, followed by more killing – something it could still understand.

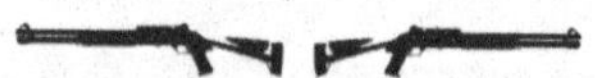

"The switches are all hardwired with redundancies. You can either set them off based on section – forward starboard, aft port side, center..."

"I get it," Andrea said.

"They can be set to a timer too, if need be."

She shook her head. "Probably too much to hope that thing will keep still long enough to use it."

"That's what I figured," Vakovsky, the ship's engineer and one of their top demolitions experts, replied. "So, in that case, you can also set them all off at once with this switch."

"And the charges themselves?"

"Each has been positioned for maximum outward dispersal. Keep in mind, though, they'll still deal catastrophic damage to the ship. I can't guarantee she'll stay afloat if you set off more than a few."

"If I have to resort to using this, you can be certain there's already little chance of staying afloat."

"That's why I wanted to talk to you again about using the remote."

Andrea shook her head again. "I already told you, we can't rely on it. Not now. If we do and it fails..."

Vakovsky nodded, his thick pug-like face not looking happy about it. "Fine. But take it anyway. Use it as a backup in case this room gets compromised or the hardwire fails. It's plugged in to the frequency of each pack, so even if a few get knocked loose, you'll still be running hot."

"Good work. I mean it." She allowed herself the ghost of a smile toward the man. "Now get your ass onto a launch and over to the Sun Angel. That's an order."

He nodded and left, leaving her alone with her thoughts.

It wasn't for long, though. She looked up a few minutes later to find Mitchell standing in the doorway. She just hoped he wasn't here to try and talk her out of it. "How goes the transfer?"

"Two more and we should be done," he said, stepping in. "I have them running another headcount on the Sun Angel. If anyone is missing we'll do one last sweep for them."

"Good. Make sure you're on one of those launches."

"You got it. Unless, that is, you could use the company."

"I appreciate the sentiment but this is a one person job."

"Captain goes down with the ship sounds so eighteenth century."

She shrugged. "More like I won't ask my crew to do anything I'm not prepared to do myself."

He nodded, allowing an uncomfortable silence to descend between them.

"You know," he said, after several seconds, "they say these workplace romances never really pan out anyway ... especially once the girl blows herself up."

"You do realize how much you suck at this, right? Oh, and call me a girl again and I'll break your collarbone."

He held up his hands. "I prefer to remain unbroken, thank you."

"Good, because don't think for a second I..."

They were interrupted by a commotion going on somewhere above them. A moment later, another agent popped his head in. "Ma'am, I think it's back."

"Saved by the octopus," Mitchell remarked as she pushed past him, making it a point to grab the remote detonator just in case.

The last thing they needed was to be caught with their pants down. She only hoped she wasn't forced to use it before everyone was offloaded.

Fortunately, there was little need to tell anyone to make a hole as she made her way up onto the deck. Mitchell hadn't been lying. There was maybe a handful of people at best left aboard.

Those that were, however, were at the ready, most with weapons while a few manned the ship's high powered spotlights.

Close by, the roar of outboard motors could be heard – one of the launches was headed toward the Sun Angel, another was on its way back.

"Someone give me a report!" she cried out as the medic caught up to her.

"We caught sight of a wake off the port stern."

Damnit. That wasn't much to go on, but it wasn't anything she could dismiss either. "Step up our efforts. Cover those boats. I want everyone off this ship within the next..."

The attack came without warning.

One moment the spotlights were sweeping the area behind the ship, the next the water around one of the launches exploded in a spray of froth.

Sadly, she saw it was the outbound one, still full of personnel – most of them the crew responsible for wiring the Nest into a floating bomb.

A tentacle rose out of the water directly in front of the raft, like the hand of some malevolent giant. Up it went, until it towered over the launch, then it slammed down right on top of the unlucky bastards.

In the dark it was hard to tell, but she could have

sworn at least a few of those aboard had managed to dive off right before being hit.

"Spotlights!" she cried. "Look for survivors."

"There!" Mitchell shouted, pointing out over the water.

She saw them a moment later, a pair of survivors. One of them looked to be Vakovsky, who she'd spoken to just minutes earlier. He was holding onto another man who appeared to be injured, trying to keep him afloat.

"Launch number two, Launch number two," Novak said into his radio. "We have men in the water in need of rescue. We will cover you. I repeat, we will cover you."

The second launch started to turn as the water around the two men once more began to froth and churn. Vakovsky let go of the other man and began fumbling with something attached to his vest.

A spotlight lit upon him just long enough for Andrea to see the small metallic cannister in his hand.

"Belay that order!" she cried at Novak.

"Launch number two, abort. I repeat. Abort!"

A spray of water temporarily blocked Vakovsky from sight as another tentacle rose from the water directly behind him.

Then there came a much larger spray as the grenade in his hand went off, booming like thunder. A heavy chunk of flesh was sheared off the massive appendage, and it quickly disappeared beneath the water again. The surface continued to churn for several seconds before finally calming down.

Where the hell is it?

Sadly, the spotlights weren't able to detect any other movement at the surface. The octopus appeared to be gone, but so were Vakovsky and the agent he'd been trying to save.

"Fuck!" Andrea cried before she could rein in her

temper. "Have launch two circle the area for survivors," she said, despite knowing it was pointless. "Once only. Then I want it back here and the rest of you on it. Let's pray Vakovsky bought us the time we need."

The few people remaining on deck double-timed it at her command. She backed away, wanting nothing more than to go below deck and put her head in her hands until such time as that beast came back. At that point she would happily go to Hell if it meant taking it with her.

Too many had been lost on her watch. No more.

In her haste she turned and almost bumped into Mitchell.

"I thought I gave you an order," she barked, although there wasn't much fire in her voice.

"Yeah, well, I don't work for you. And, like you said earlier, this is more my team's ballpark than yours. So ... I'll be taking it from here."

Andrea made to respond but, before the words could come out, a stabbing pain shot up from her thigh. She looked down to see a syringe sticking out of her leg, the plunger already depressed.

"Sorry about this," Mitchell said, his voice sounding as if it were coming from far away. "Just do me a favor when you get back to shore. Have a cheesesteak in my honor, and try not to hate me too much. Or you can hate me. Just make sure to have that cheesesteak."

She took a stagger step forward, her tongue suddenly too heavy to form words.

"Youuuu..." She meant to call him a son of a bitch, but instead toppled forward into his arms.

"Someone help me over here!" he cried, holding onto her. "I think she passed out."

Had she been capable, she'd have gladly shot him right then and there. Instead, her head lolled back as he laid her on the deck – the lightning flashing above the last thing she saw before darkness claimed her.

"I've never seen someone argue with themselves quite like that before," Derek said as he led the way through the halls of the alien vessel again, following the trail of tape markers they'd left.

"Consider yourself lucky," Mitch replied. "At least you get to go back to your universe with the one who *wasn't* willfully trying to blow us to bits."

Derek nodded. "As I've often said, the downside of any government job is the government."

"Can't argue with that one."

They'd retrieved Mitchell's radio before leaving. Since then, though, the only communication they'd had was with the other Norah, her promising to keep hailing their Jacob.

As for their Norah, if she had anything new to tell them, it would have to wait for one of those outages to…

Speak of the devil.

He'd no sooner thought it than the lights began to dim around them. A second later, it felt like he was walking through waist deep mud from the change in gravity.

This time, however, it was accompanied by a sound like that of rushing water – which, considering what Danni had shown them earlier – likely meant it *was*.

Just great.

What happened next did little to improve that sentiment. Rather than the normal lighting resuming once the glitch ran its course, the walls began to pulse with color – lighting up brightly in spots before dimming again.

This went on for a minute or so before they finally stabilized back to their original hue.

"That can't be good," Harrison said from behind him.

"Nope," Mitchell replied. "I have a feeling this tinker toy is starting to break down faster."

Derek turned toward him. "What do you think that means for the outside world?"

"Beats the hell out of me. Just don't be surprised if you're met at port by an orangutan named Doctor Zaius."

"Eh, I could think of worse fates."

"Does that count?" Harrison asked, pointing ahead toward where water collected in the hall. "Pretty sure that section was dry when we came through last time."

He wasn't wrong. The water was definitely rising faster now.

"Come on. We need to hurry."

As if that wasn't bad enough, the hallway ahead remained dark as they approached it, aside from a quick sputter of light that didn't last.

"Flashlights it is then," Derek said. "Everyone stick together. I have a feeling we're gonna be swimming in the dark before this is over."

Mitchell let out a chuckle. "A moonlight swim. How romantic."

"Minus the moonlight. Come on."

Derek led them onward, the seawater cold around his ankles, definitely a far cry from the tropical currents near the shore. Worse, though it was gradual, he could tell it was getting deeper as they continued on, the slight incline of the floor working against them as they continued searching for markers on the wall.

Though he kept his opinion on the matter to himself, Derek was starting to get creeped out. Several of the rooms they'd explored during their first tour of this section were still open. The walls of some were lit, allowing them some illumination as they walked, while others were as dark as the hall, giving the place a feel somewhere between a sewer and a haunted house.

The water was approximately knee deep when he finally announced, "I think that room over there is where we split off from Jake. Everyone wait here for a second."

Derek stepped in, the lighting there seemingly broken now as well. He shone his flashlight around, hoping he wouldn't find his friend floating face down, and instead saw there was more than one exit. "This is it. I think I know which way he went."

"Okay, so how do we do this without getting caught?" Harrison asked.

"Far as I can tell," Mitchell replied, "that seems to only happen when the ship glitches out."

"Except it's pretty much glitching out constantly now."

"Good point."

"We cross through one at a time," Derek said, interrupting their banter. "So far, the doors seem to be opening up again for anyone on the outside. Long as that holds, we should be okay."

Almost as if mocking him, the lights in the room sparked to life for a moment before going out again.

"Famous last words," Mitchell replied.

Derek laughed as he walked to the far doorway. "Trust me. If I have any last words, they'll be a hell of a lot better than that."

50

Jacob desperately pulled himself through the hole in the wall then surfaced, gasping for breath.

That was too close.

Sadly, there was no cause for celebration. Only a few more feet of air remained in the room, the unreadable display on the one wall having gone dark a while back. He'd done his duty, though. He'd planted some explosives here, then had risked swimming into the flooded room to plant the rest.

On that front, he'd gotten lucky. Though they were hundreds of feet underwater, the pressure in the other room seemed to be the same as the rest of the ship – meaning it hadn't been much different than diving in a swimming pool, at first anyway.

There was some kind of massive machinery in the other room, something he couldn't begin to understand. It was glowing at the top, no doubt the source of the illumination he'd seen – pulsing in a strange chromatic hue that made it uncomfortable to look at. Further up, at the ceiling, he'd been able to dimly make out another breach – possibly the same one caused by the ZarroGreen drill.

There hadn't been time to tell, however, whether beyond it lay the open ocean or another deck. As he'd neared the strange mechanism to plant the charges, the temperature rose considerably – likely the only reason he hadn't succumbed to hypothermia yet. At the same time, the water became thick and viscous – like swimming in motor oil. Though Jacob was an accomplished diver with excellent lung capacity, the strange viscosity had slowed his progress greatly, using up precious air.

He'd pushed himself as far as he'd dared, planting another charge, and was about to turn back when there came a blinding flash from the alien mechanism.

A moment later, Jacob felt a rush of water from above forcing him back. Far worse, though, was the pressure. It instantly intensified to several times what it had been, the shock forcing most of the remaining air from his lungs and almost causing him to black out.

It was only through his experience and training that he was able to keep a fingerhold on consciousness, realizing he had perhaps seconds at most to escape this place or become a permanent resident.

Thankfully, the sudden rush of water had managed to push him back toward the hole leading to the first room. As he fought to pull himself out, though, a face – his own – bobbed into view in front of him. The other Jacob's eyes were once again open – his sightless stare seeming to silently convey that this was the fate they both deserved.

Jacob had screamed, expelling the last of the air from his body before frantically pulling himself through the breach in the wall – the pressure instantly dropping again as he made it through, as if there were some unseen force keeping the power of the ocean at bay.

Whatever it was, though, it wasn't enough to keep the ship, and more importantly this compartment, from flooding.

His mission accomplished, he turned his eyes to the nearby backpack, still thankfully afloat and now considerably lighter having been relieved of its explosive burden.

He could rest now, knowing he'd done what was necessary. There was just one thing left. Jacob unzipped the pack and pulled a remote detonator from it. It was different from what he was used to – *from a whole other world* – but it wasn't so alien that he couldn't figure it out. If anything, he was a bit jealous as it seemed to be of higher quality than what he'd brought. *Guess the suits aren't as cheap over in the mirror universe.*

He studied it for a minute or two, until he was certain he wasn't going to blow himself to kingdom come by accident.

Soon enough for that.

Then he set the digital timer for one hour and locked it in. That finished, he pulled out the radio again and turned it back on.

If this was to be his final mission, he had no regrets – except one. However, fate had been kind enough to provide him with the means of learning how that mistake may have otherwise played out. It was a small consolation, but one he was glad for nevertheless.

Sorry I took that away from you, buddy. He glanced back toward the flooded chamber then lifted the radio to his lips. "Norah, this is Jake. Come in."

He repeated the call a few times over several minutes until there finally came a response.

"Oh, thank God," she said. "I was getting worried."

"No need to. Just taking care of business. How're things looking on your end?"

"You know there's such a thing as taking care of business and answering your damned radio, right?"

Now she sounded like his Norah. "Sorry. But you know how I get. Distractions make for a poor partner." He hoped the lie was a convincing one, since it was mostly the truth.

"Yeah, I get it." She paused before continuing, giving him an opening.

"Hey. I need to tell you something. I set the charges and..."

"Listen, hon," she interrupted. "The others know."

That caught his attention. "Know what?"

"Our orders ... your orders. What needs to be done to this place."

They did? "How'd they find out?"

"Norah, the other one. She put two and two together with their Derek's help."

Of course she did. "How'd he take it?"

"Go figure. About as well as ours did."

Jacob didn't know exactly what that meant, but he could guess. Derek was a good guy, but too much of a straight shooter for government work.

"Listen to me, Jake. They're coming to find you. Please tell me you didn't plant all the charges."

"Yeah. Why?"

"Shit! That means we're trapped in here. Mitch was working with the other team, to figure out how to open the outer doors. The only idea they could come up with was..."

"Blowing them open," he finished for her. "Goddamn it."

"That's it then," she stated flatly. "Well, we knew going in this could be a one way trip. Won't lie. I was hoping it wouldn't be, but I also won't ask you to disarm anything you've already set. This place has to go. We both know that."

Can't argue, he thought. But then he remembered what lay just outside the door to this room. "Listen to me, baby, I have good news and bad news, but I need you to hear me out because there isn't much time."

"What do you mean?"

"There's another backpack with explosives and it's still half full."

"What?! Where?"

"It's in the hall outside of where I am." He closed his eyes, hating the words he was about to say but unwilling to stop them. "I-I found the other Jacob. He ... he was already dead. Drowned."

"Oh my god. I ... need to let her know."

"No, don't! It's just..." He paused as he considered things. What would it hurt? He was fucked either way. Why not just be the other guy for the short time he had left? "It would be best to tell her in person, but you're right. I suppose she should know. I ... I know you would want to."

She let out a deep breath. "I'll take care of it. But what I need you to do is grab that bag and get your ass back here."

"I'm sorry, Nor, but that's part of the bad news. I'm locked in. Door shut behind me and won't open. The room's flooding and there's no way out of here without a dive suit. Way I see it, I've got maybe twenty minutes before the air runs out, thirty tops."

"Hold tight. Mitch and Harrison are looking for you. Maybe they can get the door open again and..."

"No!" he snapped. "I mean, there's no time. You tell them to find that bag and bring it back there. You know how to set the charges. Do it and get out of here."

"What do you mean there's no time? Is...?"

"I already set mine to blow, and I can't change it ... not knowing how much time I have left."

"How long until...?"

"Less than an hour. So please tell them to hurry. I ... I love you, Norah."

"I don't get it," Mitchell said. "This is obviously a different part of the ship serving a completely different function. Why didn't he radio this in and let you know?"

Danni shrugged. "He didn't have a radio. That, and he was probably too busy trying to figure out how to break it." She quickly glanced at Derek. "Sorry."

"It's okay," he said. "I've known Jake for a long time. Doesn't mean we haven't had our disagreements. And, just for the record, this almost definitely counts as one of them."

She reached out and squeezed Harrison's hand in the waist deep water. Their forward progress had slowed to a crawl, partially due to the rising seawater, but also because she could barely feel her feet anymore.

The lighting in this part of the ship was just as unpredictable as the way they'd come. Some sections of the hall were well lit, others dark as a tomb. Though they didn't dare venture into any of the rooms they passed, they paused long enough to call out Jacob's name and take a look inside.

Danni was no engineer, but she agreed with Mitch's assessment. She could also tell he wanted nothing more than to explore, but time wasn't something they had a lot of.

It was especially hazardous now because the lights had been their cue that a glitch was coming. Now, whether gravity was doubling itself or the other way around, by the time they felt something it was already too late. They had to ride it out and hope for the best.

"There's another tape mark," Derek said, pointing his flashlight at a section of wall. "He definitely came this way."

"See any signs of duct tape?"

"Not yet. You think your Jake might be around here, too?"

"Hoping for it, but hard to say," Mitch replied. "Far as I can tell, we docked on kind of the opposite side of this section compared to where you guys are. But also, so far as I can tell, that would place the room your sub's in somewhere beneath a huge pile of sand."

"Safe to say it's not," Derek said. "Or at least I hope not."

"Thanks. I could probably figure that part out myself. I'm thinking maybe it's some kind of mirror effect caused by the dimensional breach. We probably entered in the exact same spot of our respective ships, but because of the way things are it actually seems like we're on opposite ends of..."

"Hold that thought, and not just because it doesn't make any sense," Derek interrupted, shining his flashlight further down the hall. "What the fuck is that?"

Danni and Harrison both took aim with their weapons as Mitchell followed Derek's lead with his own light.

"Stand down," he said a moment later, pointing toward the juncture ahead of them. "Is that ... some kind of mirror?"

"No idea," Mitchell replied. "Definitely reflective, but looks pliable, almost like ... water. But that's..."

"Mitch, are you there? Come in," Norah's voice blurted from the radio.

In that same instant, Danni felt as if a great weight were taken off her shoulders, albeit not of the emotional variety, as water droplets began to rise up around her. Sadly, just then, whatever Derek had been shining his light on seemingly erupted, becoming a raging wall of white water that rushed their way.

Oh shit!

There was no time to brace herself as it slammed into them, scattering them back down the hallway like bowling pins. Danni had been in rough surf before, but never in a way where she was boxed in like they were now.

She was slammed against the wall, knocking the air from her lungs. Before she could begin to choke on seawater, though, she righted herself, pushing off with her feet. A moment later she burst through the surface, continuing to rise thanks to the greatly lowered gravity, until she bumped her head on the ceiling.

"Ow!" She splashed back down as the torrent began to subside, the water falling around them as if it were raining in the hall.

"Y-you okay?" Harrison choked out, pushing himself up about ten feet away, the water now rising to past his stomach.

"I'll live."

"And this is why I hate surfing," Mitchell said, likewise standing back up.

Danni looked around, not seeing Derek. She was about to tell the others when she saw a flashlight beam coming from within one of the side rooms, causing her to let out a sigh of relief. "Derek? Are you...?"

"I'm okay," he called back. "The flood knocked me in here. Just stay where you are and ... oh, that's not good."

"What's not...?"

She was interrupted by a flash of bright green from within the room.

Derek came splashing out in a hurry a moment later,

just before the door could close on him. "That was too close," he said, gasping for breath. "Good news is, Jake definitely came this way."

"And the bad news?"

"There's C-4 wired to a bunch of cylinders in there."

"Cylinders?" Mitchell asked. "What kind?"

"The big alien kind." He shook his head. "I don't know. There wasn't time for a close look. We should probably call this in, though."

"Easier said than done." Mitchell held up his now empty hands. "I must've lost it when that tidal wave hit us."

Harrison let out a coughing sigh. "I'm sure Norah was just calling to chat. Probably nothing important."

"Hold on. I still have...," Derek unclipped his own radio, only to find the antenna had been snapped off. "And, so much for that idea. Guess I hit the wall harder than I thought."

"Nice to see our luck is the same as always," Danni remarked.

"Come on," Mitchell said, looking around. "Someone help me find it."

Derek, however, shook his head. "Leave it. There's no time. Look at this place. It's going to be unpassable before you know it. We need to find the Jacobs ASAP, along with any charges they have left. After that, we say our goodbyes. Any objections?"

Mitchell took a quick look around at their group. "None? Good. Because I'd prefer we get moving before someone turns on the wave machine again."

"No argument here."

They pushed forward once more, reaching the intersection. Ahead was out, that much was obvious, unless they suddenly grew gills – something Danni wasn't about to rule out in this weird-ass funhouse. "Right or left?"

"In D&D they say righthand rules," Harrison replied, to which she raised an eyebrow. "I took it up as a hobby to honor Rob's memory."

"Aww. That's sweet, in a nerdy sort of way."

"Even Allie plays."

"The couple who games together...," Mitchell started.

"Would still be wrong," Derek interrupted. "Look." He pointed his flashlight toward the left corridor. There, just barely hanging onto the wall, was a strip of electrical tape. "This way. Hurry."

"Is nobody going to talk about the freaky-ass wall of water back there?" Mitchell asked, following.

"No, but I have a feeling you are."

"That's not just a quirk of gravity. Otherwise it would've been floating in every direction. Something was holding it back."

"Yeah, something that almost drowned us. And is probably going to try again if we don't hurry."

"True, but you gotta admit the technology is incredible."

"Says the guy from a whole other freaking universe," Danni replied.

"Nobody likes a snot."

"Hey, be nice to my sister," Harrison said. "Otherwise she'll kick your ass the next time she sees you."

"Quite the optimist, aren't we?"

"Hey, what's that?" Danni pointed up ahead, where it looked like something was floating in the water.

"Come on." Derek reached it first, his light illuminating it enough for her to see it was a backpack, one she'd seen before.

"Is that...?"

"Jake's," he finished for her.

"But where is he?"

"No idea. Here, hold my light for a second." She did

while Derek unzipped the backpack. A humorless smile lit up his face a moment later. "Ladies and gentlemen, I do believe we haven't yet exhausted our supply of good luck."

Almost immediately after he said it, though, Danni's stomach dropped. *Oh crap!* "Brace yourselves!"

They managed to flatten themselves against the wall as another torrent of water hit them, muted a bit by the corner they'd passed, but still hard enough to almost pull her off her feet.

"You just had to say it, didn't you," Mitchell complained.

"Oh shut up," Derek replied, holding onto the backpack for dear life.

When it had finally passed, the water was once again higher. As the shortest member of the team, Danni figured she had maybe one or two more outages before she'd be forced to swim back the way they'd come.

Derek quickly resumed what he was doing, pulling out a brick of C-4. "There's more. Hopefully enough for both teams to escape."

"Great!" Harrison replied. "Now let's go find..."

"No," Derek said flatly. "This is where we part ways." He began pulling charges and detonators out of the bag, handing them to Mitchell. "Hold on to these, preferably better than you did the radio."

"Never going to let me forget that, are you?"

"Not in this universe." He turned to Danni, handing her the backpack. "Take the rest back to basecamp."

"But..."

"That's an order."

Danni shook her head. "I don't even know what to do with them."

"Norah will. Trust me on this. She's been playing this game a lot longer than you."

"I'm kind of with Danni on this one," Harrison said.

"Then that's an order for you, too." He held up a hand as if not in the mood for debate. "We know our Jacob came this way, but it's getting worse by the minute. I'm not willing to risk all of us to find him."

"Just yourself," Danni said.

"Pretty much. He's my friend. But I also need to make sure someone gets back with these."

"And then what?"

"Wait for us, obviously. Unless things get bad ... or start blowing up. Then you get the hell out of here and do what you can to avoid the angry calamari on the way up."

"I won't leave without you," she said defiantly.

"I know, which is why Norah's in charge. Now go." He turned toward Mitchell, likely hoping, Danni noted, that the senior member of the other team would agree with him. "Same with you. Finding your Jacob from here is probably a snipe hunt. Head back the way you came. I won't tell you how to run this mission, but you'll probably have an easier time tracking him from that end. Do what you can, but if it gets bad..."

"Yeah yeah, angry calamari. I get it," Mitchell replied before holding out his hand. "It was awesome meeting you, man. I'm just sorry you're a prick in two universes."

Derek took it and laughed. "The feeling's mutual, my friend." Then he turned to Harrison. "You have no idea how good it's been to see you."

Harrison nodded, likewise grasping hold of his hand. "Thanks for looking after my little sister."

"Always. Now it's your turn. Make sure she heads back the way she's supposed to. And no detours." Before Danni could say anything to that, he added, "I know you."

Danni wasn't happy to leave him, and he could no doubt sense that.

"Please. Go and make sure those charges are planted. I'll be able to search a lot more efficiently if I know you're safe. And before you say anything, I'm neither suicidal nor stupid. If things get bad, I'll turn back. I promise."

She was about to argue, but instead she waded forward and grabbed him in a big hug. "I'm gonna hold you to that."

51

ndrea's eyes slowly fluttered open. She expected a headache, but the truth was she felt good — damned good. Hell, she couldn't remember feeling like this since her college days.

Above her, she spied what seemed to be a wood paneled ceiling, although it was hard to tell with all the colors swirling about.

"She's coming to," a voice said from somewhere close by ... maybe. They could have been fifty miles away for all she knew.

Yep, no doubt about it. She was stoned outta her gourd. *Goddamned sorority parties.* Hopefully she didn't have an early class this...

A familiar face leaned over hers. "C-Cortez?"

That was weird. She didn't recall ever going to any parties with him. She made it a point not to fraternize with members of her team while... *Wait! My team.* "W-what happened?"

"You passed out on deck. Harkness checked you out. Had us bring you over here after he..."

Harkness?! "T-that son of a bitch." She tried to sit up,

noting that the cabin was full of people, but didn't make it far before the room started spinning.

"Hey! Take it easy."

"Get your hands off me," she snapped, swatting him away, or trying to. "Where am I?"

"T-the Sun Angel, ma'am."

That made sense. The place was packed to the gills, no pun intended, as she'd expected it to be – the smaller vessel acting as a shelter while she...

Shit! "I need to get back to the Nest."

"You're in no shape to go anywhere," Patel said, stepping in. "Besides, the launch is already battened down. We're to keep our distance and defend this vessel if need be."

"According to who?"

"According to you, ma'am."

Oh yeah.

"And from Agent Harkness as well."

"He's not in command." The agents around her turned and looked at each other, as if refusing to meet her eyes. "What is it?"

"Um, well...," Cortez said. "Agent Caseman, the other one, made it pretty clear this was a DoCC operation. With you down, that left Agent Harkness the ranking operative and..."

"You let him take over." Little by little her head was starting to clear, probably the anger helping to push away the effects of whatever that bastard had drugged her with. Still, it was hard to be mad at her people. They'd just been following protocol. "Where is he now?"

Unsurprisingly, the answer was the Nest, as she knew it would be.

What he'd done had been a slap in the face to her authority, disregarding the chain of command – all for macho bravado and an overinflated sense of chivalry.

The reality was Andrea didn't want to die, but she'd accepted it as part of her duty, the same way she and her team accepted it for every mission they were sent on. Sure, if one of them was able to save another, they would do so without fail, sometimes at the risk of their own...

Goddamn it.

Her own logic betrayed her.

Nevertheless, she found herself hoping he survived, just so she could kick his ass when next she saw him – or at least so she tried to convince herself.

For now, though, there was nothing she could do. It would be the height of hypocrisy for her to betray her own orders and risk her people just so she could get back and right this wrong.

The reality was she'd been played and had no choice but to accept it.

"Someone get me a status report and something to drink."

Fortunately, her team was ready with both. Patel handed her a bottle of water as Novak stepped forward.

"There's armed lookouts on deck, and the crew is ready to make sail at your order. The ... um ... phenomenon above us seems to be holding steady. No change that we can tell."

"Radio chatter?"

"Not good. We can't call out, but we've been able to pick up reports of power outages and freak weather patterns up and down the East coast." He paused for a moment. "Another plane went down, this time over Florida."

"Fuck!"

"Um ... and we're in the process of taking another headcount."

"Another? Why?"

The obviously stressed out agent looked momentarily embarrassed. "Because we seem to be one person short."

"You know, if you're going to pull shit like this, you could at least let me know first."

Mitchell turned from the railing, back toward where Julie stood facing him.

He stared at her for several seconds before sighing. "You might want to think twice before surprising the guy with the detonator."

"What? Did you think I was a giant octopus?"

"That, or Andrea decided to swim back and kick my ass."

"And you'd deserve every second of it."

"You saw what happened?"

"No." She shook her head. "But I heard enough to figure it out. The whole delayed concussion bullshit, followed by you volunteering to take her place was a bit too convenient to ignore. I mean, I know I haven't been a part of the team for long, but I think I have your M.O. figured out. So what did you do? Drug her coffee?"

"Nah. Too pedestrian. Palmed a needle."

"What did you shoot her up with?"

"A little concoction of my own making. Same stuff I used on Derek back in Jersey, just a bit more concentrated."

"Oh. She's gonna be high as a kite."

"Yep," Mitchell replied, turning back toward the water. "Hoping it keeps her happy enough to not try anything stupid."

All of the Nest's spotlights were on, lighting up the area around the cutter, further helped by the lightning still flashing overhead. Unless that monster came up right beneath them, they'd have a hard time missing it.

Julie shuddered at the thought. "Stupid? Like what you did?"

"Not going to deny it," he replied. "Although, I'd be remiss in pointing out that I'm not the only person reporting for suicide squad duty today. So, how'd you manage to pull it off?"

"Hid below deck. Pain in the ass with these things." She gestured at her crutches. "But I managed. After that thing attacked the launch, it was chaos. The few people left were scrambling to get out of here as fast as they could."

"Can't say I didn't notice." He glanced back at her. "You do realize that if we have to swim for it, it's going to be hell on wheels dragging you with me."

"Do you honestly think we're going to get a chance to dog paddle away from this?"

"No. I got a look-see at some of their demo-guy's handiwork. He knew his stuff. We're basically standing on a two-hundred foot long pipe bomb. We're talking burial at sea *and* cremation, all for the same price."

"I always did like a bargain."

"So why are you here, Jules? I mean, I know why I am, even if I don't want to be. It's part of the job. This is what we do. We take down the threats, no matter what it takes."

She hobbled up alongside him. "Exactly. *We*."

"This is a one person job."

"That doesn't mean you should have to do it alone."

He nodded as they both looked out over the sea, calm for now, but she had a feeling that could change at a moment's notice.

"Thank you," he said.

"You're still an asshole."

"Yep. But if you're looking for me to change my ways

while there's still time, you're going to be highly disappointed."

Julie turned her attention toward the stern, albeit there wasn't much to be seen. Then there came a peel of lightning and she caught sight of the Sun Angel – just a dark spot on the water. They were keeping their distance with lights out, as ordered.

She found herself wishing them well. Though she personally hadn't given up hope, she realized at this point it was likely futile to expect the sub to reappear and miraculously save the day. Julie instead said a silent prayer, hoping that whatever had befallen their friends had been both quick and painless.

On the upside, it seemed likely they'd be seeing each other again soon.

I wonder if they have cryptids in the afterlife.

She realized she might get an answer to that question in short order as her ears caught the sound of waves breaking from the direction of the bow.

Turning that way, she didn't notice anything strange, but then she felt the ship rock beneath her, almost causing her to stumble.

"Was that...?"

"There!" Mitchell cried, pointing.

He needn't have bothered, though. The wake was far too large to miss, along with the dark shape beneath it, easily visible in the glow of their spotlights. Lightning flashed again, illuminating the submerged beast as it swam past where they stood, its body seeming to go on forever.

"Goddamn that thing's big."

"And terrifying," Mitchell replied. "Let's not forget that."

"Kind of hard to. What's it doing?"

"I don't know. Maybe trying to figure out the safest angle to attack after we smacked it last time."

"Pretty sure that thing takes up all the angles."

"You and I both know that, but we've given this thing enough bloody noses by now that I think it's grown a bit wary." He shook his head. "Not wary enough to leave us alone, mind you."

"I had a feeling you'd say that."

He stepped back from the railing and turned toward the door leading below deck. "Come on. Let's get back to the command center. Everything's hard-wired there and I'd prefer there be no screwups when the time comes."

She began hobbling after him. "Don't wait for me to pull the trigger."

"Let's not be too hasty."

"You think there's still a chance for us?"

"Nope, but I want to be certain we get it. So we wait for it to give us the last bear hug of our lives, then we all take a walk on the wild side together."

Llanzo considered his day. So far, all things considered, he thought he'd managed to cope fairly decently with being repeatedly smacked in the face by the impossible.

Here now, though, watching Norah stare out into the hall, as if expecting her husband to come back to her, well, he truly had no idea what to do.

The news had come only a few minutes earlier – the other Norah radioing in, relaying that Agent Caseman's body had been found. The message had been garbled but he'd heard enough to understand as she'd tried to express her sympathies.

She'd said something after that, but Llanzo hadn't listened, having retreated to the sub so as to give them a few moments alone.

Several minutes of silence passed before he'd popped

his head out to find Norah trying unsuccessfully to raise the rest of her team, receiving nothing but more static in return.

Llanzo debated whether he should return to the sub and check it again, but he realized that was just busy work. The moment they'd decided upon their course of action, he'd hopped in to run diagnostics. They'd taken some damage during the initial attack, nothing he could hope to fix even if he had the proper tools. However, so far as he could tell, their ability to navigate wasn't compromised badly enough to keep them from escaping.

He didn't like their odds if that beast was out there waiting for them, but they had a shot if they could get clear and make a break for the surface.

Any further preparation on his part would do nothing more than drain their batteries.

"Are you okay, Agent Caseman?" he finally asked from behind her.

"I'm not sure." She turned back toward him. He'd expected to find her face stained with tears, but her eyes were dry. "I'm not really even sure what to think. I mean, I know how I feel, but there's also a reason it didn't work out."

"You know, it's okay to..."

"I'll stop you right there, Doctor," she said, steeling her voice. "Because it's *not* okay, at least not now. I have a duty to perform, people to get to safety. And by God I will see that duty through. Anything else can wait until after."

She turned back toward the hall, as if trying to force her team to return by sheer force of will.

"I'll tell you what. Once we get back to the surface and confirm all threats have been neutralized, then you can ask me again. For now, though, please make sure that sub is able to get us out of here, because my gut is telling me we're running out of second chances."

Derek was certain he must've had rocks in his head to continue onward. At the same time, he was pretty sure Jacob would have done the same for him. Hell, he already had in years past, more than once.

Because of that, they'd both walked out of tough spots time and again.

Derek didn't care to bet on the odds of a repeat performance, but he still intended to search until the last possible second, taking care to note where the water seemed the deepest so as to not end up trapped when he was finally forced to turn back. Despite that, he knew his timetable was short and growing shorter by the second.

Jacob was nothing if not practical. Derek had seen the charges that had already been set. The fact that his friend hadn't returned yet told him he'd likely pushed on ahead, hoping to keep going until he was certain he'd ensured maximum damage. That, or something had befallen him.

Either scenario seemed likely, especially considering how he and Mitch had almost become permanent roomies. At least now he knew to take it slow, walking in a zigzag pattern to ensure he didn't miss any closed doorways by mistake.

Therein lay another potential problem – staying prepared in case he accidently opened a door to a room that had previously been dry, realizing he could easily be dragged in from the ensuing rush of water. Knowing his luck, that would happen just as another outage hit and he'd end up being served seaweed salads for the rest of his short life.

"Good thing I'm not a picky eater," he said to himself, continuing to wade forward. "Just gotta hope they're not serving snails as an..."

His thoughts were interrupted as a nearby section of

wall retracted into itself. However, where he'd been prepared for rooms that were bone dry, he hadn't expected to find one that was nearly full – the deluge from within forcibly shoving him back into the opposite wall.

Nor was he even remotely prepared when something roughly grasped hold of him from below and dragged him beneath the surface.

52

"You're going to get in trouble when he finds out."

"And how's he going to find out?" Danni asked. "Are you going to send him a postcard from the mirror universe?"

"I might," Mitchell replied.

"Let me know how many stamps that takes," Harrison remarked.

Even though she realized she should have broken off earlier and headed back to the sub, Danni decided to accompany the others back to the point where they'd first met.

It was a stupid risk and she knew it, but there was no way she could just up and leave her brother knowing they had a few more minutes together. Hell, she had an entire lifetime to wonder what had become of him in that other place. If that made her selfish, so be it. She'd deal with the consequences.

"All right, that's far enough," Mitchell finally said. "Pretty sure this is where we ran into each other."

The water in this part of the ship wasn't too bad yet, still below waist level, although it had been completely dry

493

when last she'd been there – a testament to how quickly things were turning to shit.

That didn't mean she was ready to say goodbye, though. "But…"

"He's right," Harrison interrupted. "We can make it back from here, but I won't risk you going further."

If anyone else had said it she'd have told them off. But for him, she gave a single nod.

"All right," Mitchell said. "I'm going to head down the hall a bit, scout out the way back and make sure there's no xenomorphs waiting to plant eggs in our chests." He turned to Harrison. "Make it quick, otherwise I'm drugging your ass and dragging you back with me."

"Thanks, man."

"Thank you," Danni said, stepping in and giving him a quick hug. "I'm glad I got to meet you."

"Same here. It's good seeing you again, kiddo. I just wish I'd gotten a chance to meet myself as well."

Mitchell waded down the hall, leaving them alone, but she knew their time was rapidly running out.

Harrison met her gaze. "We knew this was coming."

"Doesn't make it any easier."

"I know."

"Did I tell you that I carry your picture with me on every mission?"

"I have one of you in my wallet. I like to pull it out after a hunt and tell you how things went. It's probably silly, but I remember how much you loved the woods and all, so I figured you might like that."

"I do … and I'm sure she would."

He paused for a moment. "God, this is weird."

She nodded. "Yeah, but it's a weird I wouldn't trade for the world."

"Same here."

"Come on, kid!" Mitchell called back. "Time's a

wasting ... assuming time is even still a thing in the outside world."

"Gotta love his optimism," Danni said.

"Yeah, but he's right. I've gotta go."

"How will I know you made it out okay?"

He shook his head. "We'll just have to trust that we're both survivors. Deal?"

He held out his hand, but she wrapped her arms around him instead, which he returned a moment later. "Deal. Just do me a favor. Give one of these to Frank and Allison, too. Maybe two to Frank."

"There something I should know?" he asked, pulling away. "Didn't you say earlier that...?"

"Yeah. The Jersey Devil is real, but it's a person not an animal. And he's not alone. There's a whole clan of them. Oh, and the governor is trying his damnedest to cover it up."

"Shit. Really?"

"It's ... not good. Do yourself a favor, go in there with lots of backup." She paused as she tried to keep the memories from overpowering her. *Not now!* "Don't be fooled by anything they say either. They're pure evil. They won't hesitate to shoot, so neither should you."

"I – I'll let Derek know." He must have seen the haunted look in her eyes, because he started to ask, "What did they...?"

"Don't. Just remember what I said. Okay?"

"Okay. I promise."

"Good. I love you, Harrison."

"Love you too, Danni."

She turned away, noting that the water had risen in the short time they'd spoken. There was no time left, and far too much still left unsaid.

She needed to get the explosives back to Norah and hope she knew how to use them.

"Oh, one more thing," Harrison said. "Be careful if you ever end up looking for the Mongrel Man of Morganberg."

"We just did that one. It was a bust."

"Yeah, well, if you ever get back there, be extra careful. It's not nearly as fake as you might think."

And with that, he threw her a wave and began making his way back the way he'd come – leaving her with more feelings to unpack than she'd probably ever be able to.

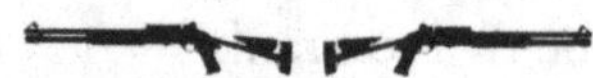

Jacob surfaced gasping for air, the wind knocked from his lungs from the sudden rush of water.

Way too close.

Added to it had been the panic of thinking his body double had washed out of the other room and he'd gotten entangled with...

A moment later, a face broke the surface – a familiar one, but not his own, thank goodness.

"D-Derek?"

"Y-yeah. Who'd y-you think it was?"

"Shit, man. If you ain't a sight for sore eyes, I don't know what is. Sorry about that by the way. Didn't expect for that damned door to open again. Thought I was gonna drown in there, so when I got sucked under I just sort of grabbed hold of whatever was in reach."

"W-which was me," Derek sputtered, spitting out water. "I guess I should be flattered. Holy shit, Jake. You had us worried."

"*You* were worried? Another fifteen minutes or so and I'd have been a floater."

"What were you doing in there?"

Jacob narrowed his eyes, making it a point to keep his voice measured. Even now, with so little time left, duty came first. "Just checking the place out. The door shut on me a little while back."

"How little of a while? I mean, we've been wondering what you've been up to all this time."

Goddamn it. Son of a bitch always was too smart for his own good. "Quit the bullshit and just spit it out. I'm growing tired of this alien swimming pool."

"You could have told us you were planning to blow the ship."

"And you would have objected."

"Probably."

"Which is why I didn't tell you."

"You could have at least told Norah."

Norah... "Stuff like this is need to know. And neither of you had that need."

"I tend to disagree when the fact-finding mission I'm on is actually more search and destroy."

"That's rich coming from you, the man with more squatch kills to his name than Teddy Roosevelt."

"Different thing entirely and you know it. It's not like I invite anyone out for a picnic and then use them as bait."

"Welcome to the government. It doesn't care about anyone's hurt feelings."

"Yeah, well, we're supposed to be friends."

"Tell me where my oath includes a friendship clause."

Derek shook his head. "We can argue about this on the way out. Come on. We found your pack. I sent Danni and the others back with it."

"Others?"

"Long story short, there's another ... group on this ship who are in the same boat as us, no pun intended."

Jacob was well aware, but so far as the rest were concerned he didn't have a radio on him. It also brought to mind the lie he had told the other Norah – a lie which, it would seem, she hadn't shared.

There was little doubt about it. No surprise showed on Derek's face at having found him alive. Either that or... "You want to radio in and tell them you found me?"

He shook his head. "Can't. Had a little accident. We should just get..." His words trailed off as there came a flash of light from inside the open doorway.

Jacob himself wasn't surprised to see it. The outages had grown far more frequent in the last half hour alone, making him wonder if this place was going to blow before his charges had the chance to... *Shit!* He'd almost forgotten about that. *Where is it?* He glanced back toward the room, not seeing the backpack anywhere, the depth of the water inside now equalized with the hall.

Either way, he knew there wasn't much time left.

"What the hell is that?" Derek asked, his attention focused on the pulsing lights visible through the water.

Jacob ignored him. He was considering his options, having just gotten an unexpected reprieve. Just because Derek hadn't heard the news didn't mean the same was true of Norah. If he just showed up there at the sub, fit as a fiddle, she might start asking...

No! That wasn't going to happen, because he wasn't going back. This was it. A second chance to make right what he'd done wrong – a chance at a better life. "This other group, where are they? Anywhere close to where we docked?"

"Huh?" Derek asked, wading toward the room. "Pretty much the opposite direction. We ran into them exploring. Surprised you didn't see their Jake. Sounds like you and he had the same orders."

Jacob had been on the verge of warning his friend away from entering, but the words died on his lips. What he'd said had been a little *too* on point.

Derek stepped into the room, no doubt noticing the hole in the opposite wall, through which there came intermittent flashes of multi-hued light. "What on Earth...?"

"Come on, man," Jacob mumbled, almost too softly to be heard. "We don't have much time."

He was debating how to convince Derek that they needed to split up, assuming he could even find the other group in time. However, then he realized that second problem might not be an issue after all. Derek had even said as much. The other Jacob had been on a similar mission. These people were just like them – a bit different due to circumstances, but essentially the same.

His people had figured out how to mark their way back. That meant the other team must've as well. He just had to look for their signs and follow them. It was so simple a child could've figured it out. As for that first problem...

"What's this?"

He looked up to see Derek reaching for something off to the side, outside his field of view. He reappeared a moment later holding the other Jacob's backpack.

Derek examined it for a second or two. "If the pack we found was yours, then who's is...?"

Even as his friend spoke, Jacob felt the water around him churn as small droplets began to rise, the gravity of this place going all trippy again.

He knew he should've said something, should have warned Derek about what was coming next, but his lips refused to form the words.

And then it was too late.

A surge of water from the opposite wall slammed into Derek from behind, shoving him off to the side and out of view as Jacob braced himself against it.

Once it finally subsided, allowing him to regain his footing, he saw the walls back in the room once again light up bright green.

Shit! Jacob's sense of duty flared to life, momentarily quieting the war being waged in his conscience. "Derek! Get out of there before..."

He was too late and his friend a bit too slow, however. As Derek reappeared near the doorway, still looking dazed, the portal closed up tight again – leaving behind nothing but a very solid looking wall.

Panic flared in Jacob's mind. They'd been so close to getting clear, only for Derek's damned inability to let shit go get in the way.

He took a deep breath, pushing his frustration to the side and trying to think clearly about the situation. Derek had obviously figured out a way to open the door from the outside. That meant it was possible. All he had to do was figure out how...

Jacob paused mid-thought. There was still one major problem to consider. Even if he got Derek out, how could he convince his friend to let him go? That particular problem was twofold. Derek wasn't an idiot. He'd already seen the other backpack. There would be questions. Hell, even if Jacob said nothing, the over-inquisitive son of a bitch would likely put two and two together.

Therein lay the conundrum. He could see no way out of that lie, not when he'd played dumb as to the existence of the other group.

It would only snowball from there. Derek would tell Norah. Then, assuming they were still in radio contact with that other team, she'd almost certainly pass the news on. The other universe's Norah would know, erasing any chance he had of righting the missteps he'd made.

She would never accept him if she knew he was a fake, especially if she suspected for even a second what he'd done. His only chance was making sure she never found out. The rest, well, he'd infiltrated drug cartels and hostile governments. He had no doubt he could infiltrate his doppelganger's life and make it his own. But in order to do that...

He began to back away, turning in the opposite direction he'd first come – realizing he needed to trust that his double had marked the way.

Though he couldn't hear Derek's cries – the walls too thick or soundproofed – he knew they were likely there. Just as he also knew that opening the door had lowered the water level somewhat, but it wouldn't take long before it filled again, silencing the secrets within forever.

Jacob shook his head. Derek had known the risks coming down here, had accepted what could happen.

However, that wouldn't be the case in his new life. There, Derek was safe aboard his version of the Nest, waiting for them to return.

That was the image he held onto as he began to push his way through the cold water – that everything would be okay in that other world, one that was so like his, yet different in the ways that mattered most.

If he was to be that universe's Jacob Caseman, then that was where he needed to focus his loyalties. Everything about his old life would have to be buried, one more ghost to add to the many that already haunted his dreams.

53

The leviathan continued circling the surface thing. Confused and in pain, its need to kill warred with the simple desire to rest and recover from its wounds.

After it had attacked the tiny surface things roaring back and forth between their larger brethren, it had gone deep for a time – albeit not so deep as to confront the massive thing.

However, then it sensed something happening above. The large surface thing continued to thrum deep within its bowels, telling the leviathan it still lived. But there was something strange going on with its smaller fellow.

Ever since the activity with the tiny things, it had fallen silent. There were no lights, no hum from deep within, and now it lay much lower in the water – as if it were dead.

Or pretending to be.

The leviathan's senses had been greatly impaired by the damage wrought to it by the massive thing's thrumming, but every so often it seemed to catch a hint of sound that suggested the smaller surface thing wasn't as dead as it thought.

Perhaps it was lying in wait, hoping for the leviathan to turn its attention away, so it could then attack from behind.

Impaired as it was, its mind feeling slow and sluggish, it still remembered the pack hunters, still understood their tactics.

The large surface thing was badly wounded, of that it was certain. But it had mostly left the smaller one alone, dismissing it as a threat.

Perhaps that was an error on its part, one in need of rectifying.

"What the fuck is it doing out there?" Julie asked. She didn't want to die, and she certainly didn't want to give Mitchell a reason to throw the switch too early, but she'd accepted her fate – taking the time to say a prayer that her mother and sister might eventually find peace in her passing.

However, several long minutes had passed, with little more to show for it than the boat rocking a bit as the beast continued to circle them.

"I don't know," Mitch replied, shaking his head. "We're dead in the water, an easy target. There's no reason it shouldn't take the bait."

Julie limped out the door to the railing. After a few moments, a massive wake passed by her spot, the dark red mass below visible in the beam of the spotlights. "Think maybe it's too dumb to know that?"

"Or we are," Mitchell said, grabbing the remote detonator. "Shit!"

"What's wrong?"

"Us," he cried. "We're wrong. I don't mean you and me specifically, just this whole scenario. Maybe it realizes this is too easy."

"Not following."

"Good. I don't want you to. I need you to stay down here. Keep your finger near the trigger so..."

"Like hell. I already told you I'm sticking by your side no matter what."

"Fine. Then just try to keep up." He stepped past her, heading toward the helipad.

She hobbled after him up the stairs best as she could. "Care to explain?"

He let out a sigh. "Octopi are intelligent, but we, humans that is, constantly underestimate them. Happens all the time. Aquariums are full of stories about the things they can do. I read about one that used to sneak out at night so it could visit the other tanks and snack on the fish there. Then there was another that set up a distraction so it could slither down a drain pipe and escape back to the ocean. That's the problem. Because they don't look like us, we assume they can't think like us despite all the evidence suggesting otherwise."

"Meaning?"

"Meaning we spent all this time setting a trap, not realizing that maybe it looks just like that – a trap."

"You can't be serious."

"I wish I wasn't. In the meantime, the Sun Angel, which has, until recently, been manned by a skeleton crew, is now packed to the brim with people. And quiet as they're no doubt trying to be, they're still walking around, talking, and doing whatever it is black-ops spooks do when no-one is watching."

Julie raised an eyebrow, a sinking feeling beginning to settle into her stomach. "And sound carries extra far in the water."

"Exactly."

"But we don't know for sure that…"

Mitchell pointed. "We don't, but it does. Look!"

The pair watched in horror as the creature broke off, the massive wake changing direction toward where the catamaran waited.

"Go grab the guns and whatever ammo's left, quick!"

Mitchell shook his head. "A few rounds aren't going to change that things mind. Here!" He shoved the detonator into her hands. "Keep that warm for me, but try not to lean on it."

"Where are you going?"

He turned away from her. "The engine room. I'm going to see if I can coax this baby back to life."

"I thought the propellers were shot."

"They are, but maybe that can work in our favor for once."

Danni wasn't happy to see the water was now far past where it had been when she and the others had left just a short while ago, but she was far from surprised.

Finally, though, as she made it to a spot where it was only ankle deep, she was able to break out into a run, keeping her flashlight pointed ahead as the lighting continued to be sporadic.

The outages seemed to be coming much more frequently now. So far, she'd been able to handle the fluctuations, but Danni worried what might happen if the ship went completely bonkers, hitting them with ten times Earth gravity or worse.

Don't think about that. Focus on getting back.

Finally, she turned a corner to the straightaway leading to their basecamp. She could see both Norah and Llanzo silhouetted in the doorway, no doubt waiting for their return. *Theirs, not hers.*

At least the lights were still on for the final thirty feet or so.

Norah's face was unreadable as she reached their base-camp, stepping over the metal plate still in the doorway. However, Llanzo was far more an open book.

"Where's Jenner?"

"He still looking for Jacob," she said. "As soon as he finds him, he's going to..."

"Jacob's dead," Norah replied flatly. "The other ... guy found him. I tried letting you know but couldn't get through."

Danni simply stared back, letting the senior agent's words sink in. "W-we had an accident. Lost the radios." However, right then she was more concerned for Derek. Despite his assurances, she knew him. He was the type to keep searching long past the point of no return.

She stripped off the backpack and handed it to Norah, already considering her options. "We found this."

"Isn't that...?"

Danni nodded. "Yeah."

"But you didn't find him? What about the other...?"

"There was no sign of either of them. We found this floating in the hallway. Derek split up the contents and ordered us all to head back. He said you'd know what to do with it."

Norah unzipped the bag, looked inside, and offered a tight grin. "I wasn't always a desk jockey, you know."

"Good. Do whatever you have to. I need to go find..."

"You don't get to give the orders here," Norah stated flatly. "And you're not going anywhere."

"But..."

"What you are going to do is join Dr. Reid in prepping the sub for launch while I set these."

Danni wasn't surprised, but she was also in no mood for games. Had their positions been reversed, Derek wouldn't have hesitated to come looking for her. Could she do any less?

Norah, however, seemed ready for that, positioning herself between Danni and the door. "I know what you're thinking. Believe me, because a part of me is thinking it, too. It's not happening, though. I can't have two of you running around out there."

"We can't just leave him."

"We won't. But he has to make it back on his own. We don't have time to send you out there looking for him and I won't risk losing you both."

"What do you mean we don't have time? The water's rising, yes, but there's still…"

"I'm not talking about the water." She held up the bag. "I'm talking about these. My namesake had more than one bit of bad news to pass along. Her Jacob set his explosives for a one hour delay."

"Then he can reset them."

Norah shook her head. "No. He can't. He was trapped and running out of air. He … wanted to make sure he fulfilled his duty before it was too late."

Danni paused in her attempt to sidestep the senior agent. "How long ago was that?"

"About forty minutes. Closer to forty five, if we're playing it safe."

Danni's heart sunk as she realized Norah was right. Had the ship still been dry, she could've easily made it to where she'd last seen Derek, and gotten back with time to spare. But the rising water made it a slog. She'd be lucky to reach him again in the time they had left, and that was assuming he hadn't made it much farther than that.

"Do you understand?" Norah asked.

Danni didn't say anything, she couldn't trust her voice right then. All she could do was nod.

"Good. Then please go help Dr. Reid. Believe me, I'll give him until the very last possible second. But all we can do until then is pray it's enough."

Several long minutes passed, the water level in the room already dangerously higher than it had been when the door first closed. Yet Derek still refused to believe it. Maybe the ship was breaking down to the point where his friend was pounding on the other side to no avail.

The problem was, no other room had acted that way before now, not even this one. Then there was the other backpack he'd found, right before getting trapped – one that had produced a look of near panic on Jacob's face upon seeing him holding it.

It didn't make sense.

"All right, enough of trying to rationalize this, Jenner," he told himself. "Figure a way out then the rest can sort itself later."

He took a look around, using his flashlight to orient himself. It was another room that appeared different from the others. However, with chest deep water, it was difficult to see what, if any, operations it might have once served. That said, he could see where a few explosives had been planted, telling him Jacob thought this place was important enough to...

That strange strobing light once again caught his eye, coming from the spot opposite of where he'd come in. It was why he was trapped to begin with, having drawn his attention like a moth to a flame. Wading closer, Derek noticed the large hole in the wall – partially submerged.

What was more interesting, though, was that it

seemed to be *fully* submerged on the other side. It wasn't all too different from that phenomenon they'd seen in the hall — a solid wall of water held back by seemingly nothing.

Though this was one area where his experience failed him, he'd seen enough episodes of Star Trek to conclude there was some sort of barrier or force field holding it at bay — one which seemed to falter in time with the outages.

Which meant it wouldn't be long before he'd be in dire need of a set of gills.

Whatever was in that other room continued to pulse with light, making the space beyond plainly visible thanks to the relatively clear water. He could see enough to know the other chamber was massive compared to the room he was in, far larger than anything he'd encountered so far.

That it was also flooded caused Derek to raise an eyebrow. This wasn't some slow leak — not with how long this ship had likely been down there. If that was the case he could have counted how long he had in decades not minutes. No. This had almost certainly been recent — a result of that ZarroGreen ship, the creature, or maybe both.

Not that it really mattered at this point.

Between the water, the flashing, and the weirdness they'd encountered on the surface, it wasn't hard to put two and two together. He could understand why Jacob had judged this a worthy place to plant his charges.

Speaking of which, something told him that drowning might be the least of his worries. Derek pulled the backpack close and unzipped it. Almost immediately upon peering inside his curiosity was raised, as well as his stress levels. There was a handgun as well as a radio — one equipped with the same high-gain antenna Mitchell's had been sporting.

Strange. And yet the Jacob he'd encountered was theirs. He was certain of it.

That was probably of lesser importance than the pack's final surprise, an ominous looking device with a digital display that was rapidly counting down. Derek had frowned on the use of explosives during his tenure as team lead, citing them as overkill against the beasts they hunted – most of the time anyway. That didn't mean he wasn't familiar with them, though.

He'd seen detonators before. This one was different, more advanced, but still recognizable for what it was. Derek studied the device for a moment then attempted to disengage the timer, only for the display to ask him for a passcode.

Son of a bitch.

It wasn't hard for him to imagine the scenario – Jake locked inside with the room rapidly flooding. He'd planted the explosives, trying to give the team enough lead time to escape. But, not knowing if he'd live long enough to set them off manually, he'd made it a point to ensure he fulfilled his goddamned duty either way.

Except now he was out there and Derek was the one stuck. He was still having trouble reconciling that his friend had likely left him to rot. Surely, he wouldn't have...

All at once, his body felt heavy.

Shit! Here we go again.

He glanced back to see the strange lights from the other room pulsing that much brighter. Knowing what was coming, Derek quickly pressed himself flat against the wall just as the proverbial flood gates opened. Water began rushing into the room from the other chamber, adding a good foot of height to what was already there, before the outage finally passed.

Derek wasn't ready to give up yet, but he knew what had to be done. The others needed to know that time was running out, and Jacob had inadvertently left him the means to do so.

He pulled out the radio, noting it was on the wrong channel, and was readjusting it when something from the other room caught his eye – the glow from within partially obscured by something pressed up against the hole.

Probably some piece of flotsam that got shaken loose.

His curiosity got the better of him, though, and he found himself wading over, pointing his flashlight to give himself a better look at whatever was there in silhouette.

Derek couldn't help the scream that escaped his lips as he beheld eyes staring back at him – eyes that belonged to the man he'd thought his lifelong friend.

How the fuck did he get in there?

Had Jacob tried to free him after all, perhaps circling around to find another way in, only to fall victim to the rapidly rising waters of this place?

His first reaction was to reach through and pull Jake out, see if perhaps there was a chance he could be resuscitated, but then he hesitated as he took in the full picture.

This man was dressed slightly different than what his friend had been wearing.

Far more damning, though, was the bullet hole smack dab in his forehead, one which Derek would've bet good money hadn't been self-inflicted.

What the fuck happened here?

Unfortunately, there was only a dead man left to tell that tale, and soon there'd be two if he didn't figure out something fast.

He did have one avenue to check first, though. Derek pulled out the gun, pretty certain it had come from that other universe, and checked it out. There was no bullet in the chamber and it had a full magazine.

That told him whatever had happened, it had been

quick, unexpected. The question now was whether his death had been an accident or an execution.

Sadly, that would be a moot point in short order if he didn't stop playing Nancy Drew.

He turned on the radio and depressed the button. "Derek to Norah. I hope you're still listening on this channel. I know you probably can't respond right now, but that's fine. We don't have time to debate this or wait for another glitch. I just need you to listen. I'm trapped with no way out, and no I'm not telling you where. There isn't time to reach me anyway."

He took a deep breath, not enjoying having to deliver his own eulogy. "I found the explosives Jake set. They're on a timer and locked in. There's no way to disable them remotely and we have less than ten minutes until they go off. I need you to set your charges and get the hell out of here. I repeat, get out of here. This place is going to blow."

Then, after a pause, he added, "Please don't let Danni try anything stupid. I need for you all to get back to the surface." He considered whether he should add anything profound, but decided to finish with, "Tell my team that I'm proud of each and every one of them, and that they can honor me best by continuing to fight the good fight. It's been both an honor and a pleasure. Derek out."

With that, he turned off the radio, not wishing to hear a response, garbled or otherwise.

He was about to turn his full attention toward figuring some way out of this mess when another thought hit him, something the other Norah had said — implying that perhaps things between her and her universe's Jacob had worked out differently.

She deserves to know.

He quickly tuned the radio back to the channel it had been on when he'd found it.

"Norah, this is Derek. Come in..."

54

"We have a ... *situation* on deck, Ma'am. I think you should see this."

That didn't bode well, especially since she hadn't heard any fireworks yet.

The upside was it meant Mitch was still alive. Sadly, the downside – for all of them – was the same was likely true of that fucking monster.

Andrea made her way up on deck, the effects of whatever that bastard had injected her with still making her feel all loopy.

The asshole knows his drugs. I'll give him that.

The current watch was on deck along with several other agents, probably a result of them all being crammed into the limited space of the yacht's interior.

Not all, she reminded herself.

Perhaps unsurprisingly, the one person left unaccounted for from their last headcount had been that Wilhelm woman. An inability to follow orders was apparently considered a virtue in the DoCC.

Someone handed her a pair of binoculars. The cutter itself was easy enough to see without them, its floodlights

513

alit making it a beacon in the darkness – not that darkness was an issue with lightning continuing to flash like crazy.

What was less obvious without an enhanced view was the unnatural swell of water that was heading away from the Nest and seemingly in their direction – silhouetted by the bright lights of the cutter behind it.

Oh god!

The damned octopus hadn't taken the bait. She wasn't sure how or why, but it was coming straight for them.

"All hands on deck! Battle stations!"

There wasn't really much standing protocol for something like this, other than getting every agent aboard into the fight. It was far from ideal, a good way for someone to get hit with friendly fire once the shit hit the fan. However, she knew their chances weren't good regardless.

Like it or not, this was their best bet for survival, even if just a handful of them made it.

"Prepare the launch!" she shouted. "Secure the wounded in it."

It was all she could do and it wasn't enough. She'd seen what that thing had done to one of their rafts. They were nothing to it, bugs to be swatted.

"I want all the heavy ordinance we have left focused on that thing," she ordered. "Don't hold back. If we're going down, I want this thing to know we fought it every inch of the way."

There came muffled cheers and cries in support of that as the wake approached them, visible now without the need for binoculars.

As lightning crashed above, she was able to see just how large it was – the beast's body visible below the surface of the water.

Here it comes. "Hold for my mark."

She was about to give the word when the creature turned at the last moment, passing them by – the boat rocking so much from its wake that she was sure they'd be swamped.

All across the deck, men and women grabbed hold of whatever they could – each other in some cases – to keep from falling overboard.

"What the hell?"

"It's coming back!" someone cried from the stern.

Sure enough they were right. The creature turned and passed on their other side, once again rocking the boat.

"Secure yourselves! I don't want anyone falling overboard."

Fortunately, there was a high railing around most of the deck. Good thing, too, as she was forced to grab hold of it to keep from losing her footing as the boat pitched and yawed like some sort of amusement park ride.

"It's coming back again. I ... think it's circling us."

There was no doubt in her mind that's what was happening – almost as if their mission had somehow turned into a bad *Jaws* knockoff. *But why?*

"I have a clear shot!" another voice cried out.

"Hold," she repeated, trying to push past the cotton in her head so she could think.

There was no reason for it to hesitate. They were an easy target.

Unless ... it was assessing how big of a threat they were.

Is that even possible? "Everyone listen to me," she hissed. "Hold your fire. Keep as quiet as possible."

"What...?"

"I said be quiet, mister! Make like a hole in the water."

She couldn't begin to understand what this monstrosity was thinking, but she was certain of one thing – once it attacked they stood absolutely no chance. So the very last thing they wanted to do was provoke it.

"Steady," she said, barely loud enough to be heard. "Everyone stay calm. We need to..."

There came a sound in the distance, a low rumble, almost certainly not thunder.

Wait, I know that sound.

Of course she did. She'd heard it nearly every second since being assigned to the Nest. Its engines were coming online.

What the hell?

She lifted the binoculars to her eyes. Sure enough, smoke was beginning to rise from the stack. At the stern, a spray was beginning to kick up from the waterline.

Then the rumble changed, replaced with what could only be described as the grind of metal against metal, muted by the water but unmistakable nevertheless.

"Are they trying to make a run for it?" someone asked.

Andrea didn't bother to answer. She knew that was impossible. Harkness was talented, she gave him that much, but he wasn't a miracle worker. He'd have needed to be Hephaestus himself to get the screws spinning again.

So what the hell is he...

"It's veering off," Cortez said from alongside her.

Andrea lowered the binoculars and turned his way. Amazingly enough, the wake at their stern abruptly collapsed in on itself – the beast changing direction back toward the cutter.

The octopus passed by directly on their starboard side, the wake nearly capsizing them from its sheer size and ferocity. There came cries as several of her team toppled overboard.

Whatever the two DoCC agents had done, it had worked, as the creature was making a beeline straight for the wounded cutter.

They weren't out of the woods yet, though.

"Pull everyone out of the drink. I want all hands

accounted for," she cried as her people scrambled into motion. "Just do it as quietly as you can."

"This isn't right," Danni said, feeling as helpless now as she had the day she'd lost her brother.

"There's a lot about this job that isn't right," Norah remarked from next to her in the minisub. "But we do it anyway. Doctor?"

"Prepped and ready to go," he replied, nervous sweat beading on his forehead. "Are you sure those explosives won't...?"

"I'm not sure of anything. For all we know, those charges will go off and barely leave a dent. I'm simply doing the best I can here."

Danni was certain that was false modesty. She'd watched the woman at work — meticulously placing charges in the same spots where the doors had retracted to let them in. If there were structural weak points, as Norah had said, those would be it.

Their only hope now was that whatever happened next didn't damage the sub enough to cripple it. The front bubble, arguably the weakest point of the submersible, was facing away from the blast site. However, if they accidentally destroyed their propulsion in the process, they might as well just shoot themselves and be done with it.

Danni wasn't sure if she could do that, but it was a kinder fate than slowly suffocating as the oxygen scrubbers finally gave out.

She'd fought tooth and nail to give Derek every last minute she could, but in the end his garbled voice over the radio had been the deciding factor. Even then, had Norah not been there to press the case, she was certain she'd have made one last effort to reach him – doomed as it would have been.

Instead she sat there, tears gathering in her eyes as his seconds counted out. Norah had done the math with Reid's help, figuring out the minimum safe margin for escape – assuming Jacob's charges did the trick. However, she'd sounded pretty confident in his abilities.

Even if that didn't cripple the alien ship, his explosives were almost certain to flood it, she'd seen enough to not question that.

"You should know how highly he thinks of you," Norah said, looking away from her watch to face Danni.

"Excuse me?"

"Both in his official reports and unofficially. I've never heard him throw a negative word your way. I think ... I think he was grooming you to take over the team."

"What?"

Norah held up a hand. "Not yet of course. You've still got a bit of growing to do. But he was damned proud of how far you've come. I figured ... you'd want to know."

"Thank you."

It didn't make the hurt go away or even sting less, especially knowing he was still out there, alive but trapped, but she appreciated Norah telling her all the same.

She glanced up at the hatch. It was foolish, but she couldn't help but imagine herself making a last minute run for it, finding Derek, then making it back just in the nick of time.

Time, however, was something none of them had.

"Brace yourselves," Norah said, her eyes focused through the front bubble at the open door beyond, as if expecting Derek to step through it. In the next instant, though, she lifted the remote detonator. "God forgive me. Three ... two..."

The charges went off, obscuring all they could see with

light, smoke and, a moment later, a deluge of rushing water.

Jacob could've kissed his other self. He'd been right. The other team had left a clearly marked trail the way they'd come, even if, in the decaying light, he'd had to hunt for them.

It had been hard going. Outside of the flickering lights, some sections of the hall were now almost fully flooded. But finally the tide had begun to slake. The water became shallower the further he walked, until at last he found himself on dry ground again.

The annoying slosh from his shoes was quickly forgotten once he turned a corner and saw *her* – Norah, his wife.

She was standing in the middle of the empty hallway as if waiting for him.

"You made it!" she cried.

He ran the rest of the way, throwing his arms around her and hugging her tight – not realizing how much he'd missed holding her until that moment. Then, after several long seconds, he finally let her go. "Um, sorry for getting you all wet."

"It's okay. I-I have to admit, I didn't expect to see you. But you're here."

"Yeah," he replied. "I got lucky. Managed to jimmy the door open."

"Really? How?"

Jacob had already anticipated that, though. "I dunno. Got lucky I guess. Once the pressure on both sides equalized, a crack appeared. Managed to pry it open before my air ran out. Close one, though."

"I tried calling you. Couldn't get through. I was beginning to fear the worst."

"Had to leave it all behind. There was just enough room to squeeze my butt through."

"And here you were complaining the other night about barely fitting into your fatigues."

He let out a laugh. "Guess I'll be going on a diet once we get out of here. Speaking of which." He did a quick mental calculation, realizing he'd probably eaten up more time than he'd thought. "Shit. We gotta get going, babe. You set the charges, right?"

She nodded. "All done. Just waiting to set them off."

"Great. Then let's get out of here. Can't wait to see Derek again and tell him all about this shit." He looked around, seeing nothing but partially lit hallway and unbroken walls. "Where's the sub?"

Norah inclined her head. "The sub? Oh, that. I must've gotten turned around out here. Hold on. I know what to do." She unhooked a radio from her belt and held it up. "You ready, Mitch?"

"Yeah," came the reply. "But..."

"Then hold tight. Please know it's been an honor. Tell Derek I said the same."

"What was that about?" Jacob asked.

"Oh nothing. Nice shirt by the way." She reached behind her with her free hand. "When did you get a chance to change?"

"This? Tore the other one, had a spare in my pack."

"Convenient. You're quick with the excuses, I'll give you that."

"I don't understand."

However, a moment later, realization dawned as she produced a familiar looking detonator.

"Wait, don't..."

"By the way, you started a diet last month," she said flatly before depressing the kill switch.

There came a muted *boom*, and then it was as if the entire ship shook around them, knocking him off his feet. The lights dimmed and then finally went out, leaving them in total darkness.

He heard the sound of something clattering to the floor, then saw the faint light of a display from a few feet away.

"Report," Norah said.

"You did it. We're free!" came the reply.

"Glad to hear it. Now get your asses back to the surface. That's an order. Over and out."

The light on the radio went dead and Jacob heard that too fall to the ground.

"What the hell did you do," he cried. "Why...?"

"Because I spoke with Derek a few minutes ago, via the radio you left behind when you *escaped*. He told me what he found. What you *did*."

"Norah, it's me. I'm..."

"I don't know why you did it," she continued, sounding closer, "but I really don't care either. You took him from me, then lied about it. And then you had the nerve to think I would be stupid enough to fall for this charade."

"No! You're wrong. I swear, I..."

"I got the impression talking to that other Norah, *your Norah*, that things didn't work out. I think I understand why now. You're nothing like him, a pale impersonation at best."

He scrambled to his feet, hoping to find her in the dark. "That isn't true."

"You wouldn't know this, but it was touch and go for a while with us, too. We came damned close to calling it quits, but then we somehow managed to pull back from the abyss – rediscovered our love for one another, that we meant *the world* to each other. And now ... that world is gone forever."

"It doesn't have to be. I-I did this for you!"

"Really?" There came the familiar sound of a slide being racked. "Well, I'm doing this for Jacob. *My* Jacob. I don't know you."

An explosion rang out in the hallway, momentarily alit with muzzle fire, but Jacob Caseman was too busy cradling his gut to care.

He'd been around enough enemy fire, seen enough wounds to know what his fate would be if he didn't receive medical attention quickly, something that seemed unlikely.

He gasped for breath while trying to staunch the blood with his hands, hoping he still had enough strength to make Norah understand, to make her...

Another gunshot rang out – the flash just barely enough to give him a momentary glimpse of Norah as she crumpled to the ground in front of him.

He felt a warm wetness on the floor, expanding from where she lay, one that had nothing to do with the seawater he knew would soon find its way there.

She'd condemned them both to death, but had then turned her weapon on herself, leaving him to die alone in an alien Hell of his own making.

The screeching clang of metal enraged the Leviathan.

What angered it far worse, though, was that the large surface thing had only pretended to be dying. Now, it was attempting to run, leaving its smaller podmate to die so it could flee.

It was a race the surface thing couldn't hope to win.

As it sped toward its foe, the screeching growing ever louder in the water around it, the leviathan realized the surface thing's ruse had been for naught. It was too crippled to do much more than weakly turn in the water, lurching to the side as it feebly attempted to swim away.

This time there would be no question of the leviathan's superiority.

It dove as it raced toward its enemy, planning to come up beneath it and use its weight to drag it down. It understood the surface things. Tip them over and the fight would end, leaving only the screaming things flailing in the water – easy pickings for a creature of its vast might.

Though they tasted foul, it was growing hungry again, having expended too much energy in a short time. Their bodies would nourish it, giving it the strength to turn back and destroy the smaller podmate. Then, at long last, it would be left with only the massive thing below remaining to challenge its supremacy – a challenge which would soon be met.

The screeching grew ever more irritating as it closed in, but it used that annoyance to fuel its anger, it's fury ... until finally it was within striking range.

It came up beneath the surface thing, grasping hold of it, knowing this time there would be no escape.

However, just as its massive arms found purchase on its wounded enemy, a distant pressure wave hit it from below – from the depths where the massive thing lay.

It knew it should finish the job, that the surface thing was easy prey, but its true ire lay with the massive thing. And if something had just happened to wound it further, then perhaps that meant it was finally ripe for the taking.

The leviathan's confused and damaged mind warred with the decision. It had a foe within its grasp, yet the massive thing was by far the greater threat to its domain.

Both needed to die, but it was unsure which to kill first.

But then, in the next instant, the rage subsumed all thought. It made up its mind and prepared for the carnage to come.

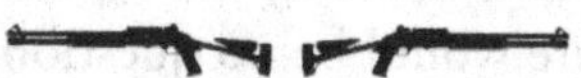

What the hell just happened?

"You ... did it! We're ... free!" came Mitchell's garbled voice over the sub's radio, barely audible, as if broadcasting from a great distance ... perhaps a whole universe away.

Either way it was the confirmation Danni had prayed for, but hadn't dared hope to ever know. The other team had made it, their gambit had paid off. Yet, she was also forced to wonder why the same hadn't happened for them.

Derek had been right about Norah's skills. The explosion had been loud, rocking the sub hard enough that she'd half-expected it to crack like an egg. Fortunately, it hadn't.

As smoke from the blast surrounded them, there came the rush of water ... for a few moments anyway. Then it had abruptly stopped

When it was finished, there was maybe two or three feet of seawater around them, not even enough to lift the sub from the floor.

Thud.

"It didn't work."

"That's not possible," Norah replied. "Even if it didn't blow the doors completely this place should at least be filling up, but look at it. The water's settling."

Thud.

"Hold on. What's that noise?" Llanzo asked.

The *thud* sound came again.

At first, Danni wondered if perhaps that creature had returned. Maybe it had been lying in wait for them to emerge, and was even now plugging the hole with its massive body as it tried to get at them.

Thud.

There was just one problem with that theory.

"That sound's coming from in front of us," Norah said, echoing Danni's thoughts.

They peered out the front bubble as the smoke started to clear, until Danni was certain she could make out movement ahead of them.

Thud.

Then she saw it. The wall began to close – the four sides of the door beginning to slide shut, only for there to come that *thud* and then they'd open up again.

It was like an elevator door that someone blocked to stop from closing, except it was doing it again and again.

"Guess your plan would've worked after all, Doctor," Norah finally said, reminding Danni that they'd shoved a hunk of metal into the doorway earlier, to keep it from locking them in.

But what does that have to do with us being stuck here now? Unless...

"What are you doing?" Norah cried as Danni sprang into action.

She started working to unlock the hatch. "Testing a theory."

"You'll drown us all."

"And yet what we're seeing outside says otherwise." She turned, not wishing to be either tackled or shot, and held up her hands. "Trust me, okay. I haven't gone insane and this isn't some stupid hero play." Norah narrowed her eyes, but nodded for her to go on. "How are we looking on time?"

The senior agent glanced down at her watch. "Shit! Just make it quick, whatever it is you've got planned."

If I'm wrong, you can say I told you so. She kept that thought to herself as she popped the hatch, ready to close it in a hurry if need be.

However, no rush of water greeted her.

That didn't mean there wasn't a lot to be seen, though.

"Holy shit. You need to check this out."

Danni climbed out to make way for Norah, staring at what remained of the wall holding them in – which wasn't much. Of far greater interest was seeing a massive wall of water, the might of the entire ocean, held at bay by the power of some unseen force.

She'd been afraid of finding the creature trying to block their escape, but this wasn't much better.

"What in the name of hell?" Norah gasped. "This isn't..."

"Yes, it *is* possible," Danni replied, cutting off the senior agent but not caring one iota in that moment. "Remember that wall of water I told you about earlier? The one you dismissed as some sort of optical illusion."

"I take it back." Norah finished pulling herself out of the sub, kneeling there with Danni as they viewed the bottom of the sea through the blown wall. "What the hell is it and why is it keeping us in here?"

As they watched, the room flashed bright red. Sections of the wall attempted to slide out, covering a few feet of the breach before retracting again.

Is it trying to repair itself? If so, it seemed the damage was either too great to fix or the ship too far gone to compensate for it. Whatever the case, it wasn't in their best interest to wait around for whatever happened next.

"Some kind of force field would probably be the sciencey answer," Danni said. "As for why, I don't..." A thought suddenly hit her, a crazy one. But with no other solutions in sight it was all she had. "Hold on. You know how ships have bilge pumps?"

"Yeah. What does that have to do with anything?"

"Maybe nothing. But what if this is kind of the same thing, some sort of emergency system to keep the rest of the ship from flooding?" She remembered what happened to them in front of the water wall. "An emergency system that's been glitching out at random. Meaning this one will probably do the same at some point."

Norah glanced down at her watch again. "Not sure we have time to wait. We need to find some way to turn it off now, otherwise..."

Thud.

Both of them turned back toward the door to see it once again attempting to close.

Of course! "I think I know how to..."

"Get back in the ship and lock the hatch," Norah said, apparently coming to the same conclusion.

"No, I can..."

"*Now!*"

Danni turned back to find the senior agent pointing a semi-automatic handgun her way. "Are you for real?"

"I understand you, Agent Kent," Norah said, her voice calm and collected. "And while your penchant for self-sacrifice is admirable, it's ill-timed here. Derek was right about you. You're the future of this organization, a future we're going to need."

"But..."

"Say another word and I'll put a bullet in your knee cap. Don't even think of testing me on this. Now get in there and seal the hatch. Doctor," she called out. "If Agent Kent tries anything stupid before you reach the surface, you have my express permission to do whatever it takes to stop her."

Danni stared hard at her, until the other woman lowered her voice. "We don't have time for this. Please. If not for me, then for Derek."

That finally broke the impasse. Danni began to climb back into the sub, stopping only long enough to say, "Thank you, Norah. For everything."

"You too, Danni. Just do me a favor and tell them we died in the line of duty."

Danni nodded just before closing the hatch. She hesitated for a moment, hating what she was being forced to do, then sealed it.

"What is she doing?" Llanzo asked from the pilot seat.

"Saving us." Danni wiped her eyes then steeled her voice. "I need you to be ready, Doctor. This ride's about to get bumpy."

She could do nothing but watch as the senior agent

made it to the doorway and then stepped through. The senior agent bent low, straining as she tried to drag the piece of ballast with her, moving it little by little as the door continued trying to shut.

Norah finally cleared it, though – standing up tall on the other side of the doorway and throwing them one final salute as the door shut in front of her, this time likely for good.

A moment later, they were lifted from the floor as an angry tidal wave of water hit them, sending the minisub tumbling to the far wall with a heavy clang.

"Get us out of here!" Danni cried.

"I can't. Not until the pressure is equalized. Just give it a few..."

However, she'd stopped listening the second she noticed movement in the water from in front of them – catching sight of something she'd hoped to never see again.

"Get us out of here! Now!"

Julie watched in horror as the sea erupted in a mass of enormous tentacles rising up over the stern of the ship.

Mitchell's plan had worked in spades – serving them a lot better than firing a few ineffective rounds at the creature from a distance.

Now it was her turn. There was no chance of making it down to the control room, not with this beast giving them its full attention. The remote detonator had to work. If it failed, then they'd be in God's hands, although she doubted their chances of receiving either a miracle or mercy.

She steadied herself on her crutches as there came the groan of metal fatigue from all around her, the stern of the

Nest slowly being dragged down – the lower deck already in danger of being swamped.

This is it. Please take good care of Sophie, Mom.

Julie held up the remote detonator, hoping that it did its job quickly. The last thing she wanted was to be left floating in the water, mortally wounded yet still alive – not that she'd probably have much choice in the matter.

She began to put pressure on the trigger when suddenly the ship bobbed up again, the stern rising so violently that she lost her footing and fell. The detonator clattered out of her hand as a wave of fresh agony raced up her leg, causing her to see stars.

Do not black out! Gritting her teeth against the pain, she reached out and grabbed hold of the detonator again. When she looked up again, however, there was no longer any sign of the beast or its tentacles. Nevertheless, she knew in her heart it was near, ready to finish the job.

She aimed to beat it to the punch.

Julie closed her eyes and prepared for the end as she once again began to apply pressure to the switch.

Derek felt the distant explosions, a series of subtle shockwaves that shuddered the room and sent ripples through the water around him – one after the other, from opposite directions.

A few moments passed and then his radio squawked to life.

"You did it! We're free!"

It sounded like Mitchell's voice, but it was hard to tell – staticky and low, as if he were picking up the signal over a vast distance.

Vaster than anyone would ever believe, he considered

before switching off the device and dropping it into the water.

He'd done what he could. Now he had to trust that his team – *both* of them – could handle the rest. Fortunately, they were in capable hands.

As for him...

The last outage had been a few moments earlier, leaving him with less than a foot of breathable air. One more and he'd be done for.

It was time to take the bull by the horns.

He turned toward the hole in the wall, took a couple of deep breaths to ready himself, and then submerged.

Nothing ventured, nothing gained.

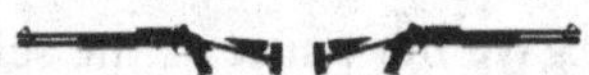

"It's just the fragment," Llanzo said, working the controls.

"What?!"

"Calm down! It's the tentacle fragment. That's all."

Danni let out a deep breath as she realized he was right. The sub's powerful lights illuminated the chamber bright as day, showing her that all she'd seen had been the piece of the creature's arm caught up in the same rush of water that had caught them. "Sorry," she meekly replied.

"All things considered," the scientist said with a nervous chuckle, "I'm not ashamed to say I'll probably need a new pair of pants myself once this is over."

"How do we look?" She dreaded his answer as the control panel lit up with what seemed like dozens of red lights.

"Another thruster is out, and there's definitely a microleak somewhere in the main housing. Our oxygen levels seem to have taken a hit, too."

"Okay, and the good news?"

"I think I can still get us out of here."

"Then don't think about it. Do it."

"Yes, ma'am."

Llanzo pulled on the controls and then there came a hollow thud as the sub bounced into the wall.

"Sorry. The controls are a bit different than what I'm used to." The scientist began to turn the sub toward the opening leading outside – sections of the wall continuing to slide and retract as the ship's crippled systems reacted to the damage.

"Aim for the center, away from all of that."

"Will do my best," he said, wiping sweat from his brow. "I think I have a handle on this now."

"You sound like my brother after his first driving exam."

That thought gave her pause as the scientist worked to maneuver the sub.

Harrison. She'd heard their transmission. That meant they'd gotten out. They were safe. She could take comfort in knowing he was still out there, ready to take on whatever the world threw his way.

Sadly, he couldn't say the same about her. *At least not yet.* "Where's the mic on this thing?"

Llanzo thankfully didn't question her. He just pointed then went back to the task of getting them out, the open portal looming ahead as he applied power to the remaining thrusters.

She flipped on the switch, took a breath to steady herself, and said, "I don't know if you can hear this or not, Harrison. But we made it. We're out. Love you always."

Then she turned it off, knowing she'd done what she could. They'd either heard her or they hadn't. There wasn't anything she could do about it now.

"Hold tight," Llanzo said. "The second we're clear, I'm dropping our ballast."

Danni nodded as they passed through the opening

into the sea beyond, trying not to focus on all those they were leaving behind. *I'm so sorry, Derek.*

"Controls are sluggish. That ... heavy water, I guess, we hit on the way in is still around us."

"Let's get clear of it before blowing the plates. Just to be safe."

He nodded. "Starting to ascend. We should be clear in roughly..."

The sub shuddered violently, causing Danni to slam into the side, bruising her arm as they came to a halt.

"W-what happened?" she asked. "Did we lose power?"

"No," Llanzo said, panic beginning to once more color his voice. "I don't understand it! Controls are operating fine. We ... we just stopped."

The sub lurched in the water again, and then it began to descend.

What the fuck? "Angle the nose down."

"Why?"

"Just do it," Danni ordered.

Llanzo worked the controls, giving them a view straight out of Hell, their lights illuminating it all – despite Danni wishing to god they hadn't.

A thick fleshy tentacle extended from the sub, continuing an impossibly long distance away, to where the rest of the creature, *Otoctopus giganteus,* sat.

It had a hold of them, the rest of it splayed out over the alien ship, its tentacles grasping and probing for purchase, one of them inside the very hole they'd escaped from.

She watched in horror as it flexed two more of its arms, tearing chunks of metal plating off and widening the hole. Multihued lights flared up from inside the spot it attacked.

Danni had no idea what had transpired while they'd been trapped, but the creature clearly hadn't survived unscathed – battle damage visible upon its massive form. Sadly, it wasn't nearly enough to help them now.

Though it was impossible to know the beast's thoughts, Danni could have sworn its one remaining eye turned malevolently their way as they were dragged down toward it.

Derek felt vibrations from the water all around him, making him wonder if he'd misjudged the timing for the explosives. However, still finding himself intact and not blown to pieces, he continued to focus on swimming – knowing he had maybe a minute or two of air in his lungs at most.

He pushed forward, toward the strange pulsating lights, hoping to find a way out or perhaps a pocket of air beyond it, as he saw little hope in any other direction, the chamber far too large to explore before his time ran out.

His only chance was if he got lucky and found...

The water suddenly took on a sludge-like consistency as he neared the massive device pulsing with its alien energies, just as it had been in the area directly outside the ship. Derek floundered, kicking his legs ever harder – expending precious oxygen with the effort – while moving forward at barely a crawl.

His head began to grow fuzzy as his lungs screamed for air that wasn't to be found.

And then, just as he was about to give up and accept his fate, he sensed even more light – except now it was coming from behind him.

Oh crap. Time's up.

Thunderous sound and a pressure wave of bubbling water followed, pushing him forward toward the alien device as everything in the room seemingly lit up –

consuming him in bright multihued energy and leaving nothing behind in its wake.

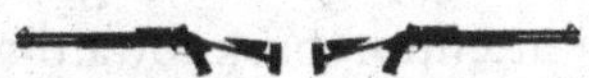

Danni was sure her eyes were playing tricks on her as she spied the first flash of underwater fire – from the part of the ship where they'd seen the broken off drill, now missing.

The explosives! Did they...? Her mouth dropped open as that section of the vessel began to come apart, rupturing in multi-hued light and strange white flames.

The destruction only spread from there. As the first shockwave rattled the sub, tiny cracks began to form in the bubble around them.

"We're coming apart," Llanzo cried. "We can't take any more of this."

No we can't, Danni thought, *but neither can that thing.*

The devastation continued to expand. Whatever Jacob had done had worked far better than he probably could have hoped, setting off some kind of chain reaction. Danni could only watch, a barely contained smile on her face, as the flames reached the first of the beast's tentacles, setting them ablaze as if in mockery of the ocean around it.

The sub jerked downward as the creature reacted to this, trying to pull away, thrashing in obvious pain, yet seemingly stuck with two of its arms deep within the alien structure – the ship's systems still trying to close the breach the great beast had penetrated.

The ruination spread unhindered, white flames and strange lights reaching out as if hungry to consume all in sight.

"Drop the ballast plates," Danni cried. "And give the thrusters everything you've got!"

"That won't help us..."

"NOW!"

Llanzo began frantically working the controls while Danni turned her attention back toward the massive beast, watching with no small amount of satisfaction as its body was consumed in white fire while the ship disintegrated beneath it, clouding the water with smoke and dark blood.

She thought it a fitting pyre for Derek, her friend and mentor, even as the chain reaction reached critical mass – the water in all directions seemingly alight in unearthly flame.

And then they were free of the creature's grasp, only to be sent spinning out of control as the world seemingly descended into Hell around them.

EPILOGUE

J ulie was just about to blow the ship when she heard frantic footsteps racing up behind her, causing her to hesitate for a moment — long enough for Mitchell to rip the detonator from her hands.

"What the hell?" she cried, swinging one of her crutches at him. "It's right there!"

"*Was*! And now it's not," he replied, clutching his chest as if miming a heart attack. "We get one chance at this. One. And if we screw it up, everyone over on the Sun Angel dies, too."

After a few moments, the panic retreated, allowing his words to finally reach her.

He helped her back to her feet. Then together they stood in the middle of the helipad, scanning the horizon for any sign of the beast's return.

They didn't have to wait long, although what happened next was nothing they could have ever expected.

The ship began to rock beneath them, side to side, as if they were on a toy boat in a kiddie pool.

"I think this is it," Mitchell said. "Be ready."

"I am," she lied, letting go of a crutch so as to grab his hand.

And then, just off their port, the ocean seemingly exploded. Water rained down on them as a massive wave rocked the Nest dangerously to one side, hard enough so that they both fell to the deck before the ship righted itself again.

"Fuck that hurts!" Julie cried out.

"Not as much as it could have. Look!"

She turned her head, ignoring the pain as best she could, to see a column of what appeared to be pure white flame rise from the sea. It shot into the sky where the clouds continued to swirl overhead, as if seeking to challenge the freakish lightning that continued to flash.

Plasma, energy, or the hand of God itself. Julie didn't know which, only that it continued to rise until it hit the very center of the vortex. There it flashed brightly, enough to make them both shield their eyes.

She was still blinking the spots from her vision when Mitchell gasped, "Holy shit. I don't believe it."

"Don't believe what?"

He didn't need to elaborate, though. She looked up and saw it clearly enough – stars, already visible as the cloud cover began to break apart. A few errant bolts of lightning flashed but that was it. Within minutes there was nothing but clear sky above them.

"What the fuck did they do down there?" Julie asked.

"No idea. But my guess is we're going to be sorry we missed it."

"Maybe." As the sea continued to roil, something caught Julie's eye, a flash of color among the darkness, momentarily lit by their spotlights. "Help me up."

"Why?"

"Just do it!"

It was slow going, the pain of her injuries almost

unbearable against the unsteady deck, still rocking from the aftermath of whatever the hell had just happened. Once they were both up again, though, he was quick to follow her gaze out over the side, where the small submersible could be seen bobbing in the waves.

"Holy shit. They made it," she cried, the strangeness of what was going on above them quickly forgotten.

The sub looked banged up to all hell, barely able to stay afloat, but it was there. A few more moments passed and then the top hatch popped. Julie caught sight of a mane of blonde hair as Danni emerged, turned toward the Nest, and began waving her arms.

"Come on," Mitch said after a second or two. "Let's go see if this tub has anything left that can reel them in. I don't know about you, but I can't wait to hear what Derek has to say about all of this."

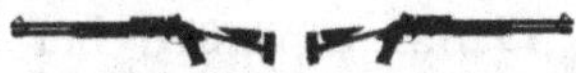

The mood inside the Nest's temporary command center was somber, but there was no doubting the quiet sense of relief among the crew.

After Danni told them what happened, Mitch had radioed the Sun Angel from the sub – finding the comm channels once again crystal clear.

Andrea was the first back aboard, where she resumed command – after popping Mitchell in the face and dropping him to the deck like a sack of potatoes. Though Danni half expected her to throw him in the brig, that was the extent of her wrath. She'd then turned her attention toward debriefing the remaining sub crew on what had happened.

Over the next few hours, Danni relayed their strange tale to the others, oftentimes to disbelieving stares, informing them of what had occurred as well as the sacrifices that had been made – having to pause several times as the crew interrupted with status reports.

Communications had been restored via the Sun Angel's radio. Along with it came news that their calls had finally been heard. The U.S. Coast Guard was dispatching ships to monitor the area, as well as assist in whatever could be done to make the Nest seaworthy again.

Andrea didn't hide any of it from Danni and her team – sharing with them the news of power outages and electrical interference that had seemingly permeated the entire Gulf region – as well as the innumerable strange occurrences that their respective agencies would likely be tallying for days to come, off the record of course.

Whatever damage had been done, though, the worst seemed to be over now, having died along with the strange ship below – leaving them with far more questions than they'd found answers to.

Despite that, Danni expressed her hope that there wasn't anything left to salvage. Judging by the looks of the others in the debriefing room, however, she knew it was unlikely they'd ever know the full truth of whatever happened next, especially now that their mission was officially over.

At least she knew enough of the truth for it to hurt, even if that truth would soon be covered up as well. She respected Norah's final wishes, filling in the others on the senior agent's final fate, as well as that of her ex-husband, letting both teams know their respective leaders had sacrificed themselves in the line of duty – even if she was uncertain as to the exact circumstances behind Jacob's death.

It was Derek who occupied the bulk of her thoughts, though.

It broke her heart to think about him, alone and trapped in that place, knowing his time was running out.

But she also realized he'd been right to send her away. Had she heeded her instincts, she'd have likely doomed them all – and not just her own team, but her brother's as well.

Derek had died protecting them both, just as she knew he sometimes wished he had back in Bonanza Creek.

His sacrifice hadn't been in vain either. Not only had she survived, but she now had newfound hope helping to burn away the darkness inside her. She knew her brother was out there somewhere, continuing to fight the good fight alongside his own world's Derek.

Though she knew his death wouldn't be easy to accept for any of them, she took some comfort in knowing that somewhere, beyond the veil of this world, there was a Crypto-Hunter still out there saving people.

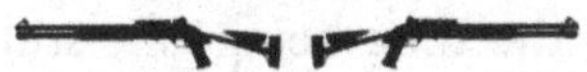

"Hurry up. It's about to start."

"Hold your horses. The popcorn's almost done," Julie said from the kitchen of her modest New Jersey apartment. A minute or two later she came walking out with two full bowls. "Here. Butter for us normal folk." She handed one to Danni. "And kettle corn for the rest." She passed the other to Andrea, who was seated next to Mitch on the love seat.

"Your definition of normal leaves a lot to be desired," Mitchell said.

"Yeah, well, cheesesteaks still suck," Andrea replied, elbowing him gently before reaching over to grab some from Danni's bowl.

"Pretty sure saying that within a hundred miles of Philly is a crime."

Danni smiled, their constant bickering having rapidly grown comforting to her ears. It was nice to be together in a place that didn't require either autographs or loaded rifles, even if they'd just barely dodged a bullet on that first one.

The execs from the Adventure Channel had wanted to celebrate the season premiere with a live event in New York City. They hadn't been happy when the cast had balked, but fortunately hadn't pushed it either."

As for the rest, things were still in limbo. Though the three of them were technically still employed by the Department of Agriculture, the status of the DoCC was up in the air. With both Derek and Norah gone, so too was their entire chain of command.

Though he denied it, rumors had reached Danni's ears that Mitchell had gone to D.C. to argue that she be placed in charge of the field team. However, so far little had come from it, which wasn't entirely unexpected. *Maybe someday*, she thought. For the time being, she still had a few miles to go before the higher ups would probably even consider such a thing.

For now, they were temporarily under another director's charge, some bean counter who seemed to always change the subject whenever cryptids were brought up. Hell, the poor sap would've probably wet his pants at the sight of a squatch. But that was okay. Eventually the world would need them again, and when that happened they'd be ready.

At least the Adventure Channel had no such hang-ups about moving forward – even if she knew it was only a matter of time before they started bugging them about photoshoots again.

She just hoped they chose more wisely this time. No sign of either Kerry Klipsch or the Rogers Will-Do had been found in the days following the incident. However, a subsequent search of the Nest had discovered Julie's missing minicam – complete with Alvita Guerrero's final moments, as well as Klipsch's hand in it.

That poor woman. She hadn't deserved what she'd gotten. But that had been the case for everyone lost that day. They'd simply been doing their jobs to the best of their...

"It's starting," Mitchell said, turning up the volume.

Dark thoughts such as those could wait for another day. On this night Danni was among friends and family – those she could see and those she could feel, even if they were forever just beyond her reach.

She turned her attention toward the TV, smiling as her own voice blared from the speakers.

Since man first walked the Earth, people have seen the unexplainable:

Lights in the sky, ghosts from the past, monsters in the mist.

Do they exist, or are they merely our imagination?

Science has scoffed at these stories ... until now.

My name is Danni Kent, and I along with my teammates, Mitchell Harkness and Julie Wilhelm, dare to believe.

Together we will continue the work of our mentor Derek Jenner.

We will discover what is out there. The truth cannot hide from us.

We are ... the Crypto-Hunters.

THE END
... in one world

Another Place

Everything hurt. It felt like he'd been run over by a truck, only to have it back up over him again. There was a strange buzzing in his ears and his body felt weird – alternately light then heavy, then light again.

Worse, he was uncomfortable as all hell, the hard floor rough and damp beneath his head.

"I think he's waking up."

"Give him some space."

"Screw that. You need to explain this now, mister."

"I will, Agent Chalmers, but I'm not sure you're going to believe me. Although maybe you can back up a bit and let us work while you try to keep this floating asylum from sinking."

"Don't think I'll hesitate for a second to write your ass up, Harkness."

"Ooh, look at me shaking."

"That's enough, Mitch."

"M-Mitch?" Derek gasped, his throat feeling dry and cracked.

"Take it easy there, boss man," the medic replied. "You swallowed enough seawater to drown a horse."

"W-what ... h-how?" Derek's eyes cracked open, although he couldn't see much – blinking at the bright lights shining down from above.

"Sorry about that. They don't believe we blew Oswald the Octopus to smithereens down there, so they're still sweeping the water for it."

"And the deck, too," another voice added. "Because why would we need working retinas to do our job?"

Derek focused on the other man, his eyes opening wide. "Harrison?"

Sure enough, Danni's brother was there looking down at him. He smiled, then began helping him up to a sitting position.

"Easy, kid," Mitchell scolded. "He's had a hell of a jolt."

"Yeah," Derek gasped. "But how?"

"Your guess is as good as ours," yet another voice answered, one so disturbingly familiar that Derek felt a chill run down his spine. He could only watch slack-jawed as his own double stepped forward and offered him a hand. "Dr. Derek Jenner, I presume."

Derek let the other man, identical save for some superficial details, pull him to his feet, where he managed to stay up, if just barely. "It's ... a pleasure ... Dr. Jenner."

The other him chuckled. "This is weird as fuck, isn't it?"

"You have no idea."

"Eh, maybe I have some."

"So how did I...?"

"We have no idea," the other Derek said. "All I can say for certain is you got lucky as hell. That thing blew, nearly capsizing the ship in the process. Next thing we knew the sub came up. Then, just as we were trying to pull it back aboard, someone shouted, 'man overboard,' and I looked to see me, meaning you, floating in the water like someone's pet goldfish. You're lucky Mitch here is a fast talker, otherwise I might've dismissed you as a hallucination and let you drift away."

"Just for the record, I'm glad you didn't."

"Me, too."

"So ... what now?" Derek asked, looking around and taking in the scene around him – familiar, yet strangely different at the same time.

"That's the million dollar question, isn't it? But I guess the short answer is we'll have to try to figure out a way to send you home."

"And do you have any idea how to do that?"

"Not even the first fucking clue," Mitch replied, "But, there *are* two bits of good news."

"And that is?"

"One, you're alive. And two, now we know for a fact

that there's a parallel Earth out there and it's possible to reach it. So … we just have to figure out how."

Derek sighed. It wasn't much, but Mitchell was right. He was alive. Not only that, but he was in a world where lost friends had survived, giving him a chance to… "Oh shit."

"What is it?"

"Danni. She…"

"It's okay," Harrison said, smiling. "We caught a faint transmission just before the ship blew. It was from her. They got out."

"Thank God."

"Exactly what I said."

"And that octopus?"

"Dead as the proverbial doornail," Mitchell replied. "Can't say for sure, but I'd bet the same thing happened over in your world."

"Let's hope so." Derek let out a deep breath. For now, that would have to be enough, knowing Danni had made it out and that she and the rest of the team were hopefully safe. Anything else was speculation, nothing more. "So what does that mean for me?"

"First things first," Mitchell said. "We try to keep the government from dissecting you."

"Then," the other Derek added, "we have our work cut out for us. I won't lie. It could be years, decades, or never before we figure out a way to get you home. And until then, the world keeps spinning."

"Meaning?"

"Meaning," he continued, "what do you think about growing a beard … one kind of like mine?"

"Can't say I ever really thought about it. Why?"

"Well, as they say – the show must go on. And I think I might just be able to convince our producers it's time to hire a rather convincing stunt double."

THE END
for now

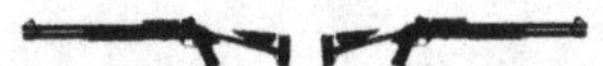

If you enjoyed this story, I invite you to sign up for my newsletter. Not only will you be kept up to date on new releases, but you'll get awesome freebies, too. CLICK HERE to gain join today!

AUTHOR'S NOTE

And thus we come to the end of the Crypto-Hunter's journey ... for now anyway.

So, what exactly does that mean?

Exactly what it sounds like. Derek and Danni's tale was always meant to be a trilogy. So indeed, this is the final chapter of Tales of the Crypto-Hunter. That said, I think I dropped enough not-so-subtle hints – in this book, and in the other series I write – that there's a much wider world out there with plenty more stories waiting to be told. And there's little doubt some of those stories are still in need of heroes.

Will Derek ever make it back to his world? Who can say? For now, he's got a whole new journey ahead of him, as do Danni, Mitch, and Julie. Whether their paths may cross again, well, we shall see.

The future is, as they say, full of possibilities.

Outside of that, I want to thank you for sticking with me through the conclusion of this trilogy. In a day and age when entire book series are released, consumed, and forgotten in less than a year's time, it's heartening to know I was able to craft a tale that kept people's interest over the years between releases. And for that I am grateful ... even more so if I was able to keep you on the edge of your seat for most of it.

All in all, that's not too bad for a story that started out as little more than a response to all the ... well, *not so great* Bigfoot movies available on cable and streaming services. And who knows? Maybe one day we'll see team Crypto-Hunter gracing either the big or small screen. And, if so, then perhaps someone else will find themselves similarly inspired to write their own tale of backwoods terror.

One can dream.

For now, though, please accept my thanks for reading, as well as my hope that I was able to entertain you with these tales of bloody mayhem and adventure.

Until next time...

Rick G.

ABOUT THE AUTHOR

Rick Gualtieri lives alone in central New Jersey with only his wife, three kids, and countless pets to both keep him company and constantly plot against him. When he's not busy monkey-clicking words, he can typically be found jealously guarding his collection of vintage Transformers from all who would seek to defile them.

Defilers beware!

Also by Rick Gualtieri
TALES OF THE CRYPTO-HUNTER
Bigfoot Hunters
Devil Hunters
Kraken Hunters
Boar War

HIGH MOON
The Girl Who Punches Werewolves
The Girl Who Fights Witches
The Girl Who Hunts Fairies
The Girl Who Defies Fate

THE TOME OF BILL UNIVERSE
THE TOME OF BILL
Bill the Vampire
Scary Dead Things
The Mourning Woods

Holier Than Thou
Sunset Strip
Goddamned Freaky Monsters
Half A Prayer
The Wicked Dead
Shining Fury
The Last Coven
BILL OF THE DEAD SAGA
Strange Days
Everyday Horrors
Carnage À Trois
The Licking Hour